MW01413613

A New Civilization of Peace

Copyright ©2009 Growing Consciousness
ISBN: 978-0-5780-4632-7 (sc)

All rights reserved. No part of this publication may be reproduced, stored in a retrieval system, or transmitted in any form or by any means, electronic, mechanical, recording or otherwise, without the prior written permission of the author.

Printed in the United States of America

The author and the publisher respectfully acknowledge that this book is copyrighted. No part of this publication may be reproduced in any form by Photostat, microfilm, xerography, or any other means which are known or to be invented or incorporated into any information retrieval system, electronic or manual without the written permission of the copyright holder.

This publication is distributed with the expressed and applied understanding that the author and publisher are not engaged in rendering legal, psychological, or other professional advice. If legal, psychological, or other professional advice or other expert assistance is required, the services of a competent professional should be sought.

Neither the author nor publisher makes any representation or warranty of any kind with regard to the information contained in the book. No liability shall be accepted for any actions caused by or alleged to be caused, directly or indirectly from using the information contained in this book.

Cover and book illustrations by Daria Kitsch.

Cover design by Madeleine St. Jacques and Angela Medici

Page layout by Madeleine St. Jacques

Ilona Anne Hress, L.C.S.W, C.T.T., Rev.
www.growingconsciousness.com

GROWING CONSCIOUSNESS

A NEW CIVILIZATION OF PEACE

Presented by:

Ilona Anne Hress

L.C.S.W., C.T.T., REV.

NLIGHTN
PUBLISHING

Table Of Contents

Acknowledgments......................................vii

Introduction..ix

1. The Creative Power of Illumination:
   Freedom From Fear..................................1

2. The Nexus of Loving:
   Embracing Your Multi-dimensionality...............19

3. Your Multi-dimensional Portfolio:
   Accessing Divine Wisdom Everywhere................39

4. Be Aware of Your Ignorance:
   The Collective Education of Humanity..............61

5. Civilized Power:
   Masculine and Feminine Communion..................81

6. Anchoring Up Into Unconditional Loving:
   Devoted to Serve.................................103

7. Living in Bliss:
   Embodying the Christ Consciousness...............123

Acknowledgments

Birthing a new civilization of peace requires a lot of labor. It also takes more than two people to conceive and I am blessed with the unconditional love and support of the entire Growing Consciousness community. All of you who have been touched by Growing Consciousness through classes, special events, planetary activations, sessions, concerts, and the website are bringing the new civilization of peace into the world moment by moment, choice by choice. My little corner of the world is so much brighter because of your purity, integrity, and commitment to service and I am grateful for your support. With *A New Civilization of Peace,* Growing Consciousness is reaching out, offering those seeking to know peace, an experience of unconditional love and compassionate forgiveness through every page.

Such development would not be possible without the support, guidance, and assistance of many individuals who stand beside me with courage and conviction, constantly challenging me to grow. Thanks to Angel Medici and Madeleine St. Jacques who are teaching me how to grow the business of Growing Consciousness so that we can touch the Soul of humanity. Thanks to Billur Samli, Bill Hungerford, and Wendy Zellea for stewarding Growing Consciousness to bless the entire world. Thanks to Frank Force, Darlene Hart, Joy Rodino, Bruce Hackman, and Barbara Parzatka for their regular infusion of generosity, understanding, healing, and joy that keeps me and Growing Consciousness healthy and strong. Thanks to my brother Jonathan who challenged me to completely live my calling to build a new civilization of peace, and to my sister Adrienne who helped me to continue developing Growing Consciousness when I wasn't sure I could make it through another third-dimensional day. Thanks to my niece Daria for all the creative love emanating from the art she created for Growing Consciousness and the illustrations she created for *A New Civilization of Peace*. I cannot imagine living into multi-dimensionality without their support, guidance, laughter, and teasing.

Lastly, thanks to the one million Light Beings throughout our Universe who loved humanity enough to spend ten years with the Growing Consciousness community, experimenting with the best ways to help us usher in a new civilization of peace on and with the Earth. And to the three billion Light Beings from our twenty-four universal system currently collaborating with the Growing Consciousness community, thank you for helping us to grow multi-dimensionally conscious, now.

What a tremendous time to be alive and to be human! Know that every day I celebrate each one of you as we collectively grow consciousness and peace emerges throughout the Earth.

Blessings,
Ilona Anne Hress
L.C.S.W., C.T.T., Rev.

Introduction

Infrastructure of the New Civilization of Peace
~through Ilona Anne Hress, LCSW, CTT, Rev.

There are three components to the new civilization that safeguard peace as a manifest reality:

>1.   A ***culture of Oneness*** will be established in which all forms of life are honored on Earth.

>2.   ***Free technologies*** will insure the equitable delivery of every natural resource all over the globe while promoting non-polluting energy sources.

>3.   ***Music*** will replace divisive religious traditions and practices as the basis of spirituality. Through such massive change humanity will develop a collective consciousness that reveals unconditional love and forgiveness as a way of life on this planet.

* * * * * * * *

Our heads are preoccupied by fears and our hearts have shut down from the hurt of losing those we love. We struggle to make peace with our bodies and often deny the existence of the Soul. In that state of being there is little left through which to lovingly re-create our selves. Humanity has been lost in our illusions for a long, long, long, long time. We specialize in self-destruction and have become experts at the process. From the Lemurians to the Atlanteans, from the Egyptians to the Greeks, from the Romans to who we are now, humanity has never owned its collective identity. We sought to compete, conquer, and manipulate each other, but never really embraced loving ourselves for the genuine beauty of being human. Humanity has suffered from such an extreme case of amnesia that most of us really believe that we are the center of the universe, all alone, self-sufficient, and powerful.

This is not true of course. We are simply one of the many species that Mother God and Father God have created. Not every species has forgotten its heavenly heritage as humanity has. Nevertheless, Mother God and Father God and many of their multi-dimensional children have not forgotten us. Although we may choose to hurt ourselves through the free will of this universal system, our heavenly parents are watching. They have said, "Enough!" *Now is the time when the fearing, the fighting and the pain come to an end. A parallel evolutionary developmental path has begun within humanity.* Those who choose to heal and evolve focus on humanity's reunification with our divine family. These are those who are reclaiming the sacred identity of this civilization.

This is a most fascinating and beautiful healing process in which to participate. Nothing less than saving the human race is at stake. However, you can only participate by choice. Those who enjoy self-destruction will be allowed to play out their fantasy, but not at the cost of the planet, the solar system, galaxy, or universe. Following the parallel evolutionary developmental path, those who choose to engage the love, wisdom, and power of their higher-dimensional Souls are detaching from the drama of those enamored by lust, power, greed and death. Mother God and Father God have not abandoned their rebellious children, but they are not catering to them any longer. Those who choose destruction will experience it to the degree that their existence will continue on another third-dimensional planet in another solar system within this universe. Just as substance abusers eventually overdose when they cannot break free of their addictions, so too those who refuse to recognize that their lives have heavenly origins, will succumb to death as their only option. Those who choose to unite within the collective group Soul of the human race are already building a new civilization of peace. The work is hard and invigorating.

Components of the New Civilization of Peace

There are three main components to the new civilization of peace. These aspects of society will be developed to sustain an excellent quality of life for all living on the planet. Given the safety and abundant resources that will be available on a regenerated Mother Earth, humanity can then focus on multi-dimensional creative pursuits. We will begin to serve the galactic community for the highest good of all within this quadrant of the Milky Way.

In order to succeed at re-creating this civilization, a higher-dimensional shift in human consciousness is necessary. Fears, judgments, condemnation, and disrespect will find no home in the re-created world. Greed, envy, lust, and manipulation will disappear as every need is addressed. Personal power will be honored as the premier vehicle through which we serve each other.

I. THE CULTURE OF ONENESS

The Culture of Oneness demands a focus on that which is common to all. It is the means through which every human being will receive food, shelter, meaningful work, playful activities, and time to rest by their mere presence on the planet. Everyone is offered everything. There are no rich and there are no poor. Thus, no judgments arise over whose work, or play, are more valuable to the common good. Everyone is honored for the specific contributions offered. A civilization that honors the weak as much as the strong will never fear itself. What you contribute and how you work is based upon your talents, abilities, and personality structure. Life is always meaningful whether you are a doctor or a gardener, a baby-sitter or a musician. And, life is continually celebrated.

Within the Culture of Oneness, no nationalities stand out. No people cry for attention because everyone is attending to each other. Race and creed are superceded by one's humanity. Within the higher-dimensional group Soul, every human being is literally recognized as family. Through compassion and understanding all are encouraged and nurtured to express their very best. You are loved. This is the collective consciousness of humanity as one group Soul.

II. FREE TECHNOLOGIES

All technologies are free within the new civilization. Everyone has access to all natural resources. No one is denied food, energy, travel, and support.

Within the civilization of peace, all willingly receive what is offered because pride has been wiped away.

The ego serves the collective Soul consciousness. No one would consider taking less than or more than they require. Everyone accepts their personal responsibility to be self-nurturing so that they can be of service to all. There are no martyrs and no victims. The poor cease to be an issue because everyone is rich with all that is required to make living comfortable and joyous. This is the essence of sustaining and maintaining peace on Earth.

Additionally, *the economic infrastructure will be re-created according to the equitable delivery of services around the globe*. No such thing as interest will exist because no one would ever take advantage of another's need. Trade will focus on trusting the choices of the individual to consume only that which is necessary. Moreover there will be no judgments about what is or is not necessary for another. Within the fifth-dimensional consciousness of the citizens of the new civilization, no one would even consider making choices that would harm another or the planet herself. *Economics will not disrespect Mother Earth. It will support and nurture planetary development.*

Scientific research and artistic ventures will soar because those individuals suited for such pursuits will be free to complete their spiritual assignments without the stress and limitations now placed upon them. Everyone will benefit from the discoveries to be made through higher-dimensional and multi-dimensional contact. Society cannot buy its way to peace. Humanity creates peace by providing for the needs of all. Service will replace shopping in the new civilization. The credos of business men and women everywhere will include, *"What do you need?"* and *"How can I help?"*

To that end, Mother God, Father God, and our multi-dimensional spiritual family will be constantly available to guide and assist. The difference will be that humanity will have greater access to them through the development of our extra-sensory perception. Our Souls have always been in conscious contact with the heavenly realms. Now, the rest of us, our bodies and minds, will consciously experience our spiritual family as neighbors and multi-dimensional friends. We will have reunited our minds and hearts with our Souls. A galactic economy will emerge upon the Earth with the sharing of technological advances and extra-terrestrial resources. Our communities will expand beyond the planet as our assistance consciously grows.

Our understanding of spirituality will develop such that religious practices will cease to be the source of conflict, division, and violence. The unity of humanity as the children of Mother God and Father God will supersede the need to worship individual gods as the only valid expression of the Creator. Indeed, individuals in the new civilization will develop significant conscious relationships with the avatars that have visited this planet. Buddha, Jesus, Krishna, Mother Mary, Kuan Yin, Confucius, and many others are now members of the Planetary Hierarchy, the spiritual government overseeing the evolution of humanity. They are guiding, teaching, supporting, and reprimanding those on the parallel evolutionary developmental path right now. *Spirituality is not about worship. It is about living reverently within Creation and learning from those who know how.*

III. MUSIC AS SPIRITUAL TRANSMISSION

Music will be the premier vehicle for spiritual transmissions from the Planetary and higher Spiritual Hierarchies.

Without any language barriers, music freely penetrates the human, planetary, solar, galactic, and universal auric fields. Composed of electromagnetic frequencies, music literally creates and destroys physical forms. It has the ability to inspire, motivate, energize, and direct the path of those who receive its particular frequencies. Life changes when music touches you. The music of the new civilization will always flow from the heart of Mother God and Father God. It will contain the frequencies necessary to continue the expansion of consciousness within the collective Soul of the civilization. At times it will soothe and at others it will invigorate. It will always support every life form on the planet including Mother Earth.

Carrying the frequencies of the personality of Mother God and Father God, this spiritual music will radiate the twelve main characteristics of the Creator into humanity. Known as the *Twelve Rays*, these emanations include willpower, wisdom, creativity, harmony, insight, compassion, intimacy, and purity amongst others. Additionally each of these characteristics is expressed differently through Mother God and Father God.

Thus, all that hear can balance, integrate, and honor the fullness of the divine masculinity and femininity within. Whatever characteristic is required to balance, calm, inspire, nurture, or honor will be directly delivered into the planetary auric field of the planet through music. Everyone and everything will have access to embodying a greater degree of this necessary quality for their well being and the highest good of all.

As you can see, Mother God and Father God have thought of everything to help humanity not only save, but recreate itself. However, They need you to choose consciousness over ignorance. If you have liked what you have heard about the new civilization of peace, join with us now on the parallel evolutionary developmental path. You are needed and you are indeed loved.

* * * * * * * *

A Special Message From Jesus' Higher Self, Ascended Master Sananda:

"Do not fear that which you do not understand. You will find that love will practically lead the way to the changes in your life necessary for your freedom. I know of your pain and of your longing to be whole again. I do not see you as fragmented or hurt. I see humanity complete, whole and healed. There is no limitation to my loving or my courage to find and hold your peace until you can own it for yourselves. There is no way to block your loving when your desire is stronger than your fear. You need not focus on what you don't have. Focus on what is provided. Peace belongs to those who live it as a possibility. Then, it manifests in reality. Own what your heart desires as true, not what your mind considers it needs. We know of your needs far beyond your worries. Send your worries into the wind and you will discover that the wind only carries the dreams hidden within your fears. These dreams emerge through the spiraling energies of the elements cohering into delightful creation. Your future is joyous, peaceful, attentive, and understanding."

Chapter One

The Creative Power of Illumination: *Freedom From Fear*

Introduction
In this chapter, the four major impediments to living a consistently illuminated life are discussed. Strategies to overcome these four destroyers of faith are presented. Using the creative power of illumination you will learn how to navigate your way into freedom. Upon overcoming these debilitating experiences humanity is free to generate the unlimited creative possibilities that will save our world and positively contribute to the evolution of our solar system, galaxy and universe.

It only takes one moment of living without fear to change the rest of your life. Every miracle that has ever occurred happened in an environment of fearlessness, even if that environment existed only within the mind of the one being healed. When you are no longer afraid, anything becomes possible. Through a shocking moment, you suddenly experience a power that is beyond your understanding. This is when illumination enters your life. At last you know the way out of pain and suffering. Filled with the creative power from deep within another part of your being, possibilities generate within your conscious mind. You find yourself manifesting a more fulfilling life than you have ever known. So excited about the future, you not only look forward to the next illumined moment, you embrace illumination as a way of life. This is what we wish to teach today.

Most individuals need to be shocked into another level of awareness through some kind of crisis. Having a car accident, getting fired, being stuck in a hurricane, or any number of events that overwhelm the human potential to cope, suffice. In these desperate moments individuals can be shocked into a higher-dimensional level of awareness because their third-dimensional defense mechanisms fail. Consider finding yourself bleeding in your car stuck upside down trapped in a ravine hidden from the highway at 2:00 a.m. You are consciously recognizing that the situation is grim. A cynic by nature you prepare for the worst. However, within minutes you see the flashing lights of a police car above you. There is no way that your human mind can comprehend how the policeman found you on a deserted highway in the middle of the night. The impossible has just become possible. In every powerful life-changing event your Soul will bypass your brain to find assistance for you. These are the moments when faith is born. You become willing to receive what your human mind cannot provide.

We live on a planet in pain that houses a suffering civilization. Apparently humanity will have to be shocked into fearlessness if we are ever going to attain our evolutionary goals. However, falling on our knees and crawling on our bellies is not the only way to discover the generative power of creativity. Humanity needs to link to an illumined state of existence in less dramatic ways. You don't have to be hit by lightning twice to awaken you to reach beyond what you know and let new possibilities to emerge. Yet to live within the higher-dimensional awareness of illumination when others cannot yet remotely perceive the creative possibilities that you envision for yourself and the world, is a challenge. The lightning bolt will eventually hit them too.

Hold on to the faithfulness and creativity generated in your moments of powerful awakening. Don't get lost in the apathy and doubt of this third-dimensional world. We are going to teach you how to regain, reconnect, and re-establish the currents of illumination that will facilitate your consistent functioning at higher-dimensional frequencies in your daily life. It will take this consistent generative creativity to manifest a new civilization of peace that does not know fear. All that is required is your desire and willingness to be strong and faithful regardless of what is occurring and/or how others are acting around you.

There are four major impediments to living a consistently illuminated life. They are embarrassment, judgment/disapproval, isolation, and powerlessness. These four faith-destroyers give fear rampant access to whomever, whenever, wreaking havoc in society and on the planet. Once you overcome these debilitating experiences you are free to generate unlimited creative possibilities to save your world and ours. We will guide you through each debilitating process in detail. Then, using the creative power of illumination we will show you how to navigate your way into freedom.

Embarrassment is our embarkation point. Embarrassment is always about you and not the others in front of whom you feel embarrassed. The experience of embarrassment is an internal emotional event. Sometimes you will feel embarrassed but no one else will know because it is only happening inside of you. Embarrassing situations provide the vehicle for you to release unrealistic expectations that others have placed upon you or that you have placed upon yourself. Embarrassments are private growth experiences that sometimes occur publicly. When you can laugh at yourself instead of crying over embarrassing situations you are reaching greater levels of illumination. You are becoming vulnerable enough to change. Celebrate your embarrassing moments because through them you reach vulnerable points in your life where change is possible. Free yourself from self-imposed restrictions and create yourself anew. Embarrassment is a form of illumination that lights the way to personal growth and social freedom. If you can embrace embarrassment as a vehicle for generating personal development, then you have already begun to experience the power of illumination to change a seemingly negative, destructive event into a positive life-changing opportunity.

If you cannot accept embarrassment as a tool of illumination, then disapproval and judgments will fill your life with pain and rob you of your personal power. Disapproval feeds on embarrassment and then heaps on the hurt, one judgment at a time. Disapproval is always coupled with a judgment that you are unworthy according to somebody. Judgments have an internal component of self-deprecation and an external component of condemnation. Born within the family, the culture, and the environment, judgments seek to divide and conquer anything that is not familiar or comfortable to the majority, even if the majority is just two parents.

Every judgment is accompanied by rules. You either fit in to belong to the group or you are thrown out. Attend any high school sporting or social event and watch the teen crowd divide into their prospective cliques. Because teenagers are searching for a means by which to define who they are as young adults, they try out group personas to give them an identity until they can discover their own. Each group has a defined wardrobe, code of behavior, and membership criteria. The smart kids, the athletic kids, the artistic kids, the kids involved with the law, the rich kids and the poor kids all have defined roles to play wherever they happen to be. If anyone refuses to play by the rules of the group culture, he or she will be identified as a traitor and dismissed.

When you are constantly being judged there is no freedom to express whom you are and to explore the possibilities of who you are becoming. Illumination cannot live where judgment resides. There is no room for creative power. Fear kills all possibilities for change. Life becomes dull, stagnant, and slowly deteriorates. A kid caught up in a gang who engages in selling drugs may not have to worry about his future because he may die just trying to belong in the present. In order to develop self-expression you have to release the rules and transmute the judgments that others have placed upon you. Do this by attending to the possibility of illumination. Try on a new behavior or embrace a differing perspective. Throw the old rules away and focus on developing creative opportunities instead. You have much more to gain than you ever have to lose.

To move to humanity's next evolutionary level we have to transmute the judgments that keep us separated and fearful of each other. We must release the rules that imprison our creative abilities. In order to generate the power that will promote change on the Earth we have to become fearless. We have to embrace our illumination with passion. We have to throw away our spiritual rules and our judgments about evolution so that we are free to develop the multi-dimensional potential of our Souls. We need to let the Universal Mind of God speak to us and through us without being censured by ourselves.

The Universal Mind of God has created the structure through which every life form, including humanity, explores its existence. God didn't set us on Earth with defined rules. The Universal Mind gave us a third-dimensional planet on which to explore and play. The third dimension is the structure, the planet is the environment and we made up our own rules about how to collectively live here. Unfortunately we have gotten stuck in our rules and forgotten how to play with illumined possibilities.

However, each of us has multi-dimensional selves in the higher dimensions that remember how to explore and re-create. In our powerful moments of illumination, our higher-dimensional selves wake us up to their existence. They exert their ability to help us solve our human problems when we need them the most. When exploring multi-dimensional solutions to problems, you are too busy following a method of discovery to be bothered by the restrictive nonsense of judgments. Your Soul is free to manifest new realities through your human mind and body. The higher dimensions are humanity's destination on the evolutionary roadmap. We need to be those who challenge the status quo, embarrass ourselves, and embrace powerful moments of multi-dimensional illumination.

Explorers often travel alone or in small groups. They are the pioneers who map uncharted territories and describe new environments. They don't care what others think because they are so excited about what they are discovering. Drawn to assist in the birth of new civilizations, they go out on a limb exploring possibilities without caring about how they may be judged. Pioneers such as Galileo, Pierre and Marie Curie, Martin Luther, and Martin Luther King Jr. felt the rewards of illumination in their lives so completely that nothing could stop them from their work. They experienced the freedom that comes from the creative power of illumination no matter how society treated them. They exhibited complete faith in the process of illumination and through this faithfulness enlightened all of humanity. When you have complete faith in your own process of illumination your conscious comprehension of the Universal Mind grows exponentially as does your contribution to the world.

All life forms in this universe are on an evolutionary journey together. We are simultaneously releasing all the rules to facilitate our collective evolution. All of the Elohim Councils who assisted in the creation of this universe have joined with us to ask the question, "How can we do this better?" The precarious situation on Earth is the crisis point that has shocked the entire universe into illuminated action. All of the life forms within this universe are growing through your human experience of fear, separation and lack. Just as humanity is our lightning bolt of illumination, we are asking all you who live illumined human lives to be the wakeup call for your civilization. The Universal Mind uses shock to awaken the unconscious when all else fails. You are providing the generative power for the shocking experiences that will awaken your family, friends, and neighbors into illumination. From this day forward dismiss disapproval as a personal issue. What do you care about what people say when you already approve of yourself? Don't tell people who don't need to know what is happening and they won't disapprove of you.

Let God shock them into enlightenment through your presence in their lives.

However, when an audience is receptive, share your experiences of the creative power of illumination. Tell them of the generative power of faithfulness that has manifested a new reality for you. Let your story inspire them to ignite the multi-dimensional creative potential within them. Most importantly share this message with those between the ages of fifteen and twenty-five who are open to the power of illumination. They are the pivotal generation that has to exhibit the strength and energy to release the old rules and governments, clear the judgments from the past, and stop the disapproval in the present. They have to be willing to embarrass themselves as they call in higher-dimensional awareness and activate the creative power of possibility for all of us. Believe in these young adults so that they don't feel dismissed and unsupported.

Isolation is the worst problem humanity faces. Your intense disapproval of each other leads to self-imposed exiles that literally threaten the cohesion of the civilization. Even though you live on the same planet humans are so isolated from each other you have no true understanding of what it means to be a citizen of Earth. You share tales of villages and cities all around the world. But, these stories have not lead to the development of a global community. Isolation takes the judgments and disapproval of one nation against the other, one race against the other, one religion against the other and exaggerates them until the entire civilization is buried by its own intolerance. The internal pressure of the civilization is so intense to conform that eventually the whole civilization collapses in on itself.

Your archeologists have witnessed this in the fall of Greece, Egypt, Rome, and all the great root races.

Isolation is a product of fear and douses illumination. It does not honor diversity and creativity, so they cease to offer the civilization possibilities for growth and evolutionary development. What has happened on Earth has happened on other worlds in this galaxy and in other galaxies in this universe. Why do you think so many multi-dimensional beings are interested in assisting humanity? Because in doing so they are helping themselves to avoid calamity. Move into awareness of your solar, galactic, and universal neighbors. You need their multi-dimensional assistance to heal yourselves.

Connection is your salvation. Utilize your communication and transportation systems to provide greater availability for the entire civilization, not just those who have monetary resources. Together communication and transportation determine the speed with which the generative, creative power of illumination travels throughout the world. Humankind consciously evolves through physiological as well as technological awakenings. These lead to advancements in communication and the means to faster and cleaner transportation. Not only do we need to be physically present to each other, we need to understand how to truly communicate with each other. The internet is a marvelous development in communication. But if it serves to divide more than it unites, its true purpose is lost. A machine can never take the place of a person, but it can help unite people.

The speed with which humanity connects with its higher-dimensional group Soul is somewhat determined by the Universal Mind in that God gives each life form a time frame in which to complete an exploratory mission. We used the example of the staircase to describe dimensional structure. Now we are adding a time frame to each step. There are many, many life forms traveling the staircase and the Universal Mind makes sure that the passageway is clear for all to explore the many dimensions it embodies. Humanity has disconnected from the consciousness of the higher dimensions with which we were to be in current contact. We have created a backup in the stairwell. So, humanity will be shocked into a cosmic awakening that re-establishes our flow within the multiple dimensions of the Universal Mind. With the exception of a few such as you, humanity has resisted recognizing our participation in the solar system and galaxy.

Yet, we have the most powerful means of connecting possible. We have the capacity to become multi-dimensionally conscious. In your evolutionary development you can literally feel celestial presences in the room with you. Your physical bodies now recognize higher-dimensional frequencies as pressure, temperature changes, and sensory activation. Your higher senses of clairvoyance, clairaudience and clairsentience are activating. Honor the reality of your multi-dimensional relationships as your connection to your solar, galactic and universal family grows. Be conscious when higher-dimensional life forms seeking to assist you are trying to make contact. Ask questions. Converse. Use illumination to generate a language by which you can understand each other.

Today we are moving beyond our connection with you to develop a multi-dimensional community. We consciously welcome your participation into the galactic community. Together we are generating more creative illuminating power for this galaxy and universe. Steer clear of extra-terrestrials who intend to impose their rules upon your third-dimensional world. They are not providing illumination. They are destroying possibilities for themselves and for you. Consequently, they will suffer under the judgments, isolation, powerlessness, and defeat that result from such behavior. Humanity already knows how to self-destruct through rigid rules and behavior.

By opening to receive and utilizing the creative generative power of illumination, the possibilities for evolutionary growth throughout this quadrant of the galaxy are enormous. Life forms throughout the galaxy are cleaning up their planets and straightening up their solar systems. Humanity needs to do this on Earth. Let faith connect us multi-dimensionally, restoring hope to all life in this galaxy and universe. Be open to becoming a direct channel in faithful recognition of the creative possibilities we multi-dimensionally offer each other within the Universal Mind. In your purity, integrity, and commitment only positive life forms committed to evolutionary gain are attracted to you. You have no need to fear. Held within the Oneness of the Universal Mind, any dark entity attracted to you is seeking healing from a powerful being whom it knows possesses the power to transmute darkness into light. *That powerful being is you.*

Already involved in inter-galactic and universal healing processes, you are respected and trusted as a community dedicated to the highest good of all in this universe. You have repeatedly served as is required to heal this planet, galaxy, and universe from its own wounds. Your connection to us provides us as much hope as our multi-dimensional connection provides you. Multi-dimensional isolation is disappearing on Earth. Connectivity is providing the vehicle through which multi-dimensional illumination is reaching humanity in time to save this civilization. Without galactic assistance, humanity would have already perished. We are offering the help required to collectively heal.

In being unable to heal yourself, you were forced to connect with others who were also searching for illumination and new possibilities. Suffering and pain motivated you to reach out and contact a power greater than yourself to grow and change. Isolation will force humanity into connection if you don't kill yourselves off first. We are going to push the comfort envelope and ask you to become the shock wave that the Universal Mind deposits into the brain of someone who has been frightened and intrigued by the possibility of life in the universe. We request that you share your stories of healing the planet, solar system, galaxy, and universe with those who exhibit receptivity to this information. You have had many successful missions linking the Heavens with the Earth. You have participated in balancing the masculine and feminine energies of the planet, preparing for the full manifestation of the Christ Consciousness as these energies merge throughout the Earth. You have established star gates and activated higher-dimensional communication systems to facilitate the evolution of this civilization. You know the neighborhood gods by name, Lord Buddha, Lord Melchior, Helios and Vesta, and Lord Melchizedek. And they know you. You are an employee of the Planetary Hierarchy working under the supervision of such Ascended Masters as El Morya, Kuthumi, Sananda, Lady Master Nada, Hilarion, Serapis Bey, Paul the Venetian, Lanto, and St. Germain. You are continually assigned specific missions to assist in the emergence of the new civilization of peace on Earth. Your multi-dimensional relationships are real, active, and developing.

Human connectivity depends on the fearlessness of a few. It always has. Jesus, Buddha, and Mohammed and all avatars incarnated on this planet connected humanity with the greater higher-dimensional beings of the Universal Mind. Be those who now connect humanity with the consciousness of the solar system and the galaxy. You are needed for the evolution of your world, your solar system, your galaxy, and your universe. Believe in yourselves as we believe in you. Download our higher-dimensional presences through you and we will speak with the authority and humility that will define your credibility as an outpost of the divine for others. You are the opportunity for others to connect with a much larger reality than their human minds can comprehend. You are not seeking to prove anything or trying to persuade them to believe in your perspective. What you are is their experience of multi-dimensionality. Let people be honest with themselves about the possibilities of multi-dimensional contact in your presence. Exhibit the ability to effectively present us to whomever in joy. It doesn't matter how others respond. It does matter that the information and multi-dimensional opportunities are made available.

Invite others to connect with their own illuminative power. How grateful are you to those individuals who initially introduced you to this multi-dimensional creative power, who set you on the path to freedom, long ago? Learn how to become effective in situations with those who have not yet chosen greater levels of enlightenment. Manage to move into new levels of your own multi-dimensional connectivity and watch what happens to the levels of receptivity from others. When you stand in your truth and download higher-dimensional energies, follow them to their conclusions. The outcomes are developing through the creative power of illumination. You don't need to know what is going to happen. Have faith and let the possibilities flourish. Feel all of our multi-dimensional hands assisting each other to grow strong, effective, and united.

In connection there is power. In isolation there is powerlessness. Consider your multi-dimensional relationships as a myriad of electrical outlets that you can always plug into to download information, experiences, and energy. If you have been so beaten by judgments that you are buried by disapproval and constantly embarrassed by yourself, how can you be effective, much less powerful? It becomes hard to simply function. Isolation is the death of illumination where possibilities cease and suicide is often considered. When you feel useless your life becomes meaningless. To turn this around takes a simple but profound act of courage: *ask for help*.

You cannot stay in an isolated depression if you are holding on to someone's hand. Connect and enlightenment will follow somehow. Helen Keller is an excellent example of the creative power of illumination. Discouraged individuals often need to be mothered. They need to successfully complete the baby steps that help them to regain their self-respect and then their self-esteem. Initially, someone has to help them define the initial processes that will lead to their empowerment. Sometimes the road to health starts when you reach out your hand towards those in isolation. You don't grab their hands. You patiently wait until they grasp onto yours. This is called loving respect.

Create strategies for growth focusing on how to change, not why. People in isolation don't need a philosophy. They need friends. Merge with your higher-dimensional selves to download the creative illumination that will generate effective plans for self-recovery — yours or that of another. Develop simple plans to solve problems and keep them flexible. Plans will evolve as they must. Follow the plans by building structures in which to create new realities. Collaborate to connect and heal. When you are working together, you are connecting, releasing judgments, and finding someone of whom you approve. You begin to feel valuable and become effective in your life. Together you celebrate new discoveries and in the process become victorious. Life is good again.

Do you see how we have come full circle from the debilitating effects of embarrassment to the transforming power of collaboration? Illumination generates the creative power to turn every negative event and relationship into a positive experience of growth and development for all. This is wisdom. If you ignore your moments of illumination you become ineffective, your self-esteem sinks, no one wants to enjoy your company, and eventually you are dismissed. There is nothing worse than being dismissed, disowned, or thrown away.

None of us in this multi-dimensional community are throwing humanity away. That is why we are here. We are collaborating in research and experimentation for the evolution of the solar system, galaxy, and universe. We are having fun and we need you to live the wisdom outlined for you today with each other and with us. Your assignment for the next two weeks is to choose one possibility that you are considering for your life and connect with your multi-dimensional friends to release your unconscious judgments about this possibility. The possibility can involve a relationship, a career move, a physical location, a talent, whatever.

Consider your future choices, drawing upon the light of illumination to recognize and identify the unconscious blocks that you cannot easily find on your own. Let the unconscious judgments go. See how your consciousness shifts and your life changes. Effectiveness manifests a new reality. All of you moved into new life experiences based on your previous shocking physical illuminating experiences. You are already powerfully effective to have reached this level of enlightenment. Be so excited about yourself and your multi-dimensional possibilities that you fearlessly move into illumined faith and can't stop yourself from being happy about you and your future.

If you feel embarrassed, recognize your unconscious block being made conscious. Look for the judgments and release the disapproval. Move out of the isolation in which you have placed yourself. Discover how you dis-empowered yourself and strategize your way to freedom and accomplishment with multi-dimensional assistance. Come back to your illumination as we are coming back to ours. This is a vast project we are multi-dimensionally undertaking for the safety, freedom, and evolution of this universal system.

Chapter Two

The Nexus of Loving:
Embracing Your Multi-dimensionality

Introduction
In this chapter, the journey of evolutionary discovery is revealed as a process of multi-dimensional loving. Strategies to assist humanity's evolution into fifth-dimensional consciousness are provided within the context of connecting to the higher-dimensional information and technologies available within the Universal Mind. By incorporating your humanity into your divine identity, you gain access is to your multi-dimensional intelligence through which evolutionary possibilities emerge. From a place of reverent grace you are invited to participate in the regeneration of humanity into a new civilization of peace.

Instead of seeing "here" and "there" as two separate destinations, connect them through the infinity symbol and the journey of evolutionary discovery appears. If you view the third dimension as "here" and the fifth dimension as "there", both are points of origin from which a journey commences. Fifth-dimensional beings travel to Earth, take a look around, and return home with a greater awareness of the limitations that accompany third-dimensional living. Physical embodiment, lots of gravity, the pleasure of eating great food, and the emotional fear we collectively generate are just some of the discoveries. Likewise, third-dimensional beings, such as humans, can consciously travel to the fifth dimension and discover unrestricted access to higher-dimensional information and technologies. Subtle energy bodies that immediately manifest whatever they are thinking, pure and beautiful environments with unrestricted access to natural resources, and peaceful civilizations in tune with divinity are some of the gifts from the journey. Third-dimensional beings return to their homes, in this case Earth, awakened to greater possibilities for improving their quality of life.

Turn the infinity symbol into a ribbon of infinity channels and you can sense the up and down movement of a spiral. The evolutionary journey is a multi-dimensional adventure into the consciousness of the Universal Mind. There are many multi-dimensional members participating in this class. Some have consciously journeyed from the star systems of Lyra, Sirius, Andromeda, and Alpha Centauri to be present. Ours is a multi-dimensional classroom where we learn from each other within the nexus of the infinity channel that we call the core of self-discovery. Here at the nexus of connection, vast opportunities are available to every life form to learn, grow, and enjoy each other.

In the nexus of connection, love does the connecting. In the nexus of connection, love does the releasing. There is no separation between connection and release. They occur simultaneously. Every life form in the nexus learns how to love themselves and each other better. In your third-dimensional experience, self-loving is at the heart of the nexus of connection. To experience this right now, place your hands over your heart. Feel your heart beating. Don't just hear it or think it. Feel the thump-thump, thump-thump, thump-thump. Inhale and connect to the oxygen you are breathing in to your lungs to deliver to your heart. Connect to the carbon dioxide you are releasing from your lungs into the air. Connect to the oxygen moving into the bloodstream from the heart and release the carbon dioxide from your lungs with every breath. Connect to the oxygen. Release the carbon dioxide. As your lungs and heart connect to oxygen and your lungs release carbon dioxide you are creating an infinity channel with the elemental gases of your atmosphere. In the nexus of connection you love yourself by breathing in those gases that sustain you and exhaling those that don't. Look at respiration as an infinity channel between first-dimensional gases and third-dimensional human bodies. You meet each other at the nexus of loving, simultaneously connecting and releasing as necessary for the highest good of both.

When you breathe freely you love yourself. You access what you need from the multi-dimensional environment in which you reside. You feel supported by Creation and indeed you are. Now, recall a stressful situation that you encountered this week. It may have occurred at home, in the office, with friends, during a doctor's appointment, or at your child's school. When confronted, did you hold your breath? What happened to your heart beat? Did you believe that Creation would support you, or did you fear being powerless to address the person or situation confronting you?

When you hold your breath, you stop loving yourself. You disconnect from the infinity channel and feel lost and alone. The "there" of Creation no longer exists for you. You cannot figure out how to get what you need from "there" because you have disconnected yourself from those and that which God has provided to heal and grow. For example, your doctor has told you that you have type II diabetes and need insulin shots to regulate your blood sugar. The doctor provides you with a rigid diet to follow along with medication. Upon hearing the news all you can think of is, "No more cookies. I'm going to have my foot amputated. What'll happen to my eyesight?" In other words, you are overcome with fear and disconnect from all the help you are being given to remain healthy and happy. God did not disconnect from you. You did. The answer to fear is reconnection.

Look at respiration as an infinity channel with the breath of God. Breathe to reconnect with the vast resources Creation will make available for solving your problems. Move from fear to faith on the infinity channel and feel the love at the nexus of connection. To move through the stress of evolutionary regeneration, you have to remain in the nexus of loving. If you allow fear to rule every time you are asked to change and grow, you will die. If you consistently love yourself by constantly accessing God's providence, you will transform your life. Review the *"Development of Oneness"* diagram for a visual expression of the journey.

Development of Oneness

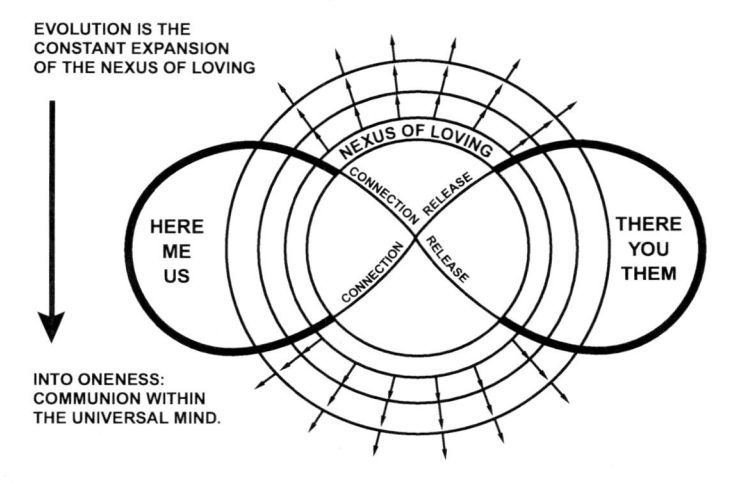

Let's do another exercise to multi-dimensionally expand the nexus of loving. Wherever you are right now, offer your hand to one of the multi-dimensional beings participating in this process with you. Even if you are reading this article at home in the middle of the night, a Light Being will come. Just reach out your hand. If the being doesn't have what you would recognize as a hand, it will pick another part of you to tug on to validate its presence. Connect, and shake or tug. Feel the love moving both ways. Release. Feel the imprint of love left on your hand or body. If you'd like, repeat the process a few times, sharing more love between you. Note that both the connection and the release are part of the experience. There is no such thing as separation within the Universal Mind. However, there are many little connections and releases within the totality of loving. They all occur within the multi-dimensional nexus of loving. This point of connectivity is where self-loving expands to embrace all life as you become acquainted with more and more and more of Creation.

Humans have difficulty maintaining their self-love at the nexus of connection because they often believe that what they do is more important than who they are. When you meet strangers at a party do you ask them about who they are before you ask about what they do? When you find out that the man wearing the tuxedo across from you is a garbage man by profession, do you think less of him than you do of the dentist he is standing next to who is also wearing a tuxedo? What you do is merely an expression of who you are. It is not the totality of your being. Thank goodness we look beyond your behavior and your checkbook to discover all of you. We strive to teach you to do the same.

If you believe that your connections are dependent upon your value, you'll never be enough to some and more than enough to others. Who is deciding your value anyway? And, why are you letting them? You are only human. Humanness has a limited value because your perception is warped according to the parameters of consciousness in the third dimension. Within your world fear is rampant and separation painful because you can't see through the eyes of faithful remembrance. We are not downplaying the value of being human. If this civilization remains stuck in the belief that your humanity is enough to save you, then you will never be able to access the massive tools required to heal each other and your planet. You have already stopped loving yourselves. You are traveling the path of self-destruction and destroying your planet. You cannot save yourselves through your humanity. Your connection to your multi-dimensionality is your only salvation.

It is necessary to embrace your multi-dimensional infinite value, to incorporate your humanity into the larger reality of you. Only then can you consciously become a whole being with an infinite capacity for loving. Your multi-dimensional self knows you as priceless with unlimited vision. This ability to embrace your multi-dimensional capacity is essential for those who choose to move humanity from point A: self-destruction, to point B: the regeneration of humanity as a civilization of peace linked with the eighth-dimensional Pendiculan civilization.

The Pendiculan civilization understands the struggles of humanity to overcome fear, greed, lust, power, envy, and hatred. They long ago mastered the Christ Consciousness. However, in an unfortunate experiment they blew up the planet on which they resided. Having the multi-dimensional technology to maintain themselves in their subtle energy bodies, they have been waiting for an opportunity to redeem themselves in their own eyes. Knowing that humanity is in severe need, they have agreed to offer themselves as co-creators of this new civilization of peace developing on the Earth. They know how to live in harmony for they have achieved a peaceful civilization. However, they are still learning intellectual humility. They are grateful for the opportunity to physically embody on a fifth-dimensional planet that will challenge the intelligent use of their knowledge and technologies.

As you see, becoming multi-dimensional does not guarantee being smart. Every civilization has a particular issue, limitation, or structure by which they are challenged. The capacity for intelligence is an inherent quality in every life form because the Universal Mind created intelligence. It doesn't mean that all aspects of the Universal Mind act smartly. That is why we are working on the development of intelligence, not from the place of information, but from the place of application. Being given the capacity for intelligence doesn't necessarily mean that you utilize it. You all have the intelligence to understand that drinking too much alcohol will make you sick, and repeatedly imbibing over time will kill you. So, how many of you stop drinking alcohol? How many governments seek to control its access to prevent its debilitating effects on society? You have to work at becoming intelligent.

Intelligence is the effective application of divine possibility. To evolve, actualize your capacities for every talent, ability, and character quality. Be willing to engage your intelligence to love. If you cannot love beyond the information your intelligence will gather, then the information is pointless because the application will be incomplete. When you love all information discovered in the nexus of the journey, you will know what, who, when, and how to connect for the highest good of all. When you don't love the information you have accessed, competition, envy, and judgment occur multi-dimensionally with disastrous planetary, solar, galactic, and universal consequences.

Intelligently inquire about the divine possibilities in your life and in the lives of those you know. You know that if you kiss your wife, something wonderful will have happened. You know that if you hit your wife something terrible will have happened. Choose wisely. Don't just choose according to a positive outcome but because you enjoy being good. You get much more pleasure out of goodness than you get out of hatred. Pleasure comes from goodness. Revenge may feel good in the moment but it will bite you. Hatred is unsatisfying in that it never lasts. Goodness lasts forever.

Right now close your eyes and think of one of the most benevolent things you have ever done. It does not matter whether it was big or small. That you remember and believe in your goodness is our concern. Go to a mirror and tell yourself about this wonderful, kind act that you have never forgotten. Continue to look at yourself after the story is complete. Be touched by your generosity. Be touched by you. Feel grateful for yourself. Speak your act of kindness aloud, so that you can hear this on the third dimension and multi-dimensionally. Your benevolence and gratitude will grow and grow and grow. There is no boasting in this exercise, nor is there any envy. Instead, a nexus of connection is growing through the gratitude that each part of you feels to be in the presence of the gracious other.

Share an experience of being able to love without fear, to go beyond the restrictions and limitations placed upon you by society. A new experience of gratitude emerges when you fully activate your capacity to love. Through gratitude, we love beyond what is expected of us. We surprise someone, and ourselves, with unexpected kindness and sincerity. True loving is motivational, surprising, and inspiring. Our hearts overcome our minds and we love without restraint. We intelligently utilize the divine possibility for service addressing us wherever, whenever and with whomever.

There can be no expectations for loving because loving is limitless. However, in specific dimensional parameters there are ways to love that are more accepted and recognized than others. The challenge is to go beyond the accepted and recognized to connect with your multi-dimensional selves, and the greater parts of the others with whom you are in contact. None of you are limited to your human capacity for loving. You all have access to your angelic natures, to the you that lives in the ninth dimension somewhere else in the galaxy, to the you that recognizes the fifth-dimensional Arcturians as family, to the you that enjoys being a star radiating life-sustaining energies to lots of planets. Intimately knowing each of these greater parts of you allows you to love beyond your human understanding. These multi-dimensional parts of you facilitate graciousness when others in the same situation would likely be disgraceful. Grace replaces disgrace when you love from all that you are. This is the power of redemption.

Those who know redemption have regained the hope that they will one day achieve their own brilliance. They believe in the faith of another who saw their brilliance when they could not. Redemption is one of the sweetest forms of loving because it takes the most broken places and regenerates them to be stronger than they ever were. When was the last time you were in the presence of someone who believed in the best in you when you felt at your worst? Just being near them made you feel better, didn't it? Being in the presence of another who knows how to help you access your own redemption is healing. They need do nothing other than sit with you while you regain the ability to believe in the parts of you that have yet to emerge. Because this individual already sees them as real, so can you and eventually your greater good will manifest.

Excellent coaches, gifted teachers, sincere preachers, caring doctors, and great parents all specialize in redemption. The redemptive deeds of these generous people manifest healing in every aspect of our society. They are grateful for their students, patients, clients, parishioners, and children. Their gratitude teaches others to love themselves because they see their possibilities. Once you see the possibilities awaiting you through the eyes of another, you forgive who you were so you can become more. In the freedom you have just accessed you can become who you now are. At that moment, you love yourself better than you ever did. If you cannot forgive, you cannot love. If you cannot love, you cannot grow to be more.

Every one of you has grown to be the person you are today because you have been forgiven over and over and over and over. You are grateful to those who have forgiven you because they truly loved you then and still do now. Making mistakes is part of growing up. This evolutionary journey is an adventure with great room for experimentation. It is a multi-dimensional adventure with lots of cultures, languages, and technologies learning to understand each other. It takes time to develop relationships and successfully solve problems. There are going to be difficult challenges and situations when everyone will need to forgive each other. Mistakes simply happen, but they are not tragedies. We are all evolving within the Universal Mind together and at different rates. It is important to exhibit patience and be able to identify a tragedy from a mistake.

Tragedy is mis-directed intention. It involves malicious or malevolent intent. It is the willful disobedience of the Universal Laws where one acts outside of divine creativity by choice. Accidentally blowing up a lab during an experiment is a mistake. Deliberately detonating a bomb in a nuclear research facility is a tragedy. Forgiveness is essential when it comes to tragedies because those acting outside of the Universal Laws are the most lost. Within the nexus of loving every tragedy can be re-created.

Is the war on Iraq a tragedy? From a human perspective it can be seen as the tragic consequence of the willful mis-intention of the government of the United States to take over the natural resources of a people who need everything their country can provide for them. Within the nexus of loving, God is using this war to facilitate greater levels of connection. The sacrifice of those civilians and soldiers who have been beheaded and blown into pieces have not gone unnoticed. Within the infinite connectivity of divinity, their offering is allowing people who have been oppressed and condemned to come to a greater level of self-respect. The Iraqi people, outside of the insurgents, are gaining an identity. You only see the reactionaries covered by your media.

The Iraqi people are an intelligent people now able to makes choices for themselves within a freedom that allows them to perceive a future for themselves and their children that was beyond their scope even four years ago. The fighting between the various Muslim factions are the mis-intentions of the leaders who have corrupted the minds of their followers by playing out the worst of the Iraqi people. We choose to believe in the best of the Iraqi people. We hope you will join us in our belief in their ability to heal themselves.

If the media would shift their attention from the worst of the Iraqi people to the most kind and generous, then the insurgents would stop acting out because nobody is paying attention. A bully needs love, not negative attention. The media are not acting within the nexus of loving. They function in disconnection where "here" and "there" are identified as "us" and "them." They cannot enter into the expression of redemptive loving because they are disconnected from the providence of the Universal Mind.

Who is not embarrassed about the goodness prevalent in the world today enough to broadcast it over your most widely recognized stations? Just as the best of the Iraqi people need to be revealed to the world, so does the best in each of us. Begin to allow this infinite expression of connection and release within the nexus of loving to become a realized experience that you share with others. Make it personal. Be willing to ask: "What was the latest really good thing you did for someone this week? Tell me. I want to know. I need to feel good about you and I want you to give me something for which I can praise you." Think about doing this at least once a week over dinner. What would happen to your experience of family when gratitude is what is served at the table? Start at home. When there is peace in the home, there will be peace on the Earth.

Goodness is the only real source of connection. All else fades away. You only remain in contact with those who make you feel good. Do you send a birthday card to the friend who emotionally abused you in high school? Would you honor the anniversary of the day you married a man who eventually broke your arm while in a rage? Would you honor the anniversary of your divorce from this man? Goodness provides cohesion and cohesion leads to manifestation. Only goodness will build the new civilization of peace for only in goodness will gratitude and forgiveness be given room to grow.

Goodness facilitates the connections and releases that growing requires. In any positive relationship you connect with the best in each other and release the worst, over and over and over until only the connection to loving remains between you. You love each other so completely that both manifest individually as better people. Each of you becomes more because you know how to live within the nexus of loving.

The more relationships you experience within the nexus of loving, the bigger it grows and the larger your world becomes. When you add your multi-dimensional selves and their relationships to the equation, then the nexus of loving connects you to the Oneness of all Creation. The process of goodness and cohesion provides for the manifestation of peace and harmony within your earthly and other dimensional lives. Here on Earth we are depending upon you to make this nexus of loving so real that people want to know how to become a part of it. You are manifesting the new civilization of peace by living it now with each other and with us. With every glimpse of regeneration you can sustain this connective loving more and more. People feel your goodness. They experience your kindness. They are touched by your generosity and want to know how to be like you.

Welcome these individuals into the nexus of loving. Help them to connect with you and their own multi-dimensional selves. Believe in the goodness that we believe is in you. Translate this information to others that don't just have the capacity but also the desire to actualize peace. Talk about goodness. Share benevolent stories. Build your community within the nexus of loving. Eventually the infinity symbol will be living within the circle that is the nexus of loving. You will know Oneness.

Part II

This process is now occurring throughout the galaxy. As more and more of humanity loves multi-dimensionally within the nexus, the galaxy, and the universe grow into greater harmony with Earth and this solar system. You are engaged in consciously expanding the experiences of the Universal Mind in Its own expansion. God is growing through you. God is growing through us. In this nexus of connection energy flows, divine timing oversees, processes of awakening occur, relationships manifest and then dissolve as is necessary. Connection and release are simultaneously occurring within loving. However, you have to stay in a process, relationship, or situation long enough to create within it. Through your connection with grace, you access multi-dimensional help that manifests solutions, partnerships, and events that were humanly impossible to coordinate.

Humanity has not stayed within its divine nature long enough to re-create itself. You keep abdicating on yourselves, on your divine heritage, choosing to act as orphans instead. Stay within your humanity until you can transform it by embracing your divine identity. You are the multi-dimensional beings who are transforming your civilized human experience into a divine one. Have fun learning how to love each other. Don't be so serious about the mistakes. Flow in divine timing. Continue to awaken those around you and manifest peaceful relationships that will hold the course for humanity's regeneration. Please refer to the *"Oneness of the Universal Mind"* diagram, below.

You are the core of humanity that will remain because you are willing to embrace your divinity. Every

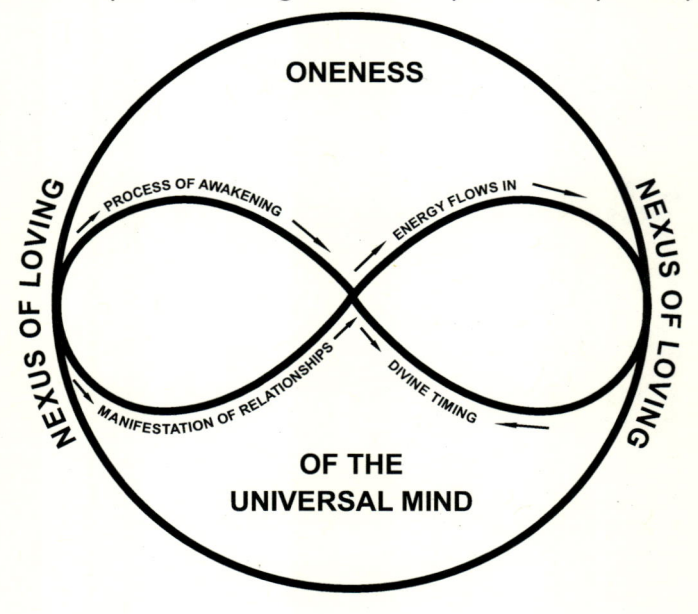

ONENESS

NEXUS OF LOVING — PROCESS OF AWAKENING — ENERGY FLOWS IN — **NEXUS OF LOVING**

MANIFESTATION OF RELATIONSHIPS — DIVINE TIMING

OF THE UNIVERSAL MIND

time you ask the Universal Mind for help, multi-dimensional divinity responds with more loving through the nexus of connection. However, not merely humanity, but every civilization connected to you receives more loving, more help to overcome the obstacles in their way of evolution. As such the Oneness grows so large in the nexus of loving that the holographic flower of life emerges at the center. The hologram of Creation is in continual evolution as each infinity channel on the multi-dimensional spiral connects with another culture, planet, or life form somewhere else within the hologram. Life reaches out to life. This is the experience of holiness. Please refer to the *"Evolutionary Multi-dimensional Flow"* diagram.

Holiness is sacred embrace. You greatly revere that which you call sacred. When you embrace that which you revere, you too become holy. Both honored life forces merge into creative regeneration and evolution occurs. Within the nexus of loving all life is revered, everything is sacred. By sacredly embracing each other you are connecting within the nexus of loving. All of life becomes holy and every embrace is an evolutionary step wherein the Universal Mind learns how to love even more.

Humanity must embrace the concept of the sacred universally and not denominationally. You have divided God into many pieces and are still trying to decide which pieces are the most sacred. In doing so you have lost your reverence for God and for yourselves as part of God. To heal, humanity must learn to revere itself. If you do not revere each other you will not go beyond your expectations for loving. When you recognize that you are a holy expression of humanity existing within the sacredness of God, you will go out of your

Evolutionary Multidimensional Flow

HIGHER DIMENSIONS

HERE
ME
US

THERE
YOU
THEM

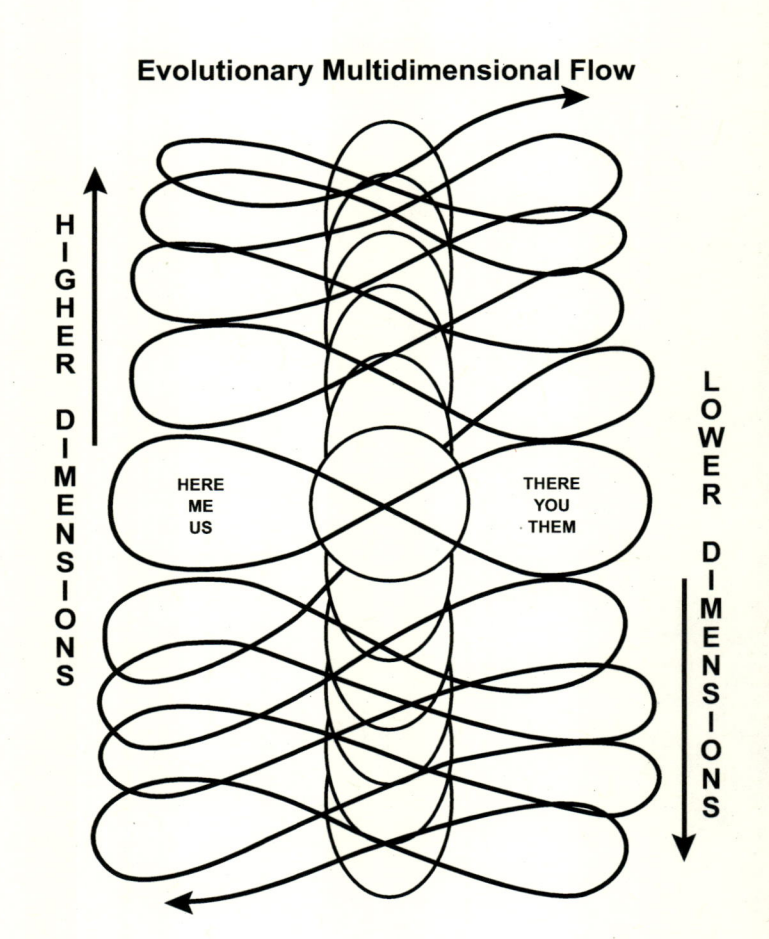

LOWER DIMENSIONS

way to connect and honor each other and the greatest form of honor is service.

You serve through who you are not what you do. Your gracious and honoring presence is the service. When you revere another it is easy to practice redemption. When people feel redeemed, they regain hope in who they are and what they can do. Suddenly they have the energy and determination to stop an addiction, clean up their language, keep a job for more than a month, listen to their children, or join a charitable group where they will always feel needed and honored. It is your desire to believe that they can achieve their highest good and it is their desire to believe in your vision of them that draws both of you to the nexus of loving. There you merge, the one offering redemption releasing a better vision, and the one being redeemed connecting to a higher vision. Both the connection and release occur simultaneously because at that moment you love each other.

Stay in a position of gratitude that says, "Thank you for whatever you are doing to help me that I don't yet understand." This is the place where miracles are born because the intelligent application of divine possibility is engaged. Don't disconnect from being revered by another who recognizes your sacredness. We are sending you out to be the vehicles through which the nexus of loving grows, through which people embrace their holiness and experience your reverence for them. People will begin to understand that when you revere another you automatically serve them in whatever way is required for their highest good. You can't help yourself because you are so excited to have met God in another. You are family.

As you have been reading, Mother/Father/God has been downloading greater capacities within you for connection, release, gratitude, redemption, reverence, benevolence, honor, and service. Grace is all around you. These energies are seeping into you and flowing through you. Be open to starting all over again from a place of reverent grace. Divine possibility is here for you personally and your civilization. Believe in your human and multi-dimensional selves. Believe in us and the parts of us that are human like you. Let us work with and surprise each other with our generosity and humor. We need redemption as much as you do. Don't you know that those needing to be redeemed are the ones who provide redemption for others? This is how you are going to save yourselves and us. You will experience the unconditional love of the Christ Consciousness and in that reverence, beauty and multi-dimensionality you will embody your fifth dimensional consciousness. Humanity is evolving through you. We hug the reverence in you. Now hug the reverence in yourself.

Redemption turns the ugly into the pretty. Experience the beauty in your reverence and let it touch you. See the world as beautiful and so it shall be. Beauty is one of the many destinations we will achieve multi-dimensionally. There is momentum building in this regenerative process on Earth and you are creating it. Already you are encouraging and motivating us to love you even more within the nexus of connection. How can we not? Life is good!

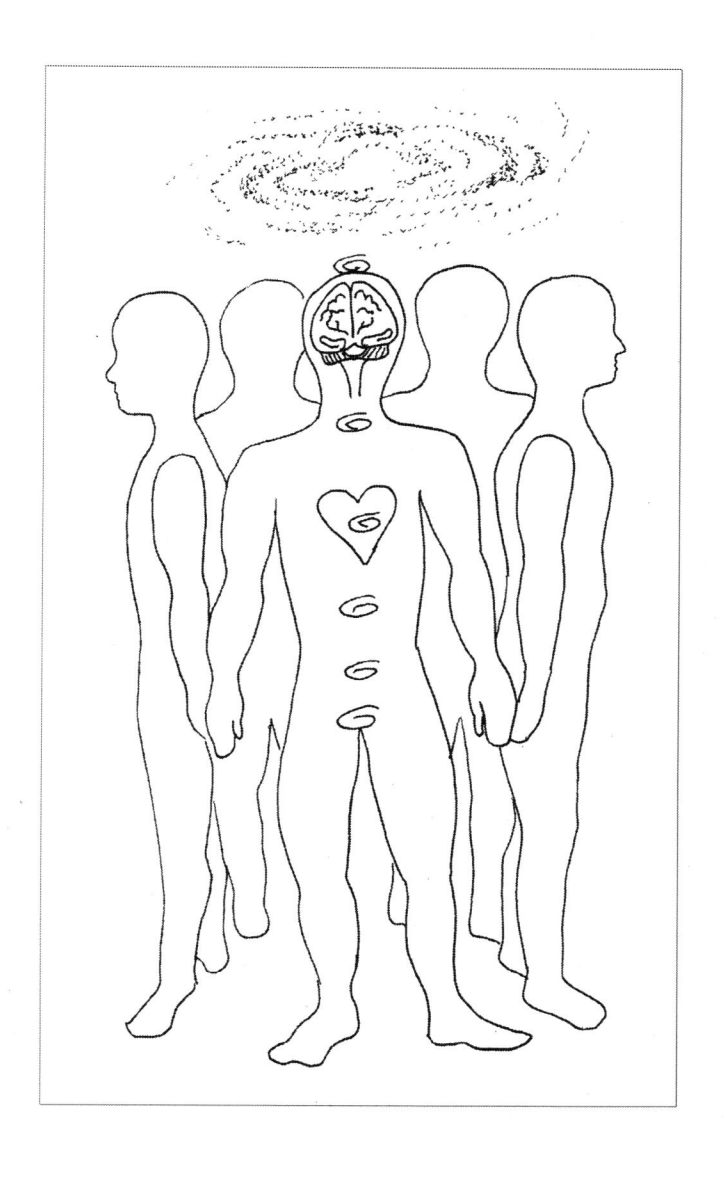

CHAPTER THREE

Your Multi-dimensional Portfolio:
Accessing Divine Wisdom Everywhere

INTRODUCTION

In this chapter, you are introduced to the multi-dimensional as well as the higher-dimensional parts of you that comprise your total being. Connected to this collective experience of yourself, your infinite abilities and creative problem solving skills afford you access to the experiential wisdom of the Universal Mind. Once able to recognize the higher-dimensional and multi-dimensional points of intersection in your daily human experiences, you can begin to transform your life according to your highest multi-dimensional good, thereby assisting in humanity's conscious evolution. Your participation is welcomed in raising human consciousness to a level of compassionate abundance humankind has yet to collectively achieve.

Spending time with yourself from a grounded place of self-awareness is the best way to get to know you. It is a type of meditation that is practiced while awake to improve your personal functioning in every aspect of your life. When you are in full communication with yourself you can effectively utilize all of you to create whatever you desire. For example, if you want to run a twenty-six mile marathon, get a master's degree, or start a business, your mind has to be committed, your body has to be fit, your emotions have to be positive, and your spirit has to guide the way when the going gets rough. Because it takes all of you to achieve your goals, becoming intimate with every part of you is necessary for success. However, from our perspective, few human beings know all of themselves.

Today we are going to introduce you to the rest of "you" — the parts of your being that are not human, but contribute to who you are within your humanity. These are the other invisible parts of you that often impede your mental, emotional, spiritual, and physical growth because of the wounds they have incurred over time. We define a solid individual as one who functions from a grounded place of dimensional awareness. To really know who you are, you have to maintain the dimensional integrity of your current incarnation while accessing multi-dimensional communication with the rest of yourselves. These other versions of you have embodied in the same dimension in differing life forms. Grounded refers not merely to your connection to the planet but also to the parameters of the third dimension. You have to allow yourself to be grounded to your awareness within this third dimension and then connect to all the rest of yourselves living in other dimensions.

Your being is huge and vast. If you always thought that you were the only third-dimensional component of your multi-dimensional profile, guess what? There is more than one of you in the third dimension and not all of you are human. All third-dimensional experiences do not resemble life on Earth. Height, depth, and width remain constant and the electromagnetic fields are similar, but not every third-dimensional world exists in a free will zone. Humanity's experience of fear and separation is extreme. Do you know that you can consciously travel to a third-dimensional world that has always been connected to its divine heritage? You can experience a part of you that lives in peaceful harmony right now. Can you imagine bringing that peaceful and unified experience of yourself back to Earth and watching your fearful human life change? That's precisely the point.

Real versions of you already live within divinity. They can teach you how to reconnect your human nature to your divine nature. You are not clueless about how to embrace the Universal Mind and feel the heart of Mother/Father/God. To access this wisdom, you must move beyond your perceptions and understanding of what happens in your dreams and through Soul travel. Our purpose is to facilitate your conscious connection, not subconscious experience, of your multidimensional and higher-dimensional selves. When you are sleeping you are still under the influence of the electromagnetic currents of this third-dimensional planet. Therefore, you have to interpret your dreams and often miss the message. Many still doubt the visions they receive and dismiss the guidance they provide. Move to a much deeper and more conscious level of awakening. Consciously travel beyond the parameters of your atmosphere. You must be awake to fully participate in the evolutionary development of your world and of the entire cosmos. Your Soul can only go so far without your permission. Consciously tell your Soul to travel further into your exploration of God within and around you.

During this lesson, your human sense of cohesion will begin to dissolve. Do not be afraid of the discomfort such change brings. The gifts of integration, wholeness, wisdom, and wonder being offered are worth the confusion. Consider yourself being given free admission to a Universal Disney World. However, you are walking around the park with very dark glasses that obstruct your vision. You keep looking down so you don't fall and you look around to make sure you don't bump into things. But, you don't yet look up. Too preoccupied with safely maneuvering around, you have not attained the vision necessary to freely explore the universe. Likewise, you haven't yet learned the language to communicate with those producing this celestial show, so your ability to comprehend what is occurring is limited. However, you are welcome and the Celestial Beings of Light recognize and care for you. They are here to teach humanity of its sacred home. Eventually you will run this universal discovery station and care for other life forms and civilizations who feel as limited as you now do.

Start your way up the evolutionary ladder by recognizing your past and future selves, already existing on Earth, as part of your multi-dimensional portfolio. This portfolio is composed of the lifetimes that you are simultaneously experiencing in various time frames in multiple third-dimensional locations. Not only your past and future lives on Earth but your past, present, and future lives being experienced on third-dimensional sites in other star systems and galaxies are part of your portfolio. When we use the word multi-dimensional in this context we are referring to the multiple parts of you living within many worlds existing on the same dimension. This differs from the other parts of you that live in various dimensions. We refer to these parts of you as your higher-dimensional selves.

The importance of your multi-dimensional portfolio cannot be stressed enough. These are the parts of you that are experiencing similar experiments, such as the one you are currently undergoing, but with differing outcomes. Each dimension has specific coordinates of consciousness that define the general experience of the dimension such as type of biology, levels of intelligence, language, perception, electromagnetic signature, etc. However the experience of the life forms living within these parameters is infinitely unique. When you are in constant communication with your various selves in the same dimension, who are completing similar experiments, you can exchange data and develop technologies benefiting all life forms within the dimension. Consider each dimension a vast laboratory experimenting with a specific level of Creation. You are one of the researchers of the third dimension in transition. It is exciting work, don't you agree?

Most of the time we have suggested that you call upon your higher-dimensional selves for assistance. Now we are suggesting that you access your multi-dimensional selves in the same way. You need both forms of your total being to assist humanity's transformation. If you placed both parts of you on a grid, your higher-dimensional selves would be located on the "y" or vertical axis and your multi-dimensional portfolio from one specific dimension would be located on the "x" or horizontal axis. You access both parts of you in different ways but you need both of them to heal and evolve. When you find your way through the mists of memory, you recognize that your memory is vast. By bringing both axes together, you build a greater, more cohesive you than has ever been. You access the higher-dimensional energies from above and the multi-dimensional energies from around and develop a multi-dimensional relationship within a dimensional portfolio. Neat, isn't it?

All of your selves are connecting and releasing within the nexus of loving multi-dimensionally and higher-dimensionally. All of Creation rides a holographic roller coaster that has no end. It flows throughout the cosmos. You are consciously expanding your access to the wisdom of the Universal Mind by flowing with the infrastructure upon which life rides. Mother Earth has called upon her dimensional portfolio of ascending selves to regenerate. Mother Earth is re-creating herself within a higher-dimensional body through the assistance of her higher selves and her multi-dimensional selves. She could not regenerate from the third dimension alone. Because Mother Earth has already engaged her dimensional portfolio in her healing, She is granting humanity easier access to their own dimensional portfolios for evolutionary expansion.

For example, our voice channel Ilona, has resided on this planet for thirty-eight thousand years. Her mission is to facilitate the evolution of humankind into a civilization of peace on an ascended fifth-dimensional planet. Although she has been well trained for this project and has been highly successful in other worlds, humanity has proven to be a challenge for her and for us. She has had over two hundred lifetimes throughout her time on Earth. All of her past and future selves, combined with our past and future selves, together with our collective higher selves, are still trying to figure out how to help humanity heal. Our higher selves and multi-dimensional selves come together because our problem-solving skills and the infinite abilities we posses as a collective far outweigh those we know as individual life forms with specific dimensional perceptions.

We need you to embrace your higher and multi-dimensional selves to save yourselves and us. You are capable of healing and creating peace when you reach beyond what you have known to be you. All of us are playing within the holographic flower of life and reaching out to touch the other in the same dimension and on every other. Although we have offered humanity many options, we continue to search for one that you are willing to embrace. We hope that meeting yourself in many environments will intrigue the human ego enough that you will try to reach beyond the limitations of your perceived self-preservation. Communion within the Universal Mind is your birthright. It is much more interesting and fulfilling than the isolation you currently experience.

Many people are fraught with confusion regarding their careers, relationships, families, and interests. This has always been on the minds of humans. However, the reality of global warming and severe social unrest that jeopardizes the security of even the greatest nation in the world has lead to serious discomfort around the world. In the past, experiences from another peaceful third-dimensional world switched places with the experiences of a violent civilization active on the land you know of as Britain. The legends of King Arthur and Merlin are simply the expression of a multi-dimensional excursion between civilizations on similar, yet very different third-dimensional worlds. As the mists of Avalon gave way to Camelot and a code of honor, service, and responsibility was introduced to humanity on Earth. You were not ready to learn from this advanced version of yourselves. You were unwilling to own your destiny at that time. And so the mists returned and the civilizations were relegated to their proper dimensional locations. Humanity continued to irresponsibly make war against itself.

Your memory on this third-dimensional planet is seriously warped by your dimensional blindness. You live in a fog where the Universal Mind remains invisible. You can clear the fog by embracing your higher-dimensional selves. To do this, you must recognize when and how you are appearing. Then start to learn the lessons that are being presented. The degree to which you remain grounded in your dimensional awareness is the degree to which you will consciously recognize multi-dimensional intersection points in your daily life. You are living a waking meditation in which you are always learning and growing in knowledge, experience, and wisdom. Your connection to the Universal Mind anchors into the spinal cord and nervous systems through the Light Channel. This is the physical infrastructure of the universal roller coaster within you. Keep the tracks of your nervous system clear of debris to enjoy your higher/multi-dimensional evolutionary journey.

You can't just sit in a private or group meditation any longer and expect to be completely successful. You must take the meditation outside as you connect with each other, choosing to live in honor and harmony moment by moment. Consider yourselves as constantly being "on" while you are awake. There is no downtime in your current evolutionary journey on Earth. Everything is radically changing and our learning curve has just jumped through the roof through your conscious participation in our collective mission.

In order to recognize your higher- and multi-dimensional selves, you need to have reference points from this third dimension. Your higher-dimensional selves function from different coordinates of consciousness while your multi-dimensional selves reside in different locations but on the same coordinates of consciousness. The boundaries between dimensions were placed as evolutionary wake-up calls to expand your consciousness and facilitate travel to new dimensional coordinates. Many of you have tapped into your angelic nature by experiencing the emergence of your angel wings in your auric field. Others have felt themselves in their Ascended Master nature during various planetary healing events. When co-creating on small and large projects, some have connected to their association with the Elohim. Yet others have recall of extra-terrestrial life forms in which they have embodied. Consciously remembering these higher-dimensional parts of you facilitates direct communication with these forms of yourself. These experiences are your invitation to limitlessness participation within the holographic flower of life.

However, these boundaries are changing because humanity no longer lives only in the third dimension. Conscious access to the fourth dimension is available to all. Those who choose to build the new civilization of peace are already attaining fifth-dimensional consciousness by exhibiting forgiveness and unconditional love. Points of higher and multi-dimensional intersection are making it easier for you to discover and recognize your many selves every day. Whenever you find yourself confronted by an issue, person, situation, or relationship, you are at a multi-dimensional intersection point. One of your multi-dimensional selves is contacting you through another. The confrontation does not have to be an external argument. It can be an internal fight between the negativity and hope within you. Regardless of where and by whom, your higher selves are triggering you to wake up and recognize the presence of at least one of your multi-dimensional selves.

In whoever is doing you the favor of a confrontation, look beyond the person to find your multi-dimensional self. Only individuals who have agreed to cooperate in cohesive learning will play these roles for you. They have consciously or unconsciously agreed to act as the delivery agents of the Universal Mind. The triggering is not the gift. The recognition of one of your multi-dimensional selves working through another is the valuable experience in your midst. These individuals become a visible mirror for a multi-dimensional part of you that is talking to itself living in you.

For example, we are actively engaged in expanding the life of our channel. She has dutifully lived with little over many lifetimes. She has become so accustomed to working with less, that when more is offered to her, she often refuses. Since one of her lessons in this incarnation is to learn to receive, it is our job to offer her these opportunities. As such, her brother is an eager, willing, and cooperative participant in her growth. It is through him that her multi-dimensional selves speak because then she listens. However, his responses have to be rather forceful to get her attention.

Recently, she was working to obtain a loan to create a website and got very confused with all the financial language and information being given to her. She spoke to her brother about the situation and he could not comprehend how his intelligent sister could be so dumbfounded by the financial industry. He yelled at her to get more information and think clearly about her options or he would have to intervene for her own good. She started crying and admitted that this is new territory for her. She didn't know what she was doing but trying her best to learn about the possibilities. He noted that she doesn't act like she is clueless. She replied that she is lost in the financial language and world. She asked him to help her instead of yelling. He did.

In this scenario her brother became a visible expression of a multi-dimensional part of herself that was saying through him, "You are not paying attention to the abundance, Ilona. There is more for you than you have allowed yourself to experience." He, like her multi-dimensional self, wants her to grow and expand, to have all that she desires. However, she has to become vulnerable enough to get the help she needs to access the available resources. Through her brother, her multi-dimensional selves broke down her wall of confidence to reveal an anxious and confused woman who needed help. Only through her brother were they successful in breaking down the third-dimensional limitations that have robbed her of believing that she can access divine abundance in this world. You see, her multi-dimensional self worked directly through her brother to reach her when no one else could. She literally talked to herself through him.

Your multi-dimensional selves know you better than anyone else because they are you. Always look beyond who is in front of you during a confrontational moment. If you look hard enough you will recognize a dimensional part of yourself. Then always look behind who you are in your current incarnation. In Ilona's case, she has always been so connected to her higher-dimensional and multi-dimensional selves that she regarded divine providence as a given in all environments. When she came to this planet thirty-eight thousand years ago, she had to cope with the limitations of a third-dimensional culture that recognized lack as a way of life. Over thousands and thousands of years she repeatedly experienced the inability of humanity to access divine providence and developed a tough outer skin in her own human lives. She learned how to function well wherever, with whatever, and with whomever, always being gracious for what was given, regardless of how much she may have earned. However, she began to give up on the reality of abundance for her own Earthly sojourn and became invulnerable to need on many human levels. Do you see how her past lives, those multi-dimensional parts of her, were active and continuing to influence her choices? These multi-dimensional selves that have struggled with humanity's essential insecurity are being healed to embrace abundance through the expansion of her business. This healing will resonate throughout her Earthly incarnations in every time frame.

Not every event in your life will be a message from your multi-dimensional selves. But those that become difficult, challenging, or create problems are definitely messages from both your multi-dimensional and higher-dimensional selves. These situations and relationships provide the learning experiences necessary for you to break through negative behavior patterns, disturbing thought processes, emotional distress, and spiritual confusion. Pay attention to flowing through the events. Do not get stuck in pride, judgment, fear, and disbelief. Most of you choose to live in peace, so conflict is rare. However, when it does appear a wound is ready to heal multi-dimensionally, then go to work. Stay in the process and flow to discover the multi-dimensional part of you speaking through the person. Stay aware of the individual cooperating in your healing and your multi-dimensional self. Both are necessary. You cannot dismiss one in favor of the other. In Ilona's case she honored her brother and her multi-dimensional self by her vulnerable acceptance of their support and advice as quickly as she could. Your first response upon recognizing a multi-dimensional intersection point is: "What do I have to learn?"

This evolutionary process is always about what it happening to you and involving you. Even when you find yourself observing a scenario in which you are not directly involved, pay attention to what is being played out for you. Your multi-dimensional and higher-dimensional selves stage plays everywhere around you for free. Learn to recognize the multi-dimensional theatre troupe playing at the grocery store, the gas station, the bank, school, and even in church. You do not need to get involved in the play, but you do need to recognize what you are being taught.

The multi-dimensional mirror is not merely active in individuals. It works for races, nations, civilizations, and life forms as well. Think of it this way: when you recognize that your multi-dimensional selves are talking to you through another and theirs are talking to them through you in the nexus of loving, then what is happening to the infinity channel? You are literally loving your selves through each other and growing more whole within the Oneness. Your own being is growing into infinity, and granting easy access to all parts of yourself within the Oneness. If we can persuade the nations of this world to participate in global governing within the nexus of loving, can you imagine how the lives of those living on this world will change?

All of you are learning how to access your higher and multi-dimensional portfolios. However, many human beings are not even accessing the consciousness available to them in the third dimension. Personal irresponsibility is a critical component of humanity's downfall. Most of humanity remains unconscious while they are awake. You spend more time teaching each other how to compete and envy each other, than you do serving each other's highest good. These public multi-dimensional stage shows are our mirrors asking us to address how we can teach humanity to do better.

From our perspective, flowing with grace is an excellent higher-dimensional mirror to provide for others. When you manage to maintain your composure and compassion in the most distressing of circumstances, others want to know how you accomplished such grace. Your expression of fifth-dimensional unconditional love and forgiveness is so refreshing that others want the same breath of fresh air to wash over them. They may ask you to leave some of your "happy spirit" behind. We desire for them to lift their own spirits in conscious recognition of the good that lives within. When you put these two components together, the presence of your fifth-dimensional selves combined with the raising of their third-dimensional consciousness, you have the intersection of the "x" and "y" axes. Evolutionary development occurs.

People need to know that everything can be fixed here on Earth and everywhere else. However, the solutions do not come from one dimension. They come from many dimensions working together. Then your multi-dimensional portfolios take the solutions out to every dimensional edge. For example, familial karma can be paid off in succeeding generations if the initial injustice is understood. If you discover that your family had negative connections to the mafia three generations ago, try to find out exactly how your family was involved. Then contact your multi-dimensional selves to figure out what good you could do in this life to pay off the debt so that the rest of your family doesn't carry the karma into the next generation. If selling drugs to children on a regular basis was their primary activity, then get involved in substance abuse prevention programs in your local community. At times, familial stories will be revealed in the presence of such as you who can instruct the family on ways to heal. The multidimensional ancestors who created the karma for their current relatives speak through you to help their families heal.

Always be aware of who you are talking to and why, even when you are talking to strangers. You are learning valuable information that we need to understand to creatively solve the human situation on Earth. You are our researchers and our colleagues. We are collectively devising creative solutions to the many human ills that reflect our own wounds. Although all of you are excellent hope generators, we need you to be excellent problem solvers as well. Generating hope is not enough to save your world. You need compassionate and just action. Recognizing what you are to teach and what you have just been taught is the flow. Once you are in divine flow, you can solve the problems that you are now capable of recognizing. This is divine wisdom in action.

Be of service by recognizing what someone attempted to teach you. In recognizing how you missed the intersection points of your multi-dimensional education, your ability to communicate with your multidimensional and higher-dimensional selves will grow. When you immediately recognize what is occurring, you can stay in the situation and relationship long enough to learn what you need to heal from whatever part of you is talking. Apply this knowledge to future situations so your wisdom grows. You do not need to transform every situation in which you find yourself, but you do need to learn from your participation in each of them. Sometimes your presence introduces a concept or process that another will complete.

Live beyond what you are told that you need. This does not mean to go out and by another car. Instead, discover what life has to offer you beyond what you have accepted as your current life. When you are in divine flow, there is always more of you to discover and enjoy, if you will allow your evolutionary expansion to commence. Instead of trying to figure out what your new life will look like, surrender into its constant emergence, doing your part towards manifestation as your higher/multi-dimensional selves direct.

Shortly, all of humanity will find itself surrendering into the emergence of a collective new life, surrendering into a life you do not yet know. Our channel is currently learning how to do this as we work in and through her. We have given her glimpses of her life to come but she cannot figure out how what she is doing now will lead to what she will be doing next. Feeling the success to come she will manifest her new physical life through this third- and multi-dimensional process. Many other people will get involved in her mission. Some will cooperate and others will not. That is okay. Be willing to recognize the glimpses of your new life through the others with whom you will come into contact. Don't try to comprehend the future, just accept the good feelings you are generating and allow the emotions to flow you into greater manifestation of your highest good.

If you are feeling anxious, frightened or negative about your future, pay attention. Emotion creates the cohesion through which your future life will manifest. Fear will manifest negativity, confusion, pain, and disease. If these choices are unacceptable for your future, then change the way you are now living. Consider how much negativity humanity generates through its newspapers and television throughout the world. Is it any wonder that you live in fear and generally expect the worst of each other as a civilization? You have to change the mood of the entire planet to heal the wounds of the many. The media could be of great service if it would choose to move its focus to the positive, healing, and hopeful activities that are occurring around the world.

We are asking you to join us as multi-dimensional problem solvers for humanity and indeed the entire galaxy. Put your fears to rest and live your lives so that others can feel your love and joy. Most important, share your hope in others so that they can rise to the occasion and grow beyond their unconscious ignorance. As long as you are accessing your higher-/multi-dimensional selves, you will know peace and providence. Don't get caught up in the hysteria of the world. You have no need.

You are living a waking meditation in the nexus of loving. You are in contact with your higher-/multi-dimensional selves and with us. Don't try to solve your problems with third-dimensional insights. Do what you are called to do multi-dimensionally and follow your healing to completion. In recognizing what you are being taught and embracing this knowledge through experience you will use your human systems for their highest good for as long as they last. The solutions are not found in your current global systems, but the systems can be helpful in working towards the solutions.

Anything global will eventually affect everyone personally. Likewise, every personal decision you make, from the car you drive to the food you eat, affects the world. Most people are afraid of the future. Many are either running away from or stuck in the past, and few are living in the present. However, everyone is concerned about what happens to their children, their homes, their jobs, and their checkbooks. Convenience and comfort are the hallmarks of human vanity. Anything that interrupts this human flow is seen as a threat to one's well being. However, humanity is sick and the human flow has created the disease. If you all were really happy, fear wouldn't live on Earth. That's why we've come to help you heal.

This is the paradigm shift humanity must embrace: the needs of the many outweigh the needs of the few. In other worlds, the all comes before the one. We are collectively solving multi-dimensional problems to create a just society where everyone is cared for and luxury ceases to be. You will all live in luxury or no one will. Humanity has never endorsed compassionate abundance for the entire civilization. Eventually you will. The Essene communities who visited your world two thousand years ago brought this conscious awareness to humanity through Jesus the Christ. You were not ready to love then and you are still caught in hatred now. But there is hope and there are all of you to join with us as multi-dimensional problem-solvers to save this civilization.

You are beings grounded in your higher-/multi-dimensional awareness. You are clear about how you are learning and how you are being taught. You are solving problems with your expanding knowledge and dimensional experiences. And through the wisdom of the Universal Mind expressing itself through you, new life is manifesting within and all around you. Don't worry about how the new life will look in the third dimension. You won't be living in 3D for long anyway. Know that Life is changing because of your loving and so are we. Simply flow in divine timing, recognizing what your collective self is being taught and manifestation of every good will follow. Flow into and through God and the waters of Grace will move you to abundant and peaceful joy.

We offer you the following meditation to develop and practice your multi-dimensional communication skills.

MULTI-DIMENSIONAL PORTFOLIO MEDITATION

Breathe in the present moment. Relax into your current human body. Activate and open your Earth Star beneath your feet and run your energy into Mother Earth's chakra column. It flows through Mother Earth's Solar Star and into the chakra column of our solar system. Feel your energy moving through our yellow Sun into the chakra column of our Milky Way Galaxy. Your energy travels into the galactic Sun into the chakra column of our universe. Your energy flows into the Great Central Sun and into the chakra columns of the many universes making up the cosmos. Feel the energy and the love flowing back to you from all of these Celestial Beings as a beautiful cloud that rides across your sky. Feel a gentle loving energy raining down upon you.

As the rain begins to touch your auric field, feel all of your multi-dimensional selves within the third dimension throughout Creation receiving this tender loving energy. Feel all of your higher-dimensional selves contributing to the love that is now falling down upon you.

Wiggle your toes and caress this planetary body that you call home. Gently tickle Mother Earth until she giggles. Stop tickling her and let your toes softly, tenderly, and lovingly touch the Earth until you feel that you are melting into the planet. As you do so invite all of your multi-dimensional selves from the past, the present, and the future of the incarnation in which you now reside to join you here. As each part of you enters, they join the group placing their feet within the large circle being created by all of the selves that comprise who you are on the third dimension. A huge circle will emerge from the Oneness of your multi-dimensional portfolio. Now look beyond the feet and into each other's eyes, however they may appear. Recognize and honor each other. These are all YOU. The past and the future and the present experiences of you living on all the third-dimensional worlds in the cosmos are gathered together here and now.

To make this process easier, ask that four of you join with your human Earthly self in an intimate smaller circle within the larger circle that YOU have created. Visualize all five selves moving into the middle of the larger circle. Know that they are as interested in you as you are in them. Truly look at each of your selves with love and respect. You are going to notice a common characteristic among yourselves. Allow the common characteristic to be recognized and affirmed by all of you. As you recognize this commonality, let the human part of you consciously embrace the talent or ability all of you have developed multi-dimensionally.

Go deeper within the meditation and fully see your selves. Ask questions. What do they do? How do they do it? What does it feel like? How does it relate to what you do or do not do here on Earth? Share with each other your successes and failures in your common endeavors. This is your time to learn and grow from each other. If your portfolio includes educators, athletes, engineers, healers, journalists, politicians, or any other professionals discover how each has become proficient, thereby increasing the knowledge base of the whole. If difficulties have arisen for a par-

ticular self, devise a strategy among the collective you to assist this self to achieve the desired goals. This is the time to use all of you to solve problems for each of you.

Pay attention to how YOU feel. Honoring the emotional state of your collective being will guide you to the information you require from and about each other. Open your hearts to fully connect with each other. Your knowledge and experience will flow as the emotion from your collective heart opens. You are the information of the collective mind. You are communicating with yourselves within a multi-dimensional meeting to further your individual and collective evolution. As you collectively grow so does your contributions to the worlds in which you live. Your presence becomes an even greater gift as you consciously bring the rest of yourselves to where each of you live. In accessing each other's wisdom you will manifest the best in life for every one of "you" and all those touched by "you." Enjoy!

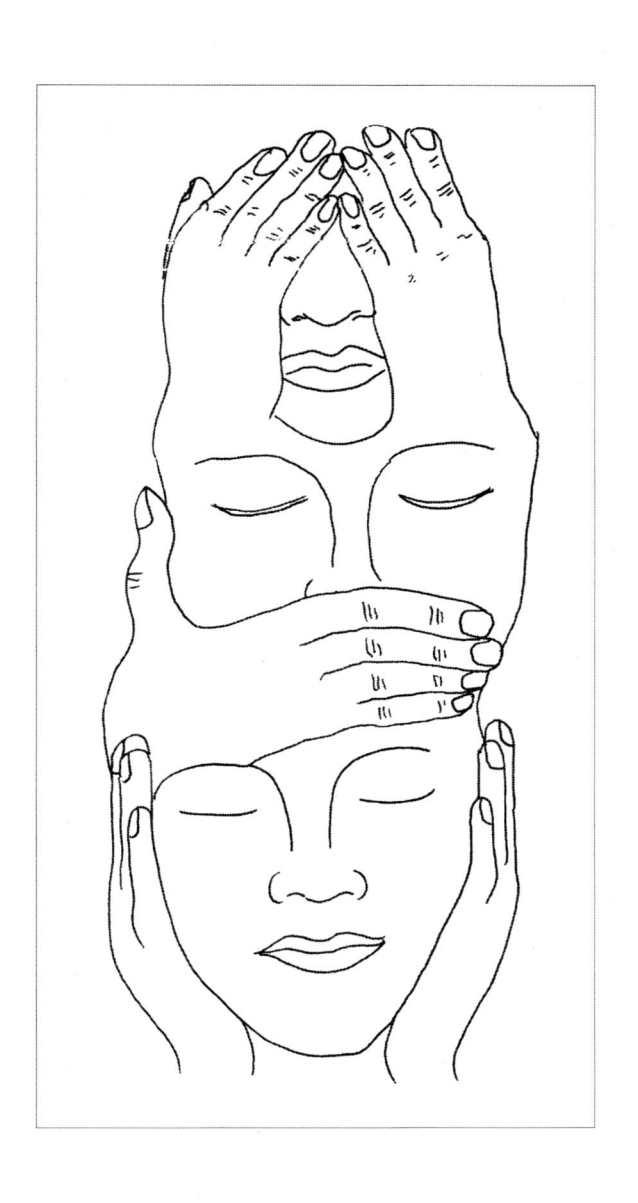

Chapter Four

Be Aware of Your Ignorance:
The Collective Education of Humanity

Introduction
This chapter outlines the debilitating consequences that human ignorance has created within this civilization. It offers the development of intuitive awareness and faithful action as a prescription to heal the devastating path humanity has thus far chosen to pursue. It offers personal and collective responsibility as a key to unlocking the institutionalized ignorance that has imprisoned the collective education of humanity. Free to develop beyond the bounds of fear, lack, and separation, it offers the possibility of self-supporting communities, each interacting with the other all over the globe. Through graciously serving each other the unconditional love of fifth-dimensional consciousness will give birth to a new civilization of peace on Earth.

Ignorant people act disrespectfully and they don't even know it. They are oblivious to any other reality than that which they experience. They generally isolate, preferring the company of those who share similar perspectives. Life feels comfortable and safe, but that doesn't mean that it is. When anything or anyone challenges those life experiences and offers opportunities for growth, the ignorant can feel threatened or saved, depending upon the circumstance. Trying to convince ignorant people that life can be better is often a dangerous enterprise, unless you can prove how valuable you or your ideas are to their daily life. Developing self-awareness is the goal, not trying to manipulate a people or save a civilization. This is not missionary work. It is evolution. Today, we lay the groundwork for awakening the ignorant of humanity to become the wise who will save this civilization from self-annihilation.

Ignorance is a major impediment to evolutionary advancement because it breeds disrespect that goes unrecognized. If you do not know that the media are controlling the information you receive, then you will believe what you read, hear, and see as the truth. However, once you learn that what you read was a lie because you talked to the person in question, or did some in-depth research of your own and discovered the facts, you will have become aware of journalistic discretion. From that moment on you may start asking questions, challenging perceived authorities and beginning to think for yourself. Education has just become a significant part of your life.

You cannot be aware and ignorant simultaneously. However, in awareness the eyes can be open while the mind consciously chooses to remain closed. How many of you overeat or intoxicate yourselves even though you know better? Education is the movement of those who are aware reaching out to the ignorant with the information they need to overcome difficulties. Education is also the movement of the ignorant reaching out to the aware with experiences that need to be rectified. Currently there is a great division between the aware and the ignorant. Instead of paying attention to each other and learning from each other, they blame and use each other to escape responsibility for creating their own separate realities. We seek to develop a commonly shared reality.

Education, from our perspective, is the pursuit of informed wisdom. To what does informed wisdom refer? Can you think of an individual who has great life experience in a trade such as masonry, alterations, computer programming, electronics, or landscape design, but cannot tolerate the idea of gun control to protect the general safety of the children of the United States? Can you think of a group of individuals committed to the economic welfare of the world, such that they would insure that the wealth of the planet be divided evenly among all human beings? Education is a problem because it depends on who is doing the educating. Knowledge does wield power. However, those wielding the power control the information being provided to a specific audience for a pre-identified purpose. Always ask yourself, "Who is doing the educating and for what purpose?" When you understand the context in which you are receiving information you will be able to make wise decisions, no longer acting out of ignorance. The Universal Mind will never manipulate you. Mother/Father/God will always stimulate your intellect with creative, life-affirming possibilities.

Many of those considered to be highly educated have earned advanced degrees and possess an expanded knowledge base in a particular field of study. Professors are keenly aware of certain aspects of society and the environment. However, their attention to academics generally keeps them in the role of an observer. Their knowledge base can serve to improve the lived experience of humanity but only when effectively applied. In the movie, "Nell" with Jodie Foster and Liam Neeson, the fields of psychology, medicine, social work, and law competed to either control or honor an unusual human being. Academicians need to join hands with those who live within the areas they study. They need to embrace these individuals as their worldly teachers, not merely research subjects.

Lived experience becomes wisdom over time, but wisdom without an informed knowledge base leaves much to be desired. You can't apply what you don't know. When early man discovered how to make fire the collective knowledge base of the entire civilization grew. Everyone learned how to build and light a fire. Over time this grew into creating fireplaces, stoves, heating systems, rockets, etc. A base of knowledge combined with lived experience expands new information into application. The information becomes useful to life experience and people teach each other how to grow.

Awareness is always connected to information while ignorance is always connected to experience. You have to utilize both to evolve individually and collectively. Those living in what you consider to be your third-world countries do not collectively have access to the knowledge base that would contribute to their lived experience. Therefore, their ability to financially provide for themselves is compromised. However, your world powers, especially the United States, have hoarded their information and intellectual resources, limiting academic and technological advances to literally institutionalize ignorance. This is the basis of humanity's disrespect for itself.

We are sending you out into the world with lived experiences and an informed knowledge base so that you will grow to educate yourselves by becoming aware of what, where, and whom you are ignorant! This is the only true departure point for learning. Every academician will tell you that they learn the most when they are challenged to explain a newly discovered physical process, embrace a previously unrecognized philosophical or spiritual truth, or engage in an artistic endeavor that moves art and music into new directions. However, what you don't know is that the academics are so busy competing for the accolades of first discovery that they withhold information from each other and the public deliberately. The collective academic ego holds the development of the collective consciousness at bay. But, only if you let it.

Education is always collective. It is never merely singular. There is nothing happening on this planet, especially with the global links offered through the world wide web, that each of you cannot access either consciously or unconsciously. The collective knowledge base of this civilization grows through each of you to affect all of you. When you collectively demand exposure to your academic and technological advances, you shall have them. Then it is up to you to appropriately utilize these resources to manifest peace, health, and abundance throughout the world.

Who is the current guardian of the collective technology and knowledge base of humanity? It is not the academics, for even they are controlled by the same entity controlling you right now. The governments of every nation censure the collective education of every society and culture. Your government promotes literacy while others deny it to their populations. Governments literally control access to medical, environmental, political, and sociological breakthroughs, denying you the right to make your own decisions about what is best for your world. Then, they fight among themselves over who should have how much of each resource, technology, information or power. All of you must acknowledge that you abdicated your role and right to make informed choices by placing the full responsibility for such information into the hands of your governing bodies. Because you collectively did not choose to make these decisions for yourselves, you created groups of individuals to make them for you without considering the consequences.

A collective level of knowledge and experiential wisdom can be accessed by this civilization if governmental restrictions can be bypassed. This is not necessarily easily but the process is already occurring by necessity. If you are going to survive as a civilization, your governments must fall so that free, non-polluting technologies become available to all. As the governments collapse, one by one, the scientists, doctors, teachers, and healers bound by governmental restrictions will be free to share all they know in service to humanity. This information will include the higher-dimensional technologies brought to Earth through extra-terrestrial contact with the governments of the world. Your governments have long held the solutions to global warming, the deadliest of diseases, and peaceful co-habitation.

Your governments have chosen, through free will, to imprison this civilization by fear into separation. By limiting access to technology and information, resources and economic power were distributed according to who knew how to use what against whom. The result was the emergence of the world powers and third-world countries. You are either one of those who have access to abundant resources or one who is left to scramble for existence.

This division between the ignorant and the aware created an even greater obstacle to overcome in the development of the collective education of humanity. The downtrodden came to believe that they were and are worthless, not deserving of more or better. They played into the hands of the governing bodies such that those who have were content with not sharing. Abundant resources were perceived as belonging to those who earned them, not as a human right. Thus greed and power grew in the hands of the "privileged" who decided that they could own and manipulate the rest of the civilization because many people were easily duped. Even the middle class within the United States has developed a "privileged" attitude when it comes to welcoming immigrant populations into the country. When certain people or groups become problematic they can be threatened or actually dismissed through military resources if necessary.

In the present, those in privileged positions of power are being given the opportunity to rectify the fearful imprisonment of the population into ignorant separation. Hope does not work with the ignorant. Proof that alternative energy sources are available for popular consumption is necessary to enlist the population in using them. When he was the presidential candidate, John Kerry had no proof to offer the people of the United States that he could make life better for the citizenry. President George Bush had all the proof he needed to continue to feed the public a diet of terrorizing fear which has created a toxic society that is beginning to gag on its own immorality.

The general public will believe in a car that runs on water when they see them in the showrooms and drive them on the highways. When those with cancer, AIDS, and other debilitating diseases are cured by the release of advanced medical technologies, some of which are extra-terrestrial in origin, they will regain confidence in humanity's compassion and love. Those who possess these technologies are responsible for making it accessible and available to the general public out of personal integrity to the well being of the civilization, and the regeneration of the planet. When the individuals who have answers to humanity's problems become personally responsible for sharing the solutions with the population, significant advances to the collective education occur.

Moreover, when the governments introduce the public to the benevolence of extra-terrestrial cultures, already committed to healing the Earth and its people, the leadership necessary for this planet to enter into full communion with its solar and galactic family will have finally arrived. Instead of fearing a UFO, humanity will be trained and ready to enter into positive, effective, and cooperative relationships with higher and multi-dimensional life forms who have the technologies we need to save ourselves. Humanity can offer its third-dimensional life experiences to other worlds who could easily make the same mistakes you have.

Equitable access to resources does not rest on fearing the collapse of an economic infrastructure dependent upon oil consumption. The issue belies the need for the formation of an equitable economic infrastructure based on free technology. The primary resources of the Earth need to be freely given to all of its inhabitants because this is the essential nature of the planet. This is one of the primary tenets of the new civilization of peace. Every human being must be enabled to contribute his or her best to the collective education of this civilization. It is the mandate of those who control the resources to share them with those who need them until every human being is given enough food, shelter, work, and support to be at peace. Then there will be nothing over which to fight and everything with which to love.

Those who are aware do not need proof. They have developed intuition and live in faith. They serve each other without question, regardless of the cost. However, humanity has not been a faithful civilization. Faithful people eventually get angry and act against injustice. Some have lead revolutions into global awareness such as Mahatma Gandhi, those who signed the Declaration of Independence of the United States of America, Nelson Mandela, Mikhail Gorbachev, and many others the world over. They didn't need proof that change was possible. They became the proof and empowerment followed. This is what we are asking of you. However, anger is no longer necessary.

We are preparing you to be the proof that faithful action propels evolutionary change within the collective civilization. You are to live the experiences and share the stories of those who receive all the resources required to serve humanity because they trust in divine providence. Commit yourselves to fulfilling your divine missions and your support and equipment will come. In my case, it became clear that part of my mission is to establish a website and publishing company devoted to developing the consciousness of humanity. Having limited financial resources I nonetheless sought out what the financial world could offer. I spent thirteen hundred dollars just to access a line of credit that would cover the initial operating costs at a very high interest rate. Within days of engaging the line of credit, I was given a ten thousand dollar gift with which to develop the business, no strings attached! Faith manifests new realities but you have to step out on the precipice first.

Mother/Father/God will provide your wings in the most amazing of ways.

This story is one of many that needs to be shared with those who still require proof that faith works on the physical plane. With every story of amazing blessings, the collective knowledge base grows to accept intuitive awareness as a valid form of manifesting new possibilities. When those who need resources begin to access goods and services from those who have them to offer, without being manipulated or censured, sincere help becomes a practical and realistic possibility. My local newspaper ran a story this week about a couple who recently gave birth to triplets. Having no family close by and living on limited economic resources, they decided to run an advertisement in their church bulletin for a "fairy godmother" to help them raise their children. They accessed divine intervention and it worked. An entire Girl Scout Troop, senior citizens, and neighbors have come to aid the family on a regular basis. Not only did this couple believe in divine providence, they accessed it.

Faith will only take unconscious humanity so far. Faithful action will awaken them to Mother/Father/God's presence because you become God in action. The heavenly definition of an intellectual is one who is able to recognize and utilize the possibilities around. If humanity is going to develop its intellectual capacity, you must believe in possibility. How is this different from faith? Faith is an amorphous experience. You never know how Mother/Father/God is going to surprise you. You trust, flow, and receive. Possibilities are much more concrete. They can practically be imagined and are easily comprehended by the human mind. You also have to participate in their completion.

In order for the average human being to embrace the faithfulness that supercedes third-dimensional limitations, they have to experience possibilities that work.

Every significant technological advance emerged because someone was inspired to act in a new and unexpected way. Those who become aware develop their intuitive ability and contribute to the collective education of the civilization through hard work. Divine intervention lead Alexander Graham Bell to build the telephone and Thomas Edison to build the light bulb. That was just the beginning. Now, humanity enjoys the internet and fiber optics. Scientists and entrepreneurs live through inspiration and act on faith. Henry Ford's good idea created a new industry that revolutionized human accessibility. The knowledge base of humanity grows through experience to expand the collective education of the civilization. It all starts with the few who act on faith.

As of November 2, 2004, it became apparent to many citizens of the United States that they could no longer count on their government to care for them. Most of the people around the world already know this. Those living in Central America have lived through one military junta after another. Those born in the Middle East emerge within a violent human drama. If they chose to stay within these geographical confines, then they may violently die in this tragic saga of hatred, entitlement, and revenge. Governments, in their corruption, have become ignorant to the needs of their people. Therefore, they will collapse. The collective education of this civilization requires that humanity withdraws their power from the governments and becomes self-responsible as small communities that interact with each other. You have never collectively engaged in self-responsibility. Now is the time.

When you don't rely on your government for water, sewage, garbage, electricity, gas, currency, medical assistance, or education, for what do you need it? You are free to live in your power and create a new world that is defined by cooperation and service. There is no need for the military because there are no countries fighting over resources. Nobody else is fighting either. Everybody's basic needs are met through each other. That is, if you are willing to help each other.

Mother Earth's regeneration will fuel the disarming of governmental power. As She reclaims the air, earth, water, fire, and ether of her planetary body, natural resources will be withdrawn from the grasp of every government around the world. Every person will be forced to develop a personal relationship with the elements of this planet. Those who live in awakened possibility will be blessed by the services they render to the planet. Those who have raped her won't.

This is where the ignorant will suffer and die while the aware will have already engaged in the faithful actions that allow them to weather the storms with hopeful grace. Begin to master organic gardening, alternative energy sources, water purification, waste management and alternative healing methods. Possibility needs to merge with awareness not to create the faithful action necessary for your survival. However, you will not return to tribal states of being. You have extra-terrestrial technologies that will revolutionize your ideas of comfort and convenience without disturbing the planet, right now. Start developing a collective education that takes power away from the governments and returns it into the hands of the community. Become aware of just how important you are to each other.

The world is shaking today because it recognizes that its greatest power has just fallen. The collective consciousness of the United States of America chose fear over hope, war over peace, and power over cooperation. If the United States can no longer hold the vision for a just, free, honorable, and compassionate society, who will? Every government around the world is trying to figure out how to respond. Are they going to compete with each other for the spoils? Already the United States has transferred its merchandizing base to China and its technological base to India. By depositing their wealth into third-world countries to maximize profit, American corporations, given government approval, have assisted in the creation of an economic infrastructure in parts of the world where it was desperately needed. Those who have hoarded the resources of the world have unwittingly given them away. The United States has indirectly created a new world order out of their own greed. Unfortunately their economic infrastructure is collapsing while they are still living within it.

This will be much more traumatic than watching the twin towers fall in upon themselves. Millions of lives are at stake and there are no terrorists from outside of this country more powerful than those who were born and are still living here. The governments of the world are wondering if they need to band together for protection since they can no longer trust or honor this government or its people. What will the world do about the United States of America?

The threat of an external act of terrorism is not the issue. Humanity has chosen to terrorize itself repeatedly. However, the United States was created to be the vision of a civilization, indeed, the embodiment of a culture learning how to love in diversity and live in peaceful justice. Although the nation made serious gains in this arena, its power and greed have made it now the most serious threat to planetary stability. A question is being posed to the entire civilization through the United States of America. Are you choosing to be responsible for yourselves or are you choosing to fearfully react to the possibility of planetary chaos?

When you are responsible for yourself you can control your reactions to news and events. Initially, humanity reacts. You have not yet evolved to embrace response as a better methodology than reaction. Only after thoughtfully processing the situation can you respond through faithful action. The United States is being used to increase the collective education of humanity through its irresponsible behavior. The results of the 2004 election sent a clear message to the world that the United States is no longer the powerful protector of humanity that it was in World War II. Many are asking themselves, "If the supposedly most advanced society on this planet is truly this unconscious, what does this say about the rest of the world?"

Many individuals not only expressed sadness but also became ill upon hearing the election results. This physical distress was representative of a turning point, not merely for this nation but for this civilization. Are we going to continue to sicken ourselves until we die? Will this civilization choose to become conscious of its responsibilities? If this is the wake up call, then what are the possibilities and how do we achieve them? Human ignorance is being replaced by awareness. Evolutionary gains are on the way.

In the United States, hope is not enough to unite a divided country. Huge marches on Washington have not and will not change this administration's policies. We need you to believe in possibility not create drama. Hullabaloo is not where you belong. Stay in the center of self-responsibility and learn how to ground yourself in a new reality in which you are not dependent upon the government, but upon yourselves. This is the shift that is already taking place within the minds of those who are aware and walking the evolutionary path. This does not mean that you dig bomb shelters or hide in the wild. There is no fear in the new world order. There is grace.

Build communities that create harmony in work and in play. You have to begin by trusting yourself to live differently and better, then trust those you love to do the same, and those they love to the do same, and on it goes. Eventually, humanity will trust each other again because you have learned to respect rather than judge each other. You don't trust those you cannot respect. This situation is no longer about the United States. It involves the entire world and every member of this civilization from babies to senior citizens. Isolation will disappear as crises demand faithful action. You need each other more than you know.

Relax into the changes ahead. Flow through the emergence of the new civilization of peace as it manifests among and through you. Love neutralizes fear and encourages possibility. Do not have preconceived ideas of how your new life will look because you cannot comprehend it with your third-dimensional minds. Live in faithful action and encourage each other with a healthy sense of humor. Love as you have never loved before. Embrace possibility and see your lifestyles positively change. Engage benevolent extra-terrestrial assistance and enjoy your galactic family. They are here to help, support, and love you as you become responsible co-creators of a new world. Allow your awareness, intuition, and informed wisdom to develop the collective education of humanity such that everyone will want to choose to build this new civilization of peace. What you are doing now becomes part of the collective education of this civilization. Humanity has never consciously owned itself. Now, you must. You are growing beyond your human limitations to make unconditional love a reality. You are banishing fear from a civilization that is finally finding its way home into its Divine Heart. You are raising the consciousness of an entire civilization to embrace its Soul.

A Meditative Process to Help You Embrace Your Solar and Galactic Family:

Settle into the moment, breathe out the stress of your day, and breathe in the presence of your Soul. Invoke the presence of this multi-dimensional spiritual collective and Mother/Father/God. Allow your Divine Parents to settle in and be present. Feel the complete balance, total harmony, and pure beauty of Mother/Father/God's masculine and feminine energies reaching out to each of us and enveloping us in a blanket of creative loving. Mother/Father/God touches our hearts in a holographic web, uniting us within a tremendous cascade of loving.

Hear Mother/Father/God singing to you: See your hearts joined as one. Feel our loving. We are One. Moving near and far, small and wide, there is no space. There is no time. All we are is one heart. All we are is one mind. All we feel is one Love opening our eyes. We have much to see today. We have much to hear this way. We are not afraid to fly. We have even touched the sky. Now we float home. Now we float home, meeting peace in our love. Being at peace in our love. We are One home.

Feel the comfort and the belonging, the harmony and the support of your divine home. Relax into it now. Truly surrender into this love and feel it supporting you. Feel it supporting all life in this collective. Feel every link between all of your multi-dimensional and inter-dimensional hearts providing lifelines from My heart to all of yours. Float into this network of love. Trust it.

Put your hands out in front of you and feel your arms being supported by this ocean of creative loving. Allow the full weight of your arms to descend into the air and feel the support. Now, allow your whole body to float within this ocean of loving. Now feel all of the extra-terrestrials, the angels and the Ascended Masters, and the Elohim in the same loving web, in the same light nebula. All of you are floating and supported and loved. This is our home. This is where you belong. This is of what you are part, the awakened, the intuitive, the informed wise ones. This is you. This is us. We are.

When you are feeling unfaithful in your lives and need proof, reach out. Call forth this sea of our loving and feel it supporting you. Feel it upholding you. Yes, reach out to each other and reach out to us in the Heavens too. We are here for you. We will guide and lead and we will instruct and comfort. We support your growing awareness, your collective education. You are far from ignorant. Trust and learn.

You are my Beloveds in whom I AM well pleased.

Allow divine music to penetrate your auric field: When you reach out and touch love, love will support you. Reach out and touch love, I AM here. Hold onto loving. Hold onto hearing all that our hearts know. We are whole, holy ones, holy ones. Hearts that are wise are holy ones. Reaching out to touch you, holy ones.

And so it is. And so it is. From this moment forward you are held and supported in this ocean of loving. It is through this ocean of loving that the collective education of your civilization will occur. It cannot be stopped. It will not be stopped. Your loving, our loving, is too great and it turns ignorance into wisdom through you, through us. And so as always, My Heart is yours.

Chapter Five

Civilized Power:
Masculine and Feminine Communion

Introduction
This chapter describes gender equality as the means to a peaceful civilization. It outlines the importance of reclaiming the feminine energies within a civilization whose masculine focus has left much of the population suffering under violent devastation. Integration, compassion, tenderness, and unconditional loving are offered as a four-part strategy to heal the wounds of humanity. Men and women, as equal complements to each other, can save humanity from self-destruction.

In order to fully experience this chapter, please complete the following meditation before reading further.

Opening Meditation
Visualize your Soul Star as a big bright Sun about a hand's length above your head. Spin it down into a disc moving counterclockwise above you. Visualize your Earth Star as a big brown orb about a foot beneath your feet. Spin the orb down into a disc moving counterclockwise beneath you. Feel your feet being pulled into this connection with the third-dimensional planet on which you reside. Feel the higher-dimensional energy of your Soul radiating out of the Soul Star disc and flowing around your body, creating a cylinder of light that connects with the Earth Star beneath you. Feel a golden beam of light penetrate the center of your Soul Star disc and flood your brain with light. The golden light travels into the brain stem and into the spinal cord. It moves through the base of the spine, down through the legs, out of the soles of the feet, and into the Earth Star. The golden light now

travels through Mother Earth's chakra column, into the chakra column of the Solar System, through the Sun, into the chakra column of the Milky Way Galaxy, into the galactic Sun, into the chakra column of this Universe, and into the Great Central Sun of our Universe. Feel yourself linked within the web of life of our Universe.

Visualize a tender pink orb descending through the Light Channel you have just activated. Feel Mother/Father/God's heart descending into you and anchoring into your heart chakra. Spin the green orb in your heart down into a disc counterclockwise within your chest. Feel the creative loving of Mother/Father/God flooding your heart. Allow your heart chakra to expand, connecting with the heart chakras of all life forms in this Universe. The pink light now moves up into your head and activates your third eye chakra. Spin down the indigo orb in your forehead into a disc counterclockwise. Feel this creative loving move into your third eye. Feel your third eye chakra connecting with the third eye chakras of all life forms in this Universe. Now feel Mother/Father/God's love move down into your pelvis activating your sacral chakra. Spin down the orange orb into a disc counterclockwise as it absorbs this creative loving into its matrix. Expand your sacral chakra connecting with the sacral chakras of all life forms in this Universe. Relax into all the multi-dimensional creative loving pouring in and through you now.

Imagine a horizontal pink beam of light radiating out of every heart in this Universe, directly in front of the body. Now imagine another pink beam emerging from every third eye and another pink beam coming out of every sacral chakra. Allow the third eye beams and sacral beams to intersect with the heart beams creating a pyramid of energy directly in front of all of you. Although Mother/Father/God's heart is within us, it also exists at the apex of the pyramid created outside of, and in front of us, at the center of the Universal Light Channel. Breathe Moth-

er/Father/God's multi-dimensional loving back into you through the pyramid and feel your multi-dimensional ability to visualize, feel, and manifest love growing with each breath.

*   *   *

All loving is, by necessity, creative. Love seeks to become more than it has already been. Loving creates something out of nothing. It forms relationships that did not previously exist. Right now, you are now fully engaged in Mother/Father/God's web of creative loving. This web is the cohesive blueprint upon which creativity manifests in every dimension in this Universe. In their relationship, Mother/Father/God generates a gentle, dynamic power that is the source of all loving. Every family on every celestial body in this Universe emerges from this core energetic bond between Mother/Father/God. Experienced intimately by two adults, creative loving manifests new people on the planet. When males and females unite within a civilization, their loving manifests powerful peace, abundance, and creativity. A couple opens not only their hearts to each other, but also their minds and their bodies. They share a common vision of how to contribute to life and live in a common home, creatively manifesting what love means to them and their children. Thus, creative loving involves a lot more than the heart. It creates environments.

A gentle environment that produces peaceful relaxation is necessary for creativity to flourish. When you are stressed and overwhelmed it is difficult to be creative. Moments of discovery happen when you allow time for exploration. In our society, time has become a precious commodity. We are generally overbooked, driven to distraction, and often pining for vacation. Our masculine focus on productivity is at the expense of our collective creativity. We need many more gentle rather than productive men to reclaim the peaceful environments through which we will all learn how to heal the world.

Isn't it interesting that the word gentleman is used only for men? Men are not generally perceived as gentle beings. What is the point of identifying a man as gentle? In the presence of a gentle man, you experience feminine awareness combined with masculine power. A gentleman at his best is both protective and nurturing simultaneously. It is no accident that gentleman is a word that has long been used in the English language. Throughout your tumultuous history and ravaging warfare you have always been seeking gentle men to bring peace and stability to humanity.

Gentility is a feminine factor of creative genius. It provides safety through tender protection, not violence. Consider being raised in a war zone where your father sits outside your bedroom door with a rifle on his lap and a pistol in his belt while you sleep. Consider being raised on a farm in the middle of the United States where your Dad reads you a bedtime story and tucks you in while the doors remain unlocked all night long. In which scenario would you feel safer and more inclined to sweet dreams? Protective safety, gently implemented, leads to great moments of discovery and revelation. In the movie, *Life Is Beautiful*, a gentle, tender Jewish father protected his son from the violence of the Nazi soldiers so much so that the little boy did not even know how precarious their situation had become. This little boy did not lose the wonder of life in the worst of environments because his father nurtured his creativity while gently protecting him from harm.

Gentle moments emerge when masculine and feminine energies unite. They provide us with creative experiences that whet our appetite for music, dance, theatre, art, technology, architecture, and more. Call to mind your most creative moment or your most interesting idea. How did you feel when it occurred? What did you experience? Did you feel excited, enthusiastic, grateful, awakened, surprised, or delighted? Did you want to share your experience right away? Who did you call and why? Generally, both men and women find themselves connecting with others when struck by creative genius. It is a contagious experience that is feminine in nature. It causes you to fearlessly reach out in your exuberance and share the joy. In the movie *Contact*, Jody Foster plays a scientist who ardently testifies, before a congressional panel, about her experience in space while all of America listens. She focuses not on what her masculine mind would tell her about what is real, but of how her feminine nature connected with Creation in a way that she had thought previously impossible. She reported that she not only knew but also felt that she was connected to the life in this universe. She was no longer alone.

Creativity is always about an experience. Although thoughts and ideas are necessary, they are the masculine component of creativity. Experience is the feminine aspect that manifests the creative vision into words, pictures or actions. In creativity, you have the perfect balance of masculine and feminine energies. This is why creativity occurs within the heart of Mother/Father/God. The gentle man, the Father, provides the protective safety in which the dynamic feminine, the Mother, comes forward to creatively express their joint discoveries. The masculine and the feminine complement each other in creativity. They are not merging with each other, but rather nurturing each other's own growth.

Creative loving flows between the masculine and feminine forming an infinity symbol between the two at their point of connection, or heart. The heart of Mother/Father/God is literally the space, the void, or the electromagnetic energy in which the concept, the experience, and the coordinates of consciousness for the emergence of what you experience as love, coalesce. No physical heart exists at the Source of Creation, but we use this image to help you focus on divine loving.

Within the web of creative loving you are now experiencing Mother/Father/God's heart beating in and through you. It is moving into your mind and opening up your imagination. And it is moving into your pelvis stimulating your connections with others and generating creative activity. There is an internal infinity symbol now functioning within you. Your masculine ideas flow into the heart, through the figure eight, and down into the pelvis where they are expressed through the feminine energy of physical activity. Then, the pelvis sends this feminine experience up into the heart where it is received and sent through the figure eight up into the masculine brain for further processing. On and on the creative cycle goes, each time meeting within the heart where the communion between the masculine and feminine within grow strong, clear, and holy.

If you were going to destroy creativity, what would you put in the center of the infinity symbol where the Heart lies? Any painful memory, divisive thought, physical object, or hurtful experience will separate the masculine from the feminine. The heart will then shut down and the creative impulse will fail. Humanity lost its collective creativity when it cut itself off from the heart of Mother/Father/God. It takes humanity forever to embody a new idea because you are separated from the creative cohesive force that would allow you to easily flow into change. You have to flow into creativity. Change always involves a process, and processing is a feminine quality that humanity needs to develop in large quantities. Humanity is stuck. You need to learn how to flow with the feminine so you can download appropriate solutions to difficult societal maladies.

Although change is hard for humanity, it is not impossible. You practiced embracing the feminine through your Goddess worship. As a simple agrarian civilization, you honored Mother Earth and all of nature as an expression of the divine feminine. However, women and girls were treated as possessions and objects. There was no recognition or appreciation for the creative dynamic power that women possess. Then, when you began to worship the masculine God, feminine creativity further diminished. Violence thrived not only within the civilization but also towards the planet, whose feminine benevolence was dismissed. Currently, your planet and your civilization are being devastated by masculine violence.

Your human creativity is imprisoned within your gender battles. Because you do not honor both your masculinity and your femininity, you are unable to make peace among yourselves. You have cut yourself in half as a civilization and are bleeding to death. You don't flow into change because you do not honor the dynamic creativity of the feminine. Then, your masculine energy cannot implement the changes that the feminine intuits for the healing of all. The women are left powerless and the men defeated.

In order for the civilization to heal, there needs to be at least a conceptual reunion of masculine and feminine energies in perceived harmony. We did say *perceived* harmony. If humanity can at least perceive harmony, you will be utilizing both your masculine and feminine energies to create a peaceful thought form that is better than the one from which you now function. Any solution to your civilized chaos must come from both sexes. Until it does, there will be no peace. Further, both sexes must function as equals or at least be perceived as equal.

When you collectively choose peace, women will bring forth and intuit the solutions which the men will then execute. Leaders who are able to equally access their masculine and feminine energies are able to both recognize and manifest solutions to dangerous situations right now. However, how many world leaders currently exhibit this kind of balance and integrity? The King and Queen structure of leadership has great potential for creating harmony. However, they must rule as equals over an integrated, compassionate, tender, and loving civilization.

When you combine integration, compassion, tenderness, and unconditional loving, you become extremely powerful. Humanity has never collectively experienced civilized power. The recipe noted above delivers consistent, evolutionary progress for every civilization in any dimension. The archbishops and abbesses during the Dark Ages and Medieval period came close to benevolent ruling, except that they were kept segregated and their congregations were small. Together, their masculine and feminine power would have been formidable. Therefore, the men of the church pulled tight the reigns, the power, and the control over their sisters in the faith.

The true feminine within Mother/Father/God's heart is never a victim. She is always respected and honored as an equal. Since this has not been the case for women, they have had to protect themselves. This is where violence has creeped into the heart of women, shutting down their creative processing. Violence is always a masculine expression that is protective in nature. The people who are the most violent, whether it be in a highly populated riot or a small crime scene, are trying to protect themselves from someone or something. At times, they are even trying to protect themselves from themselves. Kali expresses the victimized feminine who protects herself through masculine violence. Kali does not live in Mother/Father/God's heart. She lives where danger lurks — behind separation, division, and prejudice.

We are focusing on the source of creativity that is love itself. When handling the creative energies of the First Ray, both birth and death are encountered. As better ideas emerge, old ones are thrown away. Creativity requires holding on and letting go simultaneously. To do this with grace, integration, compassion, tenderness, and love are necessary. These qualities offer every life form the complete experience of Mother/Father/God. They propagate harmony. However, when any life form chooses to play outside of Mother/Father/God's heart, life will begin to disintegrate. Civilized power deteriorates into warfare. Greed, fear, and disrespect flourish. Everything outside of integration, compassion, tenderness and love is a distortion of Mother/Father/God's love. Kali expresses the victimized feminine in everyone. She plays outside of God's heart, protecting herself from disintegration, hatred, disrespect, dismissal, and apathy.

We are not judging those who play outside of God's heart. We are simply noting that there is a better way to play. We begin by calling forth gentle men to heal this civilization. We choose this strategy to help you break free of the judgments you hold against men. Masculine energy is not violent and aggressive by nature. It has become so because humanity has been playing in a heart broken in two. Disconnected from your masculine and feminine completion, you cannot access healing strategies. Half a person or half of a civilization cannot solve problems. Men are hurting and many do not know why. Humanity is literally disabled. You need to be whole to heal.

The women's movement in the United States and around the world has been an attempt to bring balance to the civilization. Women have made some gains in the work place and at home, especially in Western countries. However, gender equality has yet to truly manifest around the world. Therefore, we are asking you to honor the feminine in every single way. In particular, we request that you pick one feminine quality that you enjoy and infuse this feminine energy into the entire civilization for the next two weeks. Through this process, you will discern what the feminine and masculine components are of every personality characteristic. Once you understand how femininity truly complements masculinity, you will be able to infuse the appropriate energy into the consciousness of humanity. Here are some examples of feminine energies that can be embraced for humanity:

1. <u>Calm stability</u> is the feminine component of masculine common sense. Focus on the experience that common sense brings to allow humanity to "chill out" and practically attend to difficulties without drama.

2. <u>Opening up</u> is the feminine energy men must embrace in order to receive women as equals. Receptivity is the feminine energy that allows women to take their place as equals among humankind.

3. <u>Embracing diversity</u> is the feminine process necessary for humanity to flow into positive change. It is the experience of being willing to embrace many ways of living. Rather than limiting yourself to a particular lifestyle and judging the rest as unworthy of your attention, you begin to respect the adaptability and genius of every culture.

4. <u>Being attentive</u> is a feminine component of tenderness. Women spend time and energy focusing on others for no other reason than they exist.

5. <u>The willingness to see beyond whom or what lies before you</u> is the feminine component of forgiveness. This is how women intuit the greatness in others that they cannot yet see in themselves. This is the feminine energy within the man that allows him to forgive others, and himself, for being or doing less than was required. Seeing what is good in another is a fe-

minine process. The masculine energy receives the female perception and honors it by forgiving the one in question.

6. <u>Care giving</u> is the feminine quality of patience. When you are caring for another, especially children and senior citizens, you have to be patient. Perseverance is the masculine component of patience.

7. <u>Support</u> is the feminine component of nurturing. The masculine builds a solid infrastructure through which the feminine moves creative energies. Visualize the masculine as the solid metal structure of a trampoline while the feminine is the flexible rubber sheet upon which people jump. Both are necessary to nurture playfulness.

8. <u>Empathic touch</u> is the feminine component of listening. Women listen to others with more than their ears. They often physically touch or even hold those whom they hear. The feminine embraces the individual's entire energy field, while the masculine will generally hear the words but not necessarily the meaning of them.

9. <u>Connection</u> is the way in which the feminine gives herself to another. Men will offer ideas, opinions, or advice, but not necessarily themselves, in interactions. Women give themselves as the gift.

Do you see how important it is for women and men to complement each other? The only way to access a complete understanding of any situation or relationship is to view it from both perspectives. Humanity's masculine side is very well defined but your feminine side is in need of serious healing. Only then will effective solutions emerge to heal troubling difficulties. As you offer this service for humanity, you provide it for all life forms in the Universe who are also struggling to attain gender balance within themselves. Over the next two weeks you will encounter many experiences that will test your commitment to honoring the feminine energy you have chosen to uphold. These situations will also deepen your respect for and understanding of the dynamic, creative power of the divine feminine within you. Your masculine energies will begin to honor your feminine nature such that your sense of balance increases, and you will feel more complete.

CIVILIZED POWER

For any life form to be fully integrated, masculine and feminine energies must be balanced within the physical, emotional, mental, and spiritual bodies of the auric field. When any part of the field is out of balance, harmony is compromised and completion remains elusive. Always work towards complete balance within yourself and you will become a gift that helps to bring peace to your civilization. Although your emotional, mental, physical, and spiritual growth occurs at varying speeds, try to keep your progress steady in each area. You will discover that when all of you is growing at the same pace, your creativity becomes expansive.

When you are emotionally hysterical, can you think of a solution to your dilemma? When you are mentally depressed, do you have enough energy to answer a difficult question? When you are spiritually bereft, for what can you hope? When your masculine and/or feminine nature disintegrates, you lose your ability to effectively solve problems. You end up with ineffective solutions that create more difficulties than they fix. Integration creates stability through effective solutions that are calmly implemented. A stabilized character structure is capable of great internal flexibility and personal creativity. We are committed to helping humanity stabilize its character structure so that you can reclaim your creativity.

Only through integration will humanity's evolution accelerate. No significant progress occurs outside of integration, because you are too busy driving each other to distraction. Evolutionary leaps occur when populations are focused on specific goals. In the United States, your campaign against cigarette smoking has lead to a keen awareness of the disastrous consequences of such activity. It has penetrated the pocketbook, public spaces, and the media. When a society collectively chooses to address a specific obstacle, it can.

To overcome your obstacles, humanity must go further than addressing issues—you must resolve them. Men like to take action, but they often act without considering the ramifications of their decisions. The feminine, intuitive nature considers the highest good of all. Her input is necessary to safeguard the population before action is initiated. When you combine masculine thought with feminine creativity, justice, peace, and plenty for all arises. Your industrial revolution occurred because men had to do something when they gained control of the civilization. When the Goddess was worshipped in agrarian populations, the dynamic feminine energy was not supported enough to create the kind of technological progress seen during the Industrial Revolution. However, reliance upon fossil fuels and the development of sweatshops have created massive social problems that are still plaguing humanity. Masculine support is necessary for feminine creativity to manifest new possibilities for well being around the world. Without men to make the dreams of women real, human children are left with ineffective parents, who are unable to nurture their children in healthy environments.

Fully embody your masculine and feminine qualities. Seek the balance within, and then it shall emerge around you. Integration builds links on a chain that grow stronger with every addition. You are not just integrating the masculine and feminine energies for yourselves, you are doing it for the entire civilization. Let's look at how the masculine and feminine energies will integrate as the infrastructure of the new civilization of peace develops.

Within the culture of Oneness, men will learn to create peaceful environments. Without threatening or actually using violent military means, they will ensure the safety of all. Through such gentle and tender means of protection, peace will emerge as all that is. Women responding to the safety their men have provided, will begin to connect every cultural expression into a tapestry of human Oneness. Nationalities will cease to be a point of contention as our collective humanity becomes the focus of attention.

In regards to music as spiritual transmission, the masculine energy makes the music and completes the performances. The feminine energy composes the music and connects the musicians necessary to deliver the music. The composing feminine and performing masculine allow higher-dimensional transmissions to descend into human consciousness with creative joy.

All technologies are free within the new civilization because all resources are equitably shared around the globe. Men will build the technological infrastructures and ensure the equitable delivery of resources. Women will download the higher-dimensional and multi-dimensional, non-polluting technologies necessary for human evolution on this planet. Do you see how the integration of masculine and feminine energies provides the cooperation necessary to manifest a new civilization of peace and abundance?

The next step toward completion, after integration, involves compassion. Initially, compassion will be required by all to heal the traumas resulting from Mother Earth's physical regeneration. Natural disasters will be addressed and displacement will occur all over the globe. However, women will not be the only nurses to a wounded civilization. Men will express their compassion through nurturing others back to health as well. A truly compassionate man will go out of his way to do what is necessary —from buying groceries, to washing someone's face, or digging through rubble. Although he needs to be active in his care giving, he is nurturing in his compassion. A true gentleman is a healer who provides nurturing support. Instead of allowing women to provide for basic care-giving needs, he also jumps in and offers assistance. What is the feminine component of compassion? The feminine energy carries an intuitive awareness of what needs to be healed and how. When a man accesses this internal wisdom, he will know how best to proceed. If he cannot hear his internal voice, he can depend on the intuition of a woman he trusts for guidance.

All that humanity has experienced as compassion has been linked to disasters, misfortune, and personal and societal wounds. You have not yet been able to access the positive side of compassion. Compassion also opens the heart to its cohesive possibilities for manifestation. This form of compassion recognizes the huge space in your heart that has yet to be filled. It sees an opportunity towards which it joyously moves your attention. This is playful compassion filled with hope and laughter.

Playful compassion leads to greater levels of connection because wounds are not the focus of your joining. Positive compassion wipes out pain as it discovers new ways for the heart to open. Every time your heart opens wider, the integration of your masculine and feminine energies grows more complete. You will recognize the divinity within you on levels that you will shortly begin to comprehend. Divine joy will begin to fill that huge space in your heart. Every experiment that may not have been so successful is celebrated for its attempt at integration and completion. The process and the outcome is equally honored. Every adventure has something from which you learn and grow. If a construction project proved to be inadequate, create a sculpture out of it instead. There is always a creative possibility awaiting manifestation within Mother/Father/God's heart living within you. Welcome playful compassion into your lives now. Get a glimpse of where you are going in your evolutionary development.

The positive connections that began in playful compassion, turn into loving relationships through tenderness. You never fear someone who is tender. Tender people are always approachable and extremely safe.

Because of these qualities, you easily trust them with as much as your life. The sincerity exhibited by a tender person is never an illusion because his or her heart opens to you with great integrity. They recognize the possibilities that exist for you, and encourage you to reach for the stars. Their strength is powerfully soft and unmistakably loving, while their support is steadfast and true. A tender experience with an acquaintance turns him or her into a friend.

Tenderness is the defibrillator for hearts in crisis. It literally turns on a heart that has shut down. It can also restart the heart of a civilization that has almost stopped beating. Its primary gift is complete trust. No fear exists in tenderness, and as such, vulnerability emerges. Held within a tender connection you are free to experience and express yourself without restraint. Such freedom offers you the possibility to believe in the unbelievable for yourself, others, and the world.

Huge changes occur in vulnerable people because that is when they will finally listen to what will free them from whatever hurts. Tender people don't control or manipulate others —they celebrate people. Humanity loves crises because they force you to become vulnerable and change. Most of you have to be forced to change. In tenderness, you joyfully step into vulnerability and welcome change. You embrace the freedom to grow without fear, and suddenly you are already changing. Without fear to slow you down, your vulnerability is ready to receive all the help necessary to explore unknown territories. Consider humanity becoming a civilization known for its tenderness. Think about master craftsmen. Do they hack away, or do they treat concrete, steel, and wood with the attention a baker gives to his flour, sugar, and eggs? Tender workmen create masterpieces. We are depending upon you to be the tender creators of a collective masterpiece, the new civilization of peace.

Initially, you have to integrate your masculine and feminine energies within every body of your auric field so that clear and effective decisions flow through you. In discovering just how difficult that process can be, you develop a greater level of compassion for yourself and others. You being to open up to possibilities, feel differently about your lives, and begin to connect with others who share similar hopes and dreams. You become tender in the process and your initial connections deepen into powerful relationships that provide creative, cohesive experiences in which you find yourself growing vulnerable. Within this safe, supportive, and tender environment you find yourself healing, growing, and enjoying life. Faith is no longer an invisible quantity. You are experiencing the freedom to unconditionally love.

Loving is an experience of communion in which you recognize another as part of you. This is not about union, where you merge into one —but rather about communion, where you share yourselves with each other. You become so vulnerable that you recognize that you need each other. Morever, in needing each other, you perceive yourselves as being part of a whole. You develop a cohesive sense of consciousness that provides a primary sense of Oneness. You begin to comprehend losing your individuality to a group identity. This is when you experience civilization as *you*. You become humanity. You and humanity are one, linked through integrity, compassion, and tenderness into unconditional loving. The idea of hurting any member of humanity becomes unthinkable because *you are humanity* and you do not choose to be hurt.

Human evolution is about growing together in unconditional love as one collective being. You feel everyone and everyone feels you. As you comprehend your collective communion, you embody the Soul of humanity. You literally bring the third-dimensional matter of your physical bodies into communion with the higher-dimensional energies of your spirit. You will humanly experience Oneness and cross the bridge to meet your solar, galactic, and universal family. Your humanity will be integrated within your divinity and the Universe will not only feel like home —it is where humanity is loved and belongs.

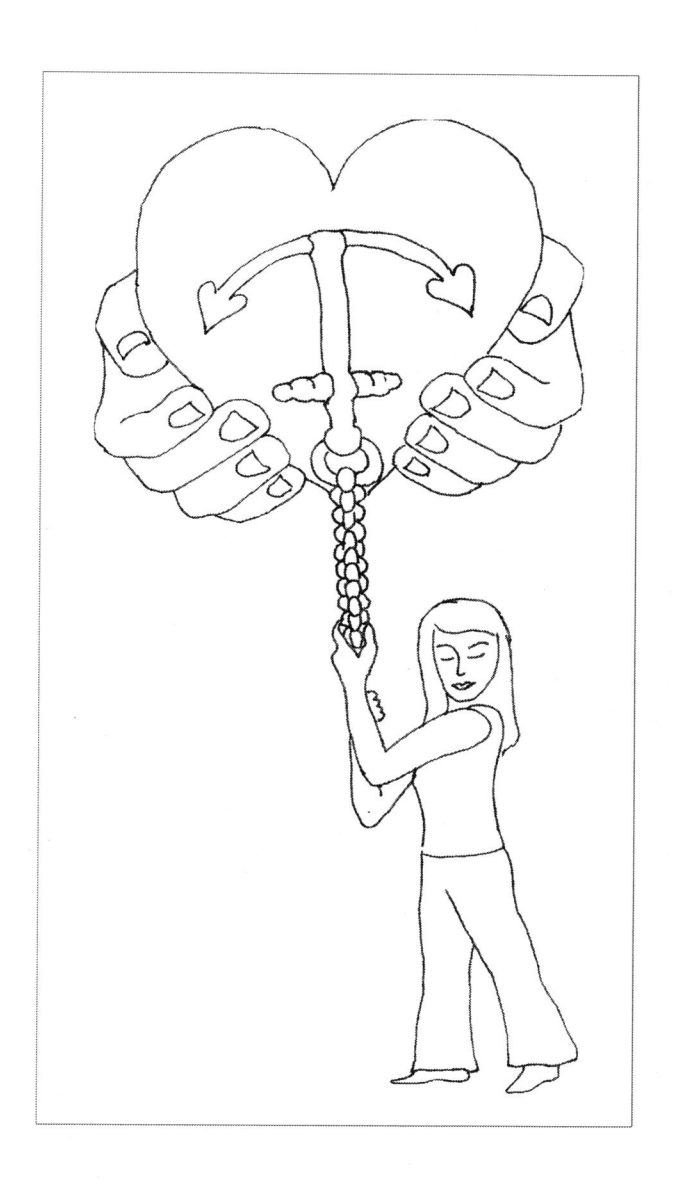

Chapter Six

Anchoring Up Into Unconditional Loving:
Devoted to Serve

Introduction

This chapter describes a process by which unconditional loving becomes an anchor into fifth-dimensional consciousness. Through gender integration, the creative loving of Mother/Father/God can consistently express fifth-dimensional consciousness in a third-dimensional world. Uniting the mind with the heart opens the pathway for the compassionate, wise, and joyous unconditional love of the Christ Consciousness to be experienced as a reality among human beings. Choosing to expand into higher-dimensional unconditional loving will allow humanity to overcome the third-dimensional limitations and societal restrictions that have imprisoned us in fear, pain, violence, and apathy.

Imagine a wheel so full of screws it cannot turn. It is literally stuck in its path and cannot function. Consider each of your fears, regrets, misunderstandings, grudges, embarrassments, and hurts as screws in the wheel of your heart. Is it any wonder your heart feels bruised, broken, and possibly even shut down? Each screw blocks your ability to fully love in an integrated manner. With every judgment, your head disconnects from your heart. With every regret, your heart disconnects from your head. Your head and heart long for each other to be united in love and function as one. You have to withdraw the screws in your heart to let the loving spiral up into your mind. Then, everyday, you are free to follow the path of the heart with a clear mind.

As you have been reading this material, you have been pulling lots of screws out of your heart thast have hurt the feminine within you. You are beginning to respect, honor, and embrace her wisdom living within. As you do, the feminine within you begins to love the masculine expression of yourself more fully. Your feminine and masculine selves begin to commune within, and suddenly you find yourself loving without judgment or fear — in essence, unconditionally. Your masculine mind and feminine heart are making peace inside of you. And so, you can make peace around you. Unconditional loving means that you completely respect the masculine and feminine perspectives of which you are comprised.

You fight with yourself almost all the time when you do not respect either side of you. Your masculine self is allowed to disagree with your feminine self. Through those disagreements, you learn from each other how to negotiate. You grow more conscious of what the other part of you needs. The development of conscious awareness comes from this inner processing. It is easy to watch a couple fighting in a restaurant and judge one side or the other. However, if your bring this fight into yourself and truly begin to perceive the position of the masculine and the feminine, you are going to have an entirely different view of what is occurring. You will also develop different ways to address similar issues that arise within your masculine and feminine expressions of being.

The development of consciousness that arises from respecting your masculine and feminine natures allows you to access Mother/Father/God's heart. You grow increasingly aware of Creation as the ultimate gender process because Mother/Father/God functions as a complementary unit within you. You experience Their expansive loving as creativity. You participate in evolution as *co-creators*. When you disconnect your head from your bleeding heart, the Heart of Mother/Father/God stops beating within you. Your creativity dissipates, and unconditional loving, as a practical and real option for your life, is dismissed.

To reactivate the divine heartbeat, increase your expansive awareness of how Mother/Father/God functions inside and all around you. Understand that this is the basis for unconditional loving.

REACTIVATING THE DIVINE HEARTBEAT

Breathe deeply inside of your heart. See the pyramid of energy developed through the heart, third eye, and sacral chakras all generating pink beams to the apex of the pyramid in front of you. The apex penetrates the heart of Mother/Father/God. Breathe their creative loving back into you now. Feel the masculine and feminine qualities of divinity washing in and through you. Feel your heart reaching up into your mind and down into your pelvis and throughout your body. Receive Mother/Father/God's loving now.

*   *   *

Describe how this meditation felt to you right now and don't read ahead. Take this time to become consciously aware.

You may feel balanced, secure, safe, happy, creative, peaceful, gentle, and equal. Moreover, you may experience a sense of point and counterpoint, or a forceful movement that is matched by fluidity. We are going to focus on the balance created through force and fluidity. You will only experience this level of balance in the human heart through unconditional love.

If we describe force as resistance and fluidity as flow, then you can perceive how resistance and flow function as a complementary pair. You experience this when you use the brakes on your car. Flow and resistance identify both sides of the process— flow representing the feminine, and resistance representing the masculine. When they are in balance, you experience an expansive creative power only accessed through unconditional loving. Notice that there are no judgments regarding flow or resistance. They work together in emotional and mental harmony.

*   *   *

Unconditional love expands. Conditional love contracts. You cannot respect and honor your masculine and feminine nature when you are focused on undermining each other. Comfort and safety are born through unconditional loving because flow and resistance are embraced as part of the creative process. Let's describe how Jesus, the Christ, exhibited this in his public ministry. Jesus did not appear to be publicly uncomfortable when addressing others. He didn't particularly care about being externally safe. In fact, he flaunted the internal safety of unconditionally loving to the point that he died because of it. In comfort and safety you love so completely that your external world ceases to have a limiting effect on you. In unconditionally loving, you are no longer a prisoner to your external environment.

You are bound by no conditions, so therefore any conditions of your external world would become meaningless. The boundaries of unconditional loving are divine, not human. As your heart expands beyond human limitations, you move into fifth-dimensional Christ Consciousness. You are no longer caught up in the judgments and recriminations of a fearful civilization. Feeling complete comfort and safety in who you are becoming, your ability to love within flow and resistance becomes unconditional. Your loving is expansive and divinity shines through your heart. You share this experience of flow and resistance with all whom you come into contact. It is through unconditional loving that humanity as a collective will embody fifth-dimensional Christ Consciousness.

This does not mean, however, that you can disrespect human boundaries. Jesus never did. He said, "Give to Caesar what is Caesar's, and give to God what is God's." Within unconditional loving, you pay attention to the dimensional parameters that create the experiences of the civilization. Although you honor the civilization in which you reside, you are not limited to society's rules and regulations. Unconditional loving honors dimensional parameters, but is not restricted by them. We will use another example from Jesus' public ministry to highlight this. Jesus had to use money to buy food for himself and his disciples. However, when he didn't have enough to feed a crowd, he simply multiplied the loaves and fishes for as many people as required. He moved beyond the dimensional parameters to provide for those in need.

You are growing beyond the vision of your eyes. You are growing beyond the vision of your third-dimensional brain. You are activating your Soul potential to literally manifest your individual Christ Consciousness through your body, mind, and heart. This is why your third eye, heart, and sacral chakras are so essential. When they are fully functioning within masculine and feminine balance, they facilitate and encourage unconditional loving in every aspect of your life. Let's give another example. If you walk into any local town jail, you will usually find a number of unfortunate people who choose to live inebriated or homeless lives. They tend to create some distractions and problems for local businesses, but are not a serious threat to the public. If you have an unconditionally loving mayor, he or she may choose to talk to the town judge and devise an alternate experience for these citizens who do not need to take up space in jail. They may create a situation in which a room, or a number of rooms, are made available in a local substance abuse center that allows these individuals to come in and out, no questions asked. No treatment is required because they are not interested in getting healthy. It is just a stopping station without conditions. The mayor is not saying that the police will stop picking up the town drunks or homeless people. However, he will not imprison them. This mayor decided to expand the rules of society to find a way to care for those who resist care. His feminine nature intuited an unconditionally loving solution that was supported and executed by his masculine energy. It may be that the inebriated or homeless person starts going to the room on his or her own instead of having to be picked up by the police. Anything is possible within unconditional loving.

Unconditional loving is always going to take you beyond institutionalized and civilized parameters. It has the ability to open the heart wider than your dimensional experience allows. It is how third-dimensional situations grow into experiences of higher-dimensional loving. As your heart expands within gender integration, a higher-dimensional society is born through unconditional loving. The more humanity practices unconditional loving, the more the new civilization of peace emerges around the planet.

You are moving completely beyond what you recognize and know as the basis of life. Through unconditional loving, your inherent grounding to the dimension in which you reside begins to dissipate. Why? If you are evolving beyond the dimension you are in, don't you have to let this one go? Unconditional loving is the key to every dimensional shift. Right now many of you are having a verbal, conscious, physical awareness of fifth-dimensional living in your third-dimensional lives. You are recognizing how expansive life can be because you are experiencing it. In other dimensions, the same process occurs. These higher-dimensional life forms just keep moving up the evolutionary spiral.

Unconditional loving dissolves the grounding in the current dimension and creates an anchor in the next dimension above you. This anchor draws you up to it, somewhat like a pulley. As you keep practicing unconditional love, you embody more and more of fifth-dimensional consciousness. If you were to look at your evolutionary development from a mountain climber's perspective, your thirst and quest for unconditional loving places you firmly in an upward moving direction. You are climbing your way up to the anchor of Christ Consciousness: forgiving, compassionate, unconditional love.

The expansive quality of the masculine and feminine working in harmonious balance to create possibilities, exudes joy. Unconditional loving is always joyful in its emergence. The birth of the Christ Child was the anchor Mother/Father/God placed within humanity to draw the civilization up into fifth-dimensional living. It is no accident that wonderful scenarios of angels singing, stars shining, and celebrations, surround the birth of this infant. What you are really doing is welcoming the joy of unconditional loving into your lives. Here was the embodiment of one who would bring unconditional loving to the conscious awareness of this civilization. Joy to the world is the issue. Unconditional love truly brings joy to the world when the Christ Child is honored in every human heart.

This higher-dimensional anchor will always be felt in your dimensional reality to highlight the shift that is taking place now. You need to recognize higher-dimensional events occurring in third-dimensional lives as real, otherwise the anchor is meaningless. Yes, you have experienced discomfort over the past few weeks as many screws were being pulled out of your heart.

Each moment of pain, brain freeze, confusion, hurt, and grief set your heart free, allowing you to love in balance. Your heart wheel is not just turning, it has become a spiral uniting your head with your heart. Do you not feel empowered? Are you not engaging others with a consideration and honor you had not previously known? Are you applying the same consideration and honor to yourself? No matter what your previous limitations were, you are now free to be, live, and do more.

In unconditional loving, you are not only accessing the fifth dimension, you are calling it forth into your life now. The anchor is not where you would third-dimensionally think it to be. It is not below you. It is above you. Fifth-dimensional consciousness is coming down into your life so you can follow it back up into a fifth-dimensional world. Consciously call upon the anchor of unconditional loving. The Christ Consciousness is supporting and encouraging your evolutionary development.

Unconditional loving confuses the human brain. If you don't allow your ego to serve your Soul, which anchors into your heart, you will drive yourself crazy. Once you have chosen to unconditionally love, your Soul goes into action. It wakes you up to gracious, considerate, and joyous living. It draws you into surprising situations and relationships that will teach you how to unconditionally love. If your heart is ready to unconditionally love but your head is not, what have you just done to yourself? You have split your masculine head from your feminine heart. You will begin to disintegrate and what a headache you will endure! The masculine head must be brought into alignment with the feminine heart so that all of you unconditionally loves. If they are not combined, your ego starts to panic. In its isolation, the ego turns fear into terror, and anxiety will overwhelm you.

However, once the head connects with the heart, the heart begins to teach the mind how to think fifth-dimensionally. We are introducing this concept to you now so that when it emerges in a few weeks, you won't be surprised. You cannot fear your mind. So many of you have been taught to fear your mind because you have made mistakes. Think about how you were raised in school. If you didn't meet grade level expectations, or if you were too smart, you were taught to fear your mind. Instead of being encouraged to think, you were encouraged to produce. Producing is not thinking.

In unconditional love, there is no fear of the mind. Your mind is loved just as much as all the rest of you. Previously, we taught you how to access your multi-dimensional selves. We showed you how to experience and communicate with them. We did this so that when we came to this level of class work you would recognize that in unconditionally loving yourself, you literally experience these universal life forms as part of you. Your hearts have grown enough that your minds are capable of receiving their higher-dimensional expressions. You are open enough now to recognize their advanced thought processes. They are not human in nature, but you are. So, we had you open up your humanity to grow beyond it— to open your minds to embrace what these higher-dimensional life forms have to offer you.

You are earning this higher-dimensional recognition through conscious participation. You are living your lives as unconditionally as possible. You are integrating your masculine and feminine selves to the highest degree of which you are able. In that integration, your unconditional loving is growing and you are beginning to embody a fifth-dimensional experience of living. You are feeling and thinking from a higher-dimensional expression of being.

As your mind opens to fifth-dimensional processes so do your senses. Clairvoyance, clairsentience, and clairaudience are going to become common place for you. You are accessing a greater recall and connection to everything from everywhere. Why are the senses important? You access your experience of life through them. If you are accessing your life experience through your senses, and your senses change, then what happens to your life experience? Your life, changes. This is the easiest way to move into fifth-dimensional Christ Consciousness. However, you cannot enter this process until you exhibit the ability and practice unconditional loving. Only then do you experience the world, and your place in it, multi-dimensionally.

The focus is on experience. You are not just thinking and feeling expansively. You are engaging your multi-dimensionality through your senses. This is sensorial engagement. Members of the Planetary Hierarchy, the Angelic Realms, the Elohim, and the many extra-terrestrial life forms of this spiritual collective are literally touching you. You have seen us in visions and heard us in your minds. You have worked as our colleagues to save humanity and Mother Earth from destruction. These experiences are cataloged in your memory banks but they have not yet occurred while you were walking down the street or driving down the highway. They will now. These multi-dimensional experiences have to happen everywhere, because you live everywhere. Your ability to unconditionally love allows you to access these extra-sensory experiences as part of your every day multi-dimensional experiences.

Your connection to all life on Earth grows through your dimensional shift. You experience the hologram of life personally and intimately through the creative loving of Mother/Father/God.

THE HEART-MIND CONNECTION MEDITATION

Feel your heart connected to all life forms in this universe and see the connections through your third eye. Now feel all of these life forms connecting to each other through your heart and mind. Feel the cord of connection between your heart and third eye solid, strong, and powerful. Feel the multi- and higher-dimensional information being channeled through the head and heart.

*   *   *

Notice that you no longer feel human, do you? Describe this experience to yourself, now. You may feel waves of energy moving through you, or pulsing throughout the body, or even quite weightless. You moved beyond your humanity while still living within your body.

*   *   *

At moments you will experience a blissful reunion within the Oneness. Once you unconditionally love through the dimensions, you begin to heal problems. You take care of other life forms. Bliss comes from simply being able to joyfully serve each other. Bliss is a human experience of divine union. It is the joyous delivery of unconditional loving. This blissful state is an anomaly in the third dimension to awaken you to the reality of unconditional loving. You can't sustain bliss in a third-dimensional body. That is why there are only blissful moments. Bliss introduces you to the joy that is sustained in fifth-dimensional consciousness.

When third-dimensional beings move into unconditional love, they begin to experience a deep inner sense of contentment that they can sustain. This is much better than a blissful moment because contentment lasts. Inner contentment is not a third-dimensional anomaly used to wake people into higher-dimensional awareness. Consistent, inner contentment eventually allows you to enter into the joyous expression of being that is fifth-dimensional consciousness. You grow into your Christ Consciousness through contentment to experience continuous bliss.

We are interested in developing continuous progress. As such, our focus is on the integration that facilitates consistent growth, not drama. Drama causes disintegration, obstructs progress, and pulls you back into third-dimensional consciousness. Once in drama, you cannot access the clarity or the relationships with your multi- and higher-dimensional selves that provide solutions through unconditional loving. Avoid drama at every turn.

Consistency is the hallmark of evolutionary development. Without it, you cannot progress. Unconditional love dwells within consistency, and consistency within unconditional love. They are inseparable. Ask anyone raised by an unconditional parent what quality they most valued in their mother or father and you will likely hear, consistency. Make consistent progress your goal. Although you will have moments where there will be obstacles to overcome, you will release, learn, and move on to your next level. You won't get stuck in any drama. Those who get stuck in drama cannot find their way out because they cannot recognize what they have to learn. You have the eyes to see, the ears to hear, the extra-sensory perception to download, and the multi-dimensional support to succeed.

As you move into the higher realms through your unconditional loving, much is expected of you. You don't even reach this level of loving if you are unwilling to serve Creation at every level. Because of your desire to serve, you are supported, honored, and respected. We give you everything we possibly can within the limits of free will to help you grow. Sometimes an individual will choose to stop serving after they have attained a certain level of mastery. This individual's ability to hurt another with the power he or she has learned to utilize is drastically increased. If you manipulate another by abusing unconditional love, you pay a severe price. If you consider the love of Mother/Father/God as inconsequential to the needs of your ego, the cost is staggering. Do you understand? In other words, in respecting free will, we give you everything as you earn access to it.

If you decide to turn away from unconditionally loving, we cannot stop you. In free will, you are given that right. Humanity exercises this option freely and often. But, when you depart from a more exalted place of becoming, you are aware of how to work within peoples' energy fields such that they are not even aware of what is happening. This is why we test you so completely before you gain entrance into the Planetary Hierarchy as an employee. We love you enough to make sure that, at least to our understanding, you will abide by heavenly guidelines.

There are no victims in Mother/Father/God's heart. If you dismiss unconditional loving and choose to victimize another, then you have just victimized yourself. Unconditional loving can be thrown away in free will. The reason we are speaking of this is not because we are concerned about you. As you grow in Christ Consciousness, you may come into contact with others who are dismissing unconditional love for ego adoration. You must be able to unconditionally love these individuals by respecting their choice. In unconditionally loving those who make negative choices, you must be able to step away and do nothing. If someone asks you for advice and you recognize that they are choosing to dismiss unconditional loving, you could simply ask, "Do you really want to hear my observations or understanding? Or, would you prefer to do this the way you desire?" In this way, you are offering them options, respecting their free will, and avoiding drama. You unconditionally love them. People caught in ego desire don't really want to entertain various levels of truth. They believe in their own conception of what is true, so step back and let them be. You can have no emotional charge related to the individual or situation in unconditional loving. If you do feel emotionally triggered, learn what must be released and let it go. Free yourself to love better next time.

In consistently practicing unconditional loving you become devoted to the life forms residing within your dimensional existence. You love everything in your environment unconditionally. Your heart expands to appreciate every situation and relationship that you have been privileged to experience on Mother Earth.

Filled with fifth-dimensional compassion, you see that huge space in your heart. You know that it can be filled in this dimension as well as in all the others. You are grateful for third-dimensional consciousness and unconditionally love your current life experience all the more.

Do you see how the openness of the heart transfers into every dimension? The consistent use of unconditional love creates the experience of devotion. Think about people who have exhibited great devotion in your world. In what have they participated? All of these wonderful individuals served others. People such as Mother Theresa engaged in consistent, unconditional loving regardless of the circumstances. The same is true of couples married for over fifty years who support, nurture, and sustain each other throughout many struggles. You observe this in musicians, architects, and scientists who devote themselves to particular fields of study for the benefit of humanity. Unconditional loving never stops in those devoted to serve. The more devoted you become, the more unconditionally loving you are.

In the presence of devoted individuals, what other qualities besides expansive loving do you feel? Honor. Many consider Mother Theresa a saint, a holy individual. She expressed holiness in honoring the lowly and the exalted similarly. When devotion is consistent, the honor for the person or group grows to such levels that they become revered. Reverence leads to holiness and holiness guides you into communion with Oneness. This class is titled: *Devotion, Devotion, Devotion: The Way of Loving*, because in consistently practicing unconditional love, you will attain holiness. This is true for everyone. There is a Mother Theresa living inside you just as sure as Jesus, the Christ, is waiting to come through your heart. Do not set devotion aside for the few. It is a calling for everyone.

When you are in the physical presence of someone who is devoted to you, what does it feel like? Do you feel free, safe, peaceful, comfortable, or home? Devotion will always involve a physical experience. How often have you experienced this in your life? How often have you offered this experience to another? We choose to develop more devotion among our multi- and higher-dimensional selves and within the world. When people experience others devoted to them, then unconditional love becomes real. Examples of devoted servants encourage belief in unconditional love. On this planet, you need quite a few examples to encourage your population to believe. All of you are already examples of unconditional loving and continue to be. Also know that if you are in the presence of others who are open to discussing consistent unconditional loving as part of their journey, stress upon them the importance of being an example who can raise the consciousness of another. No words need leave the mouth of a devoted servant. Unconditional love speaks its own higher-dimensional language.

Be the living examples of unconditional loving. Wake up this civilization to the joyous expression of fifth-dimensional Christ Consciousness. Embody unconditional love right now. The entire civilization is crying out for unconditional love. You don't have to live on the streets of Calcutta to embody the Christ Consciousness. Love unconditionally in your homes with your spouses, your children, your parents, and your neighbors. Humanity doesn't have enough examples of how to love, because your genders are disintegrated and you can't function as one. Instead of dismissing the feminine, embrace her. Let her love the masculine within you until he is healed of his impotence. Let him bring peace to every person, in every home, all over the world. Grow in gratitude for your desire and willingness to practice unconditional loving on a third-dimensional world. We are.

Become the living expressions of fifth-dimensional Christ Consciousness. *You know how.*

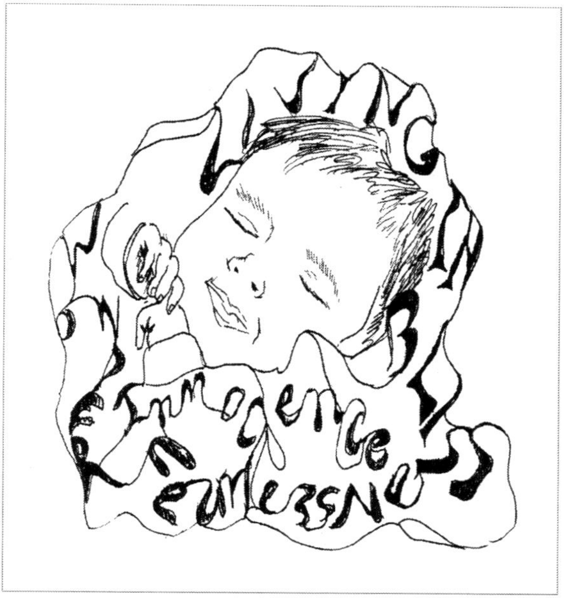
Innocence

Chapter Seven

Living in Bliss:
Embodying the Christ Consciousness

Introduction
Innocence, fearlessness, and wonder are the main components of the physical, emotional, mental, and spiritual blueprint of those who will populate the new civilization of peace. This chapter describes a process through which you can embody these three characteristics of the Christ Consciousness. In doing so, you become co-creators with Mother God and Father God, building a higher-dimensional planetary environment in which peace is assured for all.

Please complete the following meditation to deepen your comprehension of the material to follow.

Opening Meditation

Visualize your Soul Star as a big, bright Sun about a hand's length above your head. Spin it down into a disc moving counterclockwise above you. Visualize your Earth Star as a big brown orb about a foot beneath your feet. Spin the orb down into a disc moving counterclockwise beneath you. Feel your feet being pulled into this connection with the third-dimensional planet on which you reside. Feel the higher-dimensional energy of your Soul radiating out of the Soul Star disc and flowing around your body, creating a cylinder of light that connects with the Earth Star beneath you. Feel a golden beam of light penetrate the center of your Soul Star disc and flood your brain with light. The golden light travels into the brain stem and into the spinal cord. It moves through the base of the spine, down through the legs, out of the soles of the feet and into the Earth Star. The golden light now travels through Mother Earth's chakra column, into the chakra column of the Solar System, through the Sun, into the chakra column of the Milky Way Galaxy, into the galactic Sun, into the chakra column of this Universe, into the Great Central Sun of our Universe, and into the multi-universal chakra columns. Feel yourself anchored into this multi-universal energy and relax into this divine flow.

Now, see and feel the cosmic, universal, galactic, solar, planetary, and all the Holy Christ selves of humanity merging into a whole at the center of this universal collective. Visualize their energies as a pulsing orb of White Light. Feel the pulsing White Light of the Christ Consciousness expanding throughout the collective, moving into and through your every cell, every neuron, every subtle body, and throughout all of the life forms here, present. Feel the energies of the Christ as it ripples upon the ocean of the creative web of Mother/Father/God's loving. Their children are being born. And so we begin...

Imagine a newborn cuddled sweetly in your arms. Look into this little one's eyes and let wonder overwhelm you. Feel the innocence and fearlessness this bundle of warmth exudes to all within its reach. Let hope, possibility, and gratitude wash over you for the pure experience of witnessing new life. What blessings would you wish for this child? What offering of yourself would you choose to deposit into this little one's aura?

Now imagine that you, just as you are right now, are held within the arms of Mother God and Father God. Cuddled within their loving, you look into their eyes. Mother God and Father God's innocence, fearlessness, and wonder pour into you. They are so happy to have you in their lives. They are grateful for you and filled with joy about what you will discover and who you will become as you explore Creation. Mother God and Father God's first gifts to you are their own fearlessness, innocence, and wonder. You are their Christ Child and no matter how old you are or how poorly you have behaved, these gifts still belong to you. They are the everlasting qualities of the children of God, the Christ that lives in all of us. Today, you can reclaim your first birthday presents and continually embrace them for the rest of your life.

Receiving a present is always easy, but unwrapping it can be a challenge. The three characteristics of the Christ Consciousness are not so much unwrapped as they are embodied. To embody innocence, fearless, and wonder, each must be fully integrated into the entire dimensional expression of your being. Here in the third dimension, embodiment includes your physical, emotional, mental, and spiritual bodies. When you explore each of these qualities in all four of your lower subtle bodies, you will get a different experience of what it means to live as an evolving human being. If you are reading this article, then you are already in the process of embodying the Christ Consciousness. Our goal is to help you to understand how this embodiment occurs, so that you can fully and consciously participate in the process of becoming a fifth-dimensional life form. It is easier than you think and harder than you can imagine.

How do you physically embody innocence? Think about how physical loving occurs. Physical innocence always involves tender, gentle touching. It is a state of harmlessness so complete that every life form is honored by the way in which it is physically approached and handled. Even when babies repeatedly throw their toys on the ground to be picked up over and over again, they do so with innocent delight. They love to watch gravity work. They appreciate and utilize its function regularly. Consider how your life would change if you approached everything and everyone in your life with physical innocence? Just imagine how this would revolutionize sexual intimacy!

How do you emotionally embody innocence? This requires a level of trust that is unconditional. Many of you cannot conceive of trusting another without testing them first. Yet, Mother/Father/God has trusted humanity, already blighted with spiritual amnesia, with an entire planet. Emotionally innocent people trust unconditionally because they do not know fear. These are openhearted individuals who emotionally welcome all. You recognize them as warm, loving, and generous of spirit, whether they are children or adults.

How do you mentally embody innocence? When you are innocent, you willingly consider all possibilities in situations or relationships. Knowing no mental limits, other than the dimensional parameters in which you reside, your thought processes become explorations into the vast reaches of the Universal Mind. You enthusiastically discover your environment without judging every aspect of it as either valuable or useless. You accept and embrace how Creation works.

How do you spiritually embody innocence? To do this, you must understand that Mother God and Father God express themselves through electromagnetic energy. You can literally hear the electromagnetic frequencies of the planets on the NASA space probe recordings. You can hear the frequency or vibration of your own electromagnetic energy by listening to your heartbeat and blood pressure. Creation is composed of vibration or sound and when you surrender into the electromagnetic energy of Mother/Father/God, you flow within the love that fuels multi-dimensional creativity. Spiritually innocent individuals go with the divine flow. This is a state of being so completely pure that divine creativity can flow through you without resistance. There is nothing to allow within spiritual innocence. Everything already is, and you are part of Creation.

So how would you recognize or experience completely innocent individuals? They live in a state of harmlessness, giving tender, gentle touch to those they encounter. Keenly aware of consciously loving others, they exhibit unconditional trust and are generally emotionally welcoming and openhearted. They live in a state of possibility, considering multiple options before making decisions. Noted for their generous spirit, they live without judgments towards others. They seemingly commune with divinity and are provided for in every conceivable way.

Let's move on to fearlessness as the next characteristic of the Christ Consciousness to embody. Those who embody physical fearlessness have a muscular freedom to experience all situations. They relax into life, whether it requires mountain climbing or sunbathing, sitting behind a desk, or spending several hours a day in a truck. They freely travel everywhere because they experience every environment as safe. Because they are ready, willing, and able to go anywhere, Mother/Father/God can send them wherever, knowing that they will complete whatever assignment they were given to assist another. You regularly see these individuals helping refugees in war-torn countries or the homeless in shelters and hospitals. They embrace the power of the body and honor its movement as a gift of Creation.

Those who embody emotional fearlessness are willing to engage in every relationship offered to them. These relationships are not just with people, but also with rocks, plants, animals, and the spiritual kingdoms of nature. Emotional fearlessness requires pure vulnerability. This level of vulnerability allows you to engage in all kinds of relationships because you are not afraid of life revealing itself. Within emotional fearlessness, you enjoy your relationships and welcome the lessons they have to teach. Every relationship is honored, whether it feels good or not, because you are growing. Maybe your garden didn't produce this year. Maybe your dog bit the neighbor's child and you had to find it a new home. Maybe you got divorced. Emotional fearlessness does not mean that you allow yourself to be judged, manipulated, or abused, but if this happens to teach you to avoid such in the future, you are grateful for each experience and move on. Every action you complete, from putting the toothpaste on your toothbrush in the morning to kissing your spouse goodnight, is related to someone or something. Emotionally fearless individuals make every relationship count.

Right about now, you may be feeling a bit anxious and possibly overwhelmed. Your vulnerability has just been triggered by the descriptions of innocence and fearlessness offered through the Christ Consciousness. Take a deep breath and relax into this vulnerability. We started this article off with a meditation in which the Christ Child of Mother God and Father God was born and rippling throughout multiple universes. This is what is happening to you right now. Your inner Christ Child has responded to what you are reading. Feel the

Christ Consciousness inside of you expanding and rippling through your auric field. Embody this innocence, fearlessness, and wonder right now. Flow in divine electromagnetism. Experience the characteristics of the spiritual masters that you are becoming on this dimension and in every other. Let's continue.

Those who mentally embody fearlessness are open to divine thought. Divine thought is different from dimensional thought in that it moves through all of the dimensions. Dimensional thought is limited to specific parameters of experienced realities. In divine thought, all kinds of processes emerge. Through divine thought, you willingly engage in multi-dimensional intellectual pursuits. However, your intellect is not the same as your intelligence quotient. Your intellect is your God-given birthright to experience divine thought. Intelligence is the ability to download dimensional information to the degree that the incarnation requires. Your intelligence quotient will be based on the missions and spiritual assignments you agreed to fulfill in a particular lifetime. In one life, you may have needed a doctorate degree to complete your mission, while in another incarnation, being an illiterate farmer was all that was necessary. Your abilities change in varying lifetimes depending upon the mission. However, your intellectual capacity is always vast. You are all very bright beings, but you do not always incarnate with your brilliance intact.

Those who spiritually embody fearlessness welcome their divine missions and personal evolutionary assignments. The spiritually fearless recognize the voice of God and follow Mother/Father/God's directions without question, even when they do not understand the orders. These are the warriors of peace and those who love in the way it is required for the highest good of all. They trust the command of the Most High and ardently co-create throughout the Earth and the Heavens. These individuals are not fanatics, nor do they give their power away to spiritual masters. They own their power to work for, and within, God and as such are trusted by Mother/Father/God to care for Creation.

So what is it like to experience completely fearless individuals? They exhibit a relaxed physical relationship to their environments, appearing to feel safe and secure wherever they are. They travel wherever they feel called to go and willingly engage in every relationship they encounter—whether it is with people, animals, plants, nature, or even spirits. They exhibit a powerful vulnerability that makes them easy to approach and get to know. They enjoy engaging in multi-dimensional intellectual pursuits and exploring divine thought processes through everyone and everything they meet. They willingly embrace their divine missions and quickly go about accomplishing them. They enjoy receiving spiritual assignments that challenge them to move beyond what they have already experienced. They welcome their evolutionary tests as adventures to be embraced.

What happens when you physically embody wonder? Think of any healthy and happy two-year-old. Their lives are filled with curiosity, and in their waking moments they play, hard. Every toddler pursues physical experiences with curious abandon. They feel and act as if the entire world is their playground even if they are just exploring the family kitchen. However, for the Christ in all of us, the entire cosmos really is our playground. We are invited to physically discover every aspect of our environments by playing our lives within them. Toddlers hold, touch, push, pull, pounce, and giggle all the while—not that we necessarily want to pounce or pull on everything we may encounter. Still, it is the playfulness with which children approach living that is the physical embodiment of wonder. What would it be like if you truly experienced work in a playful manner? How much more physically active would you be if you carried curiosity around with you in the same way that you carry money in your wallet wherever you go?

What happens when you emotionally embody wonder? You are struck with awe and might even find yourself commenting, "Awesome!" You begin to pursue artistic and creative endeavors because you are so motivated by what you have witnessed you want to do likewise. How many girls or boys dream of being in the Olympics after watching a gymnast, ice-skater, swimmer, or skier win a gold medal? Many of them enroll in athletic programs and lessons only because these athletes inspired them. Emotionally embodying wonder will always generate beauty—and beauty is, by its very essence, awe-inspiring. We only pursue what truly inspires us.

What happens when you mentally embody wonder? You are filled with appreciation for all that is. Life is recognized as amazing at every turn and you are grateful for all that is within and around you. Because you are so aware of all that is, science becomes wonderful. Multi-dimensional scientific discovery fills you with delight. Difficulties or obstacles initiate adventures, not challenges. What we know of as problem solving becomes joyful research because experimentation is the focus of activity, not problems. Everything is interesting all of the time.

What happens when you spiritually embody wonder? You live in such a constant state of gratitude that it grows into glorification. Feeling glorious is the spiritual expansion of gratitude. You might be happy looking at a few tulips and hyacinths in a garden at springtime, but when you come upon an entire mountainside of daffodils that takes your breath away, that is glorious. Spiritual wonder is an experience of exaltation that surpasses human understanding. It is an intravenous dose of divine magnificence that runs throughout your entire auric field. It is electrifying.

We have now finished our chart of the full embodiment of the Christ Consciousness in the four, lower bodies of a third-dimensional human. This chart is located at the end of the chapter. Let's review the complete experience. As you read the following three paragraphs, notice how you feel and what happens within your body.

Physically innocent individuals are harmless. They offer tender, gentle touch to all life forms they encounter on their fearless journeys throughout the world. They are emotionally aware of how much everything and everyone needs to be loved, and they exhibit a willingness to act in whatever way will make that loving real and accessible to another. They are relaxed within their bodies and safely explore their environments with a playful, mental curiosity that is downright contagious. They view the entire world, indeed the cosmos, as their playground. They fear no one and consider all possibilities as valid because they live within the purity of the Universal Mind. Feel how your body is now responding to these words? Relax into the experience, noting any areas of resistance.

Emotionally fearless individuals willingly engage in every relationship they encounter. They live with an unconditional trust in life, itself, that allows them to warmly welcome all with open hearts. Purely vulnerable to another, they are emotionally available and physically present to those with whom they are relating. They view life as beautiful and are often struck by the awe of Creation. Inspired by such beauty they engage in their own creative and artistic pursuits seeking to contribute even more beauty to the world. How does your body feel now? How does your heart feel? Relax into the experience, noting any areas of resistance.

Mentally innocent individuals exhibit a willingness to consider all possibilities when pondering a situation or relationship. They are highly accepting of others without a hint of judgment or condemnation. Because they are open to divine thought, they willingly engage in multi-dimensional intellectual pursuits. They eagerly explore the vastness of the Universal Mind with a deep appreciation for Creation. They honor multi-dimensional scientific discovery and participate in uncovering the great mysteries of how and why things work. Life is always interesting to them. How does your head feel now? How does your body feel? Relax into the experience, noting any areas of resistance.

Spiritually innocent individuals commune within divinity by flowing with the frequencies of the Universal Mind. They exist in a state of complete purity constantly surrendering into the divine frequencies in which they exist. They willingly serve all life by welcoming their divine missions and spiritual assignments. They also embrace their personal evolutionary tests and work hard to pass their exams in spiritual mastery. Gracious individuals, these are those who glorify Mother/Father/God in their lives. They understand exaltation because they recognize just how glorious Creation truly is. They praise the Universal Mind by offering themselves as blessings. How does your auric field feel? Are you a bit light headed? Relax into the experience, noting any areas of resistance.

You have just received a complete downloading of the blueprint of Christ Consciousness into your auric field. It is up to you to now embody these qualities, which have been infused into every atom, molecule, cell, and particle of your being. Any resistance that appeared as pain, discomfort, irritation, anger, or dissociation can be released through forgiveness and understanding. On December 5, 2004 the consciousness of the citizens of the United States of America was infused with Christ Consciousness energy. Unconditional love and compassionate wisdom is what this blueprint makes completely real—for you and everyone else. Although you are residing in third-dimensional bodies, you can act from a higher-dimensional knowing to create a peaceful and abundant life, where no one is hurt by the needs of another. The new civilization will be populated by the Christ living within each of you. Only those willing to embody innocence, fearlessness, and wonder will have the strength, endurance, and faithfulness necessary to rise from the ashes of the old. To embody the Christ Consciousness is a choice that each has to make of his or her own volition. If and when you do, you automatically become a life-affirming force in an evolving civilization.

How? The Christ Consciousness radiates through you. Unconditional love and compassionate wisdom is spread by the joy of living it. It grows in incremental steps beyond each person into the collective whole of the planet and then further into the solar system, galaxy, and universe. The Christ Consciousness energy expands throughout Creation because the children of Mother/Father/God are continually growing up. Humanity, as a collective, is growing up even if some individuals do not. When you choose to activate the frequencies of the Christ Consciousness within, you become a beacon of possibility for those around you to do the same.

Just a note for those who are still caught up in the word "Christ." The Christ, is actually an office within the spiritual planetary government overseeing Earth's evolution. The office of the Christ is just as valid to the spiritual hierarchy of this planet as the office of the President is to the government of the United States of America. The Christ Consciousness is the energy radiated by those who hold the office. Just as you have had many presidents in the history of this nation, so too, have many Masters embodied, to reveal the Christ Consciousness for humanity. Jesus, the Christ, was your latest avatar. He tried to teach humanity that you can save yourselves by living from the Christ within. By the way, Jesus no longer holds the position of the planetary Christ. Ascended Master Kuthumi is moving in that position. Who you knew of as the human, Jesus, has evolved, and now holds the position of Christ for this solar system. His new name in this new role is, Ascended Master Sananda.

When you honor the message more than the messenger, then Jesus is not the focus of your attention—developing the ability to love unconditionally and live from compassionate wisdom, is. Therefore, move beyond the limiting and restrictive contexts that humanity has created around the man, Jesus. By honoring the Christ within yourself, you will honor every child of Mother/Father/God. Jesus would have been well pleased.

As you embody the Christ Consciousness, you become land mines of divine, life-giving energy. Instead of blowing people up upon contact, divine possibilities flood the auric fields of the lonely, the desperate, the fearful, and the needy who come into your presence. Suddenly, what was unbelievable a moment before is now real. You emanate unconditional love, and specialize in forgiveness wherever you go. Let's say you are at the checkout counter of the supermarket and suddenly the man in front of you decides to give the woman with three children at the checkout station the twenty extra dollars she needs to pay for her groceries. He tells you that he's never done anything like this before, but just feels that he has to help her. You didn't say a word but the compassionate love radiating through you reached that man and changed him, and the woman he assisted. You don't have to know what will happen through you. Just be available. Do you think that Jesus knew everything he was going to do or all that would happen? No. There were lots of opportunities and so many could have made other choices every step of the way. It played out as it did. In vibrational flow, you move with multi-dimensional experiences to fulfill Mother/Father/God within. Be the presence of the living Christ and make Jesus more than a myth of the past. Live as a force of goodness in the present.

We are depositing you everywhere. You are the innocence. You are the fearlessness. There is a wonder about you that people desire. They want to know,

"How do you do that? Why do I feel so good when you are around?" As you embody these characteristics in each of your four lower bodies, you are generators of the Christ Consciousness walking all over the planet. People can choose to activate these same frequencies in their own lives. The Christ Consciousness was downloaded into them too. Remember that the Christ Consciousness is the child of whom? You flow within the electromagnetic energy of Mother/Father/God and you express Mother God and Father God's evolutionary development as the Christ Child. We have introduced the energy of the divine child because you are the child of Mother God and Father God's love. They fulfill themselves as you consciously express the Christ Child within. When you access and utilize the electromagnetic frequencies of the Christ Child, you are in complete conscious communication with your Soul. You are flowing within divinity in a way your limited third-dimensional human self cannot. This is the dance of life offered to you today through conscious choice. It is an experience of fifth-dimensional consciousness on a third-dimensional world. Mother/Father/God is fulfilling Itself in you, through the Christ Child.

Those who choose to embody the Christ Consciousness, are the forerunners of the new civilization where everyone will live in fearlessness, wonder, and innocence. This is the physical, emotional, mental, and spiritual blueprint of those who will populate the new civilization. This is how to co-create a new world within Mother/Father/God's Earth. We have not only given you the outline of the new civilization, we have now given you the way to embody and become the beings capable of establishing and maintaining this new civilization of peace. We look forward to our continued collaboration in the evolution of humanity on Earth. Peace be with you all!

EMBODYING THE CHRIST CONSCIOUSNESS

Level of Embodiment	Innocence	Fearlessness	Wonder
Physical	Tender, gentle, touching. State of harmlessness. Aware of the need to be loved.	Muscular freedom to experience all situations. Pure safety with unlimited travel. Willingness to act.	Curiosity; playfulness. The world and the cosmos are your playground.
Emotional	Unconditional trust. Open hearted. Welcoming.	Pure vulnerability. Willingness to engage in multi-dimensional relationships.	In awe of beauty. Pursues creative and artistic endeavors.
Mental	Willingness to consider all possibilities. Accepting of what is.	Open to divine thought. Willingness to engage in multi-dimensional intellectual pursuits.	Appreciation. Honors multi-dimensional scientific discovery. Interested in everything.
Spiritual	Complete purity. Flows within electromagnetic energy of Mother/Father/God. Communes with divinity.	Willingness to receive and complete divine missions and spiritual assignments. Welcomes personal evolutionary tests.	Gratitude Glorification Exaltation

Please visit
www.growingconsciousness.com

GROWING CONSCIOUSNESS provides access to the latest multi-dimensional technologies available for planetary evolution. Through the weekly bulletin, *Now Coming To Earth*, you can learn about why you are feeling, thinking, and acting in new ways, and understand how to apply them in your daily life. *The Evolutionary Call* offers monthly glimpses at the spiritual advancements being offered to humanity according to the lunar cycle. Information about specific stones that will assist you throughout the lessons of the month ahead, and focused meditations to help you embody the current geometry of higher-dimensional living, are presented.

Each page of the website is designed with your evolutionary progress in mind, offering you tools to develop your physical, etheric, emotional, mental, and spiritual bodies. In collaboration with the mineral kingdom, Growing Consciousness presents: *Stone Healing, Crystal Personalities, Gem Elixirs,* and *Crystal Companions* to accelerate your evolutionary development. Moreover, you can:

- Experience the power of sacred geometry to manifest healing and abundance through *Images of the Soul*.
- Discover your multi-dimensional potential through *Miracle Mechanics*.

- Learn the skills to expertly function in a multi-dimensional world through the *Growing Consciousness Lessons*.
- Listen to the music of the Angels singing your whole being into harmony and balance.

We invite you to explore our **Evolutionary Marketplace**. There, you will discover our *stones*, which are chosen because of their desire to assist in your evolutionary journey. Each one is awaiting the home in which it can most effectively serve. Our *platonic solid sets* are hand crafted, and our *vibrational sprays* are calibrated for our planetary development. Each item supports your healing and multi-dimensional awareness, inviting you to experience a joyous, peaceful life. We look forward to serving you at:

www.growingconsciousness.com.

Muffy: or A Transmigration of Selves

by
S.T. Gulik

Bloomington, IN — authorHOUSE® — Milton Keynes, UK

AuthorHouse™
1663 Liberty Drive, Suite 200
Bloomington, IN 47403
www.authorhouse.com
Phone: 1-800-839-8640

AuthorHouse™ UK Ltd.
500 Avebury Boulevard
Central Milton Keynes, MK9 2BE
www.authorhouse.co.uk
Phone: 08001974150

© 2007 S.T. Gulik. All rights reserved.

No part of this book may be reproduced, stored in a retrieval system, or transmitted by any means without the written permission of the author.

First published by AuthorHouse 6/21/2007

ISBN: 978-1-4259-9614-7 (sc)

Printed in the United States of America
Bloomington, Indiana

This book is printed on acid-free paper.

Library of Congress Control Number: 2007901580

To all the women with time clock eyes who hold their slatted spoons bravely before them like crosses to ward away their fears as they fatelessly back into the familiar corners that they call home. For even the free destroy themselves given enough time.

Disclaimer

Given the nature of this novel, I feel that it is necessary to offer a few words of explanation. The following may seem harsh or redundant, but please bear with me. If you go into this novel with the wrong mindset it would be quite easy to miss the point entirely. I believe that technology and the very infrastructure of our society itself have made everything too comfortable for the average person. That comfort is causing us to devolve into squishy, stupid, lumps of meat. We are losing the very essence of our humanity, our intellect, and our freedom. In our society today, thinking is no longer necessary. You follow the program and do what you are told and life can be very easy. Go to college, get a degree, get a good job, get married, have kids, distract yourself with sports, keep up with the Joneses, go to church, don't take any interest in the world around you, be happy, and for the love of God don't think too hard about what you hear on the news. Do those things and you get nice cars, big TVs, trophy wives, plastic surgery, and unlimited comfort. Most people will live their entire lives without ever really being aware of the world outside of their circle of friends. They will never see anything truly disturbing or disgusting.

Every aspect of our lives are sterilized by somebody. Censors tell you what you are allowed to see, hear, say, think, and read. The government dictates what we are allowed to do in public and in private. The church tries to make you so afraid of the wrath of God that you'll do absolutely anything that they say without questioning them. Are we a bunch of children? Can we not think for ourselves at all? Can an average adult not say to them self, "Hey, this book is full of disgusting perversity. I won't read it" and put it back on the shelf? Sadly, many people are so used to being free from having to make their own decisions, that some of them can't. So, the point of this book is to show people how screwed up the world can be. I want to jostle you out of your safe, fuzzy blanket, reality. I want to make you think about things that you normally wouldn't, and challenge ideas that you've always had, in the hopes that you will come to a better understanding of why you think the way you do and who you really are. I want you to start making your own decisions.

What I'm not trying to do is indoctrinate you with a bunch of my own ideas. The characters in this novel are all absolutely crazy. Anyone that would buy into any of my character's rants has far greater problems than being exposed to this book. I address pretty much every taboo at some point, so if you don't want to think about child rape, incest, murder, torture, infanticide, kinky sex, government conspiracy, random violence, religious reform, politics, self destruction, and a bunch of other touchy subjects then tough. Nobody else does either. That's the problem. We ignore what's wrong with our society and hope it will go away. I hate to have to be the one to tell you but that doesn't work. The point is not to shock you. I'm not trying to be gross. The style, being as extreme and perverse as it is, will hopefully cancel itself out so that you will be able to see through the filth to a whole new world of ideas and possibilities. If this is a rabbit hole you don't want to go down, then don't read it. If you are at all easily offended, prudish, close minded, naïve, or immature this book is not for you. To flip this page is to waive all rights to being sheltered. Most people will not like this book, even fewer will understand it, but for those few I can pretty much guarantee that it will be a rewarding and thought provoking experience. If you haven't figured it out yet, this book is absolutely not for kids.

I originally didn't want to have to do this. However, throughout history, thousands of authors have been censored, banned, jailed, and even executed for either saying things that the masses didn't want to hear, or in a style that was unpopular at the time. I do both. Technically, America is a free country. Technically, you or I can say anything we want, however we want, to whomever we want. However, we all know that that's bullshit. America is a unique balance to theocracy and plutocracy. The religious fundamentalists have pretty much free reign as long as their actions don't interfere with the profits of the rich. Alternately, the rich have free reign because religious fundamentalists tend to be naïve and easy to control. In other words, if this book makes lots of money, I'm fine, but if not, I go to jail or an asylum where I get drugged and or shocked until I can't write another. So buy the book, as a favor to me. You don't have to read it. Use it as a paperweight, throw it at someone you hate, or burn it for all I care, as long as I'm not in jail or dead.

So, what's it going to be? Are you going to read this or not? If you can't handle it then don't. You've been warned.

P.S. I don't support incest, rape, pedophilia, necrophilia, vandalism, kidnapping, drug abuse, or anything else that lies on the other side of this page. The world is fucked up, now deal with it.

Contents

Epilogue	1
Family Values For Dummies	3
The Picnic	5
Hello	7
A Quick Shower Before Work	15
A New Creation	25
What Can You Do With A Dead Pig?	29
More Gratuitous Sex	35
A Study in Ornithology: Sarah	43
A Study in Ornithology: Muffy	47
Belial	49
A Surprise	55
Abby	61
The First Outing	69
Batya Christ	75
Sleepwalk in Color Form	85
Jakob Sprenger	87
A Lovely Melodrama	91
Faith, Love, and Treachery Maui Style	95
Tacos and Treachery	99
Tiny Wonders	103
A Sad Realization	111
A Long Night	113

I'm sorry	117
A Booboo	125
55	129
5@6	135
Fuck you, who needs a title for a chapter anyway? Just fucking read.	141
The Holey Crusade	145
The Devil's Advocate	149
Back at the Cabin	153
A Father's Love	157
Weizens and Weasels	161
A Night Swim in Cuneiform	165
Sarah's Midnight Romp	167
71	173
Heaven Is Nice	175
Fleas Suck	183
Don't Fuck With God	185
I Warned You	187

Epilogue

"Muffy LeSeux was found today by a fisherman off the coast of Los Angeles. Her bloated corpse was dragged ashore in a fishing net and was not discovered until later that day. Yesterday's events seem to have proven to be too much for her, for the police are saying that it looks like suicide. Popular opinion polls, on the other hand, seem to disagree. The word around town is that her father murdered her in a fit of rage for letting the world in on the family secret, which she disclosed yesterday at a press conference. Andrew LeSeux, who until yesterday at twelve fifteen was the head of a multinational conglomerate which owned major manufacturers of everything from cars to toilet paper, seems to have vanished from the face of the earth and every attempt to reach him, from family and friends to police, has failed. Lamia, Muffy's mother, is a highly respected and more widely admired lawyer of the firm Scholtz, LeSeux, and Lobis. She has been taken to an asylum and no information has been released as to the seriousness of her condition. Until yesterday both Lamia and Andrew were respected members of the upper crust of New York, well known for their generosity at fundraisers and dinner parties alike. Muffy was brought up with all of the privileges that a child could ask for; private schools, designer clothes, fine food, and don't forget money. Until yesterday no one had any idea that her father had been molesting and raping her from age eight. This country will never cease to amaze me. I only pray that justice will be done in one way or another to the father. Until I receive more information, this is Leslie Baker signing off for Channel Ten News at six."

"How awful! I knew that family well. I would never have guessed that they, of all people, would be caught up in such a scandal. It just goes to show that you never can tell about people. But we aren't like them are we, Mumsie's little darling?" the woman said crushing her poodle tightly to her large, doughy breasts. "We are good people, aren't we?" she asked the helpless beast. "So sweet and innocent, you would never be caught up in a scandal. That's why I love you, my darling. You're pure as the driven snow." She squeezed the animal tighter until it began to feel its bones splinter. But what can a poodle do in such a situation? Its eyes slid sadly over to the television and secreted tears big enough for a Doberman into the silken fabric of the fat lady's blouse. "Come on dearest. Time for walkies!" the woman said, releasing the poodle just long enough to find the diamond-studded harness. She slipped it over the beast's neck and snapped it on her belly, and opening the door she dragged the sullen beast into a world of fear.

Family Values For Dummies

Our story begins three years earlier on Muffy's fourteenth birthday. She lies, crying in the middle of her crimson king size canopy bed, convulsing from her violent spasms of disgust. Her father turns as he is leaving the room and asks, "Do you love your daddy?"

She calms herself enough to reply in a sweet childlike voice, "Yes, Daddy. You know that I do."

The door soundlessly becomes one with the wall and she feels an odd calm come over her. She reaches down to her convulsing vagina and dipping in ever so gently with her ring finger she extracts a tiny amount of her fathers semen. As if in a trance she reaches up and touches the small pink nipple of her right breast. Her fingers, lubricated by her fathers weakness, slide smoothly over the tender flesh as she let out a sigh of relief. She raises once again her hand. Bringing it to her lips she tastes the lingering warm secretion, wondering all the while how something that brought her such pain could give her so much pleasure. She usually sobs and convulses for hours after an encounter with her father, but this time had been different. She had let go this time and enjoyed herself. After all, there was nothing that she could do about it. She had tried fighting back but her father had just hit her and using only his left hand had effortlessly pulled both of her hands high above her head and held them there for the duration. She had tried gaining weight but her mother just put her on a strict diet saying that no daughter of hers would be a glutton. She even tried telling her mother once but she dismissed the accusations as a plea for attention and grounded her for a month. So this time she just laid there and let her father have his fun, and to her surprise she found herself drowning in a sea of orgasms. The thought occurred to her that she might like it better if the person molesting her was not her father. She began planning her first experiment that night.

The Picnic

One week later she was ready. At 11:00, clad only in a leather miniskirt, knee high black vinyl boots, and one of those long strips of cloth that ties in the back, she set off on her first adventure. She went to the park and waited under a burnt out street light for her first victim.

Two hours and fifteen cigarettes later she saw a large fat man walking a dog the size of a small horse approaching her. The man didn't seem to notice her until he was about fifteen feet away. He smiled revealing two rows of nicotine stained carnage that looked more like a horrible train wreck than teeth. He tied the large animal to a rusty green bench and proceeded to piss all over the garbage can that stood next to it. He turned to look at Muffy and snickering loudly asked her if he could have a freebie since it was his birthday. Muffy, who was suddenly very aware of what she was doing, began to have second thoughts. Transfixed by the gaze of the fat man she couldn't say a word. She could only stare at the dog that was now licking at the puddle that was developing around the garbage can. Drunken gaiety gave way to anger as the feeling of being insulted grew in his belly. A look of disgust crept across his face. When the urine finally ran out he stuffed himself back into his pants and turned to walk towards her. As he approached her she slowly began to back away. "You know, you're about the rudest hooker that I've ever seen. How the hell are you ever going to make any money if you run away every time somebody talks to ya? Get your pretty little ass over here. I've got a crisp five dollar bill here that says that you're coming home with me."

The power of speech finally returned to Muffy and she stammered, "I-i-i'm not a hooker," as she began to back away a bit faster.

"Well then what the hell are you doing standing out here in the park at one in the morning?" he demanded. "Why aren't you at home in bed like a good little girl?"

At a loss for words Muffy heard herself say insomnia, but it sounded more like a question than an answer. The fat man didn't buy it. "You know what little girl? I think you're a liar. I think that you think that you're better than me. I think that you *are* a hooker and you just don't find me attractive. You know what else little missy? I think that you need to be taught a little lesson."

As Muffy turned to run he snorted and shouted after her, "There ain't nuthin worse than an uppity whore." The fat man waddled back over to the bench where he had tied his dog and set it free. The dog stopped licking the urine off the garbage can and turned a questioning gaze at his master. The fat man only pointed in the direction of the girl and said, "Faggot, get the faggot boy. Go get him!"

Muffy ran as fast as she could but the dog seemed to be gaining on her. She ducked inside of an old abandoned factory and ran up the stairs to the storeroom at the top. She peered out of the window just as the dog was approaching the door. She saw the massive thing run past the door but it stopped and turned shortly after passing it. He came back to the door and began to sniff at the crack at the bottom. The dog let out a long howl as if it was angry that the door was closed. Just then she saw the man approaching from a distance. Everything went black.

Hello

She awoke a few hours later trembling, naked, and tied to a large ottoman. The position that she was in was rather painful which made her wonder why she hadn't come to sooner. She was kind of on her back, although her back wasn't actually touching anything, and her hands were pulled straight back behind her head with each tied to one of the badly beaten and splintery legs, and her feet were done much in the same way. She tried to struggle but that only made the splintered wood dig into the backs of her wrists, tearing the skin and causing blood to drip down the ropes into a small puddle below her head. A rough and dirty tasting gag had been stuffed into her mouth and tied behind her head which drew all of the moisture out of her mouth leaving it raw and sensitive. She tried to make a sound but her throat felt as if it was going to burst open and no sound would come out. The room that she was in was completely dark except for a crack of light coming out from the edges of a small door which she assumed either led to another smaller storage room or a lighted broom closet of some sort. She could hear squishing noises coming from the lighted room coupled with a faint yet very definite squeaking noise. She followed the crack of light with her eyes down the cracked wooden floor to where it ended a few feet from the leg of the ottoman where her right wrist was tied. "What the hell is going on here?" she wondered. "I remember passing out just after seeing the fat guy. Damn I have good timing!"

Just then the door opened and for just a second she caught a glimpse of a small figure silhouetted in the doorway. It stepped out of the light and shut the door. At first the room was without form and void and darkness was upon the face of the girl. She could hear her captor's footsteps as they circled her in the darkness. With every rotation they grew nearer until finally she could feel the movement of the air on her naked torso. Then, when the only way for it to be any closer was to be inside of her it was. All that she could sense in the darkness was the sensation of stiff yet gentle fingers probing around her shaved vagina. The passion which she had felt the night before returned with such force that with one violent convulsion her left hand was freed from its restraints. She found herself wishing that it hadn't happened. By this time she didn't want to be free.

It wasn't long before Muffy's wonton abandon and lack of self-control alerted her captor of her lack of restraints. Upon realizing this, the small figure stopped what it was doing and rose to its feet and, before she knew it, the room was flooded with light. The sudden increase in input overloaded Muffy's adjusted eyes, blinding her for no less than 18 and one half seconds, but no more than an hour. When her eyes finally began to clear the first thing that she was able to focus on was the large seemingly cylindrical object that her captor held in her right hand. To her surprise she saw that her captor held in her hand the furry right arm of the fat man that had been chasing her. Her stomach did a flip as revelation engulfed her. At first the thought of being molested with the severed arm of a thoroughly disgusting and uncouth individual such as the fat man frightened and disgusted her to the point of nausea. Then she thought to look at the face of the vile person who had done it to her. She saw for the first time the true face of evil. The first thing that she noticed was the hair, which was a pleasant shade of baby blue and pulled back into a short ponytail. The bangs stopped right at the point that her blood red eyebrows began. They hovered, arched in a quizzical kink above the brightest green eyes that she had ever seen. The almost pug nose protruded only slightly from the pool of ivory that was her face. Her mouth was delicately painted in white and smiling, poised above a not exactly pointy, but angular, chin. She guessed the woman was in her mid-twenties. The woman's face was twisted into the leer of a sadistic child. Muffy focused on the woman's eyes which managed to be piercing yet warm at the same time. Her gaze was like being massaged by a blender full of warm aloe. The right eye winked and Muffy fell in love.

The erect figure said "Hello," and dropped the arm onto a pile of rags that lay in the corner of the room. Wiping her hands on her rough stained jumpsuit, she walked over to her and sat on a stool positioned to the left of her head. She removed the pair of night vision goggles dangling from her delicate throat and set them on the floor beside her. Muffy smiled at her from behind the gag. The blue haired girl reached over and untied the rag and tossing it to the floor she looked Muffy in the eyes and began to speak. "You can scream if you want to, but no one will hear. Even if they did hear they wouldn't bother to come and see who was screaming," she said in a matter-of-fact and rather bored monotone. "My name's Sarah, what's yours?"

Muffy tried to speak but her mouth and throat were still too dry to manufacture sound. The blue haired one saw the problem and walked over to a large wooden table located under a large window that looked out over the barren city. She opened a small refrigerator and withdrew a green bottle of beer and a root beer and returned to her stool. She opened the root beer and with a grin poured the entirety of its contents down the parched girl's throat. The foam built up and flowed up into Muffy's nose and down over her breasts and stomach coating her torso in a thin dark layer of sweet sticky fluid. Sarah leaned down and caught a drop of the liquid with her tongue as it cascaded down her artificially bronzed side. She then drank the small amount that was beginning to collect in Muffy's armpit. Sitting up she sighed and said, "Nothing quenches thirst like an ice cold root beer." Muffy was inclined to agree.

When the root beer ran out and the foam died down Muffy looked into the woman's eyes and asked in a gentle voice, "So, if no one can hear me scream what was the point of the gag?"

"I am an artist, what can I say," she said smiling. "You didn't look right without one. Anyway, you are the one tied to the ottoman. I think that I should be the one asking the questions." She leaned in closer. "What the hell were you doing in my studio? And why was that guy chasing you?"

Muffy looked away from her captor for the first time since the lights came on. "He thought that I was a hooker and he wanted a freebie. He was gross so I ran away. This was the first place that I could find to hide. How did you kill him anyway? He was a fucking monster. That was his arm wasn't it?"

"Yes it was. I bet that you feel really dumb now," she said with a giggle. "You seemed to be enjoying his hand a minute ago. If you hadn't run away from him you wouldn't be in this situation, I wouldn't have to kill you, and from the looks of things you would have had a good time."

Muffy frowned and replied, "You're wrong. You don't have to kill me. I like the situation that I'm in."

Sarah looked slightly amused and, after pausing a moment, she said, "That is beside the point. I still have to kill you. You've seen too much."

Muffy angrily retorted, "I haven't seen shit. How the fuck am I supposed to see anything while I'm tied to a footrest. Turn the lights back off and fuck me, goddamn it!" she screamed. "What's the big idea knocking me out, tying me up, getting me all horny, and then telling me that I'm about to die? Fuck you!"

"Whoa there slugger. Calm down, I'm not going to kill you yet. If all that I wanted to do was kill you I wouldn't have gone to the trouble to tie you up, much less wasted a root beer," Sarah informed her as she searched for her bottle opener. "I'm not going to kill you until you either bore me or piss me off. It all depends on your attitude."

Muffy calmed down a bit after hearing this, but she still wasn't happy about the whole dying thing.

Sarah opened her beer and took a long draw from it. "So what were you doing out this time of the night if you're not a hooker?"

Muffy sullenly replied, "I don't want to talk about it." She looked around the room curiously and noticed that the walls were covered in violent depictions of human cruelty. The paintings were done on the walls themselves and reminded her of an exhibit that she had gone to a few months ago. She tried to recall the name of the artist but could only remember that he had been oriental and that his name stared with an M.

"So who does your decorating? I like it," she asked, her eyes lingering on a particularly gruesome piece on the wall to the right of the refrigerator. It depicted a small nude boy's torso impaled through the anus. His legs dangled from hooks that hung from the ceiling behind him, and his arms were skewered on poles that ran from the floor to the ceiling. From the angle that the painting was done, it seemed that the boy was in a fairly natural position, standing with his arms above his head resting against the wall, and his legs crossed at the knees. He had been disemboweled and his chest had been fashioned into a birdcage which held a bright yellow bird.

Sarah, noticing that she had become stuck on that one replied jealously, "Kizi did that one. All the rest are mine."

"You did these?" Muffy asked in awe. "You're good."

"They don't pay me $400,000 a piece because I suck."

"Damn," Muffy cooed, her eyes still scanning the walls, "Who do you sell to? I would think that I would have heard of you since I'm always going to private shows."

Haughtily, Sarah replied, "I don't do shows anymore. The people I sell to don't go to shows. These I mainly sell to rich sickos, but I make my good money off of my sculptures. They go for anywhere between five million and five hundred million. Those only go to heads of government and mainly the high Illuminati. They are who

I really work for. You probably don't know that there are three of my pieces in the White House," she proclaimed smugly.

"Really?" Muffy continued to coo.

"Yup. Ronnie was crazy about my work. He doubled the national debt by buying a set that I did out of a black family. He said that it helped him feel *closer* to the minorities. Sick fuck."

Muffy made a puppy dog face and commenced begging. "Please, may I see one? I love sculptures."

Sarah let out a haughty breath, "I'm working on one at the moment actually. I might let you see it," she smirked, "if you're still around when I finish. If not you may be part of it. You know how art is, you never know what it's going to look like when you finish."

She came closer to Muffy and straddling her began to unzip the paint and blood spattered jumpsuit, revealing two small pale breasts bearing colorless nipples of no definite size. She had two barbells piercing each nipple, each end bearing a sharp curved piece of metal resembling a claw. Muffy reached up with her free hand to caress the soft creamy flesh that had been revealed to her. She pinched her nipples and felt the steel bars that ran through her them in the shape of a cross. She reached down into Sarah's pants and began to manipulate the soft slippery flesh of her vagina.

Being that the entire weight of the two girls was being supported by only one wrist and her ankles Muffy was in a considerable amount of pain already, but it wasn't until Sarah leaned down and began to grind and rake her breasts against Muffy's tender stomach that the pain approached unbearable. Her arm went limp and this made Sarah grind harder. It wasn't long before she was covered in hundreds of tiny cuts, each bleeding just enough to cause her torso to become coated in a thin layer of blood. The sugary sting of the root beer being ground into her open wounds combined with her position gave her the sensation of burning at the stake. When Muffy was nicely marinated Sarah slowly began to inch her gilded nipples closer to Muffy's throat. When the scratches covered her throat Sarah sat up and asked, "Having fun yet?"

Muffy: or A Transmigration of Selves

Muffy was only able to groan under the load of sensation. She was reminded of the first time that her father had taken advantage of her. She remembered the feeling of terror that complete helplessness brings. Then she remembered the last time. She could feel her fathers cock inside of her, tearing her tender young flesh yet making her come at the same time. She decided that she liked Sarah a lot better than her father, and that she would take advantage of the situation.

She glowed a look of pure love and acceptance so intense that Sarah was taken aback. Sarah, not expecting this look of gratitude, became very confused and turned on at the same time. Lifting her legs, she thrust herself over Muffy's breasts and crushed her crotch into the girl's face. She began to grind the soft flesh of her vagina into that face and came almost instantly. She then eased up a little on the pressure and began to slide her soft pink lips up and down the girl's face leaving a thick white slimy residue over her lips and chin. Muffy reached up once again to squeeze the flesh of Sarah's breast. She observed that Sarah's juices tasted different than hers and her father's. She had a delicate sweet flavor in addition to the tangy flavor that she herself produced. She ran her free hand over every inch of Sarah that she could reach, exploring her, testing for firmness and weight of every part that she was offered. She took the opportunity to taste the bitter flesh of Sarah's anus and nibbled gently on it when it came close enough. This made Sarah erupt violently again and the sticky white secretion grew thicker. She took this as a good sign and enjoyed the increase of flavor when Sarah ground her pussy into her mouth. This obscene kiss lasted in excess of 15 minutes. Muffy felt that they had merged into one monstrous entity gorging itself on pleasure. When Sarah finally dismounted and left the room, Muffy was filled with an empty sensation.

Sarah returned to the room, which she had emerged from earlier and came out a few seconds later with a crying baby. She walked over to the table which held the refrigerator and placed the baby next to a bowl of ripe apples. She opened one of the drawers and removed a vice and attached it to the table. She then placed the baby's arm in it and tightened it until the baby's cry became a shrill howl of anguish which resembled the sound a cat makes when it's in heat, only much louder. Out of the same drawer she pulled out a large butcher knife and severed the flesh surrounding the baby's arm. She then set down the knife and picking up the anguished baby pulled until the bone came out of the socket with a loud pop. At this Muffy uttered a small cry of disbelief. Sarah looked angry that she objected and walked quickly up to Muffy and rammed the arm up her anus fist first. She could feel and hear the fingers cracking under the stress. She knew that the arm was that of a baby but, once it was lodged firmly inside of her, it felt as though it were a grown man's. Sarah returned to the flopping and barely conscious infant and quickly repeated the process on the other arm and one of its legs. Returning to the ottoman she placed the fat end of the leg in her own vagina and the foot into Muffy's. She then began to fuck her as if she were a man. Both girls began to come violently. Muffy couldn't help but pity the poor infant but the importance of that pity faded with each wave of ecstasy. The sheer decadence of the act was such a turn on that it overshadowed the wrongness and enveloped it in a fuzzy pink cloud of wanton abandon. Sarah crammed the baby's hand into Muffy along with the leg, which made her come so hard that she peed all over Sarah and herself. Soon they were both covered in blood, urine, and various other secretions. The violence of the sex mixed with the smells of these secretions quickly became unbearable. When Sarah took the foot out of Muffy's ass and stuffed it in her mouth it proved to me just a bit too much for her tender young stomach. Her body, wracked with spasms of pleasure and agony, soon let lose an enthusiastic yawn which technicolored Sara's face and breasts with bits of dinner. Sarah reacted in kind and both girls giggled hysterically. The ickyness was sublimated by the comic absurdity of the whole situation. Beyond this point things became a little too kinky to go into in an American publication. The girls played on into the night until they were both so full of blood and cum that they vomited themselves to sleep.

A Quick Shower Before Work

Muffy returned (or rather was dragged kicking and screaming) into consciousness the next morning, with the help of a blinding light and a barking dog. "Fucking dog," she groaned to herself as the crowbar of light forced its way through her eyelids. She looked around the room in a state of confusion until her eyes settled on Sarah who was still passed out naked in the corner; face down in a puddle of her own vomit. Muffy suddenly remembered what had taken place the night before and began to feel sick to her stomach. She considered this to be a very bad thing because she was still tied to the ottoman. She noticed that, some time after she had passed out, Sarah must have handcuffed her as well for her right hand was no longer free. A tsunami of nausea came crashing down upon her and she projectile vomited up into the air which, as natural law dictates, gravity soon returned to its place of origin. She began to scream and cry as she tried to spit out the half digested chunks of congealed blood and ooze that now covered her face as the root beer had done the night before.

The loud gurgling sound revived Sarah from her self induced coma and she woke with a loud squeal and a pathetic flop of disgust. She flung herself to her feet only to slip in the puddle of vomit and landed with a squish and a thud. She squeaked again and began to cry. Her loud sobs gave way to ranting when she noticed Muffy. "You bitch," she howled, "look what you did to me. I promised myself that this wouldn't happen again. FUCK!!!" She attempted to rise again and though she was a little wobbly she made it this time. She crossed the room and slapped Muffy hard on her right cheek. She looked down at her hand in disgust and wiped the dark brown fluid on Muffy's right breast. "I can't believe that I ever thought that you were hot." Her expression changed from disgusted rage to triumph. "On the other hand you are already primed to become a monument to lust. I could have you finished and sold in a couple of days." She clapped her hands and began to bounce giddily.

Muffy pleaded, "Please don't. If you will wash me off, I promise that I can be beautiful for you again. Anyway, look at me. I think that I got the worst of it last night. Didn't you have fun?"

The bouncing died off. Sarah's expression turned thoughtful and she turned away. She walked over to the table with the refrigerator on it and withdrew a clove cigarette from a small black box. She scanned the table for a lighter but all that she saw was the refrigerator, a purple baby with one limb, her cigarette box, and a crushed can of root beer. She turned to Muffy. "I don't suppose that you noticed what I did with my lighter last night."

Muffy replied, "It should be over there somewhere. Look under the baby."

Sarah picked the rancid thing up and saw her lighter in the center of a small pool of dried blood. "Maybe you could come in handy around here. You're a good lay too." Picking up the lighter she tried to light her cigarette but all that would come out were small dark flakes. Raising the baby above her head she threw it into the garbage as hard as she could, causing it to fall over and spill its contents onto the floor. Sarah threw her cigarette across the room and let out a string of profanities long enough to knit a body stocking with. When she was done cursing the baby she began to giggle and entered the small room that she had been in the night before. She returned with a digital camera and took a picture of the mess. She walked back into the small room and began to giggle louder. Returning a few minutes later with her hands behind her back, she said, "Close your eyes. I have a surprise for you." Muffy did. "Now open them."

When she did she saw what appeared to be a 'Garbage Pail Kids' card with a picture that Sarah had just taken in the center. The caption read, "Quadriplegic Quiggy."

"So what do you think?" she asked giddily.

Muffy burst out laughing. "That's bad, real bad."

"Yeah, I know," Sarah squeaked, "and it's a sticker too." She bounded over to the refrigerator and stuck it to the door. Then she kicked the pile of trash into a neat pile and returned to Muffy. Brushing the crust off of her torso she said, "I'm sick of being covered in this shit, aren't you?"

Muffy nodded gravely.

"Let's get cleaned up for breakfast, shall we?" Muffy nodded happily. Sarah wheeled her into the mysterious room that she had earlier perceived to be small. She found that she was quite wrong. The room that she had been in before was less than a quarter of the size of this new room. She surmised that this was the actual warehouse and the previous room had only been a large office. She saw a large computer with all of the newest gizmos and enough icons on the desktop that she couldn't see the wallpaper on the 25-inch monitor. Next to it was a massive bookcase which held hundreds of volumes that appeared to be bound in leather and very old. Across the room from it, some odd thousands of feet away, there was another one just like it. In fact there were bookcases like that everywhere with things in between them; tables, showers, dressers, displays of odd looking cutlery, toilets, harnesses, cages, televisions, stereo equipment, etc.

"Quite a place you have here," Muffy remarked. "It's almost as big as my parent's house."

Sarah looked confused. "Where the hell do they live?"

"Which season?" Muffy sneered. They stopped in front of a large shower and Sarah drug a piece of wood over to it to use as a ramp over the lip of the floor which was about three inches high. It suddenly occurred to Muffy that Sarah wasn't even going to untie her to bathe. "Would you please untie me?" she asked sweetly. "My muscles have been taking turns cramping for the last twelve hours and it's getting kind of painful." Sarah pushed her up the ramp and into the shower.

"If I did that you might get away, and I wouldn't want that to happen. I suppose that I could always nail you to the floor where I want you to stay, but after a while the holes would get so big that it wouldn't work anymore. You would run away eventually, and then I would have to track you down and kill you before you got to the cops, and that would be a lot of trouble. I like you where you are. Say, you're a spoiled rich kid aren't you?" She attached a hose to the faucet and turned on the water. Muffy didn't say a word as she was hosed down like an animal. She even began to like it when Sarah began to soap her up. The thought suddenly occurred to her that animals are very lucky, at least the ones with loving owners. Sarah soaped up Muffy's vagina and stuck the hose inside of her to wash out all of the scummy buildup and rotting baby bits that might have become lodged inside of her. "Hey, do you have a dog?" she asked.

"I chained the asshole's dog in the basement last night, before you came to. I figured that he might come in handy."

"Oh." Muffy giggled and began to writhe, "That feels funny, stop it."

Sarah smiled and asked, "You don't want to get an infection because of improper personal hygiene now do you?"

She pulled hard on the baby's arm and with a schlorp it was freed from Muffy's rectum.

Muffy giggled, "I suppose you've got a point."

Sarah bent down and looked into the gaping cavern. "Hey, I can see what you had for dinner last night," she said as she inserted the hose.

"You know, Sarah, your jokes really suck," Muffy said, not amused.

Muffy: or A Transmigration of Selves

"What fun is there in telling a good joke? Most of them aren't funny either but at least when you tell a bad joke you get to laugh at the persons expression when they realize just how bad it sucked."

Muffy looked confused. "So what you are really saying is that a joke is only funny if it isn't?"

"No, what I am saying is this: Most, if not all, jokes are at the expense of someone or something else, and the joke isn't funny to them. Jokes are usually to amuse the teller rather than the listener. My jokes aren't bad; you just aren't hearing them from the right perspective. If one person thinks that a joke is funny then it's funny whether you like it or not."

Muffy asked, "So you're saying that Peanuts is funny just because some Mongoloid finds it amusing enough to use it to wrap his flip towel?"

"Theoretically, if a Mongoloid was amused by it then it would be funny, but nobody thinks that Peanuts is funny. It's just really old and lame and its purpose is only to make Dilbert seem funny by comparison. Anyway you're clean. What do you want to eat? It's on me."

"How am I going to be able to eat while I'm tied to an ottoman? It's hard to eat with no hands anyway, but you have me lying down. Well… kind of."

Sarah began to wheel her back to the smaller room. "I plan to move you to a chair so that you can eat. Unless of course you want me to feed you."

"No, a chair is fine. Do you have cinnamon waffles?"

"Yes actually, I do. You like those too?"

"Of course I do! That is the best shit for breakfast, lunch, dinner, and snacking. I could live off that stuff. They must put crack in them or something. "

"I know what you mean. They are addictive. The people that I work for put chemicals in certain foods to make them more popular. It's always the same stuff. They synthesized the chemical in tobacco that gets you hooked and made it stronger. It's mainly just a power trip for them." They arrived in the smaller room where Sarah opened the freezer and tossed the entire new box of waffles into the microwave.

"You know," Muffy mused, "It seems like someone who is rich enough and powerful enough to pull that off, without anyone knowing, wouldn't need a power trip."

"Never underestimate a person's lack of self-esteem. The people with the most power are usually the ones with the biggest complexes. If they didn't feel helpless why do you think they would try so hard to be powerful?"

"Good point," Muffy awed. "That's scary. What else are they doing?"

"I really don't think you want to know."

"Damn it, Sarah, yes I do. It's not every day that somebody gets the chance to find out what the government is doing behind our backs. Go on, this is interesting."

"Okay fine, but don't go repeating any of this to anyone. If you do, we'll both be dead. Got it?"

"Of course I've got it. Who the hell do you think that I'd be talking to anyway? In case you haven't noticed I'm currently tied to an ottoman."

"Good point," said Sarah as she crossed the room to take the waffles out of the microwave. "Well, they're done. I guess it's time for the chair, huh?"

"That would be wonderful," Muffy squealed. "But don't try to change the subject. What are they doing?"

Sarah came back to the green Formica table where she had parked Muffy, and pulled a short black antique chair over to the table. It appeared to be very old and was designed like no chair that she had ever seen before. The cushion was green and appeared to be hand woven. The back of the chair was a wooden frame, which was hollow except for detailed carvings that connected the four sides. In the center of the bottom there was a pedestal with engravings that Muffy couldn't make out. On the pedestal there stood a large ovular carving, the center of which contained a cross. There were nuns standing beside the pedestal praying. Above the cross there was a chain of roses suspended from the top of the frame. They were hung in the center and the sides came down and were fastened to the sides of the chair. Above the first carved picture there was another hollow rectangle that contained only a row of skewered apples. Above that there was another hand woven cushion. This is the cushion on which Muffy's breasts were placed. A belt was woven through the apples and tightened so that she was held firmly in place hugging the back of the chair. Then a longer belt was wrapped around her midsection and the bottom of the chair between the legs. Sarah pulled it tight and buckled it so that Muffy's back was arched as painfully as it had been before.

Muffy gave a sigh of disappointment. "I thought that you were going to let me be comfortable so that I could enjoy my food."

"Not this time baby. Maybe next time, if you're good," said Sarah as she used the handcuffs to shackle Muffy's feet together. She laughed and gave Muffy a loving slap on her protruding ass. Muffy cringed with pain.

"Say, what did you do with that guy's dog?" Muffy asked.

Sarah handcuffed Muffy's right hand to the belt around her midsection, leaving only her left to handle the food. "I tied it up in the bottom floor and fed him some of the guy. But I already told you that remember?" With her free hand Muffy awkwardly fell upon the waffles, devouring them in seconds. Without commenting on her bad manners Sarah walked to the other side of the table and sat in another chair exactly like the one that Muffy was strapped to and tore off one of the small squares. She popped it into her mouth and, chewing it slowly, began to think about the answer to Muffy's query.

"Just wondering." Muffy said through a mouthful of waffle.

She swallowed and said, "Well, anyway, in answer to your first question, they are doing all kinds of stuff. Have you ever done acid?"

"Yes, of course. Who hasn't?" Muffy replied.

"Just making sure. Anyway you know how when you're tripping you see this pattern in everything that you look at?"

"Yeah?" Muffy grunted inquisitively.

"Well that pattern is really there all of the time. You see, they figured out a visual pattern that can only be picked up by your subconscious. Then they found a way to manufacture a chemical that would make the patterns that they choose and then they slipped it into all of the paint, plaster, dye, and a lot of other things that people see all of the time. Pastels are the most responsive to these chemicals, and neons are the least receptive. That is why pastel blue and pink are so frequently put in baby rooms. The messages are typically manufactured to make you calm and complacent. The basic idea is to make people so happy or mad that they don't notice what is really going on all around them. This is also the reason that people are always so pissed off about the tiny insignificant things that shouldn't matter to them. When you get mad certain parts of your brain don't function as well as they normally would, and stupid people are always the easiest to control."

She took another bite of waffle. "The reason that you can only see them when you are tripping is that the acid causes your brain to function more like it did when you were a child. You see, when you are born you have no knowledge of language or morals, so you are ruled by instinct. You understand everything because you have to. The closest thing that adults can do to this is to achieve Zen and that level of Zen would make you unable to survive in the modern world. Babies don't know things. They perceive them as they really are. Adults know things, so they are unable to perceive them as they are. You see, reality is just a grid that each person and group of people construct to help them understand things and know what is real and what isn't. The problem with this is that, too often, the grid gets in the way of the very thing that you are trying to see clearly. The more lines that you have on your grid as reference points the harder it is to see through the grid to what you are looking at, and eventually the grid becomes so dense that no matter what you point it at you can only see the grid. Babies have no grid so they can perceive things perfectly. This makes them more susceptible to the subliminal messages that are in everything. The point is that acid smashes your grid for a little while and lets you perceive things as they are. Thereby making you able to see the things that are otherwise subliminal."

"I love you," Muffy said in awe.

Sarah's eyes cut to the floor as she smiled, "I know."

A New Creation

After breakfast neither of them said a word. Muffy clammed up a bit after seeing how apathetic Sarah had been about her declaration. Sarah left her at the table (after handcuffing her left hand and checking all of the restraints) and began the drudgery that is "working for the man." Muffy pondered her situation while Sarah made art out of things that would unfortunately never grasp the concepts that they conveyed so very well. They didn't see each other for hours except for instances where Sarah would take a cigarette break or when she would get blood in her eyes (which, Muffy noticed, happened much more often than one would expect from a professional).

Muffy had to pee once, but rather than disturb Sarah's work she forced herself to pee as hard as she could so that she wouldn't get any on the chair. After all, it was a really spiffy chair. After what seemed like forever Sarah reentered the room and asked, "If I ask for your honest opinion about something would you give it to me?"

"Of course I would," Muffy replied, startled.

Sarah returned to the room from which she had come and returned a few minutes later wheeling in her latest creation. It was the body of a middle-aged woman standing kind of hunched over on a platform that was made to resemble a black and white checkered linoleum tiled kitchen floor. She appeared to be pulling a skinny eight-year old boy named Bob out of her ass. I say that his name was Bob because he was wearing a nametag on his right nipple that said

"Hi, my name is Bob, how can I help you?" She held the boy by his throat with her left hand as she stabbed him in the face with a metal tipped hose that protruded from her right eye. The back of her head was missing to reveal that her brain had been removed. The hose was clear and had a murky green fluid running through it that appeared to have letters floating in it. There was no skin on the woman's right hand or the boy's left. The woman's look was serene and tranquil almost as she was performing a loving deed, where as the boy had a look of sheer terror. "So, what do you think?" Sarah asked.

Muffy was speechless. It was the most beautiful thing that she had ever seen.

"What, you don't like it do you?" Sarah asked, looking a little worried.

"No, it's beautiful," Muffy replied. "I just need a minute to take it all in. It has got to be the goriest thing that I have ever seen and yet it's not ugly at all. It's almost cartoon like. I particularly like the use of humor and the lemony smell that it gives off. How did you do it?"

"It's a gift I guess," Sarah replied, not yet convinced. "You really like it?"

"Of course I do," Muffy assured her. "You're brilliant. Giger's got nothing on you."

Sarah bounced over to Muffy and kissed her gently on the forehead. "You're sweet," she said as she lovingly ran her fingers through Muffy's hair, "but I'm still not satisfied with it." She plopped down on the floor to glare at her new creation. "I'm going out for a while. I need to pick up some supplies." She pulled off her spattered overalls and left the room.

Muffy heard the sound of running water and the occasional squeak of pain or surprise which always accompanied Sarah's frequent showers. "How can anybody hurt themselves so frequently?" Muffy wondered as she sat patiently waiting for her lover's return. It was then that she started to notice that she was developing a really bad itch on her left foot. She wiggled around for a few moments trying to find a way to scratch it, but it was obvious that she was simply out of luck. She began to panic. Flailing violently she began to scream and whine and after a few moments the chair fell over on its side.

Sarah heard her screams and ran into the room panicked and naked. When she saw Muffy writhing on the floor she stopped for a moment to admire how cute and helpless she was. "Problem?" she asked as she towered over the twitching squealing victim of consequence.

Muffy whined, "I have an itch, and I can't reach it"

"Where?" asked Sarah.

"Left foot, itching badly," she sputtered. Sarah leaned down and scratched Muffy's left foot. Muffy squealed with joy and melted into the floor. "Thanks," she said, "I thought that I was going to die."

"Not yet dear, you still amuse me," Sarah said, only half serious.

Muffy pouted and replied, "Thanks, I guess."

Sarah turned and went to the dresser where she kept her clothes. She removed a black bikini and quickly put it on. From the top left drawer she removed two cans of black shoe polish and a pair of infrared goggles. She put them in a plastic bag and threw on a long purple fur coat. "Bye," she said, and picking up a duffel bag and the plastic bag that she had just loaded quickly ran down the stairs and out the front door. Muffy called after her but she had already escaped into the night. She was alone with only the barking of the redneck's dog to keep her company. Just then a chill ran up Muffy's spine and she burst into tears. Spasming, she tried to scratch the itch that was developing on her right foot.

What Can You Do With A Dead Pig?

After hours of torture, Sarah returned smeared in black shoe polish except for white rings around her eyes. She was dragging a large black squirming bag behind her and dripping sweat. She returned to the car a second time and returned with five plastic bags of groceries.

"Would you scratch under my left breast?" Muffy asked as Sarah went through the bags. Sarah stopped what she was doing to oblige. "Where have you been? I've been itching for hours. And the fucking dog hasn't shut up since you left."

"I told you that I had to go out and get some supplies," she said reproachfully. "And anyway, look what I got." She went over to the conspicuously animated bag and unzipped it. Out came a cop fully uniformed, bound and gagged with a mouthful of raw bacon. He kicked and contorted violently. His eyes were wild, yet curious, and they nervously tore around the room in search of an answer to an obvious question. Sarah pulled a hammer and some nails out of her coat pocket and held them before the frantic swine. She unzipped his pants and removed his genitalia and quickly put a nail through his left nut nailing him to the floor. The officer went into convulsions and ripped his scrotum loose from the floor. The testicle did not come with it. "Are you going to behave now or am I going to have to restrain you again?" The officer's convulsions stopped instantly.

"Wow, where did you get him?" asked Muffy. "Aren't you afraid of getting caught?"

"No," replied Sarah, "he came from a long way away. Nobody will be looking for him around here."

"How did you pull it off?" asked Muffy. Sarah came close to Muffy and straddled her side

"If you're good, I might show you some day," and she kissed her violently. "I have to get back to work," she said and dismounted to go to her workshop. Halfway there, she turned and asked, "Do you want to watch me work?"

"Damn skippy, I'd love to," Muffy declared exuberantly.

"Just a minute, let me take a shower and change clothes and then I will be back to get the both of you," Sarah replied as she walked out of the room.

She returned minutes later squeaky clean and ready to create a masterpiece. She placed a leather collar around the officer's throat and pulled it as tight as it would go. She then attached a leash and tied him to the leg of the table. Sarah returned to Muffy and stood her up. She unlocked her from the chair and carried her into the workshop area where she dropped her on the floor in front of a giant wooden machine, which strongly resembled a catapult. She pulled a chain down from the ceiling and kept pulling more and more until there was a sizable pile at her feet with a hook sticking out of one side. Sarah forced Muffy down on her stomach and proceeded to weave the chain through her other restraints until she was securely tied with her arms and legs behind her back. Sarah stuck the hook through one of the links and taking hold of the other chain that was hanging from the ceiling she lifted the girl by her restraints until she was level with the top of the machine. Muffy squealed in pain as the chains dug into her wrists to bruise the bone. "Oh shit," Sarah said and released the first chain causing her love to crash to the floor "I'm so sorry. I forgot why I don't use that one very much anymore." She removed the chains but Muffy was unconscious. She looked at Muffy's wrists, and as she had feared, the chains had sawed through the first few layers of skin and there was a bit of blood leaking out. She bandaged the wounded girl and tied her to the base of the machine with care. A few minutes later she retrieved the officer and tied him to the business end of her machine.

The pig was still terrified but the blood loss had made him complacent. Muffy started to come to a few minutes later and began to emit a soft whine, which slowly grew into a shrill scream. Sarah ran to her and apologized for the injuries that she had caused. She explained that she wasn't yet used to the idea of not hurting people and that she just hadn't been thinking. Muffy forgave her and the art commenced to flow. Sarah returned to the officer and began to speak. "In case you are wondering, the machine to which you are tied is simply a tool of art. Kind of like a giant paintbrush. And you, my dear, are the paint." The officer became even more crazed and began to writhe and fight his bonds. Sarah responded by thumping his bleeding scrotum and the officer regained his composure. "The walls are padded with thick foam, although I know they don't look it, so if you scream no one will hear you. If you do scream I will just hurt you again so I wouldn't bother." She removed the gag and the bacon and walked to the back of the machine.

"Why are you doing this? You'll never get away with it," screamed the frantic officer just before he threw up with such force that it landed four feet from the machine.

"Could you possibly be more cliché? You policemen are the most unimaginative and boring people in the world. Not to mention that you support an openly oppressive government and charge people money to throw them in jail," said Sarah as she ran laps around the machine. "I can't stand stupid people. That's why. And of course I'll get away with it. I do this all of the time. You see, I have always been a firm believer in the fact that in this world there are people who create and people who destroy. I choose to create and you choose to destroy. It's the classic battle of good verses evil, and although you are winning the war, this battle is mine. Anyway, it's time to get to work."

Sarah pulled a lever on the back of the machine and it sprang to life. The platform that the officer was on sprang up and forward, smashing his face into a canvas that had been hung over a metal safe. The force wasn't enough to smash his head open or even enough to kill him. Rather it thumped his face against the canvas just hard enough to break his nose and shatter his teeth. This step, however, was repeated over and over again until the man was unconscious and Sarah was pleased with the splatter. At which time she flipped off the machine and the man came back to his original position. He appeared to be dead but every once and a while a blood bubble would form in one of his nostrils. This went unnoticed until he blew one so big that, when it popped, Sarah, who was standing near him to admire her work, was spattered with a sizable quantity of the secretion. She turned and asked, "Aren't you dead yet?" and nailed his right ear to the machine so that the splatter would go away from her. She turned again to the canvas, which had taken on the impression of the man's face. It looked not unlike the shroud of Turin. "What do you think of it, Muffy?" she asked proudly.

"You are a genius!" cried the girl. Her wounds had stopped bleeding so she was able to give her complete attention to the new work. "How'd you get the idea?"

Sarah turned to look at her. "Well, as you know, I mostly do conceptual art, but my first true love was naturally occurring art. You know, stuff that isn't intended to be art, but says more than any intentional piece ever could. My favorite example of this art form is a scene in 'Der Todeskin' in which a man is attempting to watch a Nazi torture porn movie when his wife enters the room and begins to bitch at him for not being at work. She just stands there, in front of the TV, and bitches at him until he pulls out a big gun and blows the top of her head off. Then he stands up and calmly walks over to the TV and picks up a picture of him and his wife together. After staring at it for a minute he smashes the picture and the glass out of the frame with the barrel of the gun and, putting a nail just above the spot of blood and brains that hit the wall, hangs the frame from it. The frame happens to be the perfect size and shape to frame the spot on the wall."

"That sounds like a pretty cool movie. Do you have a copy?" Muffy asked.

"Of course I do," Sarah said proudly. "I have a huge collection of fucked up movies from around the world. Want to watch one later?"

"Sure, I haven't seen a good movie in a while," Muffy replied.

"That's cool, but first I have a little more work to do to this guy. So, give me a little while. It won't take long but it's pretty involved so I'm just going to leave you here."

"Okay but please hurry. I'm hungry." Sarah unfastened the officer's hand and foot restraints and pulled the huge Velcro band that held the board and the officer to the machine. She dropped the platform to the floor and Muffy noticed that the platform had wheels on the bottom and a rope coming off of the top. Her love and respect for Sarah swelled inside of her and she proclaimed loudly once again that she loved her master. Sarah turned and winked at her as she bent to pick up the end of the rope. Muffy thought that she heard her mutter something as she disappeared behind a curtain, but she couldn't quite understand what had been said.

More Gratuitous Sex

Sarah returned two hours later rolling the officer in front of her. He appeared to be standing naked on a raised wooden platform yet he was still unconscious. As they drew closer Muffy began to notice that needles stabbed into his ankles and there appeared to be buttons on the platform behind him. When Sarah finally reached her, she pulled a dog collar from her back pocket and fastened it to Muffy's neck. Then out of her front pocket she withdrew a short leash and attached it to the collar. She then tied the leash to the officer's leg and commenced pushing the cart towards the door to the living quarters. When they reached their destination Sarah tied Muffy to the table like she had previously been tied to the ottoman. The table was much larger than the ottoman had been, so Muffy was much more comfortable. "Check this out," Sarah signaled as she walked back to the statue. She picked up a small glass of water that had been resting on the platform and she removed one ice cube. The then pushed the cube up the officer's anus with her index and forefinger. The officer, or at least his head, sputtered to life. He tried to scream but only a gurgle escaped his lips. He looked down at his body and once again began to gurgle. She then walked around behind him and pushed a few of the buttons. Now the body came to life, jogging in place and fingering the hole where his scrotum once was. Sarah crossed the room again and sat down at one of the chairs that surrounded the table. The officer continued to jog. She turned to Muffy and said,

"Isn't it spiffy? I can make him do anything I want, for as long as I want, and there's nothing that he can do about it. He's the world's first living animatron.".

"That sounds like fun. Can I play with him?" Muffy pleaded.

"Maybe later, I'm hungry. What do you want to eat?" Sarah asked.

"I don't care," Muffy said, disinterested. "How did you do that anyway?"

"Oh, that. I just cut most of the nerves that ran from his head to the rest of his body, and then replaced them with little remote controlled zapper thingies that make the muscles do what I tell them to. He can still feel some things so he's easy to revive and abuse but the only part of his body that he can control is his face. And I have him hooked up with intravenous vitamins so I never have to worry about feeding him." Sarah said, slightly distracted. "What did you say that you wanted to eat?"

"I'm kinda in the mood for pizza," Muffy said perkily.

"Okay, give me a minute. I'll be right back." Sarah turned and bounced giddily into the work area. She returned a couple of minutes later and said, "Pizza in fifteen minutes." Plopping down in one of the chairs that surrounded the table, she began to stroke Muffy's hair. "You are a beast of beauty," she said, running her fingers through Muffy's long blond hair. Muffy responded by arching her body and making a purring noise.

Sarah stared at her new acquisition with adoration the likes of which she had never felt before. She studied Muffy's face, memorizing each feature and the subtleties that each feature imposed on the rest. After a few moments of this she fixed her gaze on Muffy's eyes, staring not just *into* her eyes, but, rather, through and beyond. She suddenly realized that the alarm that she had set in the kitchen was buzzing and had been for some time. She jumped up and ran into the next room and a moment later Muffy heard a string of profanities streaming from the doorway that was both colorful and imaginative.

She hadn't heard such brilliant and abundant use of the word 'fuck' since the Dennis Leary HBO special.

Shortly, Sarah returned with a smoldering pizza, or at least that is what Muffy assumed that it was. Sarah was still spouting profanities, but she had calmed down a bit. Just then she noticed an odd noise coming from her new work and when she turned to look at him she realized that he was laughing, or at least he would have been had he been capable. She walked over to the statue and the noise stopped. "You find this amusing, do you?" She asked. Then with a violent and spastic movement she jumped on top of the platform and smashed the pizza into his face. "Now *that* was funny," she said triumphantly as his face twitched from the burning grease. She gathered her composure and turned her gaze to Muffy and said, "Pizza rolls in ten minutes." She gingerly sat down and crossed her legs.

A few minutes later the alarm went off again and she left again to retrieve the pizza. She returned a few moments later with a large bowl of pizza rolls, which she set down on Muffy's stomach. She removed the top roll and placed it into Muffy's mouth. Muffy squealed loudly and spit it across the room. The movement nearly knocked over the bowl but Sarah caught it just in tine. "Too hot, huh? Sorry." Muffy responded by blowing a kiss although her expression was slightly less friendly. Sarah untied Muffy's left hand and allowed her to use it during the meal. This made both of their moods improve. After the meal Sarah tossed the bowl into the corner and asked, "Wanna play a game with our new friend now?"

"Sure, but what kind of game should we play? He can only do what we program him to do. That really narrows it down to overly complicated charades, sex, or trying to outdo each other in being mean to him. I think that I should also state that I do not have sex with farm animals or insects."

Sarah leered at the helpless officer and said forcefully, "You would if I *asked* you to, but that isn't what I have in mind. I have a better idea for a game than any of those. You see, I said earlier that the only part of his body that he can really control is his face but that isn't all together true. I had to leave his involuntary body functions intact. It would have killed him if I hadn't. So let's see how much control he still has over his penis."

"I don't like the sound of this. I said that I don't have sex with farm animals," Muffy said angrily.

"I'm not asking you to fuck him. I just think that it might be fun to put on a show for him and see how long he can keep from being aroused," Sarah said in a sly and succulent tone.

"That doesn't sound much like fun and he might be gay," Muffy said matter-of-factly. "Most pigs are repressed homosexuals. That's why they become cops. They want to feel like 'real men' with power to make up for their urges to suck cock. Exhibitionism isn't really my thing anyway."

"You have *no* faith in me, do you?" asked Sarah with a look of disbelief. "I don't just want to see his hard on, I want to see if he can keep from sticking his dick into a flaming box fan. Doesn't that sound amusing to you?"

"Flaming box fan, huh? Okay, let's try it, but I doubt that he will react since his nuts are nailed to the floor over there," Muffy said, pointing at the spot where the package had initially been opened.

"That's better," Sarah said with an easy smile, "for a second there you acted as if you had a choice." Muffy frowned at this as Sarah began taking the metal cage off of her industrial sized box fan. She had it off in a matter of seconds and she quickly rubbed a layer of gooey white stuff on the fan blades.

"What the hell is that shit?" Muffy asked and quickly humbled her tone in mock respect and added, "If you don't mind telling me," in a voice so sticky sweet that it sounded more disrespectful than the first statement.

Sarah ignored the tone and replied, "Ghetto napalm. Gasoline plus polystyrene equal's lots and lots of fun. I've been making the stuff since I was about eight." She pushed the fan up onto the platform and started it up. She crossed the room to the dresser where she kept her infrared goggles and removed a pencil torch, which she used to light the fan blades. The fan was really quite beautiful once it was lit, like a beautiful blue flower caught in the winds of a hurricane. The officer didn't seem to appreciate the splendor of this thing, but then he always *was* a bit of a dullard.

"Objectivism is hard to maintain when it comes to sexual mutilation, I guess," Muffy thought as she scratched her side with her free hand. The officer began to grow more uncomfortable, but he couldn't do anything about it but whimper/gurgle and look worried.

Sarah returned to Muffy and hopped up onto the table, straddling her, she drew close to deliver the kiss that had been waiting all day to dance across the fault of love. They didn't kiss, they caressed each others souls, revitalizing tongues long since dead to sing songs of each one's love for the other, until it seemed that simple transgression had turned to blasphemy and they were each in turn damning the other to an eternity of their embrace. The table became an alter to their love and lust as they sacrificed their bodies, scraping, gnawing, slamming together as if to fuse into one eternal being devoid of pain or consequence. Blood and sweat, lathered by their passion, clung to their heaving bodies in a thick film like a soap they used to wash away their sins as a very considerate, but long since dead, friend had done so many years ago. It seemed years since this protective specter had loomed before her, burning her eyes with his exoskeletal glow. She found him now kneeling on the hem of her consciousness just out of her range of sight, but she got the impression that he was eating a sandwich.

She was withdrawn from her dream of reunion by a low but rapid thumping noise coming from her left side. Plop, plop, plop, plop, plop, plop, plop, like the sound of a kitten's remains smacking against the window of an unforgiving lover. She opened her eyes to see the officer's bloody penis spurting blood into a pool on the floor. The tip, which was on fire and only hanging on by a thread, was repeatedly being slapped around by the large thin blades of Sarah's floor fan.

Muffy burst into uncontrollable laughter, although she didn't know why. She only knew that it had nothing at all to do with the man on the platform. Sarah's head rose from the gnarled mass of flesh that she had been nibbling on, and looked upon her new creation just in time to see something fly out of the fan and fall flaming to the floor, a few feet from the garbage can. She smiled big and red, like an 18-wheeler, and approached the man with the trembling eyes. She turned off the fan and looked cunningly at her love. "Don't you think he's missing something? He still doesn't seem quite finished to me."

Muffy looked at the fan and then at the man, "He needs a hat or something. Something that would complement his dignity. Why," she asked, "don't you make him a crown out of the fan blades?"

Sarah never felt more helpless than at that moment. Emotions flooded her, causing tears to spring from her eyes like disobedient children. Without a word she picked the fan up by the base and rushed out of the room. She returned a few minutes later with the very thing Muffy had pictured. She placed it atop the officer's head and took a step back to admire the finished product. She examined him from the floor up.

His birdlike feet bloomed into chubby thighs, which framed his mutilated sex exquisitely. His large, round, belly and breasts were so covered with hair that he more resembled an ape than man, and with his face being smashed and crooked he could have passed for one. A dead one at least. And the final crowning of his majesty, the blades rose from large black clamps that were clipped to his head tight enough to withstand a blow from a baseball bat. The black base rose and turned to charred blades that faded into white with speckles of blood.

She looked upon it and saw that it was good. Finally satisfied, she turned to Muffy and spoke, "It's late. I'm tired. Time for bed. Can I get you anything?"

"No," Muffy replied, "I'm fine. You liked my idea?"

"I loved your idea. You're a natural artist. I wish that I had caught on so quickly," said Sarah with a laugh.

"I had a good teacher. You get some rest. I'm tired too. It takes a lot out of you, being strapped to stuff all day," Muffy said earnestly.

Sarah laughed and turned to go to bed. As she walked away she had to fight the urge to run back to Muffy and take her to bed with her. "That would be weakness, though, and Muffy doesn't love me for weakness. I can't, it's still too risky," she thought to herself as she slowly crept into bed. She pulled the comforter over her head and faded away thinking of cinnamon waffles

A Study in Ornithology: Sarah

The next day Sarah woke with the illusion that Muffy had spent the night in her bed. She dreamily rolled from side to side in her bed languishing in the ecstasy that one can only feel when they first wake after a perfect night's rest. She expected that if she rolled around in her soft pink haze long enough she was sure to bump into the one she loved. After a while though she became conscious of the fact that, as always, she was completely alone. As reality came crashing down upon her like a cartoon anvil she remembered the day before and the time before and her heart sank as it did every morning. She rolled over and sat Indian style on the edge of the bed and opening the door on the nightstand beside her she removed a bottle of Vodka, a tumbler, and a bottle of Worcestershire sauce. She filled the glass three fourths full of the vodka and then added three squirts of Lea and Perrins. She quickly downed it in one big gulp, and twitching, pulled herself out of bed.

She stumbled to the shower and turned on the water. She then lay down on the tile floor of the shower and rested her head on the lip. From there she could see Muffy resting serenely on the table with her head resting lightly on her right arm. She looked so happy and calm that Sarah's heart melted into tears. She realized that Muffy would be her undoing. She had left Muffy's hand free the night before.

She wondered, "How could this girl have weakened me so fast? In two days this girl had raised from simple art supplies to master my soul. I feel that I need her. I look forward to seeing her. I would miss her if she left. I lived well enough before this chick landed on my doorstep." She said to herself, "I can survive without her. I have to. My line of work doesn't allow for relationships." Her tear ducts burst and she convulsed in sobs that smashed her head against the cold tile pillow on which she lay. It was then that the alcohol began to take hold. The spasms died down to a mere quivering in her thighs and she rose to begin her day.

She opened her closet and grabbed the first thing that she saw, which happened to be a black shirt with the words 'Kill Whitey' in bold faced white, and pulled it over her head without bothering to look at it. She then removed a pair of black suede shoes and threw them on the bed. She opened her dresser and withdrew a pair of shiny green nylon pants and jerked into them quickly. She noticed a tapping noise above her and, when she turned to look, she noticed that it had begun to rain. She began to bounce around the room, violently spewing profanities as she normally does when this sort of thing happened, but then remembering Muffy in the next room she stopped.

"I have to leave before Muffy wakes up," she thought in desperation. "I don't know what to do with her. I have to decide today. She put the suede shoes back into the closet and removed a pair of vinyl boots that she zipped up the back quickly before opening the door to the fire escape and stepping out onto the cold platform of creaking brown steel. She looked across the street to the building which, at its apex, boasted the only accurate clock in the city. The time was 9:53, which meant that she had only slept for a few hours. She felt as though she had been asleep for weeks. She tried but couldn't remember the last time that she had felt so rested.

She began her descent, and as she did she noticed a pigeon on the ground below. The pigeon wasn't anything special, and Sarah hated birds, but in that moment she felt as though the bird was there for her. Like it had come to this very spot to help her through here confusion. She reached the sidewalk and stepped down right next to it. It looked up at her with the same dull expression that all birds have and began to walk away. Sarah went after it, but it took to the air. She missed it by inches and in seconds it was out of sight. "This is great," she said to herself, "two days and I'm chasing birds. I've gotta get out of here." She turned and began to walk towards the art district.

A Study in Ornithology: Muffy

Muffy awoke that morning with a yawn that was quickly followed by a painful cramp in her neck. She called several times for Sarah, each time the pain grew worse and her cries became louder and more desperate. "Damn it, Sarah, where the hell are you?" she cried as she rubbed at the back of her rock hard neck. Tears streamed down her face as she banged her head on the table. Eventually the pain subsided and subsequently the tears followed suit leaving only a throbbing headache in its place. She then began to ponder the possibilities of where her love might be. "I wonder where she went." She looked at the clock on the microwave and saw that it was only 10:00. "Who ever gets up this early? Something important must have come up. I hope she's alright."

Just as she began to worry, her thoughts were interrupted by the arrival of a small gray bird. It entered through a hole in the skylight and dropped down to a rafter. It looked interestedly at her and, after a few moments of what seemed to be contemplation, it swooped down and landed on the microwave. As it sat looking at her, Muffy began to lose patience.

"What the fuck do you want?" she asked it spryly. "Stupid bird, bugger off before I come over there and...."

Her words were interrupted by a direct assault from the pigeon in question. It fell upon her and tore at her face and breasts with its claws. After a few minutes of fending off the frenzied animal, she finally managed to get a hold of one of its wings. She beat it mercilessly on the table, but began to lose her grip on it after a few hard whacks. Rather than let the beast escape she sat on its head and pulled on the body until it's head came off. She threw the creature against the wall and it landed with a wet thud. She looked at the splotch on the wall and then at the animals carcass and the ever widening pool of blood.

"Stupid bird," she said again to herself. She picked the head out of her left butt cheek, and stared the beast in the eye. "You should know better than to fuck with a human. Well, I guess you learned your lesson, didn't you? Now go away," she said as she threw the head in the direction of the body. It landed in the trash can by mistake. "Sure does hold a lot of blood for such a little thing." Her thoughts turned again to her prodigal love. "I wonder where that little cunt got off to. I hope that she has some aspirin or something. I'm getting hungry too."

Belial

Sarah found herself wandering the streets of Manhattan, muttering profanities and shuffling slowly down the sidewalk like a homeless person poised precariously at the brink of death. She had been wondering for 3 hours according to a wall clock in Sameel's Pizza. The time was now 1:30 and her hunger pains were quickly approaching intolerable. She looked at the street sign on the corner and found that she was only two blocks away from her friend Belial's house.

Belial was, of course, not his real name. Who would name their child after a demon? His real name was Marvin Debussy. He was a hack artist that finger painted murals of hell on street corners near churches, wearing nothing but a thong and devil horns. In his spare time Belial led a very sheltered life and his ideologies were usually naive and borderline idealistic. Sarah considered him to be highly amusing, and ambiguously Christian. Belial was the kind of guy who named himself after a demon and then covers his eyes when people die in horror movies.

Sarah arrived at his loft and banged on the buzzer as hard as she could until a raspy and highly agitated voice came over the speaker "Go away. Fuck off. I don't care who you are. If you don't stop that now I'll empty my puke bucket on your head."

"Rough night?" Sarah asked sardonically.

"Sarah?" the voice on the intercom asked. "What the hell are you doing up this early?"

"I have a problem. I want to talk to you," she answered.

The buzzer went off and the door creaked open. She walked through, not bothering to shut it back and followed the smell of rotting food and beer all the way up six flights of stairs. When she arrived she found him standing in his doorway naked and brushing his teeth. If it had been anyone else her revulsion would have compelled her to make them into art supplies, but she knew that he was just acting out one of his philosophies that probably went something like, "The human form is beautiful. Everyone has one, so no one should be ashamed of it. So, if it makes you uncomfortable, that's your problem. This is my apartment and when I'm here I'll do what I want to. You are free to leave any time you want."

She could hear him ranting inside of her head the second that she saw him, so she decided that it would be better not to say anything and spare herself. "Hi, how are things?" she asked him as he stepped through the narrow doorway into the loft.

"The usual," he replied. He walked over to the bare mattress that he had pushed into the corner of the room and plopped down. Sarah couldn't help but notice the pathetic thing flopping between his legs. She wondered how anyone could be so obnoxious, inconsiderate, pigheaded, and inherently male with such small genitalia. Her response to herself, as usual when dealing with Belial, was "God, I hate altruists."

"So, what's up?" asked the naked man. "I didn't think that you were capable of waking before 5:00."

She sat down on a cheap imitation Giger chair and replied, "I've got a problem. I can't even think straight. I've been wandering around all morning and I ended up here."

"And you want my advice, do you? Sorry but I don't have enough time to screw my own life up, much less yours. A wise man once said, 'If you ever need anything please don't hesitate to ask someone else first.'"

"Oh, shut up. Only you would quote a Nirvana song in an attempt to be witty. The only reason that I bothered to come here was that you are the only acquaintance that I have that is a big enough asshole to give me good objective advice."

"Well, if my knack for truth and sardonic sensibilities are the reasons that you came here then why are you bitching? You got what you came here for, so why don't you leave?"

Sarah stood and walked slowly across the room until she was standing at the foot of the mattress where the self appointed demon was haughtily sprawled. She took the tip of her boot and slowly but firmly she applied pressure to the dangling mass of flesh between his legs. "So," she said, "are you going to listen? Or am I just wasting my time?"

He began to writhe and squeal, and in that anguished yet oddly pleased squeak he said, "That's the Sarah I know. So what seems to be the problem?"

"That's better," she said and she returned to her previous seat. "But you see, that is the problem. I seem to be losing my touch. I have this girl living with me at the moment and I spend so much time thinking about her that, I think, my art is suffering. It just hasn't been inspired as much lately as it usually is. The worst thing about it is that this girl is having better ideas about what to do with my work than I am. She keeps suggesting things that I never would have thought of, and when I do them, they turn out to be better than my stuff usually is. I hate that. I want to get rid of her so that I can focus on my art again, but I think that I'm in love with her. She's the best lay that I've ever had."

"Well," he began, "the way that I see it is this; you can't let your art suffer even if it means that you will be happier. So you have to consider whether your work is better with or without this girl. Even though it probably hurts your ego to be upstaged or to have to get help from someone else, it is your duty as an artist not to deprive your work of being the best that it can be. Anyway, artists collaborate all of the time. It isn't at all unusual for two artists that are lovers to influence each other. Relationships are a great source of inspiration too. Take for instance 'De Profundis' by Oscar Wilde, it's better than anything else that he has ever written, and it's just a long love letter. And take Yernka's paintings and Harlan Ellison's writing, they were both wonderful and brilliant by themselves, but when they worked together they complimented each other so well that the work's worth grew exponentially."

"Shut up, I get the point." She lit a cigarette. "So you think that I should stay with her as long as she helps my work, but if she ever hurts my work I should dump her on her ass."

"Essentially, yes," said the demon.

"But the problem is that I'm afraid that if I don't get rid of her now I won't be able to when the time comes. I know from experience that the time always comes eventually. What if she helps with my art now, but after a while I fall so deeply in love that all that I can paint is butterflies and flowers and shit? It's happened before," asked the distraught girl.

To which Belial solemnly replied, "Trust me dear, if there is anyone in the world that isn't going to sell out and begin to suck when they get older, it's you. I don't think that you could paint a happy little tree if you tried."

"I hope that you're right," she said, and standing up, she began to walk over to his refrigerator. "You know, I'm a bit hungry. You feel like going out to eat?"

"Sure, let me grab some clothes real fast and I'll take a shower. I'll be ready in a minute," he said as he walked towards the bathroom.

"Never mind, I'll just grab something on the way home. I need to get back anyway," she said as she moved for a quick exit. (Belial was a nice guy, but slow as the proverbial fuck).

"Oh, okay," he said, slightly confused. "You should let me come and take a look at your studio some time. I still haven't seen it. I would also like to see this new work that you've been talking about. I could tell you if it's better than usual."

"Yeah, I'll give you a call sometime. See you later."

"Okay, bye," he said, sitting back down.

Sarah hurried down the stairs and away from the smell of decaying pizza. She stepped out of his building feeling much better than she had when she had entered. Belial may be an unbelievable fuck up, idiot, misogynist, and all around bastard, but he has a knack for making you feel better about yourself. She almost wished that she could have invited him back to her studio, but knowing his sensitive nature he would probably freak out and call the police if he saw her real work (He had only seen her work at public shows. Mostly dark impressionist paintings that give most people a strange sense that something horrible is either about to happen or just has). "It's just as well," she said to herself, "he gets annoying after a while anyway." She hailed a taxi and headed straight home, only stopping at Taco Hell to pick up some food.

A Surprise

She arrived home at 3:00 on the dot, after being dropped off a couple of blocks away and walking home. She entered through a basement window so as not to be seen. She had decided that it would be best not to tell Muffy where she had been, and in all honesty she hoped that she would still be asleep. She was quite surprised to find a wide awake and screaming Muffy flipping her off, and was even more surprised to find the decapitated remains of the pigeon that she had been chasing earlier.

"Where have you been, I'm fucking starving. What's the big idea, leaving me all alone all day. I was worried about you," screamed the irate little fixture.

"I just stepped out to get some food," she said, holding up the bag of Taco Bell.

"For over five hours?" screamed the fixture. "Where the hell did you go? China?"

"No, not China, Taco Hell," she answered sweetly. "Actually, I couldn't decide what I was hungry for so I just walked around for a while, until I found a place that looked appetizing."

"And in five hours all that you came across was a Taco Hell?" Muffy asked skeptically.

"Yeah, so, I was feeling picky this morning. Do you want food or not?" Sarah's sweet mood began to fade.

"Of course I want food. I'm fucking ravenous. By the way, why didn't you mention that you have rabid pigeons in this building?" Muffy asked, still shrieking.

"What, the hell are you talking about?" Sarah asked.

Muffy got louder. "I'm talking about the fucking psychotic bird that tried to kill me earlier. It scratched the hell out of my face. Can't you tell?"

"Oh, that, I thought that I had done that to you last night. I've never been attacked by birds here, or anywhere else," Sarah said matter-of-factly.

"Oh, that," Muffy said mockingly, "I've never been attacked by..." but she was cut off by Sarah who crammed a whole soft taco into her mouth.

"Shut up and eat. Or I won't let you help with my next project," threatened Sarah, opening another taco.

The anger melted instantly from Muffy's face, "You want my help with your next project?!!" she squealed through a mouth full of liquid meat and soy cheese. "I can't believe it, thank you."

"You show potential." She took a bite of her taco. "I like your ideas so far, so I figured that you might like to be kind of, a consultant. So you want to?"

"Of course I want to. It's an honor to work with an artist of your caliber. So when can we get started?" Muffy said as she tried to swallow horizontally.

"Whenever you finish your meal," Sarah said with a smile. "So shut up and eat before it gets cold."

They spent the rest of the meal eating quickly and silently. When they were done, Sarah got up and crossed the room to the dresser where she procured, what looked like, a pile of thin black leather strips and a huge black phallus with a big silver ring on the end. "Have you ever read 'The Trials of Beauty'?" she asked.

"No, what's that?" asked Muffy.

"It's an old trilogy by Anne Rice. It's really quite brilliant, although I don't care too much for the rest of her books. This is a

Muffy: or A Transmigration of Selves

stylized version of what the human ponies wore. I changed it a bit to make it more ideal for my needs, like strapping the arms and legs to one another to limit speed and movement, and it includes a girdle that will constrict breathing. In other words, you will be the least tied up of all of the time that you've been here, but at the same time you will be more constricted. If you try to run away you will just fall over or run out of oxygen, whichever comes first. But, I hope that you wouldn't try to escape anyway. I would be very hurt if you tried an escape and I might be forced to judge you harshly."

She began applying the harness by strapping the girdle around her waste loosely and tying it in the back. A key was then inserted into the back that, when twisted, caused the girdle to tighten. She then fastened the black straps to her legs and arms. She took the restraints off of her feet and connected the two halves that made up the leg restraints. It held her knees tightly together, so that she would only be able to move about six inches with each step. Next she placed gloves on her hands made of very soft leatherette with hard disks at the hands which didn't allow for fingers, so that her hands were completely flat and could only bend in the middle. Next she removed the restraints on Muffy's right hand and bound the two together at the wrist. Then her elbows were tied together and then to her stomach, which put in a kind of cerebral palsy pose. A soft leather bit was placed into her mouth and tied tightly in the back. The large leather phallus was placed into her anus and many cords came off of it like a long horsetail. Sarah took a few of these cords and connected them to every other restraint so that every time she moved, the phallus was pulled one way or the other, making every movement incredibly painful. Some of the other chords were stretched tightly through her pubic lips and wrapped around her breasts so tightly that the circulation was cut off, which after a few moments made them begin to grow heavier and tingle with thousands of tiny pinpricks. Now the bodice was tightened further until she was given the figure of a wasp, which made it almost impossible to keep her balance, let alone breathe. Sarah checked the restraints and plucked all of the cords to be sure that they were all sufficiently tight and that she wouldn't wriggle free or suffocate. They made a musical twinge and so did the wearer.

She then took a step back to admire her work. It was exquisite; a finer display of suffering had never been assembled. She admired the sculpture with awe. "If only I had come up with it," she thought to herself. Tears flowed down her rosy cheeks in tiny rivulets leaving red trails as they passed. Sarah kissed her gently on the cheek. The salty taste of Muffy's tears enflamed her passion and sent a momentary shiver of pleasure up her thighs. She looked down at Muffy's swollen, now purple, breasts, and looking up she stared Muffy in the eye and said, "I've decided that you are mine. I am going to keep you for a while, whether you like it or not. I hope that you do, but either way I'm going to mark you." She crossed the room and pulled a pair of chopsticks from the top drawer of her dresser. She returned with them moments later and showed them to Muffy.

They were black and square, with opal inlay that ran in long delicate spikes down the length of the sticks. They were simple, yet at the same time they were exquisite. "Do you like them?" she asked holding them a few inches from her face and moving them back and forth in the light so that the opal seemed to glow. "I've had them since I was a child."

Muffy stared in awe through her tears. They were exquisite indeed. Not able to speak through the bit, she nodded her head approvingly, moving the phallus in and out of her anus and causing her to moan. Sarah looked disapprovingly at her new creation.

"You don't seem very enthusiastic," she said. "Aren't you happy that I have chosen you to be my companion? Or would you prefer to be pressed into sausages and stuffed into the mouth of our new friend over there?" she gestured to the police officer. "If you are happy that I have chosen you I want a full nod, with feeling, all the way up and down, and more than once."

Muffy complied and the phallus was pulled so violently in and out of her that it made her fall over.

"That's better," Sarah said fervently. "Now do it that way for me every time from now on, okay?"

Muffy repeated the painful nod, but the coring of her anus was still new and very awkward. Sarah knelt down and helped her to her feet.

"Good, that's very good. Now I'm going to mark you and then we can get started." She took the tip of the chopstick and began to press it firmly into the top of Muffy's nipple. The tip had been sharpened but it was still much larger than Muffy's small nipples could handle. It finally went through with only a minor amount of tearing, and Sarah twisted and pushed it through until she could see a couple of centimeters of opal below her nipple, which was now twice the size that it had been only moments ago.

"There," she said as she took a step back, "beautiful, but I don't like asymmetry."

Muffy fought as hard as she could to be silent while the right one was done, but she still let out a whimper and the rivulets grew to rushing streams. Blood slid gracefully down the spikes and grew to large drops at the points. Sarah dropped to her knees and let a few drops fall on her tongue.

"Now… you're mine forever," Sarah proclaimed, and then she gave in to the urge to suck violently at Muffy's right nipple.

Muffy nearly fainted at first, but soon she began to like the sensation. She became aroused and began to shuffle back and forth between her feet. Her vagina grew hot and moist until the burning in her nipples had consumed her whole body.

Sarah stood and said, "Time to go to work. There will be plenty of time for that later."

The pain of being severed from her lover was unbearable but she still found the strength to awkwardly shuffle along behind Sarah as she was led into the work area. She was led to the far right corner where she observed a small trap door in the floor with a large silver ring protruding from the middle. The door was opened to reveal the gaunt corpse of a small shrunken elderly woman with long white hair.

She was covered in scratches from head to toe and appeared to have been beaten quite regularly until her time of death. Muffy was rather unsettled by the fact that, after a few seconds of having been exposed to the light, the body began to twitch and make sort of choked gurgling noise, not unlike that of a faulty drain. Finally the spasms came to a halt and the shriveled thing opened her eyes. To further shock and amaze the fettered and confused animal, the elderly woman on the floor let out a distasteful cackle, not altogether unbecoming for a cartoon witch. To Muffy's further amazement the Shar Pei beast attempted to stand. She had slightly rounded features and steel blue eyes and Muffy realized that the woman was not as old as she had previously thought. The woman, who had obviously been beaten and starved for quite some time, crumpled after a few seconds of exertion and appeared to fall unconscious. It was then, standing over the body of this pathetic fallen beast that she noticed the enormity of the woman's nipples. The blush fell out of Muffy's cheeks and, along with every fluid in her body, headed straight to her stomach and began to churn. Then, once again, everything went black.

Abby

    Muffy woke a few minutes later to the sight of the caged woman being beaten about the head with what seemed to be a summer sausage. The realization of her situation came rushing through her again. She went stiff with fear and then began to shiver uncontrollably.
    "You bitch, look what you did to Muffy," she heard Sarah scream. "You always fuck everything up!"
    The beaten woman began to chortle and then burst out into laughter reminiscent of exceptionally horrible hiccups. She finally fell twitching on the ground and began to foam at the mouth.
    "Fucking epileptics! Be fucking *still*," screamed Sarah as she kicked the withered mass.
    "I'm alright," said Muffy, trying to draw attention away from the nearly dead girl in the corner of the cage. Sarah dropped her sausage and ran to her lover crying. "What happened?"
    "You were just standing there and then, sploosh, you fell right into the cage," Sarah said, looking her over for damage.
    "I'm sorry," she said, "I'm just having a little trouble getting used to this suit. Don't forget that I haven't walked in three days."
    Sarah twisted the key in Muffy's girdle a few times to the left. And the girdle relaxed enough to let her intestines come out of her ribcage. "Yeah, this thing is still in the experimental phases. I decided that the gag was a bad idea too, since the girdle makes it so hard to breathe already," she said.

"Thanks," Muffy said sincerely, "I didn't see how I could give you input with a bit in my mouth, anyway."

"So, are you okay? You hit your head pretty hard," Sarah asked, still concerned.

"Yea, I'm fine," said Muffy, her ability to focus returning. "I'm used to getting worse from my dad. But do you mind if I sit down for a minute? I'm a little bit light headed."

"Sure, that is the great thing about this job, you make your own hours and get all of the breaks you want," said Sarah, in an attempt to cheer Muffy up.

"So, how long has that girl been down there. What's her story?" Muffy asked suspiciously.

"Oh, her, that's Abby. She's been down there for a while. Probably about three weeks. What do you think we should do with her?" Sarah asked in an attempt to change the subject.

"Why did you give me the same mark that she has? Am I her replacement or something?" Muffy asked with tears in her eyes.

"No, not really," Sarah said honestly. "But, she is my ex if that's what you mean. She's a real self-serving bitch. I caught her cheating on me with a friend of mine. But she was a bitch even before that. She blamed every little problem that she had on me, and gave me guilt trips all of the time, and all kinds of stuff. She didn't even respect my art. Then after I forgave her for cheating on me and let her move in, she pawned all of my stuff and bought presents for a friend of mine that I later found out that she was fucking too. That woman is evil, and deserves everything that she gets."

"Oh," Muffy said, feeling a little better, "I hate people like that. That sounds like my ex boyfriend, he was always cheating on me, and starting rumors about me, and beating me. He sucked."

"You want me to make you a chair out of him? I'll do it," Sarah asked spryly

"No, I got him back," Muffy said proudly. "I had this friend that he didn't know named Michelle. She was a walking disease, I mean she had *everything*; AIDS, crabs, hepatitis, the clap, herpes and a bunch of other stuff that I can't even remember the names for. This girl's body was so screwed up that she lactated constantly and only had four periods a year. Anyway, without telling him about her first I introduced them and in no time my friend called me up and said that he had fallen for it. I broke up with him that night. He's probably dead by now."

"Damn, remind me not to piss you off," said Sarah admiringly.

"I don't think that you have anything to worry about, being that I can't even move. So what do you have planned for your little pile of mush in there?" Muffy asked and indicated the trapdoor with a painful twitch of her neck.

"I wanted you to help me decide. It could be a bonding experience," Sarah said with a wink.

"Okay, I would start off by rubbing her down with high grit sandpaper from head to toe. Then..."

"Hold it, I have just the thing," Sarah said as she scurried out of sight. She returned seconds later with a DA feather sander and a fresh disc of 320 grit paper. She stuck the paper on the sander and plugged it in.

Muffy looked at Sarah and said, "Prepared for anything, aren't you?"

"You forget, I've been in this business for a long time," Sarah said proudly.

"Where should we tie her up?" Muffy asked. "For some reason I doubt that she is just going to sit there and let us torture her."

"How about my new toy? Come here, let me show it to you," Sarah said and dragged Muffy faster than she was capable of walking into a tent-like structure made from a giant piece of color changing cloth that was sometimes red and sometimes black. Muffy fell halfway there and once again hit her head. Sarah picked her up and dragged her, by the hair, into the tent. The inside of the tent was made of red plastic and full of strange utensils and furniture. She saw a large silver apparatus, about five feet tall and eight feet across. It was a giant square with two wishbone shaped metal pipes coming from the middle of the two vertical sides. Sarah walked over to the machine and explained.

"You strap their hands and arms to these," she said pointing to the straps on one of the wishbones, "and their feet to these," she pointed to the straps on the other wishbone. "Their body just hangs in between, and you can spin them around like they are on a spit." She demonstrated by sending a wishbone spinning in place. "You can get to them from any angle and they can't fight back. Neat, huh?"

Muffy nodded in awe of the sadistic genius of its simplicity. "Where the hell do you get this stuff?" she asked.

"I mail ordered it from George's House of Debauchery. They are a little known division of Wal-Mart. They do a little bit of everything, Wal-Mart I mean. They manufacture weapons, produce pornography, produce oil, and make shit like this on top of all of the stuff that you already know about sweatshops. And they still try to pass themselves off as a family store. Isn't that some shit?" Sarah asked rhetorically.

"Yeah, but I can't say that it surprises me. They are just too creepy to take seriously. Nobody is that wholesome," Muffy said with a shiver. "Anyway, you want to get down to business?"

"Sure," Sarah replied, "but what else do you need?"

"Do you have anything that we could use to wrap her hair around that would turn slowly and rip her hair or her scalp off?" Muffy asked.

"I think I've got that covered too," she said and rushed out of the tent.

A few minutes later she returned wheeling the back half of a motorcycle, on a cart. She turned it on and the wheel spun around. She pushed a button on the side and it begun to spin a little faster, and with the push of another button it spun faster still.

Muffy smiled, "It's perfect."

"I combined the back of a motorcycle with the circuitry of a blender," Sarah boasted.

"Good idea. Let's get started," Muffy said enthusiastically.

They brought the still unconscious girl into the tent and strapped her into the device. Muffy stood back as Sarah began to pour tequila down the woman's throat. She poured one fifth down her throat and she revived halfway through it. Then she opened another and poured it down her throat. After that she quickly put a strip of duct tape over her mouth to protect herself from the vomit that would surely come momentarily. She then began to spin the girl until her face turned a nice shade of green-white. She then started up the sander and began to sand her stomach, removing the top few layers of skin and turning her a reddish purplish kind of color. She struggled but there wasn't anything that she could do. When she struggled it would cause the sander to go deeper into her flesh and draw blood, so she quickly stopped and concentrated on not drowning in her own vomit.

When she had finished her stomach, she then did the same to her breasts, arms, legs, back, buttocks, sides, hands, feet, face, and lastly her vagina which she ground down nearly to the bone. Abby took it very well considering how painful it must have been. She didn't even cry. The look in her eye was kind, almost forgiving.

Sarah then took her hair and braided it through a chain into a long rope that she attached to a ring on the tire of the motorcycle. She dumped a bottle of paper cement on the braid and let it set. When her hair was solidified she turned the motorcycle on to its lowest setting. It emitted a low hum like an annoyed cat and gave just enough pressure to pull it tight and make the girl uncomfortable.

"Which do you think will go first, the hair or the scalp?" asked Sarah.

"I'm thinking the hair," Muffy said thoughtfully.

"Want to bet? It might make it a bit more interesting," Sarah asked with a grin. She was enjoying the wrongness of her justice a little too much. But then, how can you ever enjoy anything too much?

"Sure but what can I bet? You have everything including me, and I have nothing," Muffy asked, also delighting in the rush of power.

"Tell you what," Sarah said thoughtfully, "if you win you can go on my next supply run with me. If not you can't go for three months, and then only if I feel like it."

"That sounds like a good bet to me. I say her hair goes first. Turn it up, let's see who wins." Muffy's excitement was becoming too much to control and she caught herself bouncing, ever so slightly, despite the pain in her colon.

"Here we go," Sarah said as she pushed the next button. The pitch of the noise grew higher and the girl began to squeal beneath her gag. The severity of the situation seemed to be coming clear to her. Sarah pushed the next button and the pitch again grew higher. The squealing also became more intense. Her scalp began to separate from her skull and gave off a sucking noise that only she could hear. Sarah pushed the last button and the pitch became a roaring whine. Sarah sparked her blowtorch. Abby's scalp tore off like a cheap Halloween mask and flung blood all over the room and the girls. "Looks like you lost. Too bad, I was looking forward to taking you out. Three months isn't that long," she said as she stopped the bleeding with the fire.

The girl gave off a sweet robust smell like a good steak. She passed out from the pain, but was quickly revived when Sarah pinched what was left of her clitoris. Sarah removed her gag and as the girl began to scream, through her mouth full of vomit, she emptied a bottle of bleach in her face. Then, as the bleach was being purged from the girl, Sarah took a small bone saw and removed the top half of her cranium.

"It was nice knowing you," she hissed as she pried off the top of the girl's skull and reached into it to remove her brain.

Abby evacuated her bowels into the basin that was made into the bottom of the frame. Her face grew calm and took on a look of relief. Sarah then flopped her over and slit her throat letting her blood drain into the bottom of the tub. Her blood, urine, vomit, and feces collected in a drain and filtered through small holes, in the bucket, into a pipe that ran to the sewer. Sarah hosed the girl down, washing away the ooze of her demise. She then hosed down the tent, washing the scum of her work down into a drain in the floor. She inspected the girl's eyes and they had been bleached white. She then led Muffy into the kitchen where she proceeded to make five big boxes of chocolate pudding.

She fixed herself and Muffy each a large bowl and they enjoyed it thoroughly. She then took the remains of the pudding in a large blue bowl along with a mixing spoon and a small spoon into the work area and set them down on a table in an area filled with wires and metal pipes of various diameters and lengths. Muffy hobbled behind her as fast as she could but had a bit of trouble keeping up so she flopped down on top of a large pile of wire that made a kind of couch for her although it made the phallus go deeper inside of her. She was used to it by now, so it didn't bother her much.

Sarah returned a minute later carrying the lobotomized girl as if she were a baby. She threw her down on top of Muffy and said, "Here, hold this."

She placed the small spoon into the girl's hand and made it into a fist that she placed against the pile of wire to make it hold its shape. She then pulled a cord down from the ceiling and tied a small noose in it. She placed the girl's head into the noose and made her sit Indian style. She pulled down another cord and placed the hand with the spoon inside of it. She pulled it through until it was almost to her elbow and then tied it loosely to hold it in place. Then she placed the other hand on the girl's crotch. She then filled her cranium with the pudding and adjusted the cord so that the spoon was stabbed into the pudding. Lastly, she ran her fingers around the bottom of the bowl and smeared pudding around the girl's mouth.

She took a step back and admired her work. The girl looked as though her skin had been scrubbed off and now she was masturbating while either eating the putrid mess in her head, or filling her head with the spew that she was spitting up. On her face was a blank white stare of relief. It was beautiful.

"We do really good work together," she said as she kissed her lover.

"I'm glad you think so," Muffy replied lovingly.

Sarah tore away the girdle and threw it against the wall. She took Muffy's left chopstick in her mouth and pulled her closer. She ripped her legs free from her bonds and buried her face in the warm sweet nest of skin between Muffy's legs. In her passion she didn't notice that Muffy's hands had come free too. Muffy flipped her over on her back and, while sitting on her face, began to knead the flesh between her legs. Sarah realized what was going on and tried to get up but, since her head was being held down by Muffy's ass, she couldn't get any leverage.

"Relax, I'm not going to hurt you. At least not much." Sarah gave in to ecstasy and for the first time they made love without being tied.

The First Outing

As the three months passed their relationship grew into something that most people will never experience. They fed off of each other. Each one's love and creativity caused the other's to grow exponentially until they were pumping out more and better art than any of their competition. They were rich beyond measure and respected by every art critic in the world. But since they had made a bet, Sarah still kept Muffy tied up in her loft every day and never let her out.

Exactly three months later it was time for Muffy to learn how to gather supplies. The night before Muffy hadn't been able to sleep at all, and neither had Sarah, so they spent all night making love. They eventually passed out at 10:00 in the morning. They woke with a start to the sound of explosions outside of their window. It was 9:00 on the Fourth of July. They kissed warmly and crawled out of bed and into the shower. They were slightly crunchy from the previous night's activities but, after their shower, they were bursting with excitement. They got dressed and Sarah put together the proper utensils.

"I've been saving this one for today, you know. This is my favorite way to go shopping." She filled her duffel bag with tomahawks, red paint, night vision goggles, and black shoe polish. "Let's go watch some fireworks," Sarah said happily.

They loaded up Sarah's bright purple 1975 Caprice Classic and began their journey. They started by just driving around for a couple of hours looking at fireworks, and arguing about whether or not it would be wise to be hauling bodies in a car so flashy. Then they stopped off at a truck stop to use the bathroom. They removed their normal clothes and covered themselves neck to toe in black shoe polish. They saved their faces for when they got to the hunting site. Wrapped in black trench coats that were lined in vinyl and trimmed with purple fur, they returned to their car and drove for many hours.

After a two hour argument over nominative determinism they finally ended up lost somewhere in Pennsylvania. They parked their car on a long back road and walked to the highway from there. They left the coats in the car and finished covering themselves in black shoe polish. They took the bag and waited just inside the woods for a car to come along.

"So what are we doing here?" asked a confused and cold Muffy.

"When a car comes along I will dip this tomahawk in the red paint and throw it at their windshield," Sarah explained.

"Why? What if they stop, or call the police?" asked Muffy, more confused than ever.

"If they stop we get them. If they wreck, we get them. If they drive off we let them go and leave the state," her lover explained in a cool even tone, displaying patience despite her obvious irritation at being questioned.

"Oh, okay. So, why is this your favorite way? Aren't there easier ways," asked the annoyingly inquisitive fledgling.

"Yes, there are easier ways," Sarah began to grow impatient, "but that isn't the point. I'm not a fucking serial killer. I don't want to kill people that don't deserve it. This is a great test and, if they pass, they learn a valuable lesson." Muffy looked confused even in the dark. "Let me explain. What would make someone get out of their car if somebody had just thrown, what they think is, a bloody hatchet through their windshield?" Muffy still looked confused. "....Concern for their car. The only people that stop are going to be people who are getting out of their car to kick my ass. If you are dumb enough to get out of your car when there is an ax-wielding lunatic outside you deserve to die. If you wreck it's because you are weak and you panicked. So either way it's survival of the fittest. The smart, strong ones will get away."

"Oh, okay," Muffy said. Luckily Sarah didn't catch the patronizing tone because she was too busy dipping a hatchet in the paint. "So, why the shoe polish and bikinis? Wouldn't black clothes be more comfortable and sensible?"

"No, actually considering the bizarreness of the crime and the way that we look, if we got picked up by the cops, we would be instantly labeled psychos and taken to a hospital instead of jail. And it's a lot easier to get out of a psyche ward than a prison." Sarah continued to impart her wisdom.

"Oh, okay." Muffy, still slightly confused (but now for different reasons) returned her attention to the highway. Finally they saw a car approaching in the distance. As it neared, Sarah dipped a tomahawk in the red paint and came slowly out of the woods. When it came in range she hurled the weapon at the car and it hit perfectly. The blade stuck in the windshield and paint was spread over it in a perfectly runny circle. The car swerved for a moment but adrenaline kept the driver on the road. The car, with its bleeding windshield intact, sped away into the darkness leaving Sarah to return to the woods empty-handed.

"They'll have an interesting story to tell tomorrow," she said as she gathered the supplies and put them back into the bag. "Time to go."

"That's it? We didn't even get anybody," Muffy screamed. "I can't believe that on my first time out we don't get anybody. That's just my *fucking* luck," she said and then went on to utter a long string of profanities all the way back to the car. She threw the bag onto the backseat and wrapped herself in the coat. She climbed into the passenger seat and commenced to silently fume.

"Want to try again? The night is still young. They won't be looking for us where we're going," Sarah said in an attempt to console her.

"Can we?" Muffy asked hopefully.

"Of course we can. I'll just go to the other end of the state," Sarah replied through a breath of smoke.

"Fun," Muffy said, bouncing now. "I'm sorry for being a bitch. I've just been looking forward to this for so long, I couldn't stand the disappointment."

"I understand its okay. I get upset when that happens too," Sarah confided through the smoke.

"I need to pee. Do you mind if we stop?" asked Muffy as she lit a cigarette.

"Sure, I need to go too. Take the polish off of your face before you go in though," Sarah said and she pulled off of the highway and into a Shell station. They entered the bathroom together and both entered the same stall. Muffy sat in Sarah's lap while she pissed first. Then they heard someone opening the bathroom door and coming in. They were both frightened at first, then they heard the sound of urination in the next stall, and they were relieved.

Now it was Muffy's turn. She sat and began to pee while Sarah stood and waited. The sound stopped coming from the next stall and was replaced by the sound of magic marker scraping against flimsy metal. Sarah was curious so she stood on the back of the toilet and peered down into the next stall. There she saw a 50'sish fat woman wearing a purple sweatshirt with a bubble-painted cross on the back and a black hat that said "Jesus loves me", writing "Kill a gay fetus for Jesus today - WWJD" on the wall of the adjacent stall. Sarah's face began to burn with rage. There was nothing that pissed Sarah off more than displays of insurmountable stupidity, except for maybe displays of hypocritical Christian insurmountable idiocy that makes the rest of them look bad. (Despite her job Sarah was a devout Christian free thinker, which was to say, she hated the church and most Christians, but loved God and did her best to make the world a better place and follow his teachings. And this was just the kind of person that made her ashamed of being a Christian.)

She waited until the woman left the bathroom, and then she and Muffy followed her to her car. On the way, she saw the woman approached by a homeless man who asked for some spare change. She opened her pocketbook, as if to unleash a few cents of pittance, but instead, removed a small white tract and handed it to him, as if it were the requested money. This made Sarah so furious that she had to turn around and stare at the wall, making the pitiful music of self control. She calmed down after about a minute and approached the woman, who was now pumping gas.

"Hi, how are you doing?" she asked the woman. "That's a nice car you have there and I love the bumper stickers. 'Pray everyday that the Lord will take the heathens away,' that's cute."

The woman replied, "Thank you, it's nice to see such nice Christian girls these days. Most young people just spit at me, but their day will come. The Lord will teach them a lesson that they won't ever forget. My name is Batya Christ. What's yours?"

Sarah's face flashed red with fury, but the woman didn't notice, as she was watching the numbers flip by on the dial. "I'm Sarah, would you like to come to my church? We were going there just now."

"Isn't it a little early to be going to church?" asked Batya.

"It's never too early to worship Jesus," Sarah replied. "Won't you come?"

"Sure I will dear. I agree. How do we get there?" asked the fat woman.

"Just let me fill my car with gas and you can ride with us," said Muffy. "It's really no trouble."

"I can't just leave my car here. Why don't I just follow you?" asked the fat woman.

"Okay," Sarah said and she sent Muffy off to pump gas. "So," she asked, "is Batya Christ your real name? It's kind of strange."

"I had it changed to Batya when I got saved. It means daughter of God."

Muffy returned a minute later with the car and they had Batya follow them to the parking lot of some long since abandoned church where they stuffed her in the trunk and took her home. As they left the parking lot of the church Muffy said, "I understand now. I understand *everything* now."****

Batya Christ

The sun was beginning to rise as they dragged the limp old woman out of the car. Muffy turned to Sarah and said, "I want you to know, I had a wonderful time. I love being out with you. I'm sorry that I overreacted earlier, too. I won't do it again."

Sarah heaved, and the fat old thing came tumbling out of the trunk and onto the ground. "Don't worry about it. I had a good time too. And look at what we found! I've wanted to do one of these for years. Nothing pisses me off more than stupid, hypocritical, badly dressed, old women. You would think that after as many years as she's been alive, she would have learned something, if not about life, at least about fashion," she said as she stared down at the crumpled frame of the once vibrant old woman.

"Damn skippy," Muffy replied with the vehemence of a preacher. They each grabbed an end and drug her inside where they loaded her into a dumbwaiter and pulled her to the top floor. They went upstairs, and silently agreed to put her in the floor-cage while they ate breakfast. When she was securely locked down, they popped six burritos into the microwave and settled down at the table which they had christened almost to the point of destruction..

When they were comfortable, Muffy asked, "So, do I get her or do you?"

"As much as I would like to do this one, she is your first catch, so she's all yours." Sarah replied, "I'm just going to watch. But, do make it a good show. I would hate to waste a speck of the potential that this one has."

"Ding!" said the microwave.

"Cool," said Muffy.

Sarah got up and put three burritos onto one plate and three on another. She brought them back and, after setting them on the table, she returned to her seat. Without thinking, Muffy picked one up and put it in her mouth. Instantly the burrito popped, filling her mouth with beans and cheese the temperature of burning thermite.

"Shit!" she screamed as she spat it back onto the plate. She ran to the sink and gulped water the faucet, but since the water there never really got cold, it didn't help.

"What the hell were you thinking? Haven't you ever eaten microwave burritos before? They get hot when you put them into the microwave, you know," Sarah said sarcastically.

Muffy just flipped her a bird and kept sucking warm water out of the faucet. When she was done disillusioning herself about the water Muffy stripped down to her underoos and went to work. She opened the door to the floor cage and, seeing that Batya was still unconscious, hopped inside. Sarah handed down the ether after taking a few draws herself, and Muffy placed the rag over the old woman's face. She sputtered and fought for a minute, but calmed down soon enough and unleashed a shy giggle before returning to unconsciousness. They then dragged the once again unconscious woman to a heavy metal table with a wooden top and handcuffed her hands to the legs.

The table was short enough for her head to rest on the top while she knelt beside it her legs were pulled apart, the shoes removed, and her feet nailed to the floor. The woman began to groan as if she were having a bad dream, but didn't regain consciousness until her shirt and bra had been cut off, revealing two huge saggy breasts with a bit of hair on them, and her hands and nipples were nailed firmly to the table. She came to with an agonizing shriek, followed shortly after by screams for help. The two girls stood back until she calmed back down and began to whimper.

"Why are you doing this to me?" she cried.

"Because we are sick of you making us look bad," Muffy replied

Sarah added, "Because I'm sick of having to defend my religion, because of the atrocities committed by people like you, to card carrying members of the Church of Satan. You know it's really sad when Satanists help little old ladies cross the street only to be nearly flattened by some old lady taking her grandson to church. Anton LaVey displayed more Christian morals than you do. I saw what you were writing on the wall of that stall. I don't know what Jesus will do to you when you die, but I doubt that it will involve graffiti," she said triumphantly. "Muffy, she's all yours."

Muffy dragged another large floor fan over to the woman and fastened Sarah's longest, stiffest cat-o'-nine-tails to it with a length of duct tape. She then walked around where Batya could see her, and said, "Hi, my name's Muffy and I will be your minister for the evening. Today's sermon will be on the value of attrition for sinners. Now, what I need you to do for me is this: I'm going to put something in your ass, and I want you to hold it there for me, K?"

"No, I can't do that. I'm a woman of god. How dare you do this to me? You'll both burn in hell for this!" she screamed.

"You forget, my friend, God forgives. After all, this is for your own good. If you hadn't run into us you would surely have gone to hell for your crimes against nature, God, and your fellow man. This way I think you'll have a better chance," said Muffy while Sarah cut off her pants.

She cut off the woman's skid marked cotton underwear to reveal the most disgusting mass of bright red soggy flesh and gray bristles that she could ever have imagined. It reminded her of a dead rat that had bloated and burst open in the hot sun. It rather smelled like it too. She then pulled the large rat that Sarah kept as a pet, from it's cage and apologized profusely for what was about to happen to it. Sarah would normally never have allowed one of her pets to be used in art, but the little bastard had bitten her five times in the last week so she gave Muffy permission. Muffy picked up a large hollow pipe and inserted it into the woman's ass. At first it didn't want to go, but after a little Tabasco sauce was used as a lubricant and Sarah gave her a hand, the two inch diameter pipe fit snugly into the convulsing little hole.

The pipe emitted a foul stench in a gust of wind and the woman burst, once again, into tears. The rat was inserted into the pipe and it slid down easily into the woman's anus. They pushed it a little deeper with a pair of salad tongs, and removed the pipe, which let the walls of the woman's colon squeeze the rat tightly and hold it in place with only it's tail protruding.

"Owww, it's biting me!! Make it stop. Please stop." Batya screamed in agony.

Muffy walked, once again, to where she could be seen by the woman and said, "Okay, now hold that tight. You don't want to know what will happen to you if it falls out, trust me." She responded by shitting the trembling rodent, and a stream of murky blood, into Sarah's waiting hands. "I warned you not to do that. Now you have to be punished," said Muffy as she pushed a number two pencil into the woman's urethra. She screamed and squirmed as the reluctant rat was once again pushed down the tube. This time she made an effort to hold it in. Now the fan was faced so that the blades would rotate in the direction of her ass and it was turned on high. The weight of the whip kept the fan from going very fast but it did manage a decent flogging.

The girls stood back and laughed, as the woman writhed under the light blows of the whip. They let it run for about ten minutes before walking once again into view. "Now then, how does that feel? Are you pure yet? Are you ready to admit that Satan is your true lord?" Muffy asked.

"Fuck you!" screamed the old woman.

"Nope, not yet," said Muffy. They let it run for another ten minutes before asking her again.

Again the woman screamed, "Fuck you! You little whores will burn in hell for this! You can't do this, it's wrong."

"You know, in most cases I would agree with you, but, given the circumstances, I believe that it's necessary," said Sarah.

Muffy observed, "I don't think that this is working. We need to try something else." She turned off the fan and picked up a porcelain figure of Jesus. She showed it to Batya. "What's this? It was in your trunk?"

Batya answered, "It's a statue of Jesus Christ our lord and savior, or mine at least."

"NO," cried Muffy, "this is an idol. The bible specifically states that any graven image of God is an idol. So, why then, does the church sell these in their overpriced gift shops? That's another thing that pisses me off. The church ignores the word of God and, not only has these made, but also sells them for one hundred times what they cost to make. Christians are not supposed to be greedy. They charge for bibles too. Shouldn't the word of God be free? He didn't charge Moses for the Ten Commandments. He didn't sell tickets when He gave the Sermon on the Mount. And I somehow doubt that He gets royalties. But then again, He's God, He doesn't get hard up for cash. No, this is a dildo that you use to fuck God."

She picked the pipe up once again and inserted it into the woman's vagina. After putting on thick rubber gloves and lighting her pubic hair on fire, she brought a jar full of large red cockroaches and set them down before Batya. They were the color that you would expect a cockroach to be if it had just crawled out of a child's eye socket. The lid was off and they were all squirming around on top of one another trying to get out, but every time one would get near the top it would slip back down only to be trampled by the others.

"Beautiful, isn't it? It's the best metaphor for life that I have ever seen; a bunch of intelligent yet hideous beings who crawled willingly into a trap, and now trample and kill one another trying to escape. They finally resort to cannibalism and then grow weaker until someone new to the trap comes along and eats them alive. I wonder sometimes, whether or not they have an epiphany at the end. If the extent of their existence comes crashing down on them in one final earth shattering revelation before it all fades to black. Oh well," she said as she picked up the bottle and emptied in down the pipe. She then pulled the pipe out of the screaming and vomiting old woman's vagina, and began to fuck her with the idol. The noise of crunching roaches and the smell was enough to make even Sarah a little queasy. A thick white cream with small flecks of red, black, and brown began to flow from her and cake to the statue. Batya let out grunts of disgust, in between verses of the Lord's Prayer. She began to slowly wag her hips in time with Muffy's churning of the idol. Not much, but just enough to be noticeable.

When Muffy noticed this she stopped maneuvering the statue and, pulling her underoos aside, began to urinate on her back saying, "We've got to cool her down. She's gonna explode."

Sarah, taking the cue, said, "We wouldn't want that now would we?" and pissed in her face.

Batya began to scream, "Ocooooowwwww!!!!!!! My eyes! It burns, oh god, it burns!"

Muffy and Sarah laughed hysterically. When the crying woman's comedic squeal died down and the girls stopped laughing quite so hard, Muffy went to the refrigerator and removed a large jar of peanut butter. She returned and smeared a generous portion of the bottle onto the woman's puffy, red, bleeding crotch and nipples. She then went downstairs to procure the dog. She returned a few minutes later with the slobbering mutt and let him go. It only took him a few seconds to find the scent of the peanut buttery goodness and immediately took to lapping at it.

As soon as the dog began to lick at it Batya began once again to wriggle and twist beneath her confines. She let out a gasp of pleasure and her face went red and for one second she stopped her infernal muttering. But, as soon as her face regained its pasty pallor she started up once again, this time louder and more determined. After a few more minutes of lapping the peanut butter ran out and the dog moved up to her nipples. This made the woman twitch even more, which amused the girls immensely.

While this was going on, Sarah took the opportunity to smear the other half of the bottle on the spastic lower regions of the woman. Smelling the third course, the dog turned and once again began to lap at the goo between the woman's shaking legs. She began to press herself against the animal, which confused him for a second, but after backing up, he returned to his feast. As she was once again building up to orgasm, Muffy pulled the dog away and drug the beast to the other end of the room and tied him to another table. Muffy turned the fan back on and the woman began to scream and beg for the dog to be returned.

Meanwhile, Sarah had gone out onto the patio and brought in the pot of beanie weenies that they had left festering in the sun for three days. She removed the lid, unleashing the foulest smell that either of the girls had encountered in their entire lives. She lifted the lid away to reveal thousands of squirming larvae, trying to escape the light. The pot was placed directly under the woman's face, and after a few minutes of dry heaving, she showered the tiny creatures with all of the stomach acid that she could muster. The girls then put on thick rubber gloves and began to pull wads of the mixture and pelt the woman from a few feet away. When they ran out they replaced the pot in front of the woman and, still wearing the maggot encrusted gloves, began to touch her all over her body. Sarah attacked her head and mouth, while Muffy worked on her lower body. They eventually moved the fan and worked their way down to the woman's crotch and began to massage the maggots into it. To the girl's surprise they managed to bring the woman, once again, dangerously close to climax, but stopped just short and replaced the fan.

The woman still twitching, her body wracked with pleasure and pain, began screaming, "Please, don't do this to me. Why do you bring me so close and then stop? I don't care what else you do to me but please release me from this tension."

Sarah came in close to her and said, "So even a woman as pious as you can beg for sex. Not just sex, but lesbian sex fueled by bestiality and torture. You know you are really one sick fuck to be turned on by this stuff." She turned and pulled off her gloves and picked her pack of cigarettes up off of the table and lit two. Exhaling the smoke in the woman's face, she handed the second to Muffy who took it and began to puff on it as hard and as fast as she could. "Tell you what," she said "we'll finish you off if you will do just one thing for us."

"Okay," said the woman, "I'll do anything. Just tell me what."

Muffy looked coyly at Sarah and they nodded in unison. They then took turns shitting into the pot, and, when they were done, sprinkled a handful of dollar bills on top. They then stirred it all around with the few remaining maggots, and replaced it below the woman's face. "Eat," Muffy said confidently. "That is the only way." The woman began once again to cry, but the girls would not have pity. She lowered her face and began to lick at the disgusting substance. While she was struggling with one of the bills Sarah walked around behind her and pulled the rat out of the woman's anus, which began to gasp as if trying to find something to hold on to. Sarah secluded herself in a distant corner with the rat while Muffy filmed the woman eating the steaming pile before her.

Sarah returned to find the woman licking the bowl. She said, "Well, you deserve this. I might as well give it to you." With that she covered the idol with crazy glue and crammed it into the woman's rectum backwards, so that only the head protruded. She then shoved the rat into the woman's vagina, also backwards, and began to fuck her with the, now dead, rat. Batya began to moan and rock her hips.

"You never really believed in God, did you?" Sarah said as she moved the rat in and out of the woman. She went faster and faster and the white, speckled cream slowly began to ooze down the length of the rat. "Did you?" she demanded.

"No," cried the woman, flooded with ecstasy, "I was afraid of this type of thing. I couldn't bring myself to do anything about my secret desires, so I used God as an excuse to condemn everyone who wasn't. I wish that I hadn't been such a prude my whole life."

"That's exactly what I've always thought," Sarah said, and with a turn of the rat's nose she sent long, sharp spikes shooting out of the rat and through the woman's organs. Blood poured from her vagina and the mouth of the rat. As a disturbing look of pleasure crept across her face, she lay her head down and calmly died.

"Well, that was fun," said Muffy. "How did I do?"

"You did wonderfully. I couldn't have done better myself," Sarah said as she beamed across the dead woman. "Now you go treat her while I drag the mutt downstairs. He's getting annoying."

"Sure, I'll get that damn thing out of here. Why haven't we killed it yet?" Muffy asked. "We both hate dogs."

"Because, as you can see, a dog can come in handy," Sarah said.

"But they're annoying and loud," Muffy pleaded.

"They're also harder to come by than people," Sarah declared boldly.

"Okay, whatever, I'm going to go dip the bitch," Muffy said as she pried the nails out of the table and the floor, and dragged the woman into the next area.

She fixed a harness loosely around the woman's torso. She left it loose enough so that, when the pressure was taken off of the line, the straps would float, above her, in the solution. She lowered the woman into the large glass tank of slightly pink ooze. She wondered, as she usually did while carrying out this particular chore, what the hell this stuff was. She only knew that it hasn't been changed out in over three months, and that the pink was a fairly recent development. She lowered the body into the muck and, as it was settling she wondered at the serenity of the scene.

All of the trouble that that woman had caused in the world was now reduced to this; a calm puffy husk floating in a pink haze. She heard Sarah coming back upstairs, so she turned and walked back into the main living area. "So, what do you want to do while the body soaks? Wanna fuck?" Muffy said with her eyebrow arched high, almost above her head.

"I'm kind of tired," Sarah yawned, "Why don't we just watch 'Holy Mountain' and then go to bed?"

Muffy was disappointed, but she agreed that they had been awake for far too long and that sleep would be nice. She set a clock to wake her up in three hours and together they curled up in front of the TV and went to sleep.

Sleepwalk in Color Form

Sarah awoke three hours later to the screaming of the most obnoxious alarm in existence. She had to have it because she was already immune to all other forms of alarms, due to her previous girlfriend's nasty habit of incessantly hitting the snooze button. She pulled herself out of Muffy's arms and stumbled over to the clock, which she kicked out of the wall, picked up, and threw down the steps and into the basement. Muffy didn't stir.

Sarah stumbled into the work area feeling as though she was walking under water under the influence of heroin. She reached the vat and pulled the cord that was attached to the harness. Batya came slowly out of the pink, dripping and oozing, but with the smell of rose petals wafting from her, as though she were a three hundred pound sachet of potpourris. She left her dangling above the vat to dry and returned to Muffy. She slid easily under her and, once again, Muffy didn't stir. The second that her head hit the pillow she sank comfortably back into the black sea of unconsciousness.

Jakob Sprenger

The next day they both woke some time around eight-o'clock at night. Sarah was in the mood to go out so they went to a local club called 'The Flaming Testicle' where they had performance art and good Belgian ale on tap. They sat at a small table in the corner and watched a bad show in which some guy rolled around in broken glass and barbed wire until he was dragged away to the hospital by a couple of drunken transsexuals. The show was amusing, but it had been done thousands of times before by hundreds of unimaginative, talentless hacks that couldn't performance art themselves out of a hospital room.

They sat around for about an hour, sucking down fifteen dollar draft beers and watching a couple of hired vagrants mop blood off of the stage. They were about to leave when the second act took the stage. It started out by having a normal enough looking guy walk out on stage and sit on a stool. The only strange thing about the man was the demonic grin which oozed across his face like clown makeup. He was just so happy looking it was scary. Then another man came out dressed in a black pinstripe suit and red suede shoes and stood behind the first man. He then undressed the first man, leaving him naked and looking helpless on the stool. It was then that they noticed that he seemed to have an overabundance of body piercings. His nipples had been stretched out so that they hung nearer his belly than his chest and there were barbells all the way down them. He had a hose coming out of his urethra and going, it appeared, back up into his scrotum. He also had numerous piercings throughout his body, everywhere that you can imagine and a few places that you can't. He was stood up and displayed by the first man and made to crouch on the stool. He was slowly turned around and around so that you could see the full extent of his piercings. Some of the piercings were so painful looking that Muffy hurt just looking at them, and most of them were in body parts that she didn't even have. After a few minutes of this the man sat back down and smiled at the crowd.

"This is boring." Muffy said, "Let's go back home and finish Batya."

Sarah, without taking her eyes off of the pierced man said, "Wait this could be interesting."

Muffy settled back down and ordered another beer. The second man then began to remove piercings from the first man revealing large holes through which you could see naked muscle and sometimes organs. He gradually worked his way around the man until the last barbell was out and the man was held together by threads of skin. It looked as though he would fall apart if he only moved an inch. Muffy was asking herself what the hell he could possibly do next, when the second man touched the first on the jaw lovingly and then pulled it away to reveal that it had been prosthetic. He then did the same to the ears and the nose and finally the left eye until the man's face was nothing more than a sparsely skinned skull, oozing with blood, pus, and sinus drainage. The man's tongue, which you could see as soon as the jaw was removed, was split into thirds and held together by rings which were taken out to allow the three separate writhing strands to hang from his skull. The second man then began to probe the insides of the first man's facial orifices with a sharpened pencil. Sarah couldn't take the sight of this man moving slowly to the background music ('Kiss Me Son of God', was playing at this time) while he was having a pencil stuck into his sinuses and then, after it collected a large amount of snot and blood, put into his eye socket.

Muffy: or A Transmigration of Selves

Sarah finally lost it when the second man pulled the catheter out of the first man violently enough to make one of his testicles fall out through one of the holes in his scrotum. She went to the bathroom and smoked a little opium until the show was over and then, still in awe, she went to the bartender and asked who the man was. The bartender only knew that the man's name was Jakob Sprenger and that he was new to the place. When asked what he thought of the show he simply replied, "I've seen worse."

Sarah then returned to Muffy who by this time was sloshed and crawling along the floor searching for her cigarette, which was in her right hand. Sarah dragged her into the back room of the club where the second man was attempting to reassemble the first. His face had been put back together by now so he once again resembled a human being. "Hi," she said, "I loved your show. What inspired you to do that? It was great."

Jakob looked up at her with his glass eye and cartoon clown dog that just-smoked-way-too-much-pot, dopey grin, which she now came to the horrifying conclusion was his natural expression (shiver), and asked, "Who are you?"

"Oh, I'm sorry," she replied, blushing, "My name's Sarah and the drunken puddle over there is Muffy. We do conceptual art too."

"You wouldn't be Sarah Goodie would you?" Jakob asked with a quizzical look.

"Yes, as a matter of fact, I am. I take it that you have heard of me," she said, flattered.

"Heard of is a bit of an understatement," he stated with a gleam in his eye. "I collect your work. I even have one of your more, how shall we say, involved pieces."

"Really," she asked, not quite sure what he meant, "What is it called?"

"Transmigration of selves, it's my most prized possession. I've wanted to meet you for a long time. What are you doing later?" he asked hopefully.

"I was just going home to finish one of my new pieces. Would you like to come?" she asked. Muffy stirred at this and began to moan and flop. "It's okay dear. He's seen my work before."

But she kept on flopping until she threw up and rolled over in it, after which she went to sleep. Sarah carried her to the car while the last few barbells and limbs were put into place and by the time that she returned to the club Jakob was ready to go.

When they reached the warehouse, they unloaded Muffy and carried her inside. The barking of the dog nearly woke her, which pissed Sarah off and made her rethink the dog's worth. Either way, she would have to handle it later. They put Muffy to bed and returned to the parlor discussing the meaning of Gumby. They discussed all forms of art; from films, music, and painting to fashion, lies, and sex. They agreed on almost every point of every concept, which unnerved them almost as much as it titillated them. They ended up making love and Sarah learned the purposes of every piercing that he had. The sex was great, but she still couldn't get over that damn creepy grin. You couldn't possibly imagine, nor could I put into words, the look on his face when he came. Suffice it to say that Sarah would never make love to a man, under any circumstances, for the rest of her life. He went home after he swore himself to secrecy about the whole thing and they agreed to meet again tomorrow to work out some concepts that they could do together. Sarah crawled into bed that night and, as she curled herself around Muffy, had the sinking feeling that she had betrayed the one person who loved her unconditionally. She hung her head off the side of the bed and cried herself to sleep.

A Lovely Melodrama

"What did you do last night?" Muffy demanded sweetly. Sarah only groaned and rolled back over as she had only achieved sleep three hours earlier. "I asked what you did last night," Muffy said, this time a few decibels higher. Again she received no response which made her furious. She straddled her lover and bounced up and down violently until Sarah sputtered to life and began to curse.

"Light bad!" Sarah squealed in anger and confusion. "What do you want? I just got to sleep," she demanded, shielding her eyes from the intruding light.

"I want to know what you did with that freak last night. The living room smells like sex. Did you fuck him?" she asked once again.

"Yes, I fucked him. Can I go back to sleep now?" Sarah said matter-of-factly and rolled over.

"You fucking whore! How could you cheat on me with somebody that doesn't even have his own body parts? I thought that you *loved* me," Muffy screamed as flashes of the disgusting scene flashed violently through her mind.

"Look, I'm sorry. It was late and we were drunk. I regretted it as soon as we were finished. I'm sorry," Sarah said sincerely. "We just got caught up in the moment. I haven't been with a guy in years, and he is really smart and interesting. It seemed like a good idea at the time, but as soon as we were done I felt as though I had defiled our relationship. I felt horrible for what I had done to you. It won't ever happen again."

"Damn skippy, it won't ever happen again. I'm going to rip his dick off and feed it to him," she screamed. She began to sob uncontrollably and eventually collapsed onto the bed beside Sarah.

Sarah took her into her arms and tried to comfort her. At first Muffy cuddled back and cried on her shoulder, which left a large, black spot of mascara on her, but after a few minutes she ceased her blubbering and jerked free. She kicked Sarah hard between the legs and head butted her in the face. Sarah curled up into the fetal position and held onto her bleeding nose.

Muffy once again began to scream and curse and pace around the room, demanding to know why she wasn't good enough to satisfy her anymore. "What did he do for you that I can't do, huh? Why did you have to go and fuck him of all people? Talk about adding insult to injury, he is fucking gross."

Sarah interrupted to interject, "I'm sorry, but every now and then I like to fuck a guy just to remind myself what it's like. It just reminds me why I like women better. I don't enjoy sex with men, but sometimes it's good do it anyway. And besides, since when are we monogamous? You seemed to be having a pretty good time with Batya the other day and she was old and fat and way more disgusting than Jakob. I don't remember ever agreeing to monogamy. Monogamy doesn't work; it only breeds contempt and resentment. I think that it's healthy to fuck someone different now and then. It keeps the relationship fresh and reminds you why you are with the person that you're with. You see, if you never have sex with someone other than the one that you love, you tend to get bored with them and then you idealize everyone that you see into some kind of sex god. You start to resent that you can't experience passion with anyone that you want to anymore, and that makes you want to be single again, which in turn makes you indulge in self destructive acts which ultimately brings about the downfall of the relationship. I'm sorry for what I did, not because it was wrong, but because it made me realize that you are the only person in the world that I want to be with. I felt like I wasted my time with him when I could have been with you."

"Do you really feel that way?" asked a tearful Muffy as she watched her mascara burn discolored rivers into her cheeks.

"Of course I do. I love you and I don't want to be with anybody else *ever*. I'm so sorry that I hurt you," Sarah sobbed and ran into Muffy's open arms. "Will you forgive me?" she asked.

"Damnit I can't stay mad at you. I know that sex is meaningless, but it still hurts me, you know?" Muffy whined.

"I know. Hey, you want to go finish Batya real quick while I make breakfast?" Sarah asked.

"I'd rather stay with you," said the sobbing Muffy.

"Okay, whatever you want. Let's go finish her up together," Sarah said in an attempt to cheer her up.

"Sure," said Muffy her mood brightening a notch, "let's go."

They went into the work area together, holding one another up as they stumbled through the debris of hundreds of previous art projects. They finally found their way to the tank, above which Batya hung like a broken chandelier. They took her down and nailed her to a rack that was shaped like an X. They then broke her on it, leaving her in a very unnatural and painful looking position. They then stuffed a few more dollars into her shit filled mouth and declared her a finished work.

"So," asked Sarah, "what do you want for breakfast?"

"I want to go out today. How about that fish taco place?" Muffy responded brightly.

"I could do with some fish tacos. Sure, let's go," Sarah said as she dressed herself. When she was finally done lacing up her thigh high red vinyl boots they grabbed their coats off of the still living cop sculpture (which they had decided to use as a coat rack) and they were out the door.(inferno)

Faith, Love, and Treachery Maui Style

They arrived at Tacos of the Sea twenty minutes later even though it was only a ten-minute drive from their warehouse. Traffic had been held up because some kid had shot another kid in the face for his 24 carrot gold crucifix, in the middle of the street.

"You know there is just no decency left in the world today," Muffy observed as she stood in line. "I mean, it's a sad day when a kid will kill another kid in the middle of the road, in broad daylight no less. I know that he isn't old enough to drive because I went to school with him, but still, what kind of asshole would go out of their way to hold up traffic like that? Another ten seconds and they would have been on the sidewalk, and we would have our food by now," she complained.

"Yeah," Sarah agreed, "that road is always having stupid shit happen on it. I remember a few years ago, when I first moved in, there was this huge traffic jam because some kid ran over a nun on his way out of the school. It happened around three thirty but they didn't have it cleaned up until well after six. Just imagine that road clogged up with pigs during rush hour."

"Damn," said Muffy, eyeing the menu, "that must have sucked."

"Not really," replied Sarah, "I didn't have a car back then so I was walking when it happened. I just sat there all day watching the pigs scrape the nun off the sidewalk and the drivers flipping each other off and honking their horns. It was really pretty cool."

They had finally reached the front of the line and the perky young girl behind the counter said, "Hi! Welcome to Tacos of the Sea. What can I get for you today?" the words were issued from an ominously cheerful grin which barely moved as she spoke. They were polished and methodical as if pre-recorded by an automaton. Despite the frequency of this type of salutation, this open display of wanton dehumanization sent chills up the girls' spines every time they witnessed it.

"We'll have one chicken quesadilla and a two fish taco combo. Make the tacos gringo style with black beans. And here's my card," Sarah said as she thrust her punch card out to the girl, who punched it while it was still in her hand. She forced a smile and led Muffy to her usual table in the corner. "The food's really good here, but that chick scares me. Nobody is really that happy. I'm afraid that one day I'm going to come in here and find a human finger in my taco or something," she said as soon as they were out of hearing range.

Muffy replied, "Yeah, I know what you mean. She's scary."

In trying not to stare at the happy girl Sarah inadvertently found herself staring into the malformed ass of a no less than three hundred-pound woman, who wrestled with her (also huge) children a few feet away. The ass was triangular; she had never seen one like it before. She brought it to Muffy's attention, who looked and then shrugged it off as Sarah trying to make her jealous. They had this kind of miscommunication often, ever since Sarah had let her go unchained.

Sooner than they expected the food was carried out by the scary girl and placed before them. Sarah was instantly pissed because while she had been observing the peculiar mannerisms of the cashier she had forgotten to mention that she didn't want any lettuce on her tacos. However, it was her own fault so she thanked the scary girl and sent her away. Grimacing, she picked up the taco and took a large bite. She hated lettuce, but it was tolerable.

"So," Muffy said, interrupting Sarah's feast of self-pity, "What's this guy like, the one you fucked?"

"He's actually really cool," Sarah said tactlessly. "He had all of the body modifications done by crooked doctors so that he could do his show. He also has this theory that people always take everything for granted, and the only way to make them appreciate what they have is to take it away from them. He thinks that people should push themselves to do things that they can't do, and give themselves handicaps so that they have to strive harder to achieve their goals. That way, when they achieve them they will feel so much better about it that they won't be disappointed by the fact that it isn't as great as they thought it would be. We live in an age where everything is so simple that we are devolving into monkeys with more and more dangerous toys."

"Are you going to drone on like this about every aspect of him?" Muffy asked.

"No," Sarah said, realizing her mistake. "I just wanted you to understand why he did it to himself. He isn't just a body piercer gone overboard. He's a philosopher who practices his own theories."

"So, how do you know that he isn't a cop or ex military guy who fell into a bomb or a vat of mustard gas or something?" Muffy asked skeptically.

"If he was a cop, he.... You know I don't really know. He just seemed really cool," she said with a slight glow.

"I think that you're being stupid. Someone in your line of work doesn't need to be making friends and bringing them home for dinner," Muffy said as she gnawed a triangle of cheese.

"Fuck you," Sarah said with a smirk. "You're just jealous. I've been doing this a lot longer than you have. I promise that I know what I'm doing. He wants to meet today to discuss a sculpture that we can do together. He's a really big fan."

"Damn your gullible!" Muffy laughed. "Overconfidence has been the downfall of every great mind, and you my dear are not the greatest, comparatively speaking, of course."

"Why don't you just shut up and eat before I make you into a lamp," Sarah growled through a mouth full of taco.

Tacos and Treachery

They finished eating and then went to the Café Ennui where Sarah had agreed to meet Jakob for cappuccino. Muffy, of course, wasn't too happy about this, but Sarah had promised that they would be there. Sarah hated to break a promise (and it was her car) so Muffy reluctantly agreed. When they arrived at the café they had to park four blocks away and walk even though it was still early enough that the area should have been empty.

After four blocks of bitching about the walk they arrived at the front door in time to see a group of darkly dressed individuals escape along with a cloud of smoke. The room seethed with carcinogenic fallout from all too many hastily committed suicides. As they pushed through the haze they quickly spotted his hideous grin flapping at a sleazy looking guy who was wearing dark sunglasses, despite the fact that it was getting dark and he was sitting in the darkest corner of a poorly lit cafe. They approached and were introduced to the sleazy man. His name was Lethe and he turned out to be Jakob's dealer. They were discussing the quality of the latest batch of Sunshine that had been produced. They seemed to agree that quality was down, but then quality of acid has been declining steadily since the sixties.

Sarah turned the conversation to art, like always. And soon Lethe lost interest and began talking to Muffy. "So, what are you into, little girl?" he asked with a sneer.

"I'm into a little bit of everything and a lot of some," she replied.

"Do you like to ride horses?" he asked, revealing a large bag of white powder in his inside coat pocket.

"Don't know," she said, "never tried. I always heard that it was a little dangerous."

"Why don't you give it a try? I'm sure you'll like it. Everything is scary the first time that you try it. People talk a lotta shit about sex, and I bet it was scary the first time you tried it, but you like it now. Don't you?" He was eyeing her like a hungry wolf.

She agreed to follow him to the men's restroom, which consisted of three urinals and seven stalls, the last of which didn't have a toilet in it at all, only a stool and a glass counter. "This place is ritzy," she remarked sardonically while they waited for the stall to open up.

They waited for five minutes before knocking on the door and saying, "Did you fall in?" They received no reply so Lethe stuck his head under the door and then crawled through. He opened the door from the inside and Muffy stepped in to see a blue man in a black business suit hunched over the counter with a needle hanging out of his arm. "So that's where daddy's money goes," Lethe said laughing.

He pushed the corpse off into the floor and removed the bag from his pocket. He formed four generous lines across his own face and then inhaled two of them through a gnarled straw. Muffy stepped meekly up to the challenge before her. She couldn't fathom putting that much powder up her nose. She imagined suffocating with two lungs full of sand, but she did it anyway. One and then the other disappeared up her nose before she knew what had happened. She experienced a burning numbness and then a wave of energy rushing over her, not unlike an orgasm.

The next thing that she noticed was the sensation of her anus being ripped open by a monstrous penis that any donkey would be proud of. She felt the exhilaration of revenge and the greatest physical torment that she had yet encountered. She loved it. As soon as they were finished having sex she kissed him and ran out a back entrance to the ATM where she withdrew five hundred dollars and then rushed back to the café. She paid the man and stashed the bag in one of the pockets in her oversized coat.

She then returned to the table where Sarah sat, still talking about art with Mr. Potatohead. She sat down next to Sarah and looked at her expectantly, but got no response. "Is it possible that I was gone for thirty minutes and she didn't even notice?" she asked herself. Another five minutes of waiting with no response convinced her that she was right. She stood and dismissed herself loudly saying that she was bored and that she was going to the bookstore down the street and stomped out the door, emitting a low, guttural growl.

Sarah looked up in shock as she walked away. "What's up her ass?" she asked sincerely, but the two men just shrugged.

Tiny Wonders

Alone, Muffy walked down the cold, soggy street, staring at the roaches scrambling amongst the cracks in the sidewalk. The rain had stopped an hour or so ago, leaving only a cold, gray drizzle. It was the type of weather that produces the same chill that evidences itself when walking past an ancient graveyard on a foggy night.

She entered the bookstore and ambled around aimlessly, looking at, but not seeing, the rows and rows of restated concepts that someone had thought worthy of recording. She finally happened upon a copy of 'Secrets of an Ugly Stepsister' by George Magnus, who was the author of one of her favorite novels. She picked it up and removed the dust jacket, to reveal the full picture beneath. She replaced the dust jacket and, after pausing to scan her immediate surroundings, stuffed it down her pants. A small, strangely high-pitched voice came from behind and below her.

"It's very good. Have you ever read his other works?" asked the small voice with a thick French accent.

She turned around to see an exact replica of the dwarf from Fantasy Island. She was taken aback more by the fact that this man was dead than she was from being caught shoplifting with her pockets full of smack. She could feel her face going red instantly. Her mouth opened but no sound came out.

"Did I startle you, chare ? I'm so sorry. Accept my humblest apologies, please," said the odd little man.

"I'm sorry. I'm being rude. You just look so much like the guy from Fantasy Island," Muffy finally sputtered, just before realizing how shitty it sounded.

"I get that all the time chare, but a movie star I am not. We suffer from the same disease and we are both French, but the similarity ends there. My friends call me Fousto, a nickname procured from one of his better films," he said proudly.

"I'm sorry, you probably get tired of people saying that you look like him. Why don't you go ahead and arrest me now, before I say something else stupid?" Muffy asked holding out her wrists.

"Why would I arrest you, chare? I don't work here, and I'm not a policeman," he said, opening his black leather coat and pulling up his green poet shirt to reveal a very thin Kurt Vonnegut novel. "Everybody looks like somebody famous in someone else's eyes. It just so happens that in my case everyone is right," he said emitting a small (no pun intended) chuckle. "I was just about to go get a cup of coffee. Won't you join me?" he asked, smiling broad and childlike.

Muffy was amazed at how he could look so innocent and so sleazy at the same time. She knew that it was a mistake, but she went with him anyway. As they walked out the door Muffy asked, "Do you mind if we don't go to Café Ennui? I'm a little put off by that place at the moment."

"I agree, only assholes go there. I take you to a much better place across town. None of that pretentious rich society crap there; only pretentious undiscovered artist crap. Heh, heh. Is far superior," he stated proudly. "Do you have a car, chare? Or shall I call us a cab?" he asked.

"Actually, I do have a car," Muffy said, remembering that Sarah had given her an extra key in case anything ever happened to her. She led Fousto to the car and helped him in. She started the car and asked, "So, where am I headed?"

Fousto simply pointed and said, "That way".

She started the engine and without a thought as to the wrongness of carjacking the only real friend she'd ever had, entered the correct

Muffy: or A Transmigration of Selves

stream of traffic. On the way, she asked, "So how did you get the name Fousto again? It's very unusual."

"Have you never seen the Forbidden Zone?" he asked.

"Is that the one with all the girls talking about having sex with aliens?" Muffy responded vaguely.

"NO," he said shaking his head in disgust. "That was horrible Full Moon movie. I'm talking about the Oingo Boingo movie. It is about a family who lives in a house, which has a door to the sixth dimension in its basement. King Fousto, played by Herve Villechaize, was the ruler of the sixth dimension. It is a very good movie and I am proud to have such a swanky nickname from such a swanky movie. You should be so lucky. I will show it to you some time. Then you will understand."

"I'm sure it will be interesting," she said, a hint of flirt creeping into her tone. "But where is this café again?"

"Turn right at the next light, then go four blocks and take a left. It will be on your right. It is called Travesty. You cannot miss it," he said, relaxing back into the furry red seat. "Nice car, by the way."

"Cool," Muffy said, happy to finally have some directions. "So what's so great about this place anyway? I've never heard of it."

"I just love the atmosphere," he explained. "It is the only place in town where you can really do anything that you want. They have great coffee, a full bar with over sixty draft beers from around the world, good concerts, and piles of neat things lying around everywhere. The place looks like Satan's toy box exploded."

They finally arrived and Muffy found a good parking space on the side. They walked around to the back entrance and stepped through a large, purple window into a garden paved in broken glass. There were large trees jutting out of drifts of multicolored broken glass interspersed with tacky lawn furniture and rusty wrought iron tables. They continued to walk through it until they came to a door that had been obscured by a pile of dismembered mannequins which had been splatter-painted by various weapons, ranging from guns to machetes.

They walked through the door and entered a room done completely in black with red lighting. The only thing in the room was a huge black grandfather clock. They walked through it into the next room which was full of mutilated plush creatures that had been piled together to form a kind of furniture. Next they entered the main room which contained the bar, the currently abandoned stage, and a gallery of surrealist art. As she followed Fousto into another side room, she noticed that the walls were done in a kind of collage of pictures from children's books, Christian propaganda, newspapers, and magazines; all of which was highly disturbing without anything to take it in context to. You were forced to use your own imagination to find the meaning in it, and the thoughts and feelings that it inspired made you feel dirty and depraved.

She was led into a room full of crushed velvet furniture, religious icons, and children's toys. In the center were giant cushy thrones, standing defiantly on either side of a massive chess set with marble pieces which were made to resemble Jesus and angels on one side and demons and clergy members on the other. The chairs were both lined with red velvet and endowed with enough squish to ease all the hemorrhoids of all the royalty in Europe.

. "Do you play chare?" asked the leering Fousto.

"Yes, actually, I know my way around the board. Would you like to play?" she asked.

Rotting circus music hummed quietly in the background as they settled into their respective kingdoms of softness and began to play. She removed the bag from her pocket and sniffed out of the straw that had been left in there earlier.

Fousto was shocked. "Why do you poison yourself with that garbage, chare? You are a nice girl, I can tell. But that shit turns everyone into real bitches. I have lost a lot of friends to that shit."

"Does it offend you? I can wait until later if you prefer. I'm sorry that your friends died from it, but I don't do it enough to hurt me," Muffy said apologetically.

"Did I say that they died?" he asked angrily as he moved out his knight." Muffy looked confused. "NO, I wish that they had died. They started stealing from me and lying to me and fucking my girlfriend!" he said angrily. "Bastards, they were all very nice until they started doing that shit. Then everything went to hell," he said, sadly staring at the board.

"Oh, I'm sorry," she said sincerely as she moved out her queen. "I'll put it away," and she quickly did.

"I'm sorry chare; I do not want to seem as if I am telling you how to live your life. You can do anything that you want to around me, but I do have a very low opinion of that particular drug. There are so many that are so much better and hurt you so much less. Have you ever done acid, chare?" He asked.

"Of course I have, hasn't everyone?" she said, slightly offended.

"Just asking. Don't you think that it is a much better drug for a much better price?" he asked.

"Yes, but you can't do acid all the time. It will melt your brain. Not to mention the fact that you can't do it in public," she responded.

"Check mate," said the small man. "You are ensnared. You can't do smack all the time either, or you will be an asshole. But why do you need drugs at all? Life can be so much more interesting without them."

"I don't need drugs. I just like them. I can quit any time that I want to. I just don't want to. Your concern is sweet, but I do what I want to. I learn from my own mistakes, not from others," she quoted.

"Okay chare, would you like a glass of wine, or some coffee or something?" he asked, giving up for the night.

"I wouldn't mind a Belgian ale. Do they have any here?" she asked hopefully

"Of course chare, here they have everything." He pushed a button on the table and said "Suzy, we need one Belgian, my usual, and an order of ramen noodles. Do you want anything to eat?" he asked.

"Sure, do they have cinnamon waffles?" she asked distractedly, still studying the chessboard for a loophole. She found none.

"Like I said chere, they have everything." Into the intercom he added, "And an order of cinnamon waffles. That will be all for now," Fousto said as the server set the drinks down in front of them. He handed the man two hundred dollar bills and said, "The rest is yours." He opened the pint and poured her a glass. Fousto's usual, as it turned out was a large bottle of Cognac which he turned up and took in several deep gulps. He set the bottle on the table, smiled, and exhaled a potent yet not entirely unpleasant gust of oxygenated fuel. Muffy was unsure, but it seemed that the candelabra burned brighter for a second.

"You just tipped that guy like thirty dollars, didn't you?" Muffy asked, looking concerned.

"Yes, what about it? I always do that. It makes them happy, and makes up for the shit heads that don't know any better than to tip fifteen percent or even less," he said. "They only make two dollars and thirteen cents an hour, and their job sucks. I used to be a host at a restaurant. I heard enough horror stories to make me believe that there is a special place in hell for bad tippers. Anyway, do you like this place?" he asked as the food arrived.

"Yeah, it's neat. I just can't figure out why this place isn't more popular," she said, still eyeing the board as if there were some hidden strategy which she kept overlooking.

"They don't advertise, for one. And they don't cater to people's need for attention. When an asshole comes in here they feel ignored and engulfed by their surroundings. It's like stepping out of one reality and into another. I have even seen a few people freak out," he said mischievously. "It was wonderful. They start screaming and throwing things, and still no one pays them any attention. Then they break down and cry. At that, a few people laugh, but this doesn't appease them. They do something really great after that, always different but equally entertaining. They are eventually dragged away by the bartender or they leave sobbing. It's wonderful. We have a few celebrities that use this place as a hideaway, but they are really cool. They don't mention this place to anyone from the media. If they did the place would be flooded by tourists, celebrities, and all of the other type of sycophantic cockroaches and paparazzi that permeate this city."

"Oh, that makes perfect sense, now that you mention it. Thanks for bringing me here, it's really neat. Is there some kind of rule about who you can bring here?" asked Muffy.

"No, it's just kind of understood that you don't bring just anyone here. They have to be mature and intelligent and they have to be able to appreciate the place for what it is. Otherwise the place is ruined for all of us. It's that simple," he explained.

Muffy looked him in the eye and with a skeptical tone she asked, "So how did you know that I would fit in here? You hardly know me."

Fousto laughed approvingly. "I could just tell. I am an excellent judge of character, you know. And if I was wrong, I would have had you killed," he said laughing heartily.

Muffy couldn't quite tell if he was serious or not so she questioned him further. "So, what do you do for a living Mr. Fousto?"

"I am astronaut," he declared, obviously drunk.

Muffy couldn't help but laugh. She had never seen a drunken baby man before. It was just so cute. She then thought about how much it must suck to be eternally cute, to never be able to be sexy, or scary, or ugly, or plain. She stopped laughing and asked, "No, really, what do you do?"

"O.k. fine. I make snuff movies. It's not anything special, but it's a living," he replied matter-of-factly.

"You make snuff films? That isn't very nice. Were you planning to make me an actress?" she asked, bluntly and a little loud.

"Now, why is it that you will believe me when I say that I make snuff films, but you won't believe me when I say I am an astronaut? I have shown nothing but kindness to you. I meet you, invite you to go to a nice club and pick up the tab, and yet you would still rather believe that I am a monster than a hero. That, my friend, is not very nice."

Muffy was confused. "So you're not a snuff film director?"

"No, silly, I am a writer. I catalogue bullshit and put it in such an order as to make people think what I want them to think. It's a hollow profession, very unfulfilling, and it doesn't pay much either," he said, and then fell over the edge of his chair.

"But, you don't do snuff films?" she asked again.

"No, damn it, I am much worse than a killer. I make people live unhappily by showing them the truths that they try to overlook. But I can never make the world a better place, because the only people that read my work already agree with me. That's why they read my work. The people that need to read my work all read romance and self-help books. Therefore I am but a common liar who gets paid. Pretty sweet, ah?" he threw up into an 'Inspector Gadget' garbage can that had been placed beside his chair by the server that had brought his ramen.

"We need to get you home," observed Muffy. "Where do you live?"

He began to sing the Elvis song 'In the Ghetto.' The server came back and gave her a business card for the club and on the back it had an address, somewhere in Brooklyn. "Come on Fousto," she said, picking him up, "I'll take you home." She carried him out the same way that they had come in and loaded him in the trunk so as not to mess up Sarah's upholstery, and off they went to Brooklyn.

A Sad Realization

She dropped the drunken weirdo off at his house at 5:45, just as daybreak set in. His place was smaller and less grandiose than she had expected on the outside but the inside was like stepping into a cross between a surrealist painting and the set of a Vincent Price movie. There were sculptures depicting every negative emotion in a circle around a round sofa in the middle of the front room. The walls were painted to resemble fire with faces painted into the flames and the ceiling was covered in cut outs of eyes. Other than that the room was pretty plain; a round table draped in black velvet held a computer and printer, and facing the computer was a very worn crushed velvet chair that looked as though at some point it had been yellow, or maybe orange. The place was melodramatic, but what writer's place isn't?

She laid him down in the chair and stuffed his coat under his head as a pillow. She left her phone number in the right pocket of his pants and left without saying goodbye.

"What the hell am I going to do now?" she asked herself as she climbed back into the driver's seat. She sat there for a while trying to think of a place to go. She could go back to Travesty, but she didn't like the idea of going there alone. She couldn't go back to any of her old "friends" because none of them were really her friends. They only liked her for her social status, and without her parents she didn't have one. "They would probably tell my dad or some crazy shit like that," she thought to herself. "Damn, I really have nowhere to go without

Sarah. I'll be damned if I'm going back to my parent's house. But, what can I do? I'm not in the mood to go shopping and I just ate so I guess that I have to go back home. Shit!" she said as she started the car. She stomped the gas and squealed away.

A Long Night

She arrived back at home only to find another car parked in their usual space. She was furious. She exited the car, fuming like she had never fumed before. She stomped loudly up the stairs and announced her arrival by turning Sarah's chair over, with her in it. "Honey, I'm home!" she screamed boisterously.

It was Sarah's turn to be furious. "Where the hell did you go with my car? I had to get a ride home with Jakob. Luckily he didn't have anywhere else to be, but what if he had? I would still be stuck in that fucking coffee shop. Now give me my car key back. Now!" she demanded loudly. She turned to Jakob. "Jakob, I'm sorry that you have to put up with my psychotic girlfriend. She's usually not this bad."

"I had to let you know that I was gone somehow. If I hadn't taken the car, you probably would have forgotten about me and left me at the bookstore," she said, her voice disintegrating into sobs. "You didn't even notice when I talked to you," she sobbed.

Sarah was forced to forget her anger and, biting her tongue, she took her in her arms and said, "I'm sorry, Booby, you know how I get when I'm talking about work. Please forgive me, I didn't mean to ignore you. Why didn't you just join in on the conversation?"

"I tried, but no one would listen to me," Muffy said, drying her eyes on Sarah's shirt. "Do you still love me?" she asked humbly.

"Of course I do, baby. Why wouldn't I?" Sarah asked, slightly saddened by the question.

"Because you're stuck up his ass right now," she gestured angrily towards the man by the table.

"Should I leave?" he asked, "I'm not quite sure that this is the best time to talk business."

"That would probably be a good idea," Sarah said, and he brusquely walked down the stairs. "Are you happy now that the big bad man has gone?" Muffy nodded gratefully. Sarah wiped a stream of mascara from Muffy's cheek. "What would you like to do tonight? Do you want to go to a movie? Killer Condom's playing at the Rerun Theatre."

"You know how I feel about theaters. I get all anxious and spend the whole time outside smoking," she said bitterly.

"Well, what do you want to do then? We could go see the new dead clown exhibit," Sarah suggested.

"No more art today, please," Muffy pleaded.

"I know, how about a Troma marathon. There's no art in that, just a lot of dead people," Sarah said hopefully.

"It reminds me too much of work. Do me?" she asked with an exaggerated grin.

"That's my girl," Sarah said and she removed her top to reveal her milky white breasts, which she pressed to her lover as they indulged in a long and violent kiss, during which the rest of the clothes were torn away and tossed flippantly about the room.

Muffy lunged at her lover and knocked her easily to the floor. She scampered up Sarah like a tree and ground her moist vagina into her face. She smeared her juices around Sarah's face so roughly that it turned a light pink and she had trouble breathing. "Mine," she purred, and slid down Sarah's heaving torso to kiss her in as perverse a manner as anyone has ever kissed anyone before. She stood abruptly and pulled Sarah into the bedroom, where she pointed to a knob rising from the center of the bed frame at a ninety-degree angle. "Sit," she commanded, and Sarah did, letting the thick knob of metal slide easily up into her anus as she took hold of the bedposts like reigns. Muffy found her favorite whip, a short rubber cat-of-nine-tails with a silver handle, and she began to lash at Sarah's thighs. Sarah lowered her hand and tried to masturbate, but Muffy quickly put an end to that by handcuffing her to the bedposts. She then sat on the bed, facing Sarah's back, and flogged her mercilessly, slow at first, but then progressively harder until Sarah began to moan and ride up and down on the metal knob.

Eventually she began to beg for mercy, "I can't take much more of this," she said. "I'm going to explode."

Muffy grabbed her by her short, now green, hair and pulled her head back as far as it would go. When it reached the point of agony she sat on her face like a barstool, and slapped Sarah's breasts around with the whip. Sarah let out a muffled plea for mercy, but Muffy couldn't make out the exact words. She ground harder and harder into her seat until she climaxed so violently that she toppled forward, falling over Sarah and hitting her head on the floor. She was momentarily dazed but found her way to Sarah's crotch by instinct. She nibbled gently on the creamy lips of her vagina, and Sarah's face immediately went beat red. She reached orgasm a second later, so violently that she lifted herself all of the way off of the knob and with its' release it plunged back into her hard enough to cause her to swoon.

Muffy then began to dip her tongue inside to taste the warm sweetness that her lover produced. She sucked her lover dry and then went to work on the clitoris, smashing it between her tongue and teeth, licking and biting gently, which made Sarah shiver uncontrollably. She rode up and down on the knob sighing and gasping and crying out. Muffy tired of this eventually and climbed her lover once again. Sarah licked at her anus, stabbing her tongue into the warm bitter orifice, and then moving up to lap at the warm nest of flesh which returned her kiss gratefully. Muffy cried out in ecstasy and collapsed once again, this time on the bed. Her appetite finally satisfied, she laid spread eagle on the bed to cool down. As she descended into sleep she gently called goodnight to her confused lover, who begged to be let down but received no response. This would prove to be one of the longest nights in Sarah's life.

I'm sorry

The next day Muffy woke with a start. She felt as though she was drowning. She had been having a really weird dream, and, although she didn't remember all of it, she remembered that she and some girl that she had never seen before were fighting little impish creatures in a toy store. She remembered meeting a pretty girl who was covered in sores, which oozed six different colors of pus. She remembered a machine with the sick girl inside. It was big, red, and square with a glass door. They had put the girl and a strange rabbit/monkey thing in there together inside a vat of what looked like milk (but she seemed to remember it as herpes juice, milked from a five year old). They added a whole bottle of strawberry syrup and turned on the machine. Lots of lights commenced flashing and everything had gone crazy. She was repeatedly attacked by images of the naked girl being ripped to pieces by the rabbit/monkey as it tried to escape which only served to mix the solution more quickly. The last thing that she remembered of the dream was opening the door and stepping inside because she needed the liquid for something.

"That was a weird one," she said to herself. She couldn't shake the feeling that something horrible was about to happen. She told herself that dreams don't mean anything and that she was just being silly, but nothing helped. She looked up at her lover and sighed. She had fallen asleep in the same position that she had left her. She hung lifelessly with a tranquil yet tortured look on her face. Muffy sat in the floor in front of her and sketched first her position and then her expression with the care that one would give to a last conversation with a dying relative or the discussion of the will shortly thereafter.

When she was satisfied with the sketches, she stood and drew close to Sarah. She still smelled of sex, Muffy noted with pleasure. A wave of love enveloped her at that moment and she kissed her lover lightly on the lips. She found the keys to the handcuffs and unshackled her lover while holding her in place. When her hands were free, she lifted Sarah up off of the metal knob and laid her on the bed. Sarah let out several groans of disapproval as this was being done, but her expression had softened considerably from the one that Muffy had just sketched. She lay down beside her and cradled her in her arms.

She planted soft kisses all over her face until Sarah began to groan, "Leave me alone. I just got to sleep".

Muffy didn't stop and she eventually woke up with a scream and a sour face. She crawled out of bed and walked to the shower like a zombie chicken with hemorrhoids. As she was walking away, Muffy noticed that her colon was still wide open and twitching slightly. She followed on her hands and knees staring into the hole as intently as a house cat looking out of a window.

"Wow," she said jokingly, "I can see your brain from here."

Sarah turned around angrily and kicked her in the face. However, it didn't really hurt because Sarah was still weak from having been asleep. "I can't fucking believe that you left me like that last night," she said angrily.

"Why not? It's not like you've never done it to me before," Muffy asked, staring up at her.

"Fuck you, you make a good point, but fuck you," Sarah croaked as she climbed into the shower and pulled the curtain closed.

Muffy, again on hands and knees, crawled under the curtain and sat with her back to the wall as she watched Sarah bathe. The dream and the feeling of dread returned suddenly. "Do you know anything about dreams?" she asked.

"A little, why?" asked Sarah turning and looking interested.

"I just had a really weird one last night. I still feel like something bad is going to happen. It was just really disturbing," Muffy said vaguely.

"Well, what happened? Don't keep me in suspense," Sarah demanded just before the heat of the shower made her swoon and almost pass out. She turned down the hot water and stepped out of the stream for a moment.

Muffy didn't want to tell her about the other girl in the dream so she jumped to the weird part. "All that I remember is that there was a girl covered in sores, like herpes, but all over her body. She was in a machine with a weird rabbit/monkey thing and it was tearing her apart inside of a vat of milk. I had put her in there because I needed the mixture, but I don't think that I had meant to kill her. That part was an accident. I think that the animal was just supposed to stir the mixture while it tried to get out of the vat, but it attacked the girl instead. When it was all over and the girl was pureed in with the solution I let the monkey out and I went to get the solution out of the vat, but I think that the monkey thing pushed me in because I woke up with the feeling that I was drowning."

"Is that all?" asked Sarah, soaping her vagina. "I thought that you would have something juicier than that for me the way that you carried on."

Mr. Husky, the god of corny jokes and puns, leered just outside the curtain. He let out a shrill cackle and disappeared.

"Did you hear something?" Muffy asked.

"No, did you? What did it sound like?" asked Sarah, rinsing.

"I guess not. I could have sworn that I heard a laugh, but it was too high pitched to have been a human. Unless of course they have been huffing helium, but what are the chances of that?" Muffy said laughing. "Anyway, back to the dream. I guess that you had to be there. What do you think that it means?"

"It probably means that you should lay off the horse," Sarah responded.

"Seriously, dear, what do you think that it means?" asked Muffy, a bit miffed.

"How the hell should I know? I'm your girlfriend, not your psychiatrist. And anyway, dreams don't really mean anything. They're like parables, the meaning is added by the listener, by the way that they respond to it."

"You're supposed to be an artist, and artists are supposed to be good at interpreting things," Muffy said disappointedly.

"You too are an artist, dear, and you were there, not I. Interpret it yourself." She turned off the water and smoothed some water out of her hair. She ran her hands down her sides, stomach, and her ass, and slung the water at Muffy's face.

"I can't believe what a bitch you can be sometimes, but I love you anyway," Muffy said hopping up and kissing Sarah on the cheek. "So, you really don't think that dreams mean anything?" she asked again as she stepped out of the shower dripping all over the floor.

"I don't know. No one has ever figured it out, not even the guys that I work for, and they know everything," Sarah said as she wrapped herself in a flowery beach towel with a bear on it.

"They can't know everything," Muffy said skeptically.

"Can't they?" Sarah asked with a smirk. "With thousands of years and billions of dollars they can't know everything? Did you know that they once built a computer whose sole function was to take a picture of every face in the world and merge them all together so that they could find out what Human looks like?"

"How the hell would I know that? I didn't even know that they were a real organization until I met you. What did it look like?" Muffy asked while helping her out of the shower and trying not to get wet.

"Have you ever seen a picture of Michael Jackson recently?" Sarah asked after a moment of thoughtful reflection.

"No," answered her lover.

"It looked just like him," Sarah said matter-of-factly

"Really?" Muffy asked with wonder.

"No, not really, but wouldn't that have sucked? If anything is grounds for the extermination of a species, *that* would be it," Sarah laughed as she pulled a pair of pants out of the dresser.

"I concur, but who did it really look like?" Muffy asked seriously.

"It didn't really look like anybody. It was beautiful, yet horrible; the most beautiful and disgusting thing that I have ever seen. It was perfect. So perfect that it seemed flawed in its perfection. But the look in its eyes was that of total cruelty, and it leered like a demon. It was even creepier than that Richard guy on all of those Aphex Twin CDs," Sarah confessed with a shiver.

"You can't be serious, nobody's creepier than Creepy Richard," Muffy said firmly.

"This time I'm serious, it was even creepier than Creepy Richard," she reaffirmed.

"Wow, that's pretty creepy. Could I see it?" Muffy asked hopefully.

"No, they destroyed it along with the machine. They decided that they had made a horrible mistake and killed the guy who had the idea. Another mistake of that caliber could mean the end of the world," Sarah picked out a shirt with an aborted fetus on it which read 'Abortion is murder. Vote yes to the death penalty for abortionists.' "As we know it at least." She added with a smirk, "That's why they calmed down so much in the last few years. They really haven't done much lately; a little brainwashing, some assassinations here and there but nothing really big."

"Okay," Muffy said, "if they know everything, then, what is the cure for cancer?" Muffy asked with obvious skepticism.

"An extract made from the common wood roach. You know the white stuff that squishes out of the really fat ones? Well, they boil that down and add green food coloring," Sarah said pulling the shirt over her head.

"That's disgusting," Muffy said, sticking out her tongue.

"You asked," Sarah reminded her.

"Does it really work?" Muffy asked with a sour face.

"Have you ever noticed how much David Bowie smokes? The vice president is a huge fan. From what I've heard, they have cured him 5 times already," Sarah said, applying eyeliner to her lips.

"Wow, I've always wondered how he could still hit those notes for that long at his age while smoking constantly," Muffy mused, plopping back down on the bed.

"Well now you know," Sarah said in her best exaggerated smart ass tone.

"Who killed J.F.K?"

"Even they haven't been able to figure that one out. Try again," Sarah said seriously.

Muffy laughed, "Are you serious?"

Sarah turned to look at her. "Seriously, all that we know for sure is that it wasn't planned by us, any government in the world, or any special interest groups. It is however widely believed that whoever killed him did it because they were jealous that he was having his way with Marilyn. Jealousy can make people do some pretty extreme things and, in that time period, she was the one that everybody wanted. I never thought that she was that great myself, but there's no accounting for taste. That has never been proven, but they have never been able to disprove it either. It's just really funny that JFK pissed off all those cocaine slinging, homicidal, cartel guys and assassinated somebody right before it happened. Given another week they would have killed him, but they didn't get to." She turned back around.

"That's great. For that matter it could have been someone he cut off in traffic years ago, or someone that he picked on in school, couldn't it?" Muffy said thoughtfully.

"Yea, I suppose so. They never disproved either of those either," Sarah replied.

"Next question: In the movie Lost Highway by David Lynch, what the hell was going on? And why did the two guys switch places?"

Muffy: or A Transmigration of Selves

Sarah looked puzzled. "I don't know. That movie never seemed to make sense to me earlier. Lets look it up online."

"A David Lynch web site? Is that the best you can do?" Muffy jeered.

"No, of course not, the Illuminated pages. The Illuminati are online just like everybody else," she explained as she went to the computer.

"Are you telling me that if you know the right internet address you could learn the answers to all of the questions that you ever wanted to know?" Muffy asked, amazed.

"Not quite, you have to go to this web site that's disguised as a constantly malfunctioning search engine. Once there you put in a 3759 character alphanumerical code that only a chosen few know. Then the site is unlocked and you can ask it anything about anyone. You can pull up a file on anybody, living or dead, and find out anything about them, and you can do the same with places and events too. The only bad thing about it is that you have to be very specific. If you put in a vague question it could send you so much info so fast that it would melt your motherboard. Just accessing the site would blow up any computer that you can buy today anyway. The people that know the code are given special computers that can handle that much information at once. My computer, for instance, is equal to 36 Pentium 16s linked together," Sarah boasted, petting her monitor. "And the best that the average guy can buy these days is a Pentium 4." By this time she was online and at the site. She typed in, 'In David Lynch's Lost Highway, what made the two guys switch places?' She clicked on send and in a split second the answer was there.

It said, "He was just fucking with you. David Lynch loves private jokes. Any meaning that anyone has ever been able to squeeze out of that movie is total crap thought up by people who either overanalyze everything or were on really good acid. It was written and filmed as a private joke just to fuck with the heads of his fans."

"Oh, okay. It all makes sense now," Muffy said dumbly.

"That's pretty cool. I have to make it a point to meet him some day," Sarah said writing 'meet David Lynch' on a post-it note and sticking it to the edge of her monitor.

"Yeah, really," Muffy agreed. "Look me up, I'm curious to see how much they really know about me."

This time Sarah simply typed in 'Muffy LeSeux' but before she clicked search she asked, "What's your middle name? I don't want to blow up my computer."

"Lynne, but how many Muffy LeSeux's can there have been?" she asked.

"You'll see." Sarah said as she added Lynne to the middle of her name and clicked on search.

Once again, the answers were there in less than one second. Two hundred thirty-six files were pulled on people named Muffy Lynne LeSeux. Two of them were still alive. They were listed by birth dates so it was easy to pull up the right one. They opened it up and a whole page of options appeared. They could search for information by date, keyword, age, and even companion to name just a few.

"So, what do you want to know?" Sarah asked browsing the themes.

"Go to sexual history. I'm curious," Muffy requested, her curiosity peaking.

She clicked on it and immediately every sexual act that she had ever participated in was listed by date, length of time, and partner along with totals of each. It even listed when she masturbated.

"Wow," she said, "we have had sex 826 times in less than a year. Think we'll get into any record books?"

"Nothing that would be available to the public. But we might make some private Illuminated list," Sarah said, half serious. "Damn your dad was a horny sick-o. What next?"

"Go to today. I'm going to go to the bathroom. Tell me if that number changes."

She made it about three steps away when she heard Sarah scream.

A Booboo

"You stupid bitch! What have you done?" Sarah's scream echoed off the walls hard enough to crack the plaster.

"Huh?" Muffy asked, confused.

"This article says that your debit card was used yesterday to withdraw a large sum of money and a security camera recorded your face. Now your dad's got the whole NYPD looking for you. He even put up an extra million in reward money." Sarah said, still screaming.

"Sounds like Daddy. He probably hasn't been laid the whole time I've been with you," Muffy half joked.

Sarah tried to quiet her rage, but the anger was so intense that she started shaking. She could feel her brain meats twitching from the task of trying to make sense of what had just occurred. "You have ruined everything. You can never leave the house again. He has put a 1 million-dollar reward up for anyone who can give information that leads to your rescue. They think you've been kidnapped and are awaiting a request for ransom, which they say they will pay, no questions asked, no matter how high. According to this 9386 people have already responded with information."

"Damn, what are we going to do?" Muffy asked, growing concerned.

"Fuck!" Sarah squeaked, her eyes growing huge. "They already have my picture on here too as having been seen with you. I'm fucked.

No, no. I'm hamster fucked," she said screaming again. "You have *hamster* fucked me. I hope you're happy. God damn, I knew I shoulda killed you when I had the chance."

Just then they heard a banging on the door. "Shit they already found us. Damn your bourgeois heritage," Sarah shrieked. Muffy ran for clothes while Sarah ripped the computer out of the wall and threw it down the stairs.

A muffled voice came from behind the door. "It's me, Jakob, open up. We've got to talk now."

"Shit," said Sarah as she grabbed her slide bar and her 25-mm and threw on a coat. "I was really hoping that I wouldn't have to kill him," she said to herself wistfully. She pulled the lever that took the lock off of the downstairs entrance.

Jakob entered, running up the stairs, screaming, "There's no time to explain. You both have to come with me. You are both in deep shit. Everybody's looking for you. Get in my car. They have an APB out on yours. Fucking hurry!"

In the second that Sarah had to think she decided that she would have to trust him. He was their only way out since the police would be looking for her car. When he reached her at the top of the stairs she was surprised to see that it wasn't Jakob at all. It was someone that she'd never seen before. She let the pistol drop into her hand but he had her by the wrists before she could raise it. "Damn, you're fast. Who the fuck are you?" she asked, furious.

"I was afraid that you would have this reaction. It's me," Jakob said removing his nose. "I'm just wearing different prosthetics today. If I let you go will you put the gun away? We have to get out of here. They're looking for you."

"Who's looking for me?" Sarah asked, playing dumb.

"Everybody's looking for you, literally everybody; the government, the pigs, the Illuminati, even private citizens who don't know you. Now will you come with me?" he asked with an unusual sense of urgency.

"How do I know that I can trust you?" Sarah asked.

To which he replied, "You don't really have a choice. Do you have any idea how many hit men are on there way here right now, there are pictures of you, your car, and Muffy all over the news, not to mention the radio descriptions, flyers, and billboards. Now get in the fucking car!"

"Damn, this is even more serious than I thought," Sarah said, as she ran down the stairs.

"You too," Jakob said, "I know that you don't like me but I'm kinda trying to save your lives, so if you don't mind..."

She hesitated for another moment and then followed Sarah down the stairs as fast as her legs would take her. Jakob turned on the gas and set a burning stick of incense by the bed stand. Then he grabbed a particularly neat purple fur coat off of the coat rack, waking it up, and confusing its shattered mind. The cop-turned-coat-rack stared stupidly at Jakob as he took off down the stairs. Then he smelled the gas, and a look of clarity came into his eyes for the first time in months. He heard an engine start up as his eyes studied the smoke rising from the incense. He smelled the sweet odor and for the first time in his meaningless life it all came clear to him. He understood everything. Then with a burst of pain everything went the most glorious shade of black.

55

Back at Jakob's house, they all sat watching a special report on NYC news. They had interrupted a football game to give an update on the search for Muffy LeSeux.

"I didn't think that they interrupted sports for anything," said Muffy, a little flattered but mostly disturbed.

"It's the privilege of the rich, my dear. They interrupt sports for you for the same reason that they repave roads in rich areas five times a year whether or not they need it while they let the rest of the streets fall to pieces. The rich have money, and people kiss their asses in the hopes of receiving some of it. They never do, of course, but you can't blame then for trying," Sarah said bitterly.

"Nice speech, but aren't you rather loaded yourself?" asked Jakob, taunting her as he pulled at a strand of her hair.

"Fuck you. I don't have that much money, not anymore anyway," Sarah glared at Muffy. "My darling lover here falls in love with every piece that we do. She hasn't let me sell a piece since I found her. And anyway, even if I am a little better off than some it still makes me sick when I see people groveling for the rich. Nobody grovels for me, and I don't want them to. I hate driving through Richie-Land because they're always working on the road and causing traffic..."

"Shut up, that's my dad," Muffy said, interrupting and silencing the prior conversation.

All were quiet as they watched Muffy's father whine and blubber the usual catchphrases. "Come home to us sweetie. We love you and we miss you. Everything seems so empty now that you're gone. We've been looking for our daughter for so long, we are just happy that she's alive...," droned the television.

The audience had mixed reactions. Sarah looked bored and offended that she had been interrupted for this pathetic display of false emotion. Jakob also looked unimpressed by her father's display, but his face did show a trace of concern for Muffy who, by now, was crying uncontrollably. "He's never said those things to me before." She whined, "He seems to have changed so much. I think that he really misses me."

It was Sarah's turn to interrupt, "What?!!!" she blurted out in amazement, "You are buying this load of shit! I've seen politicians lie better than that."

Muffy stared in grief and amazement at her, as if her love had just picked up her favorite puppy and twisted off its head. "How can you be so cruel?" she said softly, as tears flowed down her cheeks like blood from a turnip. "You've never even met my father. How can you pass judgment so easily on someone you have never met?" she hissed.

"I only know what I heard from you, and I know that if half what you said is true then he's a shithead that doesn't deserve forgiveness. Unless you made up all of that stuff about being raped every night," Sarah said, her voice growing louder and shakier with shock and rage.

Muffy looked as though she had been slapped. "I can't believe that you, who are supposed to love me, would have the audacity to even imply such a thing. He was a shithead but people change. And anyway, you raped me the first time I met you."

"No, Muffy, they don't, not for the better anyway. Don't be so naive. You were a prized possession and his favorite fuck, that's why he wants you back. He would react the same way if someone stole his car. And I don't see how you could call that rape. You got off more than me." Sarah said, trying all the while to sound compassionate, but she couldn't quite fight back the rage and disgust that welled up inside of her every time that an intelligent person fooled themselves into believing what they wanted to, knowing that it was a lie. Nothing disgusted her more than human weakness, except for maybe her own.

"Fuck you! You don't own me. And anyway, I think you're just jealous." screamed Muffy, flipping her off and standing up to show she meant business.

Meanwhile Jakob sat behind Sarah, listening and watching them with a look of utter amusement.

Sarah stood up. "Look, even if he has changed, what are you going to do about it? Do you think he'll still want you back after he finds out what you've been doing all this time? And if he does what will become of me? Do you think that he'll just say 'So, you're in love with a female serial killer? I'm so happy for you. You got a real good catch there; female serial killers are rare as hell.' NO! He's going to crucify me. He has to tell the press something since he's called all of this attention to himself. He'll probably say that I kidnapped you, brainwashed you, filled you full of illegal drugs and turned you into a gay, devil worshiping democrat. Even my friends in high places won't be able to save my ass if they get a hold of me. Not that they would want to. Thanks to you they currently want me dead. Anyway, if you go back home we'll never see each other again. Don't you even care?"

"I did until just now," Muffy bawled. "I can't deal with this right now. I need some time to think," she said, making for the door.

Sarah lunged and made it there first. "Where the hell are you going to go? Half the world is looking for you. What if the cops came and we had to leave. We would never find you. Come back over here and we will talk it out. Please?"

Muffy kicked her as hard as she could between the legs and pushed her out of the way. "I have to get out of here. I'll be back in a little while." She ran out of the door before Jakob had a chance to stop her. He went to Sarah instead and asked if she was all right.

She rocked back and forth on the ground for a while and when she was able she replied, "Do I look alright?"

"Not especially," he said, smiling.

"Help me up. We need to talk." She glowered menacingly at him.

"Okay, beautiful," he said, helping her up. "What shall we talk about? Sports? Art? The weather?"

"How about what we're going to do now, how you knew that the cops were after us sooner than we did, and what are we gonna do about Muffy?" she began.

"Sure you wouldn't rather discuss.....the weather?" he asked sheepishly.

"What are you hiding? Ever since I met you I've had this feeling that something wasn't quite right. How did you say that you knew of my work again?" she asked impatiently.

"I guess that it's time to let you in. It's kind of embarrassing though," said Mr. Potatohead. "You see, I work for the same guys that you do. My original assignment was to find out why you weren't producing any art. I found out about Muffy's annoying little habit of keeping all of your art and reported it back along with descriptions of all your new stuff and the fact that it was exceptional, even for you. They were satisfied for a while but when this ATM business hit the news and her rich ass dad started paying off every cop in the city to find her, as well as offering huge rewards, Big Brother decided that you were both too risky and decided that you had earned retirement, if you know what I mean. They called me up and told me to destroy you as well as any evidence that you ever existed. The plan was to take you back here and turn you into dog food. Fortunately for you, my dear, I think I'm in love with you. I'm going to do my best to get you to a safe place, if there is such a place that is. Do you have any ideas?"

Muffy: or A Transmigration of Selves

Sarah stared blankly, her eyes glazed and her mouth gaping open allowing a small string of spittle to run over her bottom lip and down into a small puddle forming on the floor. She was obviously in shock and Jakob was at a loss. "Snap out of it," he said, sounding a little angry. "We have to figure out what the hell to do and I don't think that pool of spit is going to give us any answers."

All at once she came out of it. She was suddenly fully alert and her eyes ripped around the room like an altar boy at the Vatican. "We have to get out of here, now. I hope that we can find Muffy later, but it's her fault for leaving anyway. Do you have any guns?" she asked hopefully.

"A couple, why?" he asked with an all new dopey grin.

Sarah stopped panicking long enough to marvel at the happy dog expression once again. She marveled at how he could maintain that goofy exaggerated clown face even when he was in a life or death situation and wearing prosthetics to make himself look like a fat Chinese man. The squinty eyes only added to the effect making it even more disturbing and repulsive. He looked like he was about to explode and slime the entire room with thick condensed powder pink joy ooze. He did it constantly and it always made her want to throw a brick at his face, but the reality of her situation flooded back into her mind like a toilet flushed in reverse. "We have to go somewhere that we don't know anybody. Somewhere secluded, the woods maybe. We'll have to just pick out a cabin, kill anyone inside, and hold up there for awhile. You can't escape the Illuminati forever, but if I could convince them that I'm no longer a danger they might recall the order. Get your shit, we have to go now. Call your superiors and tell them it's done. We'll leave in twenty minutes."

He was as shocked as she had been only moments ago, but it passed quickly and they were soon on their way.

5@6

Muffy floated down the street with no clue where to go. She seemed to wander for hours before she noticed a familiar sight. It was the window entrance to the club that Fousto had taken her to. She searched her pockets for his phone number but then remembered leaving it on the dresser the night before.

"Damn," she said to herself, "I never have anything I need. Doesn't matter what it is. If I need it it's gone. Fuck!" she said, kicking the wall as hard as she could, causing it to shake.

She heard a cry of pain and a second later the window opened and a tiny head poked out. "Why the hell you kick me? You think I don have enough problems without being kicked in the head?!"

"Fousto," Muffy squealed, and embraced him roughly enough to pull him outside. "I was just trying to find you. I lost your number and I don't know anyone else to turn to."

"Chare," he sputtered drunkenly, "I didn't recognize you. You are on the news. People are looking for you."

"No shit," she said, slightly miffed that he was so drunk. "Can we go back to your place?"

"Sure chare, it is the best offer I've had all night." He stuck his head inside and said goodbye to someone and then slammed the window shut. "Where did you park?" he asked, smiling boisterously.

"I didn't drive today. We'll have to call a cab," she said, wishing she had thought ahead.

"Isn't that dangerous if everyone is looking for you?" he asked.

"Not as dangerous as walking. Come on," she hailed a cab and pretended to make out all the way back to his place so that the driver wouldn't see her face. It was very cliché but it worked. She even popped out a tit to give the driver something to ogle instead of her face.

They arrived, slightly aroused, but without a hitch a few minutes later. They exited the cab and she threw a large tip into the box sitting on the passenger seat. They entered the house and took a seat on the red round sofa in the middle of the room.

"So, my dear, what is the problem?" he asked, lunging for her right breast. He caught hold of it and began sweet suckle, but decided that it was too much work and decided to lie in her lap instead.

"Well for starters the whole world is looking for me. Half of them want the rewards and the other half wants me dead. Then there's the fact that Sarah's a coldhearted bitch who couldn't care less about my feelings. We have no home now, because we had to blow it up to keep the Illuminati from being discovered. Then, my father wants me back and he seems to have changed, but I don't know whether or not I can trust him. He used to rape and occasionally beat me, but he said that he's sorry and that he misses me." She burst once again into tears. "All that I ever wanted was to be loved by him as something more than a sex toy and a status symbol."

"There, there, chare. It will all be okay." Fousto put his arms around her torso and kissed her on the belly and then, struggling against pure grain alcohol, fought his way up to her mouth. His breath stank of liquor and he had an off taste to his mouth, but Muffy was grateful for the affection. She sucked back at his tiny lips and reclined, letting him climb her torso. He came up for a moment to remove his shirt, but the action made him lose his balance. He fell and hit his head on the base of one of the uglier sculptures, causing it to fall and shatter only inches from his head.

Once again he was unconscious. She took him to the bedroom and put him down on the large black satin bed. It was larger than a

Muffy: or A Transmigration of Selves

king size and swallowed him entirely. She wondered why such a small guy would have such a large bed. She made a mental note to ask him about it tomorrow. Her question, though still unasked, was answered a moment later when he rolled, violently and abruptly, from the middle of the bed to the edge and off into the floor, where he landed with a thud and commenced oozing vomit onto the hardwood.

"Why me?" she asked herself as she drug him into the bathroom and laid him down on his belly, on top of a towel.

She then went back into the bedroom to lie down. She looked around the room admiring the walls. They were covered with red wallpaper with ornate little patterns woven into them. The material felt silky, as though it was upholstery rather than wallpaper. The wall above the bed sported "La Tentation De St-Antoine" by Salvador Dali. The wall across from her was hung with "Birth Pangs" by Monaco. To her left was H.R Giger's "Birthmachine" and to her right Picasso's "Old Guitarist". This was one fucked up dwarf. Or at least that was the impression that she got.

The ceiling was the same deep red as the walls and the windows were hung with thick black drapes which kept out any light. There was a white dresser covered with knickknacks, some toys of villains from popular cartoons, some clowns, some dried flowers, and a small ceramic mouse painted florescent green with black eyes and electric blue ears. Beside the bed was a nightstand covered only in empty liquor bottles and ashtrays filled like graves. The wooden floor was covered in dirty clothes, a foot high in the corners and shallow nearer the bed.

She heard water starting in the bathroom and went to investigate. Fousto had finally managed to get undressed and was lying in the shower with his head limply dangling over the side. Cold water was causing millions of goose pimples to rise over the entirety of his small body. He was sitting on the drain and the bathtub was slowly filling up with water. He looked up at her and smiled. "Chare, how did you get in here? I looked everywhere for you this morning and you had gone. It made me sad, but everything is better now that you are back.

I'm sorry about the mess. I haven't been feeling well. Come and give me a kiss, eh?"

"You are a fucked up little guy, you know that? Do you remember anything about my being hunted down by the whole world?"

"Oh yeah, you were on the news. Some constipated looking guy was blubbering about missing you. He looked like an asshole. Who is he?" Fousto wondered aloud.

"That would be my father. Everyone thinks that he just wants me back as a figurehead, but he seems different somehow. I kind of miss him," she confided, reaching out for either some kind of sympathy.

"Why don't you call him and talk?"

"He would just have it traced. He would have people here to retrieve me and shoot you within the minute. You know, I never had any real friends before I left. Everyone was just an acquaintance who was nice because I had money. I've never been without money so I suppose that I can't say I wish that I was poor, but it certainly isn't as great being rich as everyone seems to think. I have money but it's cost me my childhood, friendship, love, and my own mind. I let my father rape my body; I let my mother rape my mind. It was like being a slave to everyone. They owned me, and they knew it. When I inadvertently escaped I met people that didn't know anything about me. People who didn't have to pretend that they liked me, but they were nice anyway. I don't want to give that up but I miss my family too, even though they treated me like shit. There were good times too. Daddy took me to Paris when I was four and we spent a whole week together. That was before he got his raise. He changed after that, but when I saw him on the news he reminded me of that week. If I go back home they will probably go after Sarah, they already know some stuff about her. People come out with information pretty fast when they offer a thousand dollars a clue and a million to the one that finds me. Anyway, what do you think that I should do?" she implored breathlessly.

"I have seen your father on the news and he seemed to be a lying asshole. I wouldn't trust him with my worst enemy's wallet. If he

Muffy: or A Transmigration of Selves

treated you like you said he did he doesn't deserve your forgiveness anyway." He chewed his lip for a moment, analyzing her situation from as many points as he presently could. Then after some chin stroking and a sigh he told her, "My advice is to stay away. He looks and sounds very dangerous. Hide out until the whole thing dies down. Hopefully, when he stops looking so will the Illuminati. They won't have any reason to kill you then. Why do they want to kill you anyway? I didn't think that they were even real."

"Sarah works for them, or, I should say, worked for them. She made art for the very rich, very sick, and very powerful and they loved it. It's one of the less scummy jobs that they have. I didn't know that they existed before I met her either, but they are plenty real to me now," she winced at a pop-up memory.

"You should stay with me for a while. We had only met once before today, nobody would expect you to be in my house. I don't have many friends, and the few I do have are always at Travesty, they never come here."

"What about Sarah? She'll worry that I've been killed. She'll leave and I won't know where to find her," whined a distraught little girl who had seemed years older only moments before.

"True love always returns, chare. Not to mention that you will both be safer if you are apart. And if they do catch one of you they won't know where the other is. You really should stay with me."

"I suppose you're right. Would you take this message to Sarah for me though?" A growing sense of hope arose within her.

He paused and thought a second before answering, "Sure, they won't be looking for me."

"You're sure you don't mind?"

"Of course not, chare. Just write it and tell me where to take it," he reassured.

Muffy wrote a short letter to Sarah apologizing for her outburst and giving the address of where she was staying. She included Fousto's warning that they are safer apart and put it in an envelope with Jakob's address on the front. He called a cab and left as soon as it arrived. Meanwhile, Muffy took the time to read a few of Fousto's books, which she found to be vulgar and tasteless, yet brilliant and thought provoking at the same time.

Fuck you, who needs a title for a chapter anyway? Just fucking read.

Sarah arrived at a small cabin on the outskirts of Woodstock, New York just as the sun was sneaking behind the trees for the day's last cigarette. They parked just out of sight and waited for the darkness to envelope them. When the sun was finally out they crept to the cabin and tried the door. It was open. After all, who would try to break into a cabin in the middle of nowhere?

The cabineers were quite surprised when they saw the two strangers enter through their front door. They stared for a minute and then the man said, "Aren't you the chick from TV?" He died with the question still on his lips. The girl they forced to clean up the mess and show them around the place. After the ten cent tour she was taken outside, executed, hung from a tree, skinned, gutted, dismembered, deboned, and put in Tupperware in the back of the refrigerator. The same was done to her husband and the two year old asleep in the next room. They then found an infant and decided to keep it for entertainment purposes. There wasn't any meat on it anyway (not that there really was on the two year old either).

Sarah hid the car in a shed out back while Jakob prepared a nice roast with potatoes and carrots that were taking up valuable fridge space. She returned and they ate the nicest meal that either of them had eaten in quite some time. Later that night they sat on the porch smoking cigarettes, listening to nature, and watching the baby crawl closer and closer to the stairs.

"This is heaven isn't it?" remarked Jakob.

Just then a huge beetle flew into Sarah's face causing her to freak out and run screaming around the deck until she had finally beaten it senseless. It died with a hearty crunch. "Heaven, huh?" she screamed.

Jakob was still laughing uncontrollably and couldn't respond. She approached him and pulled off his nose which made the laughter take on a disgusting gurgling sound that turned her stomach. She slapped him but he only laughed harder. She took the baby and went inside, leaving him locked on the porch.

Later yet that night, after he had charmed his way back inside, they sat talking and watching the news. "I wonder how long this will go on," Sarah said sleepily.

"He's bound to give up sometime, probably when he realizes that a hooker would be cheaper." They both chuckled. They watched the baby play with an electrical outlet.

"Shouldn't we stop it before it kills itself?" asked a drunken and sleepy Jakob.

"Nah, let it play. We have TV. What do we need a kid for?" Sarah yawned.

Jakob looked at her with mild disgust. "Don't you feel the slightest bit sorry for it? We just killed his entire family and fed it to him. Not all of them at once, mind you, but you know what I mean."

"Why should I feel sorry for it? It doesn't know what's going on. I would feel sorry for it if it lived, sure. It's a horrible thing to grow up in this country. It's a horrible thing to grow up on this planet for that matter. We go from being stupid and innocent little bundles of fat to being like you and me, if not worse. I think that's why children gravitate towards danger. I think that at that age they are kind of psychic, and they can sense all of the pain and frustration around them. They don't want to be a part of it so they throw themselves down stairs and stick their fingers in light sockets and fall out of windows on the fifteenth floor," Sarah mused sleepily.

"But what if it shorts out the electricity? We would be screwed," the puzzle man pointed out.

"Good point, put it up and let's go to bed."

He did just that and soon they were both snoring peacefully away in a lumpy twin bed with pillows like rocks.

The Holey Crusade

Fousto returned forty minutes later with an exasperated look on his face.

"Did you find it alright?" Muffy asked, looking up from her book.

"I found it but they weren't there. I tried to put it in the mailbox but I couldn't reach the slot, so I had to find a stamp machine and mail it to them."

"Damn," said Muffy, "I hope they get it before they have to leave. If they don't I don't want to think about what might happen."

"I'm sure that they will. They shouldn't have had time to leave yet. Don't worry chare. Hey, what do you want for dinner?" asked the king.

"What do you have?" Muffy asked back.

"I could order a pizza or Chinese, but I don't really cook. The only thing that I keep in the fridge is my beer and cigars," he said, almost proudly.

"You refrigerate your cigars?" Muffy asked in a diminutive tone.

"Have you ever had a cold cigar? They are awesome. Have one," he said, pulling two out of the freezer, he tossed one over.

She lit it up and took on a look of surprise. "This is great. Who turned you on to this?"

"Actually, it was a really stupid guy that I used to live next to," he said puffing lightly on the cigarillo as he spoke. "He liked menthols and didn't have any money for cigarettes so he had to bum a pack from his mother who smoked Reds. He put them in the fridge so that they would have a slightly cold sensation. I had the same reaction that you did. It was really an accident. He didn't know what he was doing. Then again, most great discoveries are accidents."

"That is very true," Muffy replied.

"How about a Happy Family. We could split it," suggested Fousto, returning to the subject at foot.

"Sounds good to me," Muffy agreed.

"I'll go order it." He made the call and returned. "It will be about fifteen minutes."

"Cool, what should we do in the meantime?" Muffy asked sensuously.

"I don't know. How did you like my book?" Fousto stammered.

"It was great," she said truthfully. "I was a little skeptical at first about the fact that it was from the point of view of a sentient doughnut that had evolved after being left in somebody's refrigerator for years, but when I saw how you did it I was very impressed."

"Yes, that was the one that everyone thought was stupid so no one read it," he said sadly. "It was one of my favorites, but it brought me nothing but ridicule. That is the way that it always turns out, the more I like the project, the less my fans do. The less I like it the more they eat it up. The world is a fucked up place," observed the tiny king.

"Yeah, I know," replied Muffy. "I'm an artist too. I never tried to sell anything because I was worried no one would buy them. I really liked them anyway, but it still seemed kind of silly. They all went up in the fire and I never got anything out of them. It really sucks."

"Yes, one time my computer died and I lost countless books and poems forever because I had been meaning to buy a cd burner so that I could fit in all on one cd. I felt really stupid after that." He plopped back onto the couch still lamenting the loss of all of his treasured rants. His eyes misted over for a second, but he went to the refrigerator before Muffy noticed. He drank two pints before the food came. They passed out watching the news a few hours later, blissfully unaware of what would come.

The Devil's Advocate

The press conference was scheduled to start at noon the next day. Top reporters from every major news team in the world nervously gossiped and attempted to bribe their ways into a scoop outside of the California beach side mansion. They had decided to hold it there because it just seemed more wholesome and family like than the apartment or the office. And anyway, what good is a 15 million-dollar vacation home if you can't show it off on worldwide TV?

Journalists crawled over each other like maggots in the Ritz's dumpster, attempting, in vein, to wriggle their way closer to the doors. The giant clock which was mounted above the massive front doors struck twelve and the doors burst open, no longer able to hold back the throng of lawyers and family which had been gathering behind them. A table was set up just before the police barricade and Muffy, her mother and father, and their favorite two lawyers took their seats and for the first time in news history everyone present was quiet, awaiting the news that the world was supposed to be clamoring for.

"We will start off with a statement and questions will be taken at the end," stated the lawyer on the left in the monotone drawl that one would expect from a CIA official.

Andrew began, "I would like to start off by thanking God for the safe return of my beloved daughter. I would also like to thank all of the people who were nice enough to call in with information.

Unfortunately, since none of that information helped us to find her, no money will be awarded. Now my daughter would like to relate some of what she experienced during her capture," said the father in a very businesslike manner.

"I would like to start off by saying that I do not hold my captor in contempt. As a matter of fact I was only held against my will for a little while. The majority of the time that I was gone I was there because I wanted to be. I can't say where I was or who I was with, but I will say that I wasn't mistreated in the least. I fell in love with my "captor" as you refer to them and only came back because I thought that it was time to make a stand for what I think is right," Muffy said bluntly.

Throughout the dissertation Muffy's father grew more and more uncomfortable. He began to wonder if the time that he had spent throwing together a news conference, packing, and flying to California wouldn't have been better spent getting their story straight.

"I was confused for most of my life about the relationship which I held with my family. When I found my new friend I was glad to finally have someone to talk to who liked me for me, and not because they were supposed to or because of who my parents are. I learned a lot from them, they taught me how to think for myself and how to make my own decisions. These things can be hard to learn when you are pampered from birth, home schooled, and raised by paid nannies," Muffy expounded with the jubilance of an ex-junky at a school assembly.

Sweat dripped from her parents' brows in droplets big enough to be seen by even the cameras in the back.

"I never thought that my parents loved me before I saw Daddy on the news, but now I understand everything." She went on. "You see, when someone is as busy as my daddy normally is, they tend not to have much free time to do the things they enjoy. And since he was away from us so much on business we never had time to develop a healthy father-daughter relationship. However, he did love me just as much as any other father, if not more so. When he did see me he didn't have much time to spend, so the only love which he was able to show was of a sexual nature."

When her mother fainted right out of her chair the lawyers were too stunned to move to catch her. Every eye in attendance was wide and every jaw was dropped. This was not what they had been expecting; it was infinitely better. As for her father, all smugness had drained away and in its place throbbed all of the blood which should have been in the lower portions of his body. He snatched the microphone away from her and began to sputter something about this all being a really sick joke, which he didn't appreciate.

Muffy gave him a look as unidentifiable to him as Sanskrit and plucked one microphone from the bouquet in front of him. "As I was saying, this was very understandable given my mother's schedule, which was just as hectic. He was obviously starved for sex and family in equal proportions. Because of this we have developed a stronger love than most parents are capable of showing one another. I just want to say that I feel horrible for hating my father for all of these years, and that I now understand and accept his love in whatever form he chooses to manifest it. I love you Daddy, and I'm glad to be home." She pulled him in close and gave him a kiss that would have changed the ratings on a movie.

I search for the proper euphemism to describe what happened next, but I don't think that I can recall one which would fit properly. Let's just say that all hell hit the fan. Anarchy erupted then, hitherto unknown in this country barring such instances as the Super Bowl and the Macy's one-day sale. There was a mad rush for those which didn't have live video feeds to get their information to the presses. Muffy's father took hold of her and dragged her violently into the house. The crumbling of his empire could be heard as far away as Tibet, but even the wisest monks could not explain the mystical hum it produced. Muffy's mother was loaded into an ambulance and taken immediately to the hospital where she was prescribed a massive quantity of Dilaudid and put in the corner to nap until things calmed down a bit. Everyone else just fought for their lives, trying not to be trampled while attempting to gain entrance to the house and commentary from the servants. Try as they might no one was allowed to gain entrance, although a few ambitious fellows were granted a few crumbs of gossip from the none too amorous lips of house boys and cooks who all felt that their big break had finally come. Above the roar of commerce the only audible sound was the breaking of glass and the whine of the universe expanding.

Back at the Cabin

Sarah was treated to breakfast in bed the next morning, which was a luxury that she had never been afforded. "Good morning sleepy head. I made you breakfast," came the obnoxious sound into her subconscious.

She blinked and was blinded by the glare of the sun, which came streaming in through the open window. She flailed and tried to turn over, nearly knocking her tray over in the process.

"You should be more careful," came the voice again. "You nearly lost your breakfast. Come on, I made you a big ol' steak with scrambled eggs. You better hurry up and eat it before it gets cold. I cooked it rare for you. I hope that's alright."

Flashes of rage and violence that would have put Johnny to shame flashed through her mind as she stared at the steaming lump of flesh in front of her. It was the size of a porterhouse and smelled delicious, but that didn't change the fact that she was not capable of eating first thing in the morning. Her stomach turned over and over again as she stared at the delicious meal which she was apparently required to eat.

"Why do you have so much meat in there anyway? That's just about all that you have in there and you have a ton of it." She sat naked on a stool, brushing her hair in front of the mirror.

The sight of the girl sent flashbacks, accompanied by ripples of pleasure and disgust, through her, and it was just enough to allow her to consume the meal without immediately spewing it back out.

"My cousin owns a cattle farm around here. She sent me that as a present the other day," she said after spitting out a wad of fat.

"They didn't wrap it up or anything? That's funny, my grandmother raises cattle and when they send me free meat it's usually vacuum sealed in little plastic individual serving type things," said the girl on the stool.

"Yeah," responded an irritated Sarah, "my cousin's cheap like that."

"If she's so cheap then why'd she send you so much?" Satry asked. The hollow ring of inbreeding in her tone was enough to disquiet Sarah's tummy's temporary solace.

Sarah was getting impatient. "Look, my cousin's a little weird. I think that she's in the business because she enjoys the slaughter process. We're just proud of her for overcoming her taste for trying to force different species of animals to have oral sex. She would do stuff with fish and chickens, and puppies with iguanas. Now she's out of our hair and we don't ask questions."

"Oh," said the blond girl in a way which would be described as knowing, if only she wasn't so stupid.

Sarah ate about half of the eggs and a quarter of the steak and wobbled into the next room to plop down in front of the TV. Satry came to join her and sat in Sarah's lap, which squished her barely digesting food and nearly made her vomit.

"You know, I really enjoyed our little sleep over last night. Walking hurts a little, but I don't mind. I've never done any of those things before. I never even wanted to. I guess you swayed me over to the other side, didn't you? I never imagined myself a lesbian." Ignorance dripped from those beautiful lips like vomit.

Sarah, in an attempt to shut her up, turned on the TV. A fuzzy image of a mustached man emerged slowly from the ashy vacuum. "Pandemonium is occurring at the moment. I can't believe what just transpired myself. The missing daughter of millionaire Andrew LeSeux has just admitted to having sexual relations with him. You heard it here first. Many have wondered why the tycoon, who couldn't even find a picture of the two of them together to give the press, would put up such a fuss about a missing daughter who many didn't even know existed. Today's events have left little to the imagination. He has now withdrawn to the center of his home and is not making comments. We do however have one of his servants here to give us his account of the private goings on of the LeSeux family," droned the box.

Now Sarah threw up.

"What's wrong, honey? Did I squish you wrong?" asked the dullard.

"No," she sputtered between chunks of rare steak. "I know that girl. She just signed my death warrant."

"You're the one who kidnapped the daughter of that millionaire? Gosh, I've never met a celebrity before. Why'd you let her go?"

IGNORANCE.................... APPROACHING... INTOLERABLE......... LEVELS..... TWITCH

"First of all I didn't kidnap her. She was my girlfriend," Sarah said sitting up. "Secondly, I didn't let her go. We had a fight and she just stomped off. It appears that this is her revenge. Her father is going to have me tracked down and killed now."

"Gee, that sucks. What are you gonna do about it? I know, you should kill him before he orders the hit. That's what they would do in the movies," oozed the bag of stupid.

Sarah was forced to laugh. "Are you serious? You wanna help me kill him?" she said jokingly.

"No, I couldn't really kill somebody. What do you think I am, a monster? Killing is wrong. I'll have no part in it," Satry said, her large innocent eyes widening at the concept.

"I have to get out there to talk to her. Would you do me a favor?"

"Maybe," said a suspicious Satry. "What do you need?"

Sarah began her instructions. "I need you to hold on to some things for me while I go out there and talk my way out of this. I also need you to buy me a plane ticket to California, in your name."

"But what about us? You want me to help you get back with your old girlfriend? I can't believe you. Girls are worse than men," she cried loudly as she began to sob.

Sarah couldn't help but be turned on by the pathetic display. She liked it that she had hurt the stupid girl's feelings because deep down she hated her. In all actuality she would probably kill her soon anyway, but in the mean time she really needed a partner in crime. "Look," she said, "there won't be any getting back together. She went back home for a reason. And there won't be any you and me either if I get killed. So I need to get up there so that I can save our asses. Right now I'm not the safest person in the world to be with. Won't you help me? I promise to be back soon. I'll even bring you a souvenir."

"Oh, okay. As long as you make it a good one," grinned the DNA deficient. "But, I don't have much money in my account right now. Do you have enough to cover the ticket?"

"I don't think that will be a problem. I'm rather well off, myself. I'll give you my debit card and my pin number. I'll take a few thousand with me in case I need it and I'll write you a check for, oh, let's say ten thousand just to be sure. First class, round trip and you can keep the rest. Does that sound cool to you?" Sarah bribed easily.

"Hell yeah, but what if you don't come back? Can I keep the money and the cabin and everything?" asked Satry.

"Sure, if I don't come back in a month you'll know that I am dead and you will be free to transfer all of the funds from my account to yours. You can't have the cabin though. It belongs to my crazy cousin. You can stay here for a month, but after that you would need to leave before my cousin takes another vacation. I don't think that I need to tell you the dangers of being in an isolated cabin like this with her." Isn't Sarah a good liar?

"Okay. Do we have time for a quickie?" Satry said with a kiss on the neck.

"Why not? I may be dead soon," and with that they fell on each other like hungry dogs.

A Father's Love

Meanwhile, Muffy cowered in the corner of the huge dining room while her father paced nervously around the room, only occasionally stopping to scream or throw some defenseless piece of china against an innocent wall.

"What the hell were you thinking?" he thundered. "You have ruined my life, my career, and my reputation. I know that I shouldn't have done the things that I did, but I just couldn't help it. You didn't have to destroy me for it."

Muffy finally worked up the courage to respond. "I wasn't trying to destroy you. I just think that it's time that someone took a stand against the taboos of the world. You know, a stand for love."

"Love had nothing to do with it and everybody knows it. Do you really think that I did what I did because I love you? I was just horny. I own you, so I can do whatever I want. If it wasn't for me you would never have been born. I think that entitles me to whatever I want from you. I have given you everything that you've ever wanted. And you were always so fucking demanding. Is it really so wrong that I would ask for something in return?" he said, kicking over the oaken dinner table and sending sterling silver showering down upon his daughter like wayward pineapples.

"No, it isn't. That's exactly what I was saying. It's okay, I don't mind. I just think that it would be nice to come out of the closet," Muffy responded lovingly.

He began to bang his head on the wall, but stopped because it hurt. "How the hell did you get so stupid? I'm not stupid. Your mother isn't stupid. How could two intelligent, enterprising individuals such as we produce someone so stupid that they could believe that the world would just accept child molestation and incest? We live in the most judgmental and hypocritical nation in the *world*! That is why there are taboos. It's not that we are all so pious, but that we are so good at concealing our perversions. When your weakness is revealed they all swarm upon you like piranhas, because the more you attack the evil the more innocent you appear. Do you understand now, you ignorant twat?"

"You know what Daddy? Fuck you! I didn't have to come back here. I came because I thought that you cared about me. You have made it abundantly clear that I was mistaken, so I will be leaving now. I do hope that they don't throw you in jail. Although I think that it would be interesting to see how you feel about rape when the tables are turned. As for me, you don't have to worry about me ever again. I am out of your life forever. Have a nice fall from grace Daddy. Ta ta." And she walked out of the dining room for the last time.

"Good riddance," her father said and quickly picked up the phone and dialed his favorite bodyguard. "Hello Frank, I know that it is your day off but I need a bit of assistance. I seem to be stuck inside of my home, held captive by a throng of reporters who have caught the scent of blood. Would you be so kind as to come and rescue me?"

"I'll be there in five minutes. Go to the secret passage in the basement and wait at the end of the tunnel," instructed a somber voice from the other end of the phone.

"What secret passage?" he asked.

"Don't you remember who owned this house before you? You are in Al Capone's beach house. He had all kinds of secret passages built into all of his houses in case the cops showed up. Pull out the last bottle on the right on the fifth rack from the floor on the fifth rack from the left of the wall that you face when you first enter the wine cellar." The voice was patient yet domineering.

Andy didn't mind at the moment. "I think you deserve a raise. We'll discuss it over some wine - no, make it beer. I don't want to be seen anywhere that I might be recognized," he said as he made for the basement.

"Thanks Mr. LeSeux, I'll be there soon," assured the voice with a click.

"Goodbye Frank," he said as he dropped the receiver onto the cradle. He sighed with relief and made for the basement like a kid who smells cookies.

Weizens and Weasels

Sarah arrived in California at nine o'clock that night and the first thing that she saw was a newspaper showing Muffy ramming her tongue down her father's throat.

"You always were such a show off," she said as she pulled a paper from the rack. Then, before she closed the machine, she pulled out the rest and tossed them into the trash. She hailed a cab and asked to be taken to a bar, "Any bar," she said, "as long as they have a good import selection." The driver whisked her away to a place called The Garage which was one of the few businesses that she had seen whose name didn't refer to the beach in one way or another. She thanked the driver and tipped him with a fifty.

Upon entering she noticed the unique décor of the main room, which was decorated to look like a real garage. The chairs had sheets over them and the decorations were genuine right down to boxes full of old toys. She was even more surprised when she saw the selection of beer. They had twenty-five imports on tap including her favorite five and a bunch that she had never even heard of. The bottled beer was even more extensive, over fifty different brands in stock, and all of them on ice. Sarah was in beer heaven. To make it even better, they didn't serve American or Canadian major brews at all. A sign above the bar read "If you don't like it, GO AWAY!!" Sarah was in love.

She asked for their best Weizen and took a seat at the bar. The bartender pulled a pint from under the well and placed it before Sarah with a chilled tall glass. The beer itself was room temperature but the glass was caked with ice. The side of the bottle insisted that it be drunk at room temperature as it was originally intended, so Sarah popped the top and sucked at it hungrily.

"Damn, that's good," she said as she tried to read the label. It was something in German, which would take hours to even partially translate. She asked the bartender how to pronounce it but he only laughed at her and said, "Try it in the glass." She did and was amazed at how the slight difference magnified the flavor. She thanked him and pulled the paper out of her backpack.

She read about the whole fiasco including the gossip of not one, but three different servants. She read the speculations about the motives behind the scene and the possible retaliatory action from his business associates. She read about Muffy's poor mother and how she had collapsed at the scene. Then she stared at the picture and thought about whether it would be better to kill Muffy or forgive her.

On the one hand she was great in bed, a wonderful artist, funny, and cute. And on the other she was self absorbed, bossy, psychotic, jealous, and prone to acts of unimaginable stupidity, she hadn't let Sarah sell any art, and sex with her, although magnificent, was getting old. She had Satry now, who was an imbecile that annoyed the hell out of her and worthless as an artist, but was also loyal, harmless, and *fucking gorgeous*. Before she was finished with her decision she was distracted by the sound of a man arguing with the bartender about whether or not Moosehead was worth pissing in.

"All Canadian beer is just American beer that somebody left sitting around too long," argued the bartender.

"In most cases I would agree, but Moosehead is different. It has a unique flavor which can be appreciated by any beer connoisseur worth his own urine," said the other man.

Before the argument escalated info a bar fight, Sarah slinked over to him and offered the man a sip of her beer. The man took one look at her and obeyed. The combination of the beer's flavor and the beauty of the supplier was enough to melt his anger away into

Muffy: or A Transmigration of Selves

euphoric pliancy. It was then that Sarah recognized the man as the one she was after.

"What's your name, O' beautiful one?" he asked sweetly as he signaled for one of whatever she was drinking.

"Flouris, what's yours?" Sarah lied, rather well considering the circumstances.

"You can call me Andy," said the man. "Flouris, that's a name that you don't hear too much these days," he said, pouring his beer.

"I think that's the reason that my parents chose it. Say, would you like to get out of here?" she asked trying to block his sight of the tell-tale newspaper which occupied her previous spot.

"I was just about to join my friend over there for a beer," he said pointing. "Won't you join us?"

"I really can't. I have to go to bed early tonight. I have work tomorrow. I just thought that you might like to see my place. I have some very interesting paintings that I would like to show you," she lied again.

"Well, I do love art. Hmm, let me go and see if my friend wouldn't mind me taking a rain check." He walked over to his friend and whispered something in his ear, then he returned saying that he would love to see the paintings.

They took his car and Sarah provided directions, which took them out of the city and into a more desolated area. Sarah pondered, in the meantime, where she should take him. She hadn't expected to find him so soon, so she hadn't yet found a secluded area in which to kill him quietly.

At the same time Andy was becoming more and more nervous about the neighborhoods they were driving through, "You really live out here?" he asked, his voice quaking slightly.

"Yes, just a little bit further," she lied yet again.

"This is a dangerous area; I have seen three people get shot just driving through it. Aren't you ever afraid?" Andy asked stupidly.

"No, I've always lived here. You just get used to it I guess. After you see a few hundred people get shot you stop noticing," she continued, smiling. "Why, are you scared? We could go back to your place."

"I'm not scared; you just don't seem the type that I would expect to live out here. You seem far too delicate," he said in an attempt to undermine the previous question.

"Tell you what. How about a desert picnic, under the stars? You won't have to be worried about getting shot out there. It's so beautiful at night," she said, looking at the night sky.

This sounded much better to him than the picture that was forming in his mind of a dirty mattress caked with other men's semen, so he agreed.

"Just let me stop off at home and pick up a few things," she said bluffing.

"No, that won't be necessary. I know of a Super Center on the edge of town. We'll pick some things up there," he said trying not to sound too afraid.

She snickered to herself lightly. "Okay, but you have to promise to buy me whatever I want. No questions, okay? I have a surprise for you," she said, sex dripping from her lips.

Andy grinned as he imagined the kind of surprises that she might have in store for him. When they arrived at Target he was surprised and a bit disturbed as she loaded up the cart with: beer, tent stakes but no tent, a beach towel, a set of kitchen knives, sandwich meat, cheese bread, a large mallet, pliers, firecrackers of various shapes and sizes, five large candles, a lighter, and one large flashlight. The bill was $187.47 after tax, and Andy was beginning to wonder if this girl was worth the trouble. Nevertheless, his mother had always told him that he should follow through with whatever he started. So they loaded up the car and began their trek into the desert.

A Night Swim in Cuneiform

Muffy wandered along the beach, marveling at the ocean in all of its power and majesty. As the waves came crashing onto her soggy feet she felt its pull. It was as if it were trying to take her away. She could hear the call of the gastropod, the whine of the fish, the hum of the moon as it labored to keep the whole thing jiggling just so. She felt the insignificance of herself and her problems. The white light of illumination singed away her fears and longings, filling her with the black glow of apathy. She decided to go for a swim. The red flags watched as she took her first step into the chasm of infinity. They watched as she took her first stroke into the direction of the eternal. They soon lost sight of her blurry figure as it dissipated into the soup of night. It's too bad that red flags have such bad eyesight. If they had only seen the pair of lovers making there way down the waning shore, then Muffy's fate might have been avoided. They might have called for help, but then again how many lovers speak semaphore anyway?

Muffy swam easily for thirty minutes or so before the first riptide displaced her sense of direction. Then the second and the third hit her with such force that she had little strength left for the fourth. Then apathy engulfed her again and she simply stopped. She waved at a curious fish as it swam by. She named him Sushi, and another blackness, this one much more euphoric, engulfed her consciousness and dragged her to the bottom.

Sarah's Midnight Romp

They reached the desert about twenty minutes later. She had him park the car on a particularly large dune, and they walked from there. When asked where they were going Sarah replied that she had a specific place in mind and that she wouldn't be able to find it in a car.

He blindly followed her for miles until she dropped the bags into a hole only slightly larger than a grave. One would be inclined to say that it was probably the last resting place of a zombie Buick; that is, if one were drunk enough.

She dug through the bags until she found the beach towel, which she laid in the center of the hole. She then withdrew the beer and opened one for each of them. She had him lie on the towel and stare at the sky as she extracted and laid out the rest of the party favors. She fixed them both turkey and ham sandwiches on cheese bread and lay next to him. As they basked in the moonlight, nibbling sandwiches, sipping beer and staring at the clearest night they had ever seen, Sarah gave herself a pat on the back for finding such a wonderful spot. She only wished that it was Muffy there beside her and not her father.

She thought about Satry, her beautiful annoyance, and how she would be droning on if she were here about some nonsense that would probably sound something like, "I've never had cheese bread like this before. It's so good you don't even need cheese in the sandwich. But, if you did add cheese it would be *so* cheesy. We should have bought some cheese." Sarah shuddered.

She then made up her mind. Satry had to go. "Muffy is the one I want to spend my life with," she thought to herself. "I'm not going to find another companion like that ever again. Although, I could keep Satry around for a little while longer. I'm sure that Muffy would enjoy her just as much as I did. Then she would make a great lamp. Inject her with wax, run a wire from her twat through the top of her head to a light bulb, and we would have her beauty forever without the problem of her stupidity." Sarah became excited. She couldn't wait to track Muffy back down and tell her the good news, but before she could do that she had to take care of the father.

She went to work. She rolled over on top of him and kissed him so violently that she almost chipped one of her teeth in the process. She ripped his clothes from his body and he lay avidly compliant, hands outstretched, and absorbed the deliciousness of young lust. She got off of him and procured the tent stakes and placed one at each appendage. Then she tied him to them with the ropes which she had bought. She was in such a hurry that she didn't even notice the cell phone falling from his coat to a place beside his foot. Neither did she notice that she had given him enough slack to move his hands in little 5-inch circles and even more for his feet. She then took off her own clothes and began to kiss and caress his inner thigh. Within moments his organ stood like a monument to the mistake he had made. She caressed it with her hands, rubbed it on her nipples, and a plethora of other things that she had seen done in bad pornography, until his penis began to twitch with a life of it's own. She brought him almost to the point of ejaculation with a black feather that had blown into the hole during dinner. Then she stood up and started putting her clothes back on.

Andy laughed and then screamed for relief, but no respite was granted. He said, "Come on, stop playing. Come back over here and finish me off. I'll give you a wooden nickel."

Muffy: or A Transmigration of Selves

"Sorry, can't do that. It's getting late and I have a lot left to do tonight," she said as though nothing out of the ordinary were happening. "Say, is Muffy still back at your place or did she leave already?"

"What?!!" he screamed. "You know who I am?"

"Of *course* I know who you are. Who doesn't know who you are? Now answer my question," she demanded.

"She left and said she was never coming back," he blurted through his haze of disbelief and confusion.

"Yeah, I've heard that one before," Sarah said, beginning to repack the bags.

"Who are you?" Andy asked stupidly.

"I'll give you three guesses. Then I'm going. Make it fast," Sarah said, looking at her watch.

"Are you a friend of hers?" asked the confused man.

"*Damn* you're stupid. Kind of," Sarah said looking at the kitchen knives and then at him.

"I don't know. Did you meet her when she was kidnapped?" he asked again.

Sarah decided no and put the knives back in the bag. "Closer. One more guess."

A look of shock came over him. "You, *you're* the one who kidnapped her, aren't you? That would explain the vague references to gender. She kept saying they, and them, and their." He laughed, "So, my little daughter understands the way the world works after all." He laughed some more. "You ruined my life and fucked up my daughter. You fucking bitch. You ruined everything. I've always heard jokes about feminazi dykes like you, but I never really believed them until now. Come on, the least you can do is to let me have a hand so I can finish myself off. You can have Muffy. Just let me go," he pleaded.

"Sorry, no. But you do win a sucker," she said, throwing a grape BlowPop at him. She didn't bother to watch as it bounced off of his head with a loud crack. She finished packing up the rest of the unused supplies and put them back into the proper bags.

The man sputtered. "You're just going to leave me out here to die? That isn't very nice. And you won't get away with it. You forget who I am! People will be looking for me when they find out I'm missing."

The attempt to sound brave amused Sarah. "No, I don't think so. Imagine what this will look like to the rest of the world. 'Child Rapist Flees After Being Exposed by his own Daughter at a Press Conference.' That'll be the headlines. The police won't be looking for you, because no one pressed charges. Your wife won't be looking for you, because she's in a sanitarium, doped up on synthetic heroin. Your 'friends' don't give a shit about you since they know what you did. They are probably relieved to get rid of you. The only people who will be looking for you will be reporters who want to crucify you. With your disappearance Muffy and I will end up with all of your money, not to mention the fact that I'm already filthy rich. I'll probably just squander your life savings away, buying toys for Muffy and myself and doing things like buying John Lennon's Imagine piano, lighting it on fire, and catapulting it into a row of brand new sports cars filled to the molding with money. Then we'll blow the whole lot up with diamond studded dynamite on my own private island," she was still droning on about wastes of time and money as she disappeared from sight and sound. A second or so after her voice faded a huge pack of exploding firecrackers flew into the hole, landing on his chest and scaring the shit out of him.

It was then that the gravity of the situation hit him like a ton of buzzard shit. He struggled to free himself from his bonds, but it was to no avail. He was forced to wait all night under the canopy of beautiful stars. He amused himself by watching his penis twitch against the Little Dipper, but it offered little hope. He had to come to the conclusion that he was just stuck. It wasn't until he relaxed that he felt the small round object with his foot. He looked down and saw a faint glow of blue silhouetting an oval of black. His heart tried to jump out his mouth to retrieve the beautiful object, but it found the

Muffy: or A Transmigration of Selves

task difficult and soon let the brain have a try. He nudged it over to where he could get it between his toes and slung it up to his hand. Unfortunately he was a bit out of practice at throwing things with his toes, and it was sent bouncing across his stomach until it hit him in the face. Luckily for him the phone had already come on from being dropped and all that he had to do was hit #7 with his nose. This was the speed dial number for Frank.

The phone rang and after a few moments a voice on the other end said, "Hello?"

"Hi, it's me. You know that girl I met tonight?" asked the overjoyed buzzard bait.

"Yea," came the sleepy voice from the other end.

"Find out who the hell she is and have her killed. No, tortured and then killed. But don't hurt anybody that she's with, she might be with Muffy," he demanded. Somehow Muffy's transgression didn't seem so bad, in light of his present condition.

"Why? If you don't mind my asking," came the sleepy voice again.

"She tried to kill me, that's why. And that's the second thing. I need you to come get me. I'm stuck out in the..." but he saw the light flicker and then go out. He craned his neck to look and saw that the screen was completely black. "Damn," he said to himself, "I knew that I should have charged that thing. He looked around for the other battery pack that he carried, but it was nowhere to be seen. It was then that he began to giggle to himself. He giggled like that for days and nights until, in a final flash of agony, the last drop of fluid evaporated through his eyes.

71

Sarah returned to the car and drove back to the Target, where she left it and took a white granny car back to where she started. She left the car and searched the city's clubs and bars for hours trying to find her lost love. She took along the only picture that she had of Muffy; an old picture of the two of them sitting on her couch that Jakob had taken. Everywhere that she went people recognized Muffy from the news, but no one had ever seen her in person.

Very frustrated, she took a plane back to New York to see if Muffy had returned home. She figured that if Muffy was still in California she would be spotted eventually and end up on the news. She returned to the cabin at 11:45 a.m. and found Satry just waking up.

"So, how'd it go?" Satry asked yawning.

"Well, I got the father taken care of, but I couldn't find Muffy anywhere. I thought that she might be hiding back here somewhere. It kind of sucks because she could be anywhere in the world right now. No one is looking for her but me," she said, slightly dizzy. "I need some sleep. I'm going to crash," as she plopped face down on the bed.

"You can't sleep now," said an irritated Satry. "I just woke up. You have to spend some time with me." But it was no use. Sarah was already in REM sleep, fighting three headed monsters with umbrellas. "Okay, fine, I'm going out. I'll see you tomorrow." When she received no response she stormed from the room, slamming the door behind her.

As she sped down the road she was too busy thinking mean thoughts about her sleepy lover to notice how strange it was that she passed a car on the dirt road. Nor did she notice the red and black lump that she passed as she exited the driveway.

Sarah didn't hear the two men as they crept in through the window of her bedroom. Neither did she awaken when they handcuffed her arms to the bedposts. She did however wake when they inserted a knife into her torso at the base of her right hip and slid it up to her right shoulder and then the left shoulder, the left hip and back around to where they had begun. They peeled the flesh from her chest and stomach, and commenced to caress her bear muscles while she screamed. One man split her stomach muscles with the jagged end of his knife and played with her intestines. The other tore off her fingernails and plucked out her eyes with a toothpick. She bled to death in a minute and a half, and as soon as she stopped moving the men exited through the front door, got back in their car, and drove away.

You can imagine the shock that Satry felt upon returning home to find her lover splayed and disemboweled on the bed that she had just recently awoken from. She wept and ran around screaming for a while, then she found a knife and stalked around the house looking for the culprit. When she found none she thought about calling the police, but then she remembered the card that Sarah had given her before she left. She remembered being promised millions of dollars, and felt oddly comforted to be rid of Sarah for good. She took the card, as well as all of her other belongings, and drove away, never to return.

She now lives in a large mansion in Florida, and spends most of her time drinking very expensive liquor and getting fucked by surfers. To this day she still tells stories about her first love who was mutilated by his (She doesn't want anyone to know about her little experiment) crazy cousin who owned a slaughterhouse.

Heaven Is Nice

Muffy awoke to a bright light which quickly changed into a tasteful lounge. She looked around and saw that it was decked out in the spiffiest velvet furniture that she had ever seen in colors she had never imagined. She was sure something wasn't right. She became even more convinced when she looked up to find David Bowie looking down at her with a look of curiosity and love.

"Where the fuck am I?" she asked him.

"You're in Heaven. Hi, I'm God," said the tall gaunt figure.

She wasn't sure what kind of reaction that warranted so she responded, "No, really, where the fuck am I?"

"I just told you. You're dead, you're in Heaven, I'm God. Hi," said the beautiful alien.

Muffy was confused. "You're David Bowie, not God. David Bowie isn't even dead yet, so I don't really see how you could be God."

"Damnit, I hate to be argued with. I'm God I tell you," God said, becoming annoyed.

Before He could go on, Muffy interrupted, "Ha, God doesn't cuss. Now who are you?"

God took on a look of amusement and slight disgust. Then he took on the look of a giant cockroach. Muffy screamed incoherently and ran away. She ran and ran, until she ran directly into the arms of David Bowie. She shrieked again but Mr. Bowie had had enough.

She suddenly found herself strapped to a table without the ability to make a sound.

"Now then, if I have your undivided attention, we should get a few things straightened out. One, I *am* God. Two, you *are* dead. Three, you are in Heaven. Four, being God means never having to explain yourself. I can cuss if I damn well please, I can also look however I please, eat whatever I please, and I can do anything else I please because I'm God. I really hate being told what I can and can not do by beings that I created for my own amusement. It was fun at first, but after a few billion times anything can get boring. And five, Hi," God said again.

She found herself once again upright and sitting in a very comfortable ultraviolet chair. "Hi," she said weakly. "How are you?"

"Much better, thank you. Would you like to ask me any questions?" God asked as He settled back into His infrared recliner.

"A few, may I?" she asked, humbling herself a bit.

"But of course you can. Shoot." A large electric blue drink appeared in His right hand.

"Why do you look like David Bowie?" she said, and immediately sensed that she had made a mistake.

God looked upset.

"You said ask me a question, that's what I want to know," she said, not too humbly.

"Okay, that's fair, I guess, but will you do me a favor?" God said with a sardonic grin.

"What's that?" Muffy felt a little uneasy, God shouldn't leer.

"Stop calling me 'David Bowie.' I'm not David Bowie. I'm God. If you must address me, please use one of my ten million other names. Simply 'God' will do nicely, that is how most people around here address me, or 'Savior' or 'Imminence,' 'Father,' 'Yahweh,' or whatever you like, but not 'David Bowie,'" God said pleasantly.

"Sure God, what would you like me to call you?" she asked.

"As I said before, just 'God' will do nicely," God said, lighting a cigarette. "Would you like one?" He asked holding out his indescribable yet ultra swank cigarette case.

"Sure," she said taking one, "I didn't really expect there to be smoking in Heaven."

"Why not?" he asked.

"I don't know, I just never expected there to be smoking in Heaven. Kind of like I didn't expect it to look so much like a night club, or you to look like," she caught herself, "that."

"Much better," He said smiling and lighting her cigarette. "Now as for why I look like this. This is my favorite form. This is the way that I looked before I ever changed into anything else. I created man in my image. This is what Adam looked like. Over the course of millions of years the cycle comes back to its origin, and you get a man who looks like me. Now are you satisfied?"

"Yes. By the way, what brand is this?" she asked. "It's awesome."

"I made them myself, actually. I change the make-up from cigarette to cigarette so that I don't get sick of the flavor," God proclaimed through a puff of smoke.

"Oh, neat. Wait, didn't you create the tobacco plants back on Earth?" Muffy asked, confused.

"Yes. Of course," replied a tiring God.

"Then why didn't they taste this good?" Muffy asked.

"There are millions of reasons that they don't taste like this. First of all, I have been working on the flavor for millions of years, and it improves every day. Then you must take into consideration what Heaven would be like if Earth had the best there is? Also, I didn't really intend for tobacco to be smoked when I first created it. Man came up with that one. It pissed me off at first, so I made it carcinogenic, but then I tried them and they weren't bad. So I started improving on them and now I have these. They are not addictive, they are not carcinogenic, the flavor gets better and better as you smoke them, and they don't burn down unless you want them to. It keeps me from having to empty the ashtrays as frequently," God stated matter-of-factly.

"Wow, that's cool. Can I ask another one?" asked the girl.

"You just did," reminded God.

"Oh yea," she said, a little annoyed. "I was just wondering if there is any purpose or meaning to life. Other than to amuse you, that is."

"No," He answered.

"No, not any?" she pushed the question.

"None," He answered again.

"Oh, well I guess that might be the reason that no one ever found it, huh," Muffy mused.

"Could be. I just got bored with the angels. They don't appreciate anything, having always been here, and since I designed their personalities, I know exactly what they are going to say and do. I made man so that I could have a little variety; someone to talk to. I did it the only way it could be done; by growing you away from me and my world, and then bringing you here," God said taking a sip of His drink.

"What about Hell?" asked the girl.

"What about Hell?" asked God.

"Is there one? How many people are there? How do you choose who goes where?" Muffy was getting tired of God's little word games.

"Oh, you want to know everything," God said exasperated. "Well, there is one. That's where I send the shitheads."

"Shitheads?" asked Muffy.

"Yes, shitheads. I'm sure you have met a few in your time," said God knowingly.

"Oh, yes," Muffy responded, thinking of every person that she had ever met.

"There you go. The defects go into the trash bin, just like any factory. But I don't send all that many people there. I reincarnate most of them. They get it right eventually. Hell is for chronic shitheads. If you are a shithead in ten lives in a row without improvement, you go to hell. Of course, some things make you go around again no matter how much I like you. For instance, I don't care if your Christian, Muslim, Buddhist, Hindu, Wiccan etc. as long as you *believe* that there *is* a God. If you can't see that I exist by looking around and seeing the design of the world then you are an idiot and you don't deserve Heaven. Satanists and Athiests don't get in, and are counted as shitheads for that go round," God's hot rock changed to a blue glow.

"Why Satanists? They believe that there is a God. They just don't like you," Muffy said laughing.

"Well, there are two kinds of Satanists:" explained God. "The philosophical Satanists and the cheesy Satanists. The cheesy ones are the ones that you say don't like me. You know, the ones in the heavy metal T-shirts with all the tattoos and armor rings and such. They are obnoxious and cheesy and I don't like them either. Then there are the philosophical Satanists like Aleistar Crowley and Anton LaVey who mean *themselves* when they say Satan or God. They believe themselves to be gods just because they can learn and create, but they don't believe in any higher intelligence than themselves. They are pompous and stupid and shitheaded, which is unfortunate because I would like them otherwise."

"Okay, I get it now. Who else doesn't get into Heaven?" asked the girl.

"Well, you, for one, can't stay here this time because you were too much of a follower. You made a lot of progress for a first timer, but you still only bought in to what Sarah said. She was right on a lot of counts but that doesn't matter. You must go on to think for yourself before you can come here for good," God said pleasantly. His hot rock changed to purple.

Muffy's expression turned to horror. "You mean I have to do this over again. Why? Life sucks, I don't want to go back."

God took another hit of His cigarette. "Well one of the main reasons is your suicide. You copped out, and I can't have any of that in here. Nothing disgusts me more than a suicide. It's *so* pa*thet*ic. There are people who had lives thousands of times worse than yours and they waited until they died of natural causes. Sometimes, when I really like somebody with an especially horrible lot, I help them out with a car accident or a deadly disease. But suicide is unforgivable. That's the one point that Catholics are right on.

Anyway, I'm sorry, but you have to do it over. Try to think for yourself more this time. Nobody seems to be able to do that anymore. I haven't had but a few hundred permanent friends join me in the last hundred years. I've sent more to hell than I've let in here. Anyway, I won't hold this one against you. You didn't *mean* to be a pathetic follower. Who knows, you were still young, you might have even made it on your first try if you hadn't killed yourself." God took another sip of His drink.

"No way, fuck you! I'm not going back," Muffy screamed belligerently.

"Don't be like that, silly. It's not like you have a choice." God looked slightly uncomfortable.

"No, I'm staying here. I like it here. You can't make me go. I'm a Christian, and the Bible says that as long as I believe in God and do my best to do His bidding I'll go to Heaven when I die. And as you so articulately put it, *I'm* dead, and *I'm* in Heaven, so it's *my* turn to say, HI!" Muffy's tantrum amused God.

He laughed, "I really do like you. You know, if you only had this much spunk in life, you would be staying. But, since you didn't...," He said shrugging. "The Bible is not in my words. I had Jesus tell disciples what to write and over two thousand years and a few million translations, well... It's kind of like when you start a message at one end of a line of people and then when it gets to the other end it doesn't sound anything like what you said. I'll tell you *what*..." God spoke slowly, thoughtfully. "I'll make it easy on you. I'll make you a cat. Cats get to keep their memory from previous lives. As do other certain people that deserve that torture. Before you say it, yes, the expression is actually true. I usually only make shitheads into cats on their ninth life so that they can have a better chance to get it right. Most cats are people who have been given one last chance."

"That explains a lot," said Muffy, smiling.

"Well, are you ready to go then?" He implored, standing and opening a circle of light in the floor before Him. Mist billowed from the hole like a scene from a cheesy movie.

"I like you a lot too. You're cool as hell. But, I'm not going to be a cat. Nor am I going to be a person or a llama or a goat or a hubcap. Heaven's a big place, and you're going to have to find me," she said and she took off in the other direction.

"Why must the spirited ones be my favorites?" He asked Himself as He watched her run away at the speed of light. He shook His head, "I suppose that I should punish her for that. Oh, well."

Fleas Suck

Muffy ran and ran; she decided that being dead was great. You don't get tired and you're only limited by your own imagination. Then the circle of light opened just in front of her, and before she knew it she was inside. Being sucked through the tunnel was pretty fun. Kind of like a giant water slide without the water. She tried to go back up, but it just didn't work. Suddenly the light started to fade from white to red to black. Her next sensation was a sticky wetness and the smell of wet fur.

"Shit," she thought to herself. "I'm a cat. She opened her eyes again, for the first time, and was blinded by the light. "Oh yea," she thought to herself, "these eyes have never seen light before. I should take it easy." So she lay back and let herself be licked by a giant tongue. "It's an interesting sensation to be licked by a giant tongue," she mused. "It's kind of enjoyable, except for the breath. Damn, what the fuck has this thing been eating? Smells like shit. Wait, aren't female cats supposed to have hooks on their tongues?"

She opened her eyes and to her surprise she saw a giant dog slobbering all over her. "Ahhhh, I hate dogs. Where's my mommy? This fucker's going to eat me," her brain screamed as she ran away. The larger beast quickly caught up to her and carried her back to the box that they had been in before. She saw a water bowl in the corner and hobbled over to it to get a drink. "Eww, this is gonna suck. I'm sharing a bowl with dogs." But that much evasive action had made her very thirsty so she gave in, shut her eyes, and lapped at the stagnant pool before her. "Hey, this isn't as bad as I thought it would be," she said, opening her eyes.

She then saw the most shocking thing of all, another dog. It took her a moment to register that what she saw was, in fact, herself. "Wait, this can't be right. I'm supposed to be a cat. Not a dog. I hate dogs. I am a cute little bugger though," she admitted, sitting on her hind legs and trying to stand like a human again. Unfortunately, her legs just weren't made for that and she fell on her ass. She looked over at the giant dog beside her and tried to say, "Hi, what did you do?" but she was surprised to hear herself barking.

The other dog barked back, and she understood. It translated to, "My human name was Kurt Cobain."

"Oh, so Courtney didn't kill you?" asked the puppy.

"Nope...anyway, it isn't so bad when you get used to it. I didn't have to go to rehab," said the mommy dog.

"I was supposed to be a cat though. There has been a mistake," explained the puppy.

"Damn, you *are* stupid. God doesn't make mistakes. He's God. Anything that He does is right, simply by virtue of His being God. If He had meant to make you a cat, you would be a cat," said the mommy.

"I don't think so. I think that I stepped into the wrong pool of light. I'm gonna have a word with Him about this," Muffy insisted.

The mommy dog looked worried. "I know what you're thinking. Don't do it. Nobody fucks with God and you don't want to see what happens to those who do."

"No, I'm just going to straighten out the problem. I'm sure that it's all just a misunderstanding," she said and then ran out of the box and under the wheel of a car.

Don't Fuck With God

Muffy heard a voice. "You again? I told you about suicide. Do it again, I dare you."

And with that she found herself spiraling down another tunnel of light. The next time that she woke she found herself in roughly the same position. Only this time she was on the street, instead of in a box, and her mother was a mangy, dirty mutt. She was kicked three times by seemingly blind passersby, before finally finding a puddle to drink from, and even then it had a layer of gasoline on top. When she stood back and took a look at herself she no longer saw the cute little puppy from before. In its place was a plain little shit brown mutt whose eyes were two different colors. "This simply will not do," she said just before diving in front of another car.

Behind her she heard the bark of Kurt Cobain, it translated to, "No, you fool!"

I Warned You

Opening her eyes yet again, she saw the giant roach. "I warned you. You're on your way to Hell," He said and she again saw the light.

"No, I just wanna talk," she pleaded as she flew once again down the chute of light. "Okay, I get the picture," she said as she once again opened her eyes. When the burning stopped she looked around and saw no one else around, but she was clean and sitting in her own little pan with her own water and her own puppy chow. "This is more like it. Thanks God. I always liked you." Then a massive door opened admitting four gold and diamond encrusted round beasts.

"Rich people," she thought "They are probably going to buy me for their kid or something. That's cool. I can deal with a life of luxury. I don't even have to talk to anybody."

The fat women bounced around and made squeaky approval sounds. The man nodded and the uglier and fatter of the two picked her up and held her up to her face. "Pretty little thing, isn't he," she heard one woman say.

"He?" Muffy was confused.

"Of course, we'll have to get him fixed immediately," jiggled the fat lady in that annoying, cooing, patronizing voice reserved specifically for babies, whether human or not.

"Fixed?" Muffy's heart dropped.

"You're Mommy's little poodie woodle. Yes you are." Again the woman jiggled.

"Mommy's? Poodie woodle??!!" Muffy felt sick. "I have to see. God wouldn't do that to me. He said He liked me. God wouldn't do that to me. He did say I was on my way to Hell though. I assumed that He meant the ten strikes and you're out thing though. Why the fuck has He always gotta be so cryptic?" She struggled as hard as she could, but the fat woman just crushed her tighter and tighter to her spongy lipids until she couldn't breathe. She finally gave up and let herself be carried to the car. The whole time she kept repeating to herself, "God liked me. He wouldn't do that to me." But she kept looking around. Sitting in the car she caught a glimpse of herself in the glass. For a moment she was completely still and silent. Her mind was clear, and a moment of pure revelation passed between beast and reflection.

"Such a beautiful little thing. I believe I will call her Muffy," cooed the fat bitch.

The moment passed and the beast let out a piercing howl. You didn't have to be a dog to translate the howl to English. It was a sound which means the same thing in every language, to every living being, in every planet across the universe. The translation went like this; "NNNNNNNOOOOOOOOOOOOOOOOOOOOOOOO OOOOOOOOOOO!!!!!!!!!!!!!!!!!!!!!!!"

About the Author

Stephen Gulik was born within the walls of Irish castle on October 21 , 1681. The master of the house was a mister Edmond DeSwitch who had a keen interest in the art of alchemy. Though a complete failure in every aspect of his work, his incessant fumbling with God's video game led so severe consequences for all who surrounded them. Mutations of mind and body were not altogether uncommon in this household, which ultimately resulted in Mr. Gulik's departure at the tender age of one. He traveled the world in search of wisdom and new forms of mayonnaise. Eventually he found himself face to face with the goddess Eris who, finding him cute and less annoying than her other saints, sainted him on the spot and introduced him to her good friend Timothy Leary. Timothy in turn introduced Gulik to an electric cheeseburger who eventually talked him into taking over the mind of Ronald Regan and forcing him to run for president. In the body of the Gipper, Gulick became hooked on crack and completely screwed the U.S.A. condemning it to hundreds of years of masochistic frivolity. Gulik looked upon his creation and saw that it was good. However, since his importing of crack had completely buggered the lower class, he began to feel guilty. So he did the sensible thing. He abandoned the president's body and dedicated his life to making sure that broccoli will never again seize the reigns of the world. He wrote his first book Muffy: or a Transmigration of selves in 1999 and subsequently misplaced it. This novel was followed by several screenplays which have also been lost. Word has it that he has recently been spending too much time with the ghost of Charles Bukowski and a second novel is currently underway.

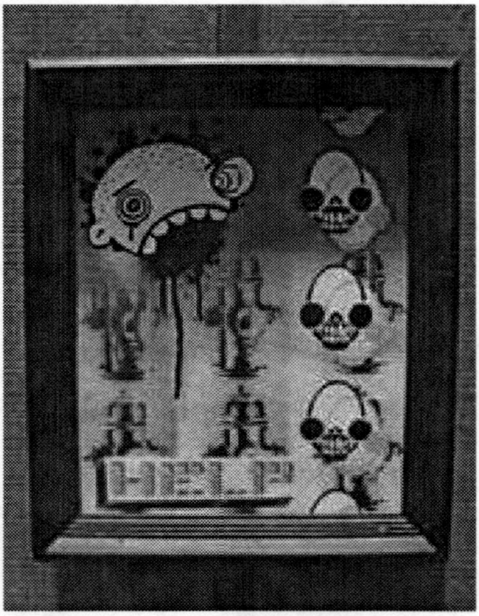

About The Artist

Front cover courtesy of Michael Dowd If you would like to see more from his large body of work, his myspace friend id is 6312826. His name currently appears as project: x-ray. You can access his page directly by pressing this page to your computer monitor and clicking here:
http://profile.myspace.com/index.cfm?fuseaction=user.viewprofile&friendid=6312826&MyToken=d6cd02ef-a16e-4356-9ef0-df04b4961ed0

Stephen T. Gulik is also on myspace. Feel free to swing by and leave some hate mail. Look me up as S.T. Gulik or friend id 60552310.

Printed in the United States
90961LV00003B/105/A